She watched h
looked so much
found him packi
stay in Gazedown and she was going to be his
secretary! *And* Esme Hatherley was going to
be put firmly in her place.

'And,' Ralph continued, 'the book will be
a resounding success and I shall become a
millionaire.'

'And then you can send the terrible Esme a
signed copy,' said Amy, 'to remind her of the
one that got away.'

'Miss Turner! You have a wicked tongue!'

They both laughed and very reluctantly
Amy stood up. 'I'll have to go,' she said.
'Even secretaries have homes to go to.'

He saw her to the door. 'And you'll come
tomorrow about two o'clock?'

'On the dot. I shall look forward to it,' she
told him.

By the time she had reached the station,
Amy was aware that for the first time for
years she was ridiculously happy. It was a
good feeling.

Also in Arrow by Pamela Oldfield

THE GOODING GIRL

THE STATION-MASTER'S DAUGHTER

Pamela Oldfield

ARROW BOOKS

Arrow Books Limited
62-65 Chandos Place, London WC2N 4NW

An imprint of Century Hutchinson Limited

London Melbourne Sydney Auckland
Johannesburg and agencies throughout
the world

First published in Great Britain by Century 1986
Arrow edition 1987

Printed and bound in Great Britain by
Anchor Brendon Limited, Tiptree, Essex

ISBN 0 09 951440 0

For Carole and David
with my love

Author's Note

In 1900 the Rother Valley Light Railway ran from Tenterden Station which was then two miles outside the town of Tenterden. When later a new station was built in Tenterden the original station was renamed Rolvenden. The line is now known as The Kent and East Sussex Railway. Gazedown village and its station are figments of my imagination, but I have set them between Rolvenden and Wittersham Street for the purposes of this novel. All the characters are, of course, fictitious.

Chapter One

Arnold sat cross-legged on the porter's trolley and surveyed the deserted station with a look of deep satisfaction. His large mouth was fixed in the smile which experience had taught him charmed friends and disarmed strangers. His wide blue eyes took in the scene with a familiar look of wonderment and the fingers of his left hand fidgeted idly with the cardboard badge which he wore pinned to the lapel of his jacket. The neat round badge bore the words 'Station Helper' and was Arnold's most treasured possession. At twenty-four, he had the large frame of a man combined with the mind of a boy but, unaware of this fact, he was happy in his own way. The coming of the Rother Valley Railway in 1900 had transformed his life, for now he spent most of his waking hours at Gazedown Station instead of drifting aimlessly around the village, as he had done previously.

His roving eye caught the signboard that hung on the opposite platform and at once his lips moved, shaping the words which Amy had taught him.

'Waiting-room,' he whispered. ' "Waiting-room" starts with a double-you.'

He was not sure exactly what this meant but if Amy said it was so, that was good enough for Arnold, for Amy was the stationmaster's daughter. 'And Gentlemen starts with a gee,' he added.

He did not know what a 'gee' was, but life was full of such mysteries and he knew better than to try to solve them. Later in the morning he would go round to the other side of the station and read his other words: 'Booking Office'.

1

He would read them in a loud clear voice just as the passengers were arriving for the train, so that no one could possibly doubt that he could read.

'A gee,' he repeated with a decisive nod of his head, then he stopped reading and practised his winning smile for a few moments. Suddenly he stood up and called out, 'Right away!'

A large ginger tom-cat on the opposite platform regarded him curiously and then proceeded to wash itself. Arnold looked around at the early morning station, which was his alone for just one hour each day. Then Mr Turner – the stationmaster – would appear, followed later by Tim and Harry and they would take over from him. Arnold did not mind surrendering the station, because he enjoyed their company and because their presence heralded further delights. If Tim was in a good mood he would allow him to help with the parcels in the office, and Arnold knew he was very good at tying on labels.

On market days he helped herd the sheep or cattle into their respective wagons and sometimes Harry let him wave the green flag, though never when there was a train in the station. Tim and Harry were his friends – Arnold knew that for sure – but he had his doubts about the stationmaster. Deep down, Arnold harboured the dreadful suspicion that if he ever did anything really wrong Mr Turner would banish him from the station for ever, and this fear cast a dreadful shadow on his precarious happiness. Mr Turner was a man of few words and even fewer smiles and Arnold could not trust him. Harry, however, had promised Arnold that one day he too would be a porter and wear a uniform like Harry's. 'Only smarter!' Tim had said and Harry had given Tim a playful punch on the arm for his sauce. Arnold grinned at the memory and allowed himself to imagine *how* exactly he would wear the smart round cap with its neat peak – perhaps pushed to the back of his head like Harry, or jauntily to one side like Tim. No, he decided after some reflection, he would wear it well forward and correct like the stationmaster himself.

Suddenly the clock on the opposite wall caught his eye and he remembered guiltily that he was supposed to be learning to tell the time. Amy had explained that he could

2

not be a member of the station staff until he could tell the
passengers the times of the trains. Not that he did not already
know the timetable by heart, but he must be able to point
to the clock and impress people with his complete understanding of the matter of time itself. He had to be able to
say things like, 'It'll be here in three minutes' or, 'You've
missed it by half a minute.' These were the things which
Harry said and it was part of a porter's job. Arnold sighed
deeply and screwed up his eyes, peering through the long
fair lashes which fringed them.

'When the big hand's on the twelve—' he began earnestly.
The trouble was that the big hand was *not* on the twelve –
it was on the ten and the little hand was not quite on the
six. He sighed again and scowled with confusion. Whenever
Amy told him about the clock and about time, she always
began with the big hand being on the twelve, yet he hardly
ever saw it in that position and was coming round to the
opinion that there was something seriously wrong with the
hands of the clock. The numbers looked all right and they
always seemed to be in their proper places, but the hands
were definitely suspect and after a few agonised moments he
gave up. He turned his attention to the cat, squeaking loudly
and trying to coax it across the tracks, but although it stared
in his direction, it seemed content to remain on the down
platform and Arnold was forced to continue his examination
of Gazedown Station.

The village station was situated between Wittersham Road
and Tenterden and the line, opened earlier in the year, had
immediately and inevitably brought about changes in the
lives of the 407 inhabitants of Gazedown. Jim Leckie at
Hope's Farm now sent his livestock to market by train and
his erstwhile drover had been lucky to find himself a new
job as the school caretaker. The village carrier no longer
conveyed passengers to and from the neighbouring villages,
except those few who were too nervous to risk their lives on
the 'newfangled' trains. He carried fewer parcels, for they
could be sent more quickly and cheaply by train, but he
did ferry passengers from Tenterden Station into Tenterden
proper – a distance of nearly two miles, and much of it
uphill. Already moves were afoot for an extension to the

3

line, to take the train right into the town. The new station would be Tenterden and the existing one would be renamed; Rolvenden seemed the most likely choice.

Other changes had also been wrought. Gerald Hatherley, a rich landowner, had sold a strip of land to the Railway Company and was consequently even richer; four of the youngsters who lived in the village now travelled to Tenterden each day to full-time work and two even travelled on to Headcorn, where they changed trains for Ashford. This meant there was less casual labour available locally when it was needed to pick Mr Burton's strawberries or Colonel Haddey's hops. Mrs Betts' eldest daughter had gone to a dance in Robertsbridge and had met and married a Roberts-bridge man instead of the Gazedown lad who had courted her very casually for two years. A few tourists from London now wandered through the village in July and August, admiring the fine church and peering inquisitively into the smithy. On the strength of this 'invasion', Mrs Betts the sub-postmistress had started selling souvenirs with 'Gazedown' painted on them, as well as some of her own honey and postcards showing local views.

And, of course, the railway had brought with it the railway staff, to impress the simple villagers with their smart uniforms and their allegiance to a large and powerful company. The head of this staff was Thomas Turner, the stationmaster, a large taciturn man who spoke only when it was necessary and who had rarely been known to smile. Harry Coombes had come as porter. He looked about sixty because he was prematurely grey, but in fact he was only forty-six, a large careless man whose uniform hung on him like the proverbial sack and whose shoes, in spite of Mr Turner's frequent remonstrances, were never polished. By way of contrast, Tim Hollis, the young booking clerk, was at nineteen a cheerful soul with a brisk, friendly manner and a decidedly roving eye. He was of medium height and good-looking in a dapper way, with dark hair slicked back from a centre parting and bold dark eyes. He had perfected a distinctive way of walking, springing from the heel and making sudden changes of direction which he rightly

4

imagined gave an impression of purpose to his wanderings around the station platform.

Bob Hart, in his mid-thirties, was officially the signalman and was paid for his duties in this capacity, but he was also a snarer of rabbits, a mender of bicycles, a gatherer of mushrooms (which he spotted from the advantageous height of the signal-box) and a repairer of boots and shoes – all of which extra activities were made possible by the long intervals between the trains which passed through Gazedown Station.

The station itself boasted a double track for the length of its two platforms, the 'up' and the 'down'. On the 'up' there was an entrance hall, a booking-office which doubled as a parcels office and a waiting-room and toilets. Further along on the same side and actually abutting the platform, was the stationmaster's house and beyond that a water tower, wind pump and Bob Hart's signal-box. A small shelter on the 'down' platform was reached by a footway across the track and further back a spur of track ran into a shed and this area served as a goods siding.

In this small kingdom Thomas Turner now reigned supreme and was paid all the deference due to a man with his undoubted responsibilities. At home, however, he found his growing son less easy to impress and relied more and more upon his daughter to supervise Sam's upbringing.

*

Amy, Sam and her father ate their breakfast in silence. It was the same breakfast every weekday: toast and boiled eggs. On Saturday it was toast and bacon. On Sunday it was bacon, eggs and fried bread. These were the breakfasts Amy's mother had always cooked and twenty-year-old Amy saw no reason to make any changes.

'Close your mouth properly when you eat,' she said sharply to Sam, who immediately pulled a face but complied.

She glanced at her father who was buttering toast with a preoccupied air, thinking that he looked pale. He was a tall man with a large frame, but was not particularly robust and recently had suffered a succession of minor ills which – while they did not pose any real threat to his health – caused

5

him considerable discomfort. His dark hair, well-greased and parted in the middle, was now touched at the temples with grey and his grey eyes were exceptionally pale. His official expression was one of permanent austerity; his staff found it difficult to judge his mood from one day to the next and therefore treated him with a certain caution. His ears were small and lay close to his head and he was determinedly clean-shaven; he frequently declared that a man with a beard had something to hide, although he excepted members of the royal family from this sweeping generalisation.

'Eat up, Sam,' said Amy. 'You'll go in the late book if you're not careful.'

'Don't care,' said Sam. He was nearly ten years old now and frequently in trouble of some kind.

'Well, *I* care,' she told him, 'and so does Papa, so do get a move on.'

She was pouring second cups of tea for her father and herself when a shadow appeared at the frosted glass of the kitchen window and a face was pressed against the pane. Sam groaned and said, 'Oh, no!'

'I've told Arnold lots of times not to do that,' said Amy irritably. 'Will you have another word with him, please, Papa? We have no privacy at all.'

'I'll tell him,' Thomas told her, 'but you have only yourself to blame – you're too soft with him. He's no business hanging about the station.'

He took out his watch and studied it pointedly and Sam took the hint, slid off the chair and jammed his school cap on to his head. The village school did not boast a uniform, but the wearing of caps was encouraged although in fact only four boys wore them. The stationmaster's son was one of these and Sam consequently suffered the taunts and jeers of his fellow pupils. In vain he complained to his father and to Amy. The stationmaster believed himself a distinct cut above most of the villagers and he expected his son's appearance to reflect this superiority.

'Off you go now,' said Amy. She thrust a small package into her brother's hands, so that at twelve o'clock he could sit in the playground and eat cheese sandwiches and a slice

6

of seed cake. In the winter he would come home to share a midday dinner with the family.

Arnold, his nose still pressed against the window, tapped impatiently on the glass.

'Not now, Arnold,' called Amy firmly and the shadow withdrew.

'I'll speak to him,' said Thomas.

'What's for tea?' asked Sam. It was always his final question before leaving for school.

'Toad-in-the-hole,' she told him. 'Now get off to school and don't dawdle. And remember, you've your Sunday boots on, so go carefully.' He went out and she heard him calling out a greeting to Arnold.

Her father took his coat from the hook behind the door and pulled it on. Amy buttoned it for him as her mother had always done, then brushed his cap and handed it to him. He had been out once at 6.30 am for the up goods train which stopped to collect Hope's Farm's milk-churns, but at that hour he did not bother with his cap because Harry and Tim did not arrive for work until after 7 o'clock, in time for the 7.34 'stopper' from Tenterden. Tim and Harry then saw that train through while Thomas went home for his breakfast. The 9.10 from Hastings was the first train to be met by the full staff at Gazedown.

When Amy was at last alone in the kitchen, she cleared the table and put down a few scraps for Snip, the young Jack Russell bitch. A tinkling bell sounded upstairs and she smiled as she crossed to the door which closed off the stairs.

'Won't be long, Grandfather,' she called and heard him mumble something in reply.

She boiled another egg and buttered two slices of bread adding tea to the large pot which was still half-full. Her grandfather liked his tea thick, dark and sweet. Then she carried the tray up the narrow wooden stairs and knocked on the door of the room which the old man shared with Sam.

'Good morning, sir,' she said with a mock curtsey. 'Breakfast is served.'

He said, 'Give over, love,' but he almost smiled and Amy knew he enjoyed her efforts to bring a little fun into his

7

rather drab life. She set down the tray on top of the chest of drawers while she helped him to sit up and propped the pillows round him to keep him upright.

'That boy,' he remarked, 'will be late for school again. I heard him go. 8.55, it was. Precisely.'

'He wouldn't be hurried,' said Amy, laying the tray across his knees. 'Here we are now – egg, bacon, mushrooms, kidney, tomatoes . . .'

'It looks like a boiled egg to me!'

She smiled. 'Just use a bit of imagination, Grandfather!'

'Where's the salt?' he demanded. 'I can't eat boiled egg without salt, you know I can't.'

'I'll fetch it,' she told him briskly and waited for the inevitable criticism.

He looked severely at the bread and butter. 'Doorsteps!' he said. 'You never could cut bread like your mother. Wafer-thin, her bread was – wafer-thin and just the right amount of butter. She may have been a wrong 'un, but she knew how to cut bread, damn her.'

Amy regarded him humorously with hands on hips and refused to be drawn into a discussion about her mother. 'Just salt, then,' she said. 'Everything else all right?'

'I'll let you know when I've eaten it.'

She went downstairs for the salt-cellar and Snip followed her when she went up again.

'And take that dog out of here,' grumbled the old man as soon as he saw her. 'You know I can't abide it. Where's that cat of mine?'

Amy crossed to the window, pushed it up and looked out over the platform. Tim saw her and waved in greeting.

'Morning, Tim!' she cried. 'Is Sandy anywhere?'

Arnold lumbered into view and beamed up at her. 'I'll find him for you,' he shouted. 'Hang on!'

'Thank you, Arnold.' She closed the window.

'And don't let him up here,' Ted warned. 'You know I can't put up with his jabbering.'

'You don't mean that,' she chided. 'Poor Arnold. He loves to come up here and hear all about the old days – and you love to tell him!'

Ted Turner had worked his way up from cleaner to engine-driver. His stories were legion and Arnold was always eager to listen to the old man's interminable reminiscences.

Now Ted pushed a piece of bread into the soft yolk of his egg and ate it noisily and with reluctant enjoyment. 'But not while I'm eating my breakfast,' he insisted. 'There's a time and place for everything, and breakfast is not the time for Arnold. Oh dammit, that'll be him now!'

Amy hurried downstairs to intercept him and found Arnold holding the large ginger cat in a grip of iron while the unfortunate animal struggled and protested loudly.

'Here he is!' cried Arnold. 'I told you I'd find him. He was in the waiting-room – Ow!'

He dropped the cat abruptly and sucked the back of his right hand, his eyes dark with instant misery. Sandy, seizing his chance, sprang up on to the draining-board and made his escape through the kitchen window. Chastened, Arnold said, 'Ow, that hurts,' and regarded his scratched hand mournfully. 'Now he's gone again,' he remarked despondently.

'Never mind,' said Amy. 'You couldn't help it. Sandy is a bit fierce sometimes.'

'It hurts,' Arnold repeated, watching fascinated as small beads of blood oozed from the scratch.

'Show me.'

Any took a clean handkerchief from her pocket and wrapped it round Arnold's meaty hand. 'There you are! You look like a wounded soldier.'

A broad smile lit up his face. 'I'd better go and show Tim,' he said, 'and Harry. Wounded soldier – that's what I am. I'll show Tim and Harry.'

'Good idea. You can keep the hanky.'

'Keep it? Can I? I'd like that.'

He lifted his hand and regarded the handkerchief reverently and Amy laughed. 'Off you go, then,' she said. 'I've got a lot to do today.'

'Shall I do my reading today?' he asked hopefully.

'It's Monday,' she reminded him, 'but if I have any spare time I'll come and find you.'

'Waiting-room starts with a gee,' he told her eagerly.

'Arnold! It does *not* start with a G!'

9

'Oh?'

'Think, Arnold. Waiting-room starts with a . . . ?'

He realised his mistake and grinned sheepishly. 'Oh, yes. Double-you.'

Amy nodded. 'Good. You do know it really; you just forgot for a moment.'

When he had gone she cleared the breakfast table and washed up, and then collected some washing from various parts of the house. She filled the copper with water and put the sheets and pillowcases in to soak while she laid paper and sticks in the grate underneath and lit the fire.

Her grandfather's bell rang and she took up a kettle full of water for his morning wash and brought down his tray. Amy hummed cheerfully as she went about these various duties and did not find them at all irksome because the familiar tasks left her mind free to think about Don Leckie.

*

A small queue of anxious people waited at the window of the ticket office, but Tim let them wait. He had already made a quick assessment of the passengers and there was not one 'tipper' amongst them. Therefore, the only way that he could make a few coppers was to short-change one or two when he sold them their tickets. He could only get away with this strategy if they had insufficient time in which to check their change, so it was necessary to delay the selling of tickets until the last possible moment. To this end he ignored the passengers' irate taps upon the window and busied himself entering details in the parcels book.

Outside in the waiting-room four passengers grumbled to each other about the delay. One of these was Mary Leckie, a rather shapeless woman who was sitting on a bench beside the unlit fire with two baskets on the floor beside her. One of these contained an assortment of salad vegetables and the other held six jars of home-made strawberry jam. The Reverend Ambrose Stokes, noticing the latter, said, 'Still picking are you?' for it was late June and the strawberry season was almost at an end.

Mary shrugged and the rest of her large body shook in sympathy.

'There's a few left,' she said. 'Mostly "jams" now, though. No point taking them into market, so I make them into jam instead. You can't sell these little ones – the flavour's there, but folks just won't buy them. Daft really, but there you are. Has your sister had all she wants this year?'

'I don't really know,' he confessed. 'I'll certainly ask her.'

'You do that, vicar,' said Mary. 'Tell her I've a few jams left and she can have them cheap. They're good in pies, too, the little ones – and I make a summer pudding too – that's lovely, that is. My husband loves a summer pudding, so does my boy. You ever had that? Line a basin with bread and fill it with soft fruits. Lovely, that is. You must have had it?'

'Er, no, I don't think so,' he said. 'I don't recollect—' He broke off to take out his watch and frown at it. 'Whatever is keeping young Hollis? The train will be here in less than four minutes.'

Mary shook her head. 'Well, he's in there right enough because I heard him talking to Arnold.'

'Ah yes,' said the vicar. 'Arnold. Poor Arnold.'

Someone rapped loudly on the ticket window and they both turned to look at Esme Hatherley, whose features were now drawn into an unattractive frown.

'It's quite disgraceful!' she declared. 'I shall have something to say to the stationmaster when I see him next. What is the point of being driven down in good time if we are to kick our heels in here and then find ourselves in a last-minute rush? It's quite absurd.'

She was a tall slim woman, almost beautiful, with delicate bone structure, hard blue eyes and smooth fair hair. Her clothes were obviously expensive and in the height of fashion and she carried a small Pekinese dog under her left arm. Esme Hatherley lived at Bates Manor with her husband Gerald and they owned a large number of cottages in Gaze-down as well as a great deal of land.

The fourth person in the waiting-room was Mrs Betts' eldest daughter, who was now Mrs Hubbard and pregnant. The Reverend Stokes turned to her with a smile and said, 'Been to visit your mother, have you, Janet? How is she?'

'Much better, thank you, sir,' said Janet, colouring shyly at the unwelcome attention. 'I could only stay a couple of days, but doctor says it was only a bit of a faint and not to worry.'

'Ah! A bit of a faint? Well, that's good news. I shall call in and see her tomorrow. And are you keeping well? And your husband?'

She nodded. 'That's good,' he said.

The Reverend Stokes was a bachelor, cared for by his widowed sister. He was a very tall, spare man in his forties with poor eyesight and very little hair, and was well-meaning in a mainly ineffectual way.

Suddenly the ticket window was opened and Tim Hollis' smiling face appeared. 'Good morning, one and all,' he said briskly. 'Come along there, then, ladies and gents. Two minutes to go!'

Esme Hatherley whirled on him angrily. 'What time do you call this?' she demanded. 'What possible excuse can you have for—'

Tim's smile did not waver and he appeared not to have heard. 'Cannon Street, was it? Day return?'

'Yes.' She fumbled angrily in her purse.

'And one dog?'

'He will sit on my lap,' she began.

'Plus one dog,' said Tim, as though she had not spoken.

They were both well aware that he could have overlooked the existence of the Pekinese and that had the stationmaster himself been present he would have told Tim to waive the extra fare. However, the stationmaster had received a bottle of passable brandy soon after his arrival in Gazedown, as a token of the Hatherleys' esteem and in exchange for favours which might be bestowed throughout the year. Tim Hollis had received nothing, though, and was therefore inclined to be much more vigilant in the matter of small dogs.

His smile broadened as he pushed Esme's change through the window and saw that she slipped it into her purse without counting it. That was sixpence so far! Her place was taken by Mary Leckie.

'Tenterden, is it?'

She nodded. As Tim reached for the appropriate ticket, he called over his shoulder to Arnold.

'Steps, please, Arnold!'

12

A pair of wooden steps, two treads high, was kept for the use of elderly and infirm passengers, to help them manage the distance between platform and carriage step. Mary Leckie was neither elderly nor infirm, but she was very bulky and found it difficult to raise her large body off the platform and squeeze it through the narrow doorway.

Delighted at the chance to be of service, Arnold seized the steps and rushed out on to the platform where the train was shuddering to a halt, with a cheerful grinding and squealing of brakes and a great rush of steam from the engine. The train consisted of the locomotive 'Bodiam' – a small tank engine – one first and one third-class carriage and the brake van.

Esme Hatherley climbed into the first-class carriage, while the vicar and Janet Hubbard followed Mary Leckie and her basket into the third-class carriage. Meanwhile Tim and Harry transferred five parcels and a basket of live hens into the care of the train guard and received three crates in return.

The stationmaster materialised on the platform at this point and walked up to the front of the train to exchange a few words with the driver and fireman.

There was a brief slamming of doors, a cry of 'Right!' from Harry and a 'Right away!' from the train guard.

With a hiss of steam the engine jerked forward and with a protesting clatter, the wheels began to roll and the train picked up speed. The entire staff of Gazedown watched it until it was out of sight and then Arnold, still clutching the steps, turned to the others, his eyes gleaming with excitement.

'I got a penny off Mrs Leckie. A penny! She gave me a penny!'

'Good for you,' said Harry.

'You'll be a blooming millionaire soon,' said Tim and in the laughter that followed, forebore to mention the total of nine pennies in his own pocket.

*

The solitary passenger alighting from the train handed in his ticket, made his way out into the station forecourt and there hesitated. He was a stranger to the village and needed to ask

13

for directions. When he noticed a woman in the garden of the stationmaster's house, he made his way towards her.

'Excuse me,' he began. 'I wonder if—'

The woman was beating the dust out of a carpet that hung over the washing line and at first she did not hear him, so he raised his voice a little.

'I wonder if you could help me?'

When she turned towards him, she was younger than he expected. She looked vaguely harassed, but her expression was friendly enough.

'You should take up tennis,' he said. 'You've got a very powerful right arm! Quite a swing, in fact.'

Amy wiped her face with the corner of her apron, laughed and said, 'I'll remember that, but how can I help you?'

'My name's Ralph Allan,' he told her. 'I'm renting The Lodge at Bates Manor. I wonder if you could direct me?'

'Renting The Lodge? How funny,' said Amy. 'Aren't they going to take on another lodge-keeper, then?'

'Apparently not.' He shrugged lightly. 'Unless I'm it – and I don't think I am.'

'I'm sorry,' said Amy. 'Perhaps I spoke out of turn. It's none of my business, but you know what it's like in a small village.'

'No,' he said. 'I don't really. I'm from London, I've never lived in a village before.'

Amy laughed. 'Oh! You're in for a few surprises, then,' she told him.

'That sounds ominous!'

'Not really. I'm sure you'll enjoy your stay.'

'I hope so, but I intend to do a lot of work so I don't suppose I shall see too much of the rest of the village. Are you a local girl – I mean, were you born here?'

Amy shook her head. 'No, I've only been here a few months. My father's the stationmaster and . . .' she hesitated fractionally ' . . . we moved here from Essex when the new line opened.'

As they talked, she was forming a mainly favourable opinion of the stranger. He seemed as though he might be in his late twenties and she liked his voice, which held a hint of shyness. He looked very thin and his clothes appeared a

14

little too large for him, as though perhaps he had lost weight recently. His intense eyes were grey above prominent cheek-bones and his mouth was strangely vulnerable. His fine hair was a pale brown. Briefly he explained that he was abandoning the bustle of London for the peace of the country, in order to work on a book.

'No, not a novel,' he explained in answer to her question. 'It's a bit difficult to explain. A certain Lord Stanisbrooke was a distant relative of ours and he left a great mass of documents and papers in connection with his work in India over a number of years. Apparently they shed new light on the Army's role during that period. I'm rather vague about it at the moment, but I think that's the general idea. His son began work on the book, but then became ill and died before he could make very much progress. My brother Elliot is with Benwells, the London publishers, and he has talked me into carrying on with it – so here I am, headed for The Lodge and a lot of hard, possibly boring work.'

'It doesn't sound at all boring,' said Amy, impressed. 'I wish you luck with it. I'll walk as far as the road with you, and point you in the right direction. Are the Hatherleys related to you?'

'Very distantly. I've never actually met them, although my brother Elliot has. Do you know them?'

'Not really, but I see them occasionally when they travel on the railway.'

They had reached the level crossing and Amy stopped. 'Go straight along the lane until you come to a junction,' she directed him. 'That's the High Street. Turn right and go past a turning on the left and the row of cottages on your right. As you start to climb Catts Hill towards the church, you'll see the drive on your right and The Lodge is right there. If you want the Manor, it's a few minutes' walk along the drive – very pretty now because the rhododendrons are still in flower. I saw them last week when I had to deliver a telegraph.'

'Well, many thanks,' he said. 'I'll leave you to your carpet-beating. Oh, you haven't told me your name?'

'Amy Turner.'

15

He held out a hand and as Amy shook it she noticed how thin the long fingers were.

'Who's going to look after you?' she asked impulsively.

'I shall look after myself,' he said. 'Don't worry about me, I can manage.'

As he left her with a friendly wave of his hand, she watched him walk away until he turned a bend in the lane and disappeared from sight. 'Ralph Allan,' she pondered. 'Nice name.'

She walked slowly back to the garden where she found Arnold wielding the carpet-beater with wild, erratic strokes. He turned towards her, beaming broadly.

'I'm helping you,' he told her. 'I can beat carpets!'

Amy hid a smile. 'Oh you can, yes,' she agreed. 'But why don't you go up and see Grandfather? He'd be pleased to have someone to talk to. I can manage the carpets.'

Arnold's grin faded. 'But I want to read,' he protested. 'I want to learn about gee and double-you. I want—'

'I don't think so, Arnold,' she told him, smothering a groan. 'You know Monday is a busy day. Tomorrow, perhaps.'

'Tomorrow? Wednesday?'

'No. Tomorrow is Tuesday.'

'And I can read tomorrow? You promise?'

'I expect so. Oh, all right, I promise.'

She led him into the house and called up the stairs to warn the old man that Arnold was on the way up. Then she finished the carpet, returned it to the sitting-room and made a start on the washing. She decided that if she finished in time she would walk down to Hope's Farm and collect the two dozen eggs she bought from the Leckies each week. Mary Leckie, she knew, had gone to the market in Tenterden; Jim, her husband, would be out working on the farm – but if fate smiled on her, she might find their son at home. At the thought of him the familiar thrill went through her, for Amy had 'taken a fancy' to nineteen-year-old Donald the moment she first saw him, four days after her arrival in Gazedown. According to Tim Hollis, however – whose sources of information were usually impeccable – Don was courting Mrs Betts' youngest daughter Lorna, so Amy held

16

out no real hopes that her affections would ever be returned. She did not believe in miracles and having seen pretty young Lorna Betts she thought her a very suitable match for Don, but Tim assured her that there was nothing actually settled between the two of them – there had been no mention of an engagement – so for the present Amy was content. While he remained single, she could still dream. If he ever married Lorna, it would be a different matter . . . but she would face that when it came. Today, Monday, was a special day because today she could go for the eggs.

*

At Bates Manor, Lorna walked backwards, scattering damp tealeaves over the landing carpet. She had already worked her way up the broad winding staircase and when she reached the far end of the landing she would knock on the study door. The carpet in the study and adjoining library would receive the same treatment as stairs and landing – *if* there were enough tealeaves and *if* Mr Hatherley was not in one of his 'frisky' moods. Lorna hoped he *was*, because the mistress had gone to London on the train and there was no chance of her surprising them together. Not that they were ever actually 'together' – not like that. Lorna prided herself in knowing how far to go. Gerald Hatherley liked to touch her, he liked to be very near her and he liked to make naughty remarks. Then he would slip her a sixpence, and Lorna saved up these tips and bought items of underwear for her bottom drawer. She intended to marry Donald Leckie and hoped he was beginning to come round to her way of thinking. Not that either of them had put the idea into words, but she believed it was understood between them.

She knocked at the study door.

'Come in.'

Her employer was not a handsome man by any standards. He was a small man, forty-two years old, almost bald and, to sixteen-year-old Lorna, an old man. His face was birdlike, with a rosebud mouth and a neat pointed nose; he had very pale blue eyes and he blinked a lot whenever he was excited. A 'dry old stick' was how Lorna had described him to Donald.

17

'I have to do the carpet, sir,' she said. 'It's Monday.'

Gerald turned from the window and beckoned her to join him. She put down the bowl of tealeaves and the dustpan and brush and crossed to the window to stand on his left. He laid a trembling hand on her right shoulder as he pointed across the lawn.

'A hoopoe,' he said. 'I'm sure of it! Lovely bird – you don't see them very often.'

'Hoopoe, sir? I can't see anything.'

His hand moved to her left shoulder and she felt the weight and warmth of his arm where it rested across the back of her neck.

'It's a migrant,' he told her. 'It shouldn't be here by rights. Should have gone back to . . . ah, there it goes! Up into the sycamore. Did you spot it?'

'No, sir,' said Lorna. 'At least, I did see a bird but it went so fast. What does it look like?'

'Tufted feathers on the head. Very distinctive.' He leaned closer and his hand moved down her shoulder and slid underneath her arm until she could feel his fingertips just below her breast. 'A very distinctive bird, Lorna. Just wait a few moments, we might get another glimpse. It was just there, below the rhododendron, feeding.'

She stared dutifully across the grass and wondered if there really *was* a hoopoe; he might easily have invented it. Last time it had been a nuthatch or some such and she hadn't seen that either.

'A handsome bird,' Gerald muttered hoarsely, 'with an O-E. Not O-W.'

'Beg pardon, sir?'

'The spelling, Lorna. H-O-O-P-O-E.'

'Oh, I see.'

He was leaning so close to her that when he turned his head slightly towards her, his mouth brushed her ear.

Lorna fought down a desire to giggle: that would never do.

'You certainly do know a bit about birds, sir,' she said, her eyes fixed stolidly on the boughs of the sycamore trees amongst which the elusive hoopoe was allegedly concealed.

'They don't breed in this country,' he told her. 'They're

18

what we call birds of passage – we're a stopping-off place for them. It's a fascinating hobby, bird-watching. Quite fascinating.'

His sharp fingers dug into her breast and she wriggled briefly to signal her disapproval. At once he allowed his arm to fall back to his side and for a moment they both continued to stare wordlessly out of the window.

'I'm sure it is, sir,' said Lorna, regretting her wriggle in case it had cost her a sixpence. 'I haven't got a hobby. It must be nice – to have one, I mean.'

She had often tried to imagine Esme and Gerald Hatherley in bed together and had failed totally.

'No hobby?' Gerald repeated. 'Oh dear, that's very sad. Everyone should have a hobby. We must find you one, mustn't we?' He turned towards her, blinking his eyes, his voice hoarse. 'What do you like to do best?' he asked. 'What do you choose to do with your free time?'

'Not much,' she confessed with a shrug of her plump shoulders. 'I help out in the shop if Ma's a bit rushed. Sometimes I cook the supper. Sometimes I see Don.'

'Don?' He frowned. 'Don Leckie at the farm? You see him, do you?'

'Yes, sir.'

He put out a small bony hand and gently pinched her cheek. 'Your young man, is he?'

'Sort of, sir. We're walking out, like.'

'You are?' He nodded and began to touch her hair, brushing the curls lightly with his fingertips. 'And what do the two of you get up to? Tell me, Lorna.'

She assumed an expression of injured innocence. 'Nothing, sir! We don't get up to anything, honestly we don't.'

He was breathing quickly and suddenly both his hands were fumbling in her hair, round her ears and neck and Lorna fought down a desire to scream.

'Nothing, sir,' she repeated firmly, thinking that surely this was worth a shilling. 'We wouldn't, not until we married. Ma would kill me if I did anything like that. You don't know my ma, sir – I mean, you don't know how strict she is. I wouldn't dare!'

Gerald thrust his face close to hers and whispered, 'Don't

19

you ever let him touch you? Surely you do? You young girls today – you let the boys—'

'I do *not*, sir!'

She thought of her sister Janet who had married in a great hurry and remembered her mother's wrath, which had been truly terrible. No, Lorna did not allow her young man to take liberties; she knew only too well where it could lead.

'You don't?'

'No, sir.' She sensed his disappointment and added, 'Well, I might just let him *touch* me.'

'Where, Lorna? Tell me. Whisper it.'

'Just like you do, sir,' said Lorna. 'My neck and my arms and round my waist. That's all.'

'Is it, Lorna? Is that all?'

She nodded. 'We're only walking out,' she repeated. 'Not promised or anything.'

'Not promised,' he said, as though in some way that explained everything. 'Well, if you do let him – when you're promised, that is – you must tell me. You understand? I'm your employer, you see, so I'll want you to tell me – in confidence of course – what you do.'

'I see, sir,' she said doubtfully.

'Good girl, Lorna. You're a good girl. And I can teach you a lot about birds, you see. We can watch them from here, like this. You'd like that, Lorna, wouldn't you? Just the two of us.'

She nodded and to her relief he finally appeared satisfied and stepped back, fumbling in his pocket for a coin. He took hold of her hand pressed a sixpence into her palm and folded her fingers round it. Then he raised her clenched hand to his lips. 'Now what was it you saw today? The bird I told you about?'

Lorna opened her mouth to say that she hadn't seen it at all but fortunately her common sense saved her and she said, 'A hoopoe, sir.'

'And what do we call it, eh? A bird of . . . what?'

'A bird of passage, sir.'

'Good girl. You're a quick learner, you know that?'

'Thank you, sir.'

They looked at each other for a moment and then Lorna

20

glanced around her, her gaze settling on the dustpan, brush and bowl.

'I'd better be getting on, sir,' she said. 'I've a lot to do.'

'Of course, Lorna. You get on.'

He turned back to the window and stared out while Lorna continued her work. She scattered the last of the tealeaves and then, kneeling, began to sweep them up into the dustpan. The dust in the carpet clung to the damp tealeaves and did not fly up into the air. Lorna worked energetically while Gerald, ignoring her efforts, pretended to watch the birds.

Before she finally left the room to extend her work to the landing, Lorna gave her employer one last glance. Outside the study she muttered, 'Poor old thing,' and then shrugged and began to think about Don Leckie.

Chapter Two

Inside the office Tim waited for the water in the tin kettle to boil and meanwhile spooned tea into the teapot.

'Milk come yet?' he asked.

Arnold shook his head and, to prove the point, waved the empty milk jug. 'I'll go and look for him' he said.

The stationmaster 'tutted'. 'Fred gets later every day,' he grumbled. 'It's quite ridiculous.' He continued to prowl round the office, making a show of tidying and checking; he collected various pens and pencils from the desk top and window sill, put the latter into the jam-jar labelled 'PENCILS' and returned the pens to the inkstand. Then he flipped up the lid of the inkwell and said, 'Ink's low.'

'Right, Mr Turner,' said Tim briskly. 'I'll fill it as soon as I've made the tea.'

'Hm.' The stationmaster sniffed loudly to let Tim know that these reminders should not be necessary.

'Got a cold coming, have you sir?' Tim asked innocently. 'You know what they say about summer colds, they last twice as long as winter ones.'

'I haven't got a cold.'

Tim winked at the kettle and mentally chalked up a 'win' as the stationmaster continued his self-appointed investigation. He returned a cork to the glue-pot; pressed a finger enquiringly on to the pan of the small parcels scales; unrolled a new poster extolling the virtues of Hastings for sea-bathing and re-rolled it; studied the entries in the parcels ledger and finally ran a finger across the top of the unlit stove which heated the office in winter.

'Where's Harry?' he asked at last. 'I want a word with him.'

'Weeding the garden,' Tim told him. 'Only two more weeks to the judging.'

'Hm.'

As the stationmaster went out, Tim pulled a face. 'Why don't you smile once in a while?' he mocked. 'Crack your face? It doesn't hurt, it's not like toothache.'

Whistling cheerfully, he made the tea and put the knitted tea-cosy over the pot. The orange and pink striped cosy, knitted in a deeply ridged pattern, was the only visible proof that there had once been a 'Mrs Stationmaster'. Amy had given it to them and Sam had said it was made by his mother.

When Tim and Harry had nothing better to do, they liked to speculate on what had become of Mrs Turner. The stationmaster never referred to her and young Sam, when questioned, said only that she 'went away'. He had obviously been told not to discuss the matter and the station staff dared not press him in case he told his father. The subject of the stationmaster's wife was obviously a delicate one.

As Tim arranged three enamel mugs on the desk top, Arnold reappeared and Tim, with a loud groan, reached for a fourth.

'The milkman's here,' Arnold told him.

'About time, too.'

Tim handed him the pint jug and Arnold came back a minute or two later, carrying it with exaggerated care.

'What did the old man tell you about this morning?' asked Tim, referring to Arnold's visit to the stationmaster's father. Arnold settled himself on a stool and screwed up his face in an effort to remember.

'About a crash,' he volunteered at last. 'A train crash.'

'Trust him! Which one was it?'

Arnold wriggled on the stool, a stricken look on his face.

'Which crash?' Tim prompted. 'When did it happen? Which year?'

'Which year,' repeated Arnold earnestly.

'You tell *me*, old son.'

'Don't know.'

23

'Arnold!' cried Tim in mock exasperation. 'You never can remember. You know what you are, don't you?'

Arnold grinned. 'The giddy limit!' he said proudly.

'Eggs-actly!' said Tim. 'Now think – was it passenger or goods?'

'Goods,' said Arnold after deep thought.

'Was it the one in the tunnel?'

'In the tunnel!' cried Arnold, a look of relief spreading over his face. 'Yes! In the tunnel!'

'The yummy meat story?'

'Yes!'

'Go on, then.'

Arnold rolled his eyes in delighted anticipation as Tim folded his arms and waited. Of course. He screwed up his face once more.

'Three trains,' he gabbled, 'crashed in a tunnel, meat in the trains and the trains crashed.' He paused and repeated, 'They were in the tunnel. Crash! And they all got on fire from the hot coals and the meat got cooked and everyone could smell the meat and it was yummy!'

In his excitement, Arnold slid from the stool and waved his arms about.

'Crash!' he cried again, bringing his right fist into his left palm. 'And all the meat cooked and everyone—' He stopped abruptly as the stationmaster came in, followed by Harry Coombes.

Harry grinned. 'Let me guess,' he said. 'The '66 crash.'

'Exactly,' said Tim. He poured out the tea, added milk and sugar and handed round the mugs.

The stationmaster said slowly, 'Two railwaymen lost their lives in that crash. It's no laughing matter.'

Arnold's eyes widened in alarm at this rebuke and he looked anxiously at Tim, who merely shrugged his shoulders without comment. The stationmaster went on, 'The Tilleys could be done today, Tim.'

'Right you are, sir.'

'Clean the glass and renew the mantles if necessary.'

'Right.'

The stationmaster raised his eyebrows and waited.

'Right, *sir*,' Tim amended sulkily. Cleaning the signal

24

lamps was usually Harry's job, but Harry was temporarily released from such mundane work in order to attend to the station garden which would be assessed shortly by three judges. One of these would be a senior railway official from London, the second a professional gardener from one of the London parks and the third the Member of Parliament for one of the Kent boroughs.

Although the station had only recently opened, Harry had begged to be allowed to enter the competition and finally had been granted one hour daily for the preparation of a strip of garden, 8 feet by 20 feet. This he had hurriedly planted with a selection of shrubs and flowers. In addition to this official time, he also put in a few hours of his own – time which his wife fondly imagined him to be spending on the family allotment, producing vegetables for their kitchen. The railway made no financial contribution towards the garden, but one or two of the regular passengers had donated cuttings. No one expected actually to win the competition – 'The perfect garden', Harry insisted, 'takes years to perfect' – but he hoped to put up a reasonable showing. Secretly he nursed a desire to be awarded a 'specially commended', although wild horses would not have dragged such an admission from him.

Now, as he sipped his tea, Harry considered the salvias and wondered whether or not to add a last-minute edging of ageratum, the dusky blue of the latter to set off the bold crimson of the former. Or he could bring some small violas from his own garden ... but would the deeper colour produce the effect he wanted?

He sighed deeply and Tim said, 'Penny for them, Hal.'

'I was just wondering,' Harry began, not meeting the stationmaster's eye, 'about the garden. I was thinking that a row of—'

'There isn't any money, I'm afraid,' the stationmaster said.

'Ah. That's what I thought.'

'Crash!' muttered Arnold. 'In the tunnel. Crash! And everyone could smell the yummy meat.' He stared at the unlit stove as though awaiting some kind of response; then slowly he pressed a fist into a palm and mouthed, 'Crash!'

At that moment there was a tapping at the booking-office window and Tim put down his mug of tea to open it. He turned back to the others immediately, finger and thumb held to his nose.

'It's Miss Peck!' he told them.

Ivy Peck was an elderly eccentric who lived at the corner of Station Lane in a small cottage which had once been an attractive dwelling but now was no better than a hovel. At least a dozen cats shared her home and the smell was enough to deter even the vicar from calling. Her mode of dress also gave scope for criticism as she wore several layers of garments at one time, all in need of a wash.

The stationmaster gave Tim a disapproving glance and said coldly that he would attend to Miss Peck himself. To do this he went out of the office and into the waiting-room, where she turned to him greatly agitated.

'I want to travel on the train,' she told him. 'Where is it?'

'Good morning, Miss Peck,' he said. 'Where is what?'

'The train, of course. I want a ticket. I'm going on the train. At once!'

He stared at her, astonished. There were still a large number of people in the village who had announced their determination to have no dealings with the railway, and Miss Peck was known to be one of them. He looked down into the beady brown eyes, trying not to see the shapeless mass of clothes.

'Where are you going to?' he asked.

'My brother's funeral.'

'No, no. I meant, which station?'

'Well, how do I know?' she demanded. 'Which stations have you got?'

'It depends where the funeral is going to be held,' he told her. 'Do you know where he is going to be buried? Do you know where he lived?'

Miss Peck eyed him frostily. 'Do I know where my brother lived?' she repeated. 'I should hope I do. He lived in the same house all his life – born and bred there. It was I who left home. I who moved away. My brother lived—'

'Where is he being buried – exactly?'

26

'St Augustine's church at five o'clock – that's where he's being buried.'

'But *where* is that?' he asked patiently. 'London? Canterbury?'

'Please don't be ridiculous!'

The stationmaster glanced over his shoulder towards the booking-office window and was relieved to see that he had closed the small wooden doors. He sincerely hoped the rest of the staff were not listening.

'I have to know,' he explained, 'where the church *is*. Then I will give you a ticket and . . .'

'It's in the letter.' She produced a purse from somewhere amongst her skirts and took from it a letter folded many times. 'It's in here.' She unfolded it and perused it silently for a moment. Then with an air of triumph she declared, 'Tonbridge. St Augustine's Church at Tonbridge.'

'And you want to go by the next train?'

'Yes.'

'And you are coming back later today?'

'Yes.' She looked around her suspiciously and glanced past the stationmaster to the platform. 'I don't see any train,' she said. 'Where is the train?'

'It's not due yet.'

'Not due?'

'It doesn't start from here,' he explained. 'It will be along later. If you catch the 3.06 you should be—'

'The *what?*' Her tone was sharp. Obviously she did not trust him.

'That's the train,' he told her patiently. 'Six minutes past three – that's the time the train leaves *this station*. You will reach—'

'But I thought you said that it doesn't start from here! If it doesn't, then where do I get on it?'

'Look, ma'am, I said—'

'Don't you "ma'am" me, young man. It's "Miss Peck", *if* you don't mind.'

'Miss Peck, then.' Becoming increasingly flustered, he ran a finger round inside his collar to loosen it. 'What I actually said was—'

'I heard what you *actually* said, Mr Turner,' she told him.

'I am not deaf. Unfortunately, what you *actually* said does not make any sense to me – nor to anyone else, I suspect – nor does it inspire one with any confidence.' Miss Peck drew herself up to her full five feet four inches. 'What you have told me only confirms what I have long suspected: that the best way to get from A to B is to go by carrier as I always have done. Therefore I shall go round to Mr Badgers at once and *he* will take me to my brother's funeral. Three-oh-six indeed!'

'But I can assure you—'

'No, Mr Turner, you cannot assure me, so you might as well save your breath,' Miss Peck told him. 'You have had your chance and I shall not trouble you further.'

With a final toss of her head, she turned and swept out of the waiting-room. A burst of hastily smothered laughter alerted the stationmaster to the fact that the conversation *had* been overheard, and he decided suddenly that he would wander over to the goods yard to make sure that all there was as it should be. Without a further glance towards the office he went out on to the platform and, climbing down on to the track, made his way across with all the dignity he could muster.

*

Amy, with Snip at her heels, knocked on the back door, opened it and called, 'It's me, Amy! Anyone home?'

Hope's Farm stood about a mile from the station and was a sprawling farm which had belonged to the Leckies for over a hundred years. Jim Leckie had inherited it from his father, who had earlier bought it from an uncle who – being childless – had no one to take over when his health forced him to give up. Originally, the farm had sustained a large dairy herd, fifty sheep and a few acres of hops. Jim's father had reduced the acreage by selling off the hop-fields and had given up the sheep. Jim, in his turn, had reintroduced sheep, drastically reduced the dairy herd and gradually diversified, planting an orchard of cider apples and growing kale and broad beans. His wife Mary fattened a couple of pigs each year, raised chickens and grew a few vegetables, mainly for their own use. They employed three men: Stan and Sid

Hollingsby – two middle-aged bachelor brothers – and Fred Williams who was almost seventy and becoming rather frail. He now drove the pony cart round the village, delivering the milk, but was not able to contribute much more.

Receiving no answer, Amy pushed open the door and found the eggs in their usual place in the old chipped wash-basin on the dresser. Carefully she transferred them to her basket and then put the correct money in the basin. This done, she let her gaze wander over the familiar, disorganised kitchen. That was Don's chair and that was his jacket behind the far door. A row of newly sealed pots of quince jam spoke of Mary's industrious ways and at the thought of her Amy smiled. Large, garrulous, warm-hearted Mary was her only friend, for Amy had not had much time for socialising and her father's position as stationmaster set the Turner family somewhat apart from the rest of the village. They inhabited a grey area in the community's hierarchy, considered 'stuck-up' by the working classes and 'jumped up' by the landed gentry. This did not worry Thomas Turner to whom this was the natural order of things. Sam was not really aware of their 'position' and Ted Turner, safely ensconced in his bedroom, would not have cared. Only Amy felt at all alien-ated and, because of this, Mary's friendship meant a great deal to her.

On a chair beside the stove a black cat stretched languidly, but the green eyes watched Snip intently as the little dog followed her nose into the kitchen. Amy allowed herself a few moments to indulge her favourite fantasy, in which Don sat in his chair at the large scrubbed table and she, as his wife, sat opposite. Meanwhile the dog edged closer to the cat, who took offence suddenly and spat, which set Snip barking hysterically. At that moment Don came into the kitchen carrying a gun, with a black and white collie at his heels.

'Oh, it's you,' he said cheerfully, flinging a brace of rabbits on to the draining-board. 'That dog of yours is a real give-away!' He sent the Collie outside.

'Where did you appear from?' asked Amy, her thoughts whirling guiltily, thankful that he could not read her mind.

'I was on the way back,' he said. 'Want a rabbit?'

'No, thank you,' she said hastily. 'At least, not if I've got to skin it and everything. I can't bear it.'

'Townie!' he teased. 'I'll do it for you. How would that be?'

'Would you? That would be much better.'

Don was stockily built, with a shock of fair hair (which would not be controlled) and a square face with full lips and blue eyes. He would take after his mother, thought Amy, and would easily run to fat although his frame was large. For such a big man his movements were surprisingly gentle, and she watched with grudging admiration as he deftly opened up the rabbit he had just shot and eased off the skin.

'Still warm,' he grinned.

Amy's heart lurched. He had a certain way of moving his head, turning it sideways and looking up at her with a request for approval that was somehow childlike. She wondered if what Tim had said about Lorna Betts was true, and if so whether Lorna appreciated him. And what did he see in Lorna, apart from her obvious good looks? She wanted to ask him, but pride kept her silent.

Don took a clean cloth from the dresser drawer and wrapped up the rabbit. 'There you are,' he said. 'A gift from me to you.'

'That is kind, but we ought to pay you.'

'No. I insist.'

'Thank you.'

Stepping backwards, he caught Snip's paw and she leaped away, howling piteously. Amy fussed over her as Don laughed.

'You should get a proper dog,' he teased, slumping into a chair and stretching his legs under the table. 'Not half a dog. Blessed noisy thing!'

'She's not half a dog!' cried Amy, obligingly rising to the bait. 'She's a dear, aren't you, Snip? You'd cry, Don, if a giant stepped on your foot!'

'I would not.' He grinned at her. 'Aren't you going to sit down then?'

'Oh – all right. Thanks.'

He was sitting in Mary's chair, so Amy sat in his.

30

'How's the station going?' he asked. 'Lost any more chicks lately?'

'Of course not,' she said indignantly, 'and that wasn't my father's fault. I told you, the label had come off the basket – we couldn't tell who they belonged to. Why do you have to keep on about it?'

He laughed at her expression. The day-old chicks had gone astray in transit from London and had ended up in Hastings. It had all been very embarrassing and Amy wished he would forget the incident.

'There's a chap moving into The Lodge,' she told him, in an effort to change the subject. 'He asked me the way. He's going to write a book.'

'That's right,' said Don. 'Military battles or some such. Renting it for six months and wants to be left alone.'

'Oh?' She was surprised and a little piqued. 'He didn't say that to me. Anyway, how did you know about him?'

'Lorna works at the Manor and Mrs H told her. She's supposed to tidy round for him once a week, but he doesn't want her to.'

So it *was* true: Don and Lorna. Tim was right. Amy tried to hide her disappointment.

'He told me he was going to look after himself,' she said. 'I thought he looked rather nice, but a bit thin. I've never met anyone who writes books before. I'd like to do that.'

'What would you write about?'

She shrugged lightly. 'I don't know. A love story, maybe.' She smiled to show she was not serious.

He laughed. 'Do you know anything about love? You look so innocent, but still waters run deep. Perhaps you're a Miss Slyboots!'

'Of course I'm not!'

'Then how can you write about it?'

'I could use my imagination. I've plenty of that.'

She was aware suddenly that he was looking at her curiously, really wondering about her.

'Will you put me in your book?' he asked.

'I'm not writing a book.' She stood up hastily.

'But if you did, would you? Could I be the handsome hero? I think I'd like that.'

31

'Maybe.' She swallowed. 'I might put you *and* Lorna in it.'

'Ah!' He clutched his heart. 'That was cruel!'

'Then stop laughing at me. You always do. What's funny about me?'

For a moment they looked at each other in silence. 'I'm sorry,' he said gently. 'I didn't know I was laughing at you; I only meant to tease. I won't laugh at you again, I promise.'

Amy lowered her eyes, then snapped her fingers, calling the Jack Russell to her.

'I must go anyway,' she said, feeling suddenly immature and out of her depth. How could he have robbed her of her self-confidence so quickly, she wondered, angry with herself. He was only a nineteen-year-old boy and she was a woman of twenty. Or was she at fault, over-reacting to his friendly teasing.

'Lorna?' he said. 'She's just a girl; she's only sixteen.'

'And you're nineteen.'

He nodded. 'And you're twenty,' he said. 'Quite an old lady!'

'Who told you I was twenty?' Amy asked.

'My mother.'

'Oh.' So he had been asking about her! The notion was somehow comforting. 'What else did she tell you?' It occurred to her that perhaps Mary would approve of a friendship between her and Don.

'Nothing else,' he said.

'I thought,' said Amy, 'that I might take him a cake or something – Ralph Allan, I mean. Maybe a pie. If he's going to look after himself . . .'

The words had been uttered without any prior thought. Until that moment Amy had not considered such an idea, but now she knew she was trying to make Don jealous.

'Lucky old Ralph,' said Don, his tone a little too casual. He leaned back in the chair, tilting it excessively and defying the laws of gravity, his eyes on Amy's face. She fancied she detected a certain wariness in them. He *was* jealous!

Just then the black cat sprang up onto the window sill and disappeared through the open window, and once more Snip began to bark furiously. Outside on the doorstep the collie whined, eager to share in the fun, but Don shouted, 'Quiet!' and there was instant silence. Even Snip was quiet, looking anxiously from Don to Amy, disturbed by the forceful command.

Amy said again, 'I must go,' but she made no move.

'Take a pound of quince jam with you,' he said. 'Please!'

'Oh, but—'

'Take two! Take four! Take as many as you can carry. Put them on your Friday stall. Quince jam – ugh!'

'I love quince jam,' she protested. 'I will take some if you're sure Mary won't mind.'

Her 'Friday stall' was a small card-table which she set up once a week on the station platform. On it she sold home-made cakes, preserves, punnets of fruit, nearly new second-hand books, bunches of flowers – in fact, whatever she could find to sell. The sale of these goods brought her the only money she could call her own and also gave her an excuse to be on the platform, exchanging greetings with the passengers. It was virtually the only time in her week when she felt she belonged to Gazedown. Set apart from the village not only by the station's situation but also her father's position, she had so far failed to overcome a sense of isolation. The Friday stall went some way to counteract her loneliness.

'Help yourself.' Don waved a languid hand in the direction of the newly-made jam and, after a moment's hesitation, Amy picked up a pound and rearranged the eggs and rabbit to make room for it in her basket. As she moved towards the door Don stood up and followed her.

'Remember,' he said, 'I'm going to be the handsome hero – and I'm *not* making fun of you!'

'I'll remember,' she said.

She called Snip, who warily slipped past the collie, and together they began to walk up the drive towards the lane.

'Goodbye,' she called back.

Don, leaning against the door-jamb, raised a hand but said nothing. Amy glanced back twice and each time he was still there, his bulky frame wedged nonchalantly in the doorway.

When they reached the lane and were safely out of sight, Amy bent to pat the dog. 'He wants to be my handsome hero,' she mused, 'but only in a book. And did he tread on

33

your paw? Poor girlie! Never mind, he didn't mean it. He's very nice, really.'

She walked back to the station with her head full of delightful imaginings, the image of Don's face in the forefront of her thoughts. She would not sell the quince jam, she decided, because *he* had given it to her. As she made her way across the level crossing, she shouted a greeting to Bob Hart who sat on the steps of his signal-box, reading the previous day's newspaper.

'How's tricks?' he shouted.

'Fine, thank you.'

'I've done young Sam's boots.'

'I'll take them. Thank you, Bob.'

He disappeared inside the box and reappeared with Sam's second-best boots.

'That's a tanner to you,' he told her. 'I've put Blakey's on the toes and heels. I don't know what he does with his boots, that brother of yours – kicks 'em to pieces! Never seen nothing like it, but I've made a good job of them.'

He came down the steps. Boots and money were exchanged and Amy duly admired the workmanship.

'Your grandfather all right, is he?' Bob asked. 'I promised I'd pop in before the week's out. Tell him I haven't forgotten – it'll be Wednesday most likely.'

'I'll tell him.'

Amy let herself in at the back door, which was never locked, and at once heard the sound of her grandfather's bell. She called out to say she would be up in one minute and then realised that Sam would be out of school soon and she had not yet made the batter for the toad-in-the-hole. Reluctantly, she allowed Don's image to fade from her mind and made a start on the evening's meal.

Chapter Three

Built in 1855, Gazedown School had never been modernised, although from time to time a new layer of whitewash was applied to the walls and ceiling; the woodwork was repainted every seven years, going from dark green to dark brown and then back again to dark green. There were three classes but only two classrooms – the top class, or seniors, having to 'make do' in the hall. Sam Turner was in the top class, but at ten was one of the youngest children who daily studied in the hall under the eagle eye of Miss Dunning, the head-mistress. He shared his wooden desk with a boy called Arthur Penn, the nephew of Miss Marriatt who taught the infants. Sam's exercise book was open in front of him and he was studying a mass of black sludge which clung to the nib of his pen. He had managed to scoop up this sediment from the bottom of his inkwell and was now finding it much more interesting than the addition of 'tens and hundreds' which should have been occupying his attention. Suddenly the nib splattered inky sludge over his own and Arthur's book and Arthur immediately thrust his hand high into the air with a strangled cry of 'Miss!'

Miss Dunning's mouth contracted. 'What is it, Arthur?'

'My book, Miss,' cried Arthur, outraged. 'Sam Turner's mucked my book up, Miss. *I* never did it, Miss, it was Sam Turner. He—'

'Bring it out to me,' she said.

With an injured expression on his face, Arthur carried his book to the front of the class, where Miss Dunning examined it in haughty silence. Everyone stopped adding up 'tens and hundreds' and enjoyed the drama.

'Samuel Turner? Have you anything to say?' she asked at last.

'No, Miss.'

'No excuse for spoiling this boy's work?'

'No, Miss, except . . .'

'Well?'

'Nothing, Miss.'

'Except what, Samuel?'

Sam fixed the infant teacher's nephew with a reproachful look. 'I don't like sitting next to him, Miss. He always makes smells, Miss. Horrible smells!'

Arthur went white with shock and then red with embarrassment as he realised the futility of denying the charge. Only very rarely did he make a horrible smell, but he knew no one would choose to believe him.

'I do *not!*' he protested feebly.

The rest of the children tittered, revelling in his downfall. Poor Arthur was a natural 'swot' and suffered accordingly, being the only child in the entire school who enjoyed his work.

'Can't I sit next to someone else?' Sam persisted, without much real hope.

'No, you can't,' said Miss Dunning. 'There is no other vacant place. You will apologise to Arthur and then you will get on with your work.'

'Apologise?' he wailed. 'But, Miss!'

'That is what I said, Samuel. We are waiting.'

Sam knew how much the interlude was being appreciated by the rest of the class and felt it incumbent upon himself to prolong it as long as possible.

'But the smells, Miss,' he cried. 'It's like poison gas!'

The class giggled and one or two fanned their faces with their hands as though personally affected by the noxious fumes.

Miss Dunning swept the room with her coldest stare. 'That will do, Form One!' she said. 'I hope no one is going to have to stay in after school, though it's beginning to seem a distinct possibility.'

36

She fixed one of the older boys with a cold stare. 'And what is the matter with you, Alan Withers?'

'Nothing, Miss.'

'Then get rid of that stupid grin. That's better.'

She took out a small blotter and applied it to Arthur's book. He leaned towards her and mumbled something.

'I'm sure you don't, Arthur,' she said. 'Now go back to your place and get on with your sums.' She raised her voice. 'And that goes for the rest of you. Samuel Turner, you will stay in at playtime and write out twenty times, "I must not tell lies". Does anyone else have anything to say? No? Good. You have each made a very wise decision.'

Arthur returned to his seat, giving Sam a baleful look as he did so, and a temporary peace descended.

Five minutes later a stubby forefinger pressed into Sam's back, alerting him to the fact that Eric wanted his attention. He half turned, keeping his eyes firmly on the headmistress who was now writing something on the blackboard about someone called Horatio Nelson.

'What?' he hissed.

'Coming down the pond after school?'

Sam hesitated. He had his best boots on and the pond was sometimes muddy and wet, but if he declined he would have to explain about the boots and they would call him 'Softy' or worse.

'All right, I'll come,' he said.

He would rather face Amy's wrath (or even his father's) than risk a name-calling session, for the latter might develop into an investigation into his past and that was to be avoided at all costs. The whole school knew that there was no wife and mother at the stationmaster's house but, fiercely loyal, Sam would never tell them why. He had sworn an oath to himself never to reveal the sordid fact that his mother had run away with his uncle; he could imagine only too well what fun they would have at his expense if the truth ever got out. Having learned by eavesdropping that 'never in a million years' would his father allow his mother back into the house, Sam knew there would never again be a mother at home and accepted that as he also accepted Amy's efforts to take her place. What he could not accept, however, was the idea that these shameful facts should become common knowledge. While the boys at school remained his friends he believed they would respect his reticence, but if for any reason they turned against him he could expect no such charity. Cheeking the teachers and playing the fool was the easiest way for him to keep the other boys' respect and since that was the price of popularity, Sam was quite prepared to pay it.

After school, the two boys set off for the pond, which could be reached in two ways. It lay in the field beyond the level crossing and it was therefore perfectly possible for them to turn right when they came out of school, walk down Catts Hill and along the High Street and turn left into Station Lane. They could then climb over the gate of the field and walk across the hundred yards of grazing land. The alternative – and this was infinitely preferable – was to cross from the school to the churchyard, sneak round beside the vicarage, push a way through the vicarage hedge into the grounds of Bates Manor, make their way through the dense shrubbery and past the stables, scramble over the rough stone wall, go through the copse and dodge through a herd of startled cows. They would then emerge breathless and triumphant beside the pond. Needless to say they chose the latter route and Sam's Sunday boots did not survive this eventful journey unscathed. However, the two boys spent a happy hour throwing things into the pond and dragging things out of it. They floated sticks and leaves and paddled warily around the edges. Finally they sat down to watch it, while they sucked gob-stoppers and considered a variety of suitable torments for Miss Dunning and Arthur Penn.

They were still talking animatedly when the closing of the crossing-gates alerted them to the approach of the 'stopper' from Cannon Street, and the two boys scrambled to their feet and set off to watch the train draw into the station.

Ambrose Stokes and Mary Leckie alighted together, followed by Esme Hatherley from further along the train. Catching sight of the two boys, the vicar called a greeting and they chorused dutifully in reply.

'Silly old fool!' muttered Eric. 'If there's one thing I hate, it's blessed choir practice. I keep on to Ma to let me give it up, but she won't.'

Sam craned his neck to look at the locomotive, resplendent in its deep blue livery, dome and chimney cap gleaming in the sun. It was a small but sturdy tank engine, one of the only two owned by the newly-opened line. Her nameplate – 'Tenterden' – ran along the side of the tank. The carriages of polished teak gleamed dully and a face peered out from the curtained first-class window.

'It's "Tenterden",' said Sam.

Eric could only bow to his friend's superior knowledge and Sam as always made the most of the chance.

'It's a 2–4–OT,' he said, 'and she's got automatic vacuum brakes.'

Eric nodded knowledgeably. 'That's what I thought.'

'You never!' said Sam scornfully.

Eric was silent.

'Came from Hawthorn Leslie,' continued Sam. 'Her and "Northiam". Good firm, Hawthorn Leslie. They make beautiful locomotives.' He had heard his father say this to Harry Coombes.

Eric looked at it critically and said at last, 'They certainly do.'

Sam could not argue with that comment. 'She's a beauty,' he said with a sigh of pleasure.

The train jerked into motion once more and rolled past them and the boys waved to the driver and fireman who, smiling, gave them the 'thumbs-up' sign. For a moment the clatter of wheels and the clash of bursting steam drowned all other sounds and then the carriages rattled past, swaying slightly as the train gathered speed.

'Pa says we shall need a third engine before long,' said Sam. 'We're getting so busy. Maybe next year. Amy says we should call her "Victoria" after the Queen, but Pa says it's always the name of a station on the line. That's the way Colonel Stephens wants it, so that's how it will be.'

'Colonel Stephens? Who's he?'

Sam looked at him with exaggerated incredulity. 'Don't know who Colonel Stephens is!'

'So what?' said Eric. 'Don't know and don't care!'

'So why d'you ask me then, if you don't care?' Having scored his point, Sam felt suddenly magnanimous and added, 'He's the man who sort of owns the railway, that's who.'

Eric, mortified, shrugged his shoulders. 'You *said*,' he reminded Sam, 'that you'd get me a look in the signal box. You keep saying, but you never *do*.'

'I will,' promised Sam. 'Honest I will. I'll ask him for next week, cross my heart.'

Eric cheered up a little at this glittering prospect. 'I wish *my* father was stationmaster,' he said wistfully and Sam grinned with pleasure.

His mother might have proved a great disappointment, he thought, but his father was obviously a man to be respected.

Just then Bob Hart tapped on the window of the signal-box to attract their attention. 'I've done your boots,' he yelled. 'I've given them to your sister.'

Sam nodded and glanced guiltily down at his feet.

'Well, I'd best go on in now,' he said to Eric, who oblig-ingly took the hint and ambled off along the lane in the direction of his own home. Sam stood for a moment recalling the better moments of his day, deciding what to reveal and what to forget when his father began his daily interrogation.

He crossed the line and began to walk slowly along the platform, arranging his face into its usual expression of deep boredom, but then he remembered it was toad-in-the-hole and, with a whoop of pleasure, he swung his bag round his head and began to run.

*

Immediately opposite the village green was a small store-cum-post office which was run by Mrs Betts, a rather talk-ative widow. She believed she knew her customers well enough to distinguish between those who would accept the odd penny added to the bill and those who would inevitably query it. The latter she considered misers, especially people like Esme Hatherley who had twice sent Lorna home with the bill and a sharply worded note pointing out the error. However, to be fair to Mrs Betts she did occasionally knock a penny off the bill of anyone she considered really 'needy' – like Arnold's mother, who took in washing, and Miss Peck.

Mrs Betts was plump with a pleasant face, but her appearance was marred by the fact that she had lost most of her hair to a scalp disease in her early twenties and had worn a sun-bonnet ever since, winter and summer alike.

'Good morning, Mrs Betts.'

'Morning, Mrs Coombes. Lovely weather!'

'Let's hope it lasts.'

Harry Coombes' wife handed over her shopping list and waited while it was checked.

Mrs Betts shook her head. 'No sultanas until Friday,' she said. 'Not making your Christmas puddings already, surely?'

Mrs Coombes shook her head. 'No, though I will be in a week or so. It's keeping that makes a good pudding; my mother always said that. Four months absolute minimum, but I like to give mine five or six. No, I was going to put a few sultanas in Harry's rice pudding. He loves a bit of fruit in a rice, Harry does.'

Mrs Betts bustled about, cutting and wrapping portions of cheese and lard and weighing the tea and sugar into bags. Mrs Coombes enquired after her health and in turn Mrs Betts asked after Harry Coombes' station garden; then the conversation turned to the newcomer, as they had both known it would.

'Seen the new fellow at The Lodge?' Mrs Betts asked.

'Not yet, no.'

'Ah, you're in for a treat then,' Mrs Betts smiled. 'Quite a charmer, our Mr Allan. Came in yesterday, as polite as you like, and introduced himself. I was beginning to wonder if he was living on air – been here a week now and yesterday was the first time he showed up. Bought a few potatoes and a couple of tins of sardines.' She frowned, ticking off the items on Mrs Betts' list.

' "Looking after yourself, are you?" I said to him – you know, joking like – and he said he was, not that he eats much. He says he's never had much of an appetite, and you can see that by how thin he is. Peaky face, if you know what I mean. Your Harry must have seen him because he came by train.'

'He never said,' replied Mrs Coombes. 'I'll have to ask him. Have I got washing soda on that list? I'm right out.'

41

Mrs Betts shook her head and added the missing item. 'A writer, he is. I asked him, straight out: "What are you doing in these parts?" I said. "Writing a book", he says.'

'Writing a book! Good gracious!'

Mrs Betts nodded. 'That's what I thought, only I didn't say so.'

'What sort of book?' asked Mrs Coombes.

'I didn't like to ask – you don't like to be too inquisitive! But quite a charmer – in his looks, I mean. A good sort of height, with such nice grey eyes and a real nice smile. A bit shy, you know, but pleasant and speaks sort of refined . . . How many candles did you want?'

'Half a dozen, please. Nice, is he, you say? Oh well, he'll set a few heads turning!'

Mrs Coombes laughed. 'And a few tongues wagging, I shouldn't wonder,' she added. 'What about your Lorna? She'll be looking for a husband before long.'

Mrs Betts snorted. 'Before long? I reckon she's already found the one she fancies.' She leaned forward and lowered her voice. 'Young Don Leckie at the farm – they're going steady*ish*.'

Mrs Coombes raised her eyebrows.

'Don Leckie and young Lorna! Well, I never! She could do a lot worse. He's a nice boy. Nice family, the Leckies.'

Suddenly the old dog in the shop doorway began to growl and then he leaped up, backing into the shop as Miss Peck came in.

'Oh, do stop it, Jacko!' cried Mrs Betts. 'It's only Miss Peck. Take no notice of him, Miss Peck. Silly old dog. Going a bit soft in the head, he is.'

Miss Peck ignored both Mrs Betts and the dog and addressed her opening remarks to Mrs Coombes.

'I went down to the new railway station a week ago today,' she said sternly, 'and I found it all quite impossible. You may tell your husband from me that the Rother Valley Railway has not impressed me one little bit. In fact, it has lost a customer. There was no sign of a train and the stationmaster himself was not at all helpful. How your husband can work for such a company is quite beyond me.'

Mrs Coombes stared at her. 'No train? I don't understand,'

she stammered. 'As for Mr Turner not being helpful, well! I can assure you he is a—'

Miss Peck shook her head firmly. 'I'm not casting doubts on your husband,' she said, 'but if Gazedown Station is typical of the rest of the line, then all I can say is it's a great pity it was ever built in the first place. I never did approve of the idea of mechanical monsters roaring through the countryside and now I can see I was right. Gazedown doesn't need a railway station. It's all been a great misuse of people's money. Railway, indeed!'

Mrs Coombes drew herself up very straight. 'But *I* have travelled by train several times,' she said, 'and I have always found it very enjoyable. Perhaps there was some misunderstanding . . .'

Miss Peck tossed her head. 'There was *no* misunderstanding. I was on my way to my brother's funeral and I was forced to change my plans and go by carrier. All at the last minute – *and* in a rush, which I hate. Now, I'll have four rashers of best bacon, not too salt and not too thin. I want to be able to bite into it.'

'I'm serving Mrs Coombes,' began Mrs Betts.

'Oh, that's all right,' said Mrs Coombes hastily. 'Serve Miss Peck; I don't mind waiting.'

As soon as Miss Peck had left the shop, Mrs Betts produced a teacloth and flapped it around the shop in an attempt to dispel the unpleasant smell which Miss Peck's unwashed clothes had left behind her. She had just finished this task when Amy arrived and she also was served before Mrs Coombes at the latter's insistence.

When she too had departed, the two women resumed their conversation, Miss Peck now becoming the natural subject for discussion.

'Take no notice of poor Miss Peck,' said Mrs Betts. 'I've always thought she's . . . you know . . . a bit touched in the head. Well, she must be to keep all those cats – and all those clothes she wears! I did hear, years ago, that she comes from a very good family but they've cast her off – you know, ashamed of the old girl.'

Mrs Coombes appeared mollified by this information. The attack on Gazedown Station had upset her.

'Well, that may explain things,' she said. 'I mean, all that nonsense about there being no train – and as for criticising Mr Turner, well! Harry thinks very highly of him and he should know. He works for him.'

'Of course he does.'

'Mr Turner would be most helpful.'

'Of course he would,' agreed Mrs Betts.

'Have you ever met the stationmaster?'

'I did see him once when I went to visit Janet. I thought he looked very helpful. Take no notice of the poor old thing, she's just a bit queer in the head.' Mrs Betts leaned forward conspiratorially. 'Poor Amy Turner,' she confided. 'She'll never marry, you know. I mean, how could she? A young brother and the old man to look after. It's a full-time job, that family, and if she left them, well . . .' she shrugged. 'She must be twenty if she's a day, and who is there anyway in this village for a girl like that?'

Mrs Coombes again felt strong stirrings of loyalty. Amy was the daughter of the stationmaster and in her eyes, as in those of her husband, the honour of the Railway Company was sacrosanct and to be upheld at all times. An adverse comment on the daughter of the stationmaster could be taken as a reflection on the railway itself, and she felt in duty bound to defend her. The railway gave Harry a respectable living wage, for which she would be eternally grateful. To their great sorrow, they had no children of their own, but Mrs Coombes took a personal interest in Amy and young Sam.

'A girl like that?' she echoed, bristling slightly. 'Like *what* exactly?'

'Why, you know – a bit la-di-da.' Mrs Betts consulted the list briefly. 'I'm afraid we're out of Garibaldis,' she said. 'What about ginger nuts?'

Mrs Coombes nodded absent-mindedly and Mrs Betts hurried round, paper bag in hand, to the row of deep glass-topped biscuit tins which were ranged in front of the counter.

'Half a pound, was it?'

'Yes, please.'

'Mind you,' said Mrs Betts, unaware that she was treading on dangerous ground, 'I've heard that Tim Hollis is sweet

44

on her, but then he's a bit young, isn't he? Nineteen, I believe. They do say that young Hollis has an eye for the ladies, if you can believe all you hear.'

'I've heard nothing like that,' said Mrs Coombes, 'but I think they are probably friendly.' She tried to control her mounting anxiety. A timid woman, she always felt out of her depth in an argument.

Mrs Betts weighed the biscuits and tossed an odd one back into the tin with unerring aim. 'There's no one in Gazedown who's in her class,' she said, 'if you see what I mean. And who'd want to take on a ready-made family, even if they could get over the business of the mother?'

Mrs Coombes almost groaned aloud. The 'business of the mother' had been a source of continued interest ever since the Turners moved into Gazedown. She herself had discussed it frequently with Harry, but they had reached no firm conclusion. No one dared broach the subject directly with the stationmaster and Amy had proved adroit at evading questions on the subject. Several boys who early on had tried to elicit information from Sam had gone home with bleeding noses.

'I think,' said Mrs Coombes cautiously, 'that a person's private life should remain private. Whatever happened, it was obviously very sad for them and in my opinion Amy has coped—'

'They say she ran off with another man.'

Mrs Coombes swallowed hard. '*They* have no right to say such things,' she said. 'There is absolutely no proof that she did such a thing – and even if she did, it's not for folks to pry.'

'Oh, don't misunderstand me,' said Mrs Betts. 'I'm not prying, I'm just telling you what other people are saying. After all, if she died, why don't they talk about her? It's not natural never to mention someone who's died. If your mother died, you'd mention her, wouldn't you? Mind you, I did hear from someone else that she went off her head and had to be . . . you know . . . put away.' She considered the suggestion for a moment and then shook her head. 'But I don't think so. I mean, the children seem quite normal and if their mother was mad, they'd inherit it, wouldn't they?'

Mrs Coombes had gone very pale. 'What a terrible slander,' she said shakily. 'I'm quite sure they're all perfectly sane and I don't think for a moment that their mother is mad. That's a dreadful thing to say.'

'But *I'm* not saying it,' Mrs Betts insisted. 'I'm telling you what *people* are saying. I hear all sorts of things in my time, you know.' She winked. 'Oh yes, I hear it all. There's a few things I could tell you that goes on in Gazedown! Not only at the station. Make your hair stand on end, it would. Now where are we? I think that's the lot.'

She added it all up and Mrs Coombes checked it with exaggerated care. Mrs Betts, seeing this and knowing exactly why she did so, said, 'They say Mr Turner came here from a very big station in Essex. Funny that, really, when you think about it. Still, I expect your husband knows all about that.'

Mrs Coombes said firmly, 'I expect he knows all he wants to know.'

Mrs Betts took the proffered pound note and rang up the change with a sickly-sweet smile.

'Here you are, then. Now, can you manage or would you like Lorna to pop it round later on her bike?'

'I can manage, thank you.'

When Mrs Coombes had gone out of the shop, Mrs Betts just had time to put out her tongue at the retreating back before the next customer came in and it was time to talk about Mrs Coombes.

*

Later that evening Mrs Coombes waited until her husband was half-way through his rice pudding before bringing up the vexed question of the stationmaster.

'I was in the shop today,' she began.

'Oh, aye.' Harry was immediately wary.

'Mrs Betts really put my back up, the way she was going on.'

'Did she?'

'About Mr Turner.'

'Take no notice of her silly tittle-tattle, love, 'cause that's

46

all it is. She's nothing better to do than gossip about folks and no one takes any notice of her.'

'But they *do*, Harry. I know they do and it worries me. I don't like to hear her going on about Mr Turner like that.'

Scraping up the last of the pudding, Harry said, 'That was nice, love!'

'I couldn't get any sultanas,' she said.

'Never mind.'

'Harry, why do *you* think he came to Gazedown? Tim says he used to have twelve staff at his last place. Twelve! There's a lot of difference between twelve and three.'

Harry pushed back his plate and reached for his pipe. 'Don't ask me, love, because I don't know. He's never seen fit to tell anyone, so I don't suppose we shall ever know, but as long as he treats us right — and he does — I'm happy to work for him.' He pushed 'Hearts of Oak' into his pipe and tapped it down thoughtfully. 'I reckon it was to do with his wife. I reckon she died and it broke him up and there are too many unhappy memories. If anyone asks you, I'd hint at that and then change the subject.'

'Then you don't think she went mad or anything like that?'

'Went mad? Certainly not — and don't let Mr Turner hear you talking like that or the fat will be in the fire!'

'Oh I wouldn't, Harry, only to you,' she said quickly. 'But that's what she was saying at the shop. And then that awful Miss Peck came in and she was on about the train and her brother's funeral and saying Mr Turner wasn't at all helpful and the railway was a mechanical monster and all that—' She stopped, breathless, and Harry gave one of his slow smiles.

'Look, love, I've told you before to stop worrying. It's early days for Gazedown. Whether they like it or not, the railway's here to stay — and plenty of folk *do* like it. It's made their lives easier and more interesting. True, it's upset some people but that's always the way when anything new comes along; they don't understand progress, some of them, and they never will. They don't like the idea of motor cars or electric light or food coming in tins, but that won't make those things go away. You can't turn back the clock, love,

47

and Gazedown now has its own railway station. They'll get used to it, you'll see.'

'I suppose so,' she said, unconvinced.

'And don't go taking it all on your own shoulders,' he told her. 'You didn't build the railway, the R.V.R. did. I only work for the Company – but I'm proud to do so and you should be too.'

'Oh, I am. Harry. I really am.'

Harry Coombes had taken what he proudly referred to as 'the Company' to his heart. His loyalty was unswerving and he would be a Company man to his dying day. He found nothing at all to complain of in his working life. The station itself was neither too big nor too small; the work was interesting and the working hours were fair. He and his wife could travel on the railway at greatly reduced fares and he could walk to work and back each day, ten minutes either way. His uniforms were provided and he could drink innumerable cups of cocoa or tea for twopence a week. With sugar! Tim Hollis was a nice enough lad to work with and Bob Hart was what Harry called "a decent sort" who would mend their boots and shoes better than anyone else and often sell them a rabbit very cheaply. He also had a station garden to attend to and he was content.

His wife sighed deeply and then stood up and began to clear the table. While she was dusting the crumbs from the cloth, she said, 'She was on about young Amy, saying she'd never find anyone to marry her.'

She expected Harry to disagree, but he took his pipe from his mouth and studied it reflectively.

'Maybe she's right at that,' he said. 'Poor lass, she's got enough to worry about, with a family to care for. Tim was saying she's bright as a button and could have been a teacher apparently. She's teaching Arnold to read, did you know that? Poor Arnold, he's as proud as a peacock.' He laughed. 'You should hear him. "Gentleman starts with a gee" – that's how he goes on. He thinks the world of Amy, Arnold does.'

'Poor girl,' said Mrs Coombes. 'There must be someone. What a worry it must be for Mr Turner.'

'I told you just now, love, it's not your worry.' He reached

48

out and caught her hand as she passed him. 'You just worry about us. You and me.'

'But we're all right, Harry.'

'Exactly!' he said and, replacing his pipe in his mouth, he reached for the newspaper while his wife bustled over to the sink and made a start on the washing-up.

*

The Lodge to Bates Manor was a single-storey building in grey stone under a slate roof. It consisted of a parlour, one bedroom, a small kitchen and an even smaller scullery. There was an outside privy and a small bleak garden, the whole property being heavily overshadowed on the north, west and east by mature elm and oak trees. Inside, the cottage was sparsely furnished but at least there was a copper in the scullery and an ancient range for cooking in the kitchen. Ralph Allan was not intending to entertain and was therefore quite content to convert the parlour – the only room to catch the sun – into a study. He had filled the two shelves with his books and folders and had opened up the small drop-leaf table to accommodate his typewriter. Elliot had had this newfangled machine sent down from London, insisting that he would find it useful; as yet Ralph was far from proficient with it, but his handwriting was poor and he hoped that practice on the typewriter would make perfect.

In the bedroom, the furniture consisted of a double bed covered with a patchwork quilt, a bedside table and chair and a rather dilapidated chest of drawers topped by an oval mirror in a pine frame. There was no wardrobe, so Ralph's one good suit was on a hanger on the wall. The rest of his clothes were neatly folded away in the drawers. He made his bed each morning as soon as he got up and his nightshirt went under the pillow.

Ralph was a quiet man and as a boy had been brought up with his brother Elliot by a nanny. She had taught the boys that a day should be well ordered if it was to be successful. Nanny Wetton had dominated their childhood while their parents travelled abroad and when Ralph outgrew the nanny, the matron of his preparatory school continued to depress his sensitive spirit and delay the development of his personality.

49

Now, at twenty-five, he had no close friends in whom he could confide and had learned to hide his feelings under an air of quiet indifference.

In the early afternoon of the following day, Ralph sat at the table staring at the blank sheet of paper he had inserted into the typewriter. Finally, defeated by it, he raised his eyes and gazed at a photograph of a young woman which he had placed on the mantelshelf, and at once painful memories flooded back to drown out all other thoughts. Forty minutes later the sheet of paper was still blank and inspiration continued to elude him. In desperation, he went into the kitchen and made some tea, carrying a cup back to his desk. He sat down, clasping the cup with both hands as he drank, but again his eyes returned to the likeness of Lydia Forrest, the girl he had once hoped to marry. Finishing the tea, he had just put down the cup when a sound from the kitchen made him turn and he was surprised to find Esme Hatherley about to knock on the open door of his 'study'.

She looked very beautiful in a pale green coat with cream lace at the neck and cuffs. Her blonde hair was swept up under a straw hat which matched the coat perfectly. 'Beautiful,' he thought, 'but unapproachable.'

'Need I knock?' she smiled.

'Why, no,' he stammered, rising to his feet.

'You don't mind me walking through, do you?' she asked. 'The door was open and I thought I'd surprise you at your work. I've never seen a writer writing!' She put her head a little to one side, looked pointedly at the blank sheet of paper and gave a light laugh. 'And what do I find?' she teased. 'Has the muse deserted you, Mr Allan?'

'I'm afraid it has,' he confessed, 'but only temporarily, I trust. I have actually filled several sheets of foolscap in the last few days but I'm still feeling my way, so to speak. I'm still at the stage of making notes and lists — what my brother calls collating material. When that's finished — and it's going to be a long job — we shall start to consider what form the book will take. Elliot's the expert, of course.' He smiled nervously. 'Can I offer you a cup of tea? Or a glass of lemonade?'

Esme shook her head. 'No, thank you, Mr Allan. I haven't

really come to interrupt your work, but just to see if you are comfortable and managing to take care of yourself. I sent Lorna down to do some cleaning for you, but she tells me you sent her away again.'

Ralph at once detected the criticism behind her carefully chosen words and formal smile.

'I really don't need her,' he said defensively. 'I meant it when I said in my letter that I was looking for solitude. I don't want *anyone* around; it's so distracting.'

Esme pouted prettily. 'Oh, Mr Allan!' she protested.

Ralph felt his face burn. 'Oh, no!' he stammered. 'I didn't mean you; of course I didn't. You are most welcome. Please don't think that . . . oh dear, I've been tactless. Do forgive me.'

Her smile returned and he found himself thinking how nearly perfect she was – but the blue eyes were just a little too hard and the smooth jaw a fraction too large.

'There's nothing to forgive,' she assured him. 'Nothing at all. Of course you didn't mean me, I'm perfectly aware of that. If you really don't want her, I'll tell her not to come again. And you aren't starving yourself?'

'No, no. I'm a reasonable cook.'

'How very unusual for a man.'

Again he imagined an implied criticism and felt bound to offer an explanation. 'I had to cook for myself for two months when I was twenty. My family was in India and I was living at home alone; the cook left suddenly to look after her ailing mother and I was left to fend for myself.' He laughed. 'Believe me, I learned very quickly! I produced some very odd concoctions at first, I don't mind admitting, but I got the hang of it eventually. No, Mrs Hatherley, the menu may not rival the Ritz but I won't starve, I promise you.'

'Just as you say, Mr Allan.' She looked round the room. 'It certainly looks tremendously businesslike. I'm very impressed. Perhaps I shall be one of the first people to buy a copy of the masterpiece when it appears. Perhaps you will sign it for me?'

He found the slim neck and poised head so disconcerting that Esme was forced to repeat her comments about the forthcoming book. Confused, he agreed hastily and then added, 'But please don't think of buying it. It will be my pleasure to give you a copy.'

'Thank you, Mr Allen. I shall look forward to that.'

Ralph suspected that she put a faint emphasis on his name whenever she used it, as though drawing his attention to the formality of the title. Should he, he wondered, suggest that she use his Christian name? She seemed to be hoping he would, yet they scarcely knew each other. His brother had met her once at a party in London and they had discovered a very slight family connection — second cousin once removed, or something equally remote. Ralph had not expected her to remember the meeting, but she had answered Elliot's letter with a promptness that was flattering and had offered a short lease on The Lodge at a very reasonable figure. He hesitated, then decided against it, reminding himself that he had come to Gazedown to find seclusion, to work and, above all, to forget.

The silence lengthened uneasily as he searched for something else to say. Esme, however spoke first.

'Well, I must let you get on with your work. Do please let me know if there is anything I can do. No, stay where you are, Mr Allan, I'll see myself out.'

At the door she paused and looked back and fleetingly he saw a new expression on her face. 'Writing is obviously a very lonely life, Mr Allan. Please feel free to call at the Manor if you are in need of a little company. Do you shoot?'

'Er . . . no, I'm afraid I don't.'

'What a pity. Gerald is always glad to have a companion — not that he's shooting at the moment. Closed season, of course. He keeps saying, "Roll on the glorious twelfth." And how *many* times he says it! Even an original remark stales with over-use and that's not even original. Poor Gerald! Oh well, I'm sorry you don't shoot — perhaps you ride?'

'I used to, but haven't done so for several years.'

She brightened. 'You must come riding with me one day,' she suggested. 'We'll arrange something. You need to have some fresh air and exercise, Mr Allan; even a dedicated writer should pay attention to his health. I warn you I won't take no for an answer!'

From the window he watched her slim figure as she walked back along the drive, pausing once to wave her hand to him.

'Damnation!' he muttered. 'I do hate interfering women.'

But even as he said it, he knew he was secretly flattered by her attention. Riding with Esme Hatherley was not an entirely unattractive proposition and after some consideration he decided that if she pressed the invitation he would accept. He imagined the two of them riding and laughing together and then wondered uneasily how her husband would view the idea. Possibly he would accompany them . . . but Ralph felt intuitively that a threesome was not what Esme had in mind. She had spoken of her husband in mildly disparaging terms and he suspected their relationship was less than perfect.

'How do two people live together without love?' he wondered aloud, and then turned back to the photograph in its ornate silver frame. He sat down heavily and, putting his elbows on the table, hid his face in his hands.

When at last he raised his head, he pulled the typewriter towards him, but the familiar doubts crowded in. Why on earth had he allowed Elliot to talk him into this book? He didn't understand the first thing about it, but Elliot had been hard to resist. As usual, his brother's enthusiasm had won him over against his better judgement and he had given up his proposed trip to Italy in order to bury himself in Gaze-down. He had been at The Lodge for two weeks now and had achieved very little, except some half-hearted note-taking and the daily perusal of letters and ledgers. If he was honest, he still had no idea how to marshal the facts into anything remotely resembling the outline of a book. All he had done was to keep at bay the dark memories. But that was some-thing, he reminded himself.

Half an hour later the paper in the typewriter remained blank and abruptly he snatched it from the machine, crum-pled it into a ball and hurled it across the room. Just as suddenly his anger left him, allowing the familiar despair to take its place.

'I can't do it,' he whispered. 'I can't write the damned thing and what's more, I don't even care!' As he stood up, his chair tilted and fell backwards and he left it there and ran out of the room.

*

The long tin bath was already half-filled with cold water and now Amy struggled up the stairs again, this time with a large steaming kettle. Although it was now July, a few coals blazed in the bedroom grate and her grandfather was sitting beside it huddled in a grey blanket.

'One more and that will do you,' Amy told him as she emptied the jug into the bath.

He looked at the water doubtfully. 'I don't want it too hot,' he said. 'I come over all faint.'

'Nor too cold,' said Amy. 'I know you. If it's too cold you'll be wanting to get out in five minutes, saying you're chilled. I'm not lugging all this up the stairs for a bath that's over before you can say "knife". You have a good soak, Grandfather, and make the most of the fire.'

She went downstairs for the second kettle, which was even larger than the first, and when that too had been emptied into the bath, she dipped her fingers into the water and expressed satisfaction with the temperature.

'Now off with the blanket,' she said firmly, 'and in you go.'

'I don't need any help,' he grumbled. 'I'm not helpless.'

'Well, if you're *not*,' she retorted, 'you shouldn't laze here in bed all day.' She dragged the blanket from his shoulders and tugged him to his feet. 'I want to *see* you in the water before I go downstairs. I know you and your tricks.' Good-humouredly she finally bullied him into the bath and put a lump of yellow soap and a piece of flannel into his hands. 'Give me a call when you're done and I'll come up and wash your back,' she told him. 'And for heaven's sake don't look so gloomy. It's only a bath — not a Chinese torture — and it's only once a month.'

Smiling to herself, she made her way downstairs and was refilling the kettle when there was a knock at the back door. Snip rushed out of her corner barking her head off as usual, and Amy found Ralph Allan on the doorstep. She stared at him, surprised, and he began at once to apologise for his

54

presence but she interrupted to insist that he come into the kitchen.

'Who's that?' shouted Ted from upstairs.

'Mr Allan from The Lodge,' Amy called back, 'but he's not here to see you, so stay right where you are. Do you hear? Snip, stop that noise – Mr Allan is not a burglar.'

Smiling, she led her visitor through the scullery and into the kitchen.

'My grandfather,' she explained in a low tone. 'He's in the bath and looking for any excuse to get out of it!' Then in her normal voice she continued, 'This is a nice surprise, Mr Allan.'

'I hope you don't mind,' he said. 'I didn't mean to come here, actually. I was out walking – just taking a walk to clear the cobwebs from my brain – just walking . . .' He stopped and she noticed for the first time that he looked very pale and agitated. 'To tell you the truth, I don't know why I came, really. It's an awful cheek,' he said.

'Are you feeling all right?' she asked.

'I beg your pardon?' He looked at her as though he had not heard the question.

'Is anything wrong? You seem a bit upset.'

'No. At least, yes . . . a little,' he confessed. 'I'm having a bad day. Do you know what I mean? I couldn't work and I felt low in spirits. I thought a walk would help, but it didn't, and suddenly I found I was heading in this direction and . . .' he faltered. 'Well, here I am.'

Amy smiled at him. 'I'm really glad you came,' she said. 'How are you settling in? Are you comfortable?'

'Oh yes, very.'

He looked very vulnerable, she thought, and he was obviously struggling to control his voice. Amy wondered what troubled him, but pretended to be unaware of his distress.

'Would you like a cup of tea?' she offered.

'No, thank you. I drink too much of it.' He attempted a lopsided grin and Amy looked quickly away for fear he might see her compassion, which she felt sure would undermine him even further.

'And the book—' she began, then with a laugh corrected herself, '—or perhaps this is not the day to ask about work.

Let's talk about something else. It's been a really wonderful summer so far.'

'Yes, it has.'

They faced each other, still standing, searching for conversation.

'If it keeps up, they'll be harvesting early,' she told him.

'I suppose so. Yes.'

With each passing moment Amy became more aware of the falseness of his composure and the possibility of some kind of breakdown. There was a tell-tale tremor in his voice and a small muscle twitched persistently in his forehead. She hoped that if she could keep him talking the crisis, whatever it was, might pass.

'Have you ever been harvesting, Mr Allan?' she asked. 'It's great fun.'

'No, I haven't.'

'I shall offer my services again at Hope's Farm,' she told him. 'Last year I helped bring in the hay and then after they'd cut the grain, Sam and I went gleaning for oats to feed his rabbit. You'll have to come along – you'd enjoy it. Afterwards we had supper of home-made cider and one of Mary's enormous pork pies. I wish I could cook like her.'

They fell silent again. 'Do you like cooking?' he asked her.

'I do and I don't!' Amy laughed. 'Sometimes when I'm in the mood I enjoy making a fruit cake or an apple pie, but at other times when I feel rushed and harassed it seems a lot of work, all to be gobbled down in a few mouthfuls and then forgotten.'

'You have your hands full, by the look of it,' he said, 'with a family to care for but in a way I envy you. I've no one except myself and it makes one rather selfish, I'm afraid; rather self-centred.'

'Are your parents dead, then?'

'Good lord, no, but they settled in India when my father retired and I wanted to stay in England. I have a brother, of course.'

The question, 'Are you married!' sprang to Amy's lips, but she bit it back. How could he be married if he said he was alone – and anyway it was none of her business. However, she thought that she detected some lessening of his agitation.

56

'I do wish you would sit down,' she smiled. 'You look as if you're going to run away at any moment!'

'I was afraid I was intruding,' he said. 'I'm sure you're busy.'

'I am, but you can help me. I'm about to start the ironing . . .' She indicated the two flat-irons heating up on top of the range. 'You can damp down for me if you like.'

'Oh?' he said, so dubiously that she laughed.

'Perhaps *I'd* better do it,' she said, 'and you can hold the sheets up.' While Ralph, following her instructions, held the folded sheet in front of him, Amy dipped her fingers into a basin of water and flicked droplets over the surface. When it was dampened sufficiently she took it from him and rolled it firmly to allow the moisture to spread evenly. Another sheet and two pillow-slips were damped down in the same way and this simple activity finally helped Ralph to conquer his emotions.

'Now, sit yourself down,' said Amy, 'and if you won't have a cup of tea you can talk to me while I'm – all right, I'm coming!' A shout from upstairs sent her hurrying back to her grandfather, who insisted he was ready to be helped out of his bath; but first Amy soaped the flannel and washed his bony back.

'Who did you say it was downstairs?' Ted demanded. 'If he wants to come up when I'm back in bed—'

'I don't know if he does,' replied Amy. 'It's Ralph Allan from The Lodge – the man who's writing a book. If he has time and he wants to chat, I'll bring him up, but at the moment he's talking to me while I'm ironing and I like his company. Now then, take my hands and stand up slowly. Oh, I'm not looking at your private parts. Don't fuss so, Grandfather. I'm family, after all. That's it, now step out and I'll give you a quick rub-down. Oh well, do it yourself then,' she said as he began to protest, 'but I haven't got all day. I can't leave the poor man sitting on his own, so just hurry up, will you?'

'The water got cold,' he grumbled.

'Well, it won't stay warm for ever.'

'My teeth are chattering.'

'Nonsense!'

'They are, I tell you.'

While he towelled himself dry, she found a clean nightshirt for him and then began to drag the bath away from the fire.

'I'll come up and empty it later,' she told him. 'You could sit up in the chair for a bit.'

'I can't manage the chair,' he began. 'You know I come over all funny if I'm not in bed. All swoozy.'

Amy snorted in a way which conveyed her disbelief, but she was in no mood to argue as she wanted to get back downstairs to her visitor. When at last she did so, she was pleased to see Ralph looking much more relaxed.

'Grandfather says you're welcome to go up and chat,' she told him, 'but I warn you he will talk non-stop about the life and times of Edward Turner and the Great Eastern Railway! He worked for them all his life and was an engine-driver for seventeen years.'

'Oh dear!' he laughed. 'Do you think I should go up today?'

She shook her head. 'Not today. Another day, perhaps — if you're going to come again that is?'

'I will if I'm not being a nuisance.'

'Of course you're not.'

She spat on the flat-iron and decided it was hot enough, then spread an old blanket over the kitchen table. Spreading one of the sheets over this, she began to iron it with practised movements while Ralph watched her.

'My fiancée died,' he said abruptly. 'Her name was Lydia.'

Amy paused with the iron poised over the sheet, immediately understanding his mood and recognising the need to talk about it. 'How dreadful for you!' she said. 'I'm so sorry.'

'A year ago today.' He swallowed hard. 'I still can't believe it.'

'Poor you,' she said simply. 'No wonder you're having a bad day. That's so sad. What happened?'

'Galloping consumption. One day she was hale and hearty and we were talking about the wedding — making plans. Seven weeks later she was dead. She died in my arms, just closed her eyes and died.'

'Oh, Ralph!'

'She was just eighteen,' he said, the words coming in a

58

rush now that he had started. 'I'd known her all my life. I even remember her being born when I was eight. My mother went to the christening, the way neighbours do. We were all living in India then, but her parents came back to England before I did. When my mother and father decided to stay on, I came back with Elliot, my brother. Her parents were living in Carshalton and they invited us to stay, but Elliot went back to our home. I accepted their offer and Lydia and I fell in love.'

He hesitated. Amy exchanged the cold iron for a hot one and said, 'Go on,' without looking at him.

He sighed deeply. 'Everyone was delighted – you can imagine.' Amy nodded without comment.

'We had even fixed the date,' he went on. 'We were going to be married at Easter – not very original but Lydia liked the idea. Then we planned to go to Italy for our honeymoon. When she became unwell with a feverish cold, naturally we all thought it would pass. But it didn't, so they took her to a specialist and he said . . .' he swallowed hard. 'He said she had six months to live, at the outside!'

'What a nightmare for you.' Amy stopped ironing and regarded him keenly.

'It was a nightmare – exactly that. Rightly or wrongly, we tried to keep it from her, but she grew so weak she guessed. She begged me to tell her the truth and at last I did, but I don't think her parents will ever forgive me.' His voice fell to a whisper. 'They said the shock hastened her death.'

'But if she wanted the truth,' Amy ventured, 'there was nothing else you could do except tell her. I would have done exactly the same in your shoes.'

'Would you? Are you sure?'

Amy considered. 'Yes,' she said. 'And if I hadn't long to live, I'd want to know. There's a time for honesty and you did the right thing, Ralph – I'm sure you did.'

'I don't know.' He shook his head. 'I hope so. Poor Lydia.'

'It's a pretty name,' said Amy. 'Poor Ralph. I can imagine how awful it was, but you mustn't blame yourself. How could you lie to someone you love who was begging for the truth?'

He did not answer, averting his eyes while Amy, resuming her ironing, shook out the sheet and turned it over.

From upstairs the bell rang again and Amy groaned and called out, 'I'll be up in two ticks!'

Ralph stood up abruptly. 'I should be going,' he said. 'I really mustn't outstay my welcome, but it's been so nice talking to you. I hope you will forgive me for telling you all my troubles. You're such a good listener, but I feel I've taken advantage of your kindness.'

'I've enjoyed your company,' she interrupted firmly. 'Will you come again? I'd really like to see you — and then you could spend half an hour with Grandfather, if you would.'

'I'd love to.'

'And tomorrow . . .' she hesitated.

'Yes?'

'Bob Hart, the signalman, snares rabbits. I could make you a small pie when I make ours.'

'That's terribly kind; I haven't had rabbit pie for years!'

She followed him through the scullery to the back door. 'I'll tell Grandfather, then. He'll be looking forward to meeting you — it will give him something new to think about!'

She walked with him along the brick path and he turned at the gate to take her hand.

'Thank you for listening,' he said, 'and for saying the right things. You've made me feel better about it all.'

'Look, Ralph,' she said slowly, 'I'm never far away. Any time you're feeling gloomy, come and find me.'

As she said, 'Goodbye' and turned back towards the house, she caught sight of a face at the upstairs window.

'I'll be—!' she muttered and flew inside and up the stairs into her grandfather's room. He was sitting up in bed looking innocent, though rather flustered.

'You were at the window!' she accused him.

'I was *not!*'

'I saw you!'

'How could you have seen me if I was here in bed?' he blustered. 'You know I couldn't make it to the window on my own.'

'But I saw you at the window. I know I did.'

'A trick of the light,' he protested.

She put her hands on her hips and surveyed him severely. 'If I ever find out that you're fooling us all, I'll have you downstairs chopping firewood and planting vegetables. I swear I will!'

Alarm showed in his watery eyes. 'Now you don't mean that, Amy, but it hurts me to think you could say such things. You know if I could get downstairs, I would.' The familiar whine crept into his voice. 'Stuck up here all day on my own, how would you like it? Nobody knows what I suffer.'

'What *do* you suffer?' she demanded, mopping up spilt water and wrapping the soap in the flannel. 'Did you brush your hair?'

'I couldn't find the brush.'

'It's on the bedside table — it would bite you if it was any nearer! Honestly, Grandfather, you're twice as much bother as Sam and that's saying something.'

She ladled water from the bath to the bucket and carried it downstairs, returning within minutes for the next bucketful.

'Is he coming again, this Mr Allan?' Ted asked hopefully.

'Maybe.'

'That means he is.'

'If you say so.'

'He's a nice-looking—' He stopped suddenly, clapping a hand to his mouth.

'You *did* see him!' cried Amy. 'You must have done, or else how would you know he's nice-looking? Oh, don't bother to deny it. I shall tell Papa when he comes home and we'll see what he has to say about it.'

She staggered out of the room with a second brimming bucket and Ted slid down in the bed and turned on his side, half covering his face with the blanket.

'If you can nip in and out of bed,' Amy continued when she returned, 'then you're not bedridden, not in *my* book.' She glanced at the bed. 'And don't pretend you're asleep just because I've caught you out. You're just a lazy old man who likes to be waited on hand and foot. What would you do if I wasn't around, eh? If there was only Sam and Papa?'

She straightened up from her labours as a faint and muffled snore sounded from the bed. 'I know you're not asleep—'

she began crossly. 'I'm just not taken in at all – do you hear me?'

Another grunt was the only reply and she bent her back once more to her task. Having made several more trips up and down, she made a final descent dragging the empty bath down the stairs behind her.

'Silly old fool!' she muttered irritably as she tugged it out of the back door and leaned it up against the wall. 'I'll get him out of bed if it's the last thing I do!'

She tidied her hair and wiped the perspiration from her face and then, remembering her promise to Ralph Allan, decided to visit Bob Hart. Her ill-humour had already left her as she took a jar of chutney from the cupboard to trade for a couple of rabbits and she hummed cheerfully to herself as she made her way along the station platform towards the signal-box.

Chapter Four

It was widely rumoured among the inhabitants of Gazedown that with fewer than half a dozen trains a day, the station staff had an easy time of it but this was far from the truth. There was plenty for Harry and Tim to do and they were kept fully occupied most of the time. The station itself had to be maintained: there were windows to be cleaned inside and out weekly, paintwork to be wiped down monthly, and floors to be scrubbed twice a week. There was brass to be polished daily and dust to be removed from various surfaces whenever the stationmaster found anyone with nothing better to do. Parcels had to be booked in and out and ledgers had to be brought up to date and checked regularly. Petty cash had to be counted and every penny must be accounted for – woe betide the unfortunate stationmaster whose books were found unbalanced when the dreaded railway inspector called for a random check!

Then there was the station water to be pumped up by hand when there was no wind to turn the sails – water for the stationmaster's house as well as for the station itself. This heavy job often fell to the lot of Arnold who positively enjoyed it, pushing and pulling at the handle with a broad grin on his face and apparently indefatigable. He could only be allowed to do it when the stationmaster was elsewhere, for he was not a member of the railway staff and therefore officially not permitted to pump up water. Rules were rules, as Mr Turner frequently reminded them, and regulations were made to be obeyed. Outside in the goods yard, there was even less enjoyable work to be done. Even goods wagons had to be cleaned out and the cattle trucks and horse boxes were particularly unpopular. If there had been a delivery of timber for the adjacent yard, there was timber to be unloaded and checked against the invoices; frequently there were bales of hay or sacks of seed for Hope's Farm and these also had to be checked and unloaded – a dusty, thankless task.

There was also the stable to muck out, for Gazedown Station – small though it was – boasted a shunting horse. This animal's job was to move the various wagons and trucks into their correct positions on the line, so that when the locomotive arrived wagon and locomotive could be coupled with the minimum time and fuss. Sometimes a special tank engine was sent to collect goods vehicles from all the stations along the line but at other times, if none was available, the wagons would be hitched to the rear of a suitable passenger train.

A week after Ralph Allan's visit to Amy, Arnold was helping Tim who was cleaning out the stable. The horse, a sturdy grey cob, stood in the yard tossing its head and eyeing Arnold balefully as he held the halter and made frequent but unsuccessful attempts to pat the horse's neck.

'Go-o-d girl, then,' he crooned. 'Go-o-d old girl! I'm not going to hurt you. No, stand still. There's a good girl.'

Tim was raking out evil-smelling straw and he glanced up briefly. 'It's a boy,' he said. 'I keep telling you.'

'A boy?' Arnold blinked vaguely.

'It's called "Prince" remember? "Prince" is a boy's name.'

'Prince?' He backed away as the horse decided to butt him with its head. 'Good girl, Prince. Whoa! Whoa, there. Stop that!' He finally managed to pat the sleek grey neck and a smile of delight lit up his face. 'I patted her! I really did.'

'*Him*, Arnold. It's a *boy*. How many times do I have to tell you?' Tim dragged the pile of oozing straw to one side and leaned on the rake, mopping his forehead.

'Can't you tell a boy from a girl, Arnold?'

Arnold's smile wavered nervously because this was the sort of 'cheeky' question his mother did not like him to ask and would never answer. He nodded and then, thinking better of it, shook his head.

Tim winked. 'I'll have to tell you about the birds and bees, then, won't I?'

'Birds and bees, yes,' echoed Arnold, feeling that this was a safer topic. 'I like birds. We had a bird once but it died. Fell off its perch, bang!'

He tried to pat the horse's rump and for a moment they went round in circles as the animal repeatedly sidestepped to avoid his eager hand.

'Give over,' said Tim. 'You're scaring him.'

'I'm not. She likes me.'

'Arnold! "Prince!" P-R-I—'

'P-R-I,' Arnold echoed, beaming cheerfully because now he was learning to read.

'N-C-E,' said Tim.

'N-C-E,' repeated Arnold.

' "Prince". Got it now?'

Arnold nodded cautiously and wondered when Amy would give him another reading lesson. He tried to remember what Tim had told him, but after 'P-R-I' his mind was a blank.

'Gentlemen starts with a gee,' he murmured. 'Waiting room starts with a double-you. And P-R-I spells horse.' He smiled at Tim, who groaned loudly. 'Bang!' said Arnold. 'It fell off its perch. Dead!'

'Stop it, you're breaking my heart!' begged Tim. 'I expect you overfed it. People do. They always give birds too much to eat and then they're surprised when it kills them.'

As he spoke Snip ran into the yard barking shrilly and Prince began to back away, tossing his head fretfully and almost pulling Arnold over. Tim shouted at the dog (who ignored him) and grabbed at the horse's halter.

'I'll hold the horse,' he said. 'You chuck down the clean straw, then we'll get him back in. Blooming animal! And get out of it, you!'

He kicked out at Snip, who had darted between the horse's legs. More by chance than design the toe of his boot met Snip's hindquarters and the little dog squealed with pain and anger and ran away to bark defiance from a safe distance.

Arnold's anxious face appeared above the armful of clean

straw he was carrying. 'Amy'll be mad at you,' he warned, 'if you hurt her dog.'

'Let her,' said Tim, with a shrug. 'She shouldn't allow it to come down here. It's a proper nuisance — yap, yap, yapping all the time.'

'She'll get mad.'

'So will I if you don't hurry up with that straw, Arnold. Just chuck it down — you've done it before. This perishing horse will have my arms off in a minute.'

Arnold, giggling, ducked back into the stables.

Five minutes later Prince was back in his stall and the lower half of the stable door was securely fastened. Arnold stood outside beside the pile of soiled straw muttering, 'P-R-I' and frowning at his boots which seemed to be on the wrong feet. Before he could finally decide whether they were or not, Snip darted away to greet Amy who was coming across the yard with an envelope in her hand.

Tim groaned. 'Oh, no! Not another telegraph?'

Amy fluttered it and called out, 'It's for the vicar. Have you got time, or shall I take it?'

Tim hesitated. If he took it he would get a tip, although the vicar was not over-generous. He might also get to know the contents of the envelope — it was surprising how many people confided in the bearer of the news. On the other hand, he *was* busy and it was a hot day.

'P-R-I,' said Arnold quickly, 'spells horse.' Amy looked at him. 'Does it? Oh, *Prince*.' Light dawned. 'Very good, Arnold. Are you coming for a lesson today? I could spare half an hour if Tim goes to the vicarage.'

Tim regarded her with narrowed eyes. She did not seem over-keen to take the message, even though to reach the vicarage she would pass The Lodge. He had heard rumours that she and 'the writer chappie' had struck up a friendship. Tim had had his eye on the stationmaster's daughter for some time but, aware of the difference in their ages (and being constantly urged by his mother not to tie himself down too early in life) had so far made no definite move in her direction.

'I might,' said Tim, 'and there again I might not.'

66

Amy laughed. 'Make up your mind,' she said. 'I haven't got all day.'

'*I'll* take it,' Arnold offered but then, remembering the promise of a reading lesson, said, 'No, I won't.'

Tim gave Amy what he hoped was a provocative look and suggested, 'We could both take it.'

Amy laughed. 'Don't be so daft, Tim! Do you want to or don't you?'

'It depends,' he said. 'What's it worth if I go?'

'What's it worth?' She stared at him.

'Do I get a kiss for my trouble?'

Amy kept her face straight. 'I suppose the vicar *might* kiss you, but I shouldn't—'

'Not him, you!'

'Certainly not.'

Tim turned to Arnold and winked broadly. 'What do you think, Arnold? Do you think she should kiss me?'

'I – I don't know,' gasped Arnold, amazed at Tim's daring. Then to his astonishment, Tim stepped forward and seized Amy's hand and kissed it with a great display of mock gallantry. 'For you, I will climb mountains and swim rivers,' he declared. 'For you I will take this blooming message to the blooming vicar! Could any man say fairer than that, I ask myself?'

Amy was laughing, so Arnold felt it safe to join in.

'And what do you answer yourself?' said Amy, a hint of colour in her face.

'I don't,' replied Tim, taking the envelope and clutching it to his chest. 'I ask myself another question. Why, I ask myself, is the beautiful Amy Turner making rabbit pies for Ralph Allan?'

'Oh!' She was taken aback. 'Why not? There's no harm in it.'

'The village gossips will be glad to hear it.'

'Village gossips?'

'Oh, it's all over the village.' He adopted what he imagined was the furtive manner of a village gossip. 'Have you heard the news, Mrs Peabody? About that young woman at the station? Yes, Amy Turner herself and no better than she should be! Isn't she the sly one? Creeping down to The Lodge and taking *pies* with her! Who'd have thought it, eh? And her so—'

'Stop it, Tim,' she protested. 'I don't believe you; they're not saying anything. I only went once – and how could they know, anyway?'

'Aha! Walls have ears and there are eyes at every window.' He was relieved to learn that she had only been once and made up his mind to pay her a little more attention than he had done recently.

'So you will take it, then,' she said, referring to the message.

'My rear wheel's got a puncture,' he replied.

'You can take mine. Thanks, Tim.' She turned to Arnold. 'Are you coming for a lesson?'

'Yes, *please!*' He turned to Tim. 'I'm going for a lesson.'

'Well, mind you pay attention. And Arnold . . .' he lowered his voice, but only a little, wanting Amy to hear it. 'Ask her to tell you about the birds and the bees.'

Arnold's reluctance was obvious.

'Take no notice of him, Arnold,' said Amy. 'He's got birds and bees on the brain! They'll be gossiping about him next. Come on.' They walked back to the platform together and Tim went off to collect Amy's bicycle, which was behind the coal-shed at the rear of the stationmaster's house. As he rode past he saw Amy and Arnold sitting on the small square of grass which served as a lawn in the tiny garden. Arnold's earnest voice came to him over the hedge.

' "A" is for apple, "B" is for bed . . .'

Tim had a mental picture of himself and Amy sitting up in bed together and he liked what he saw. As he cycled along the lane, he wondered about Amy and gave rein to his imagination. Soon they were no longer sitting up in the bed but rolling about in it and he liked that, too. It was a pity that women were so possessive, but his mother assured him that they were.

His daydream was interrupted by arrival at the vicarage, where he tugged at the bell and Mrs Jay answered the door. The vicar's sister was tall and raw-boned, with broken veins in her cheeks and a precise way of speaking.

'Well?' she demanded.

'Telegraph, ma'am,' Tim said, handing over the envelope. 'For the Reverend,' he added as she prepared to open it.

'The Reverend is out,' she said, 'but he would want me to open it. *I am* his sister and entirely in his confidence.'

She read the message. 'No reply,' she snapped and closed the door in his face.

'Miserable old bat!' he muttered, louder than he intended. To his dismay, the door opened again immediately.

'I *heard* that remark!' Mrs Jay told him furiously, 'and I shall report you to the stationmaster for insolence.'

This time the door was not merely closed, it was slammed; Tim stood on the doorstep, speechless, gazing at the brass knocker and cursing his stupidity. Mr Turner was not going to be at all pleased when he received Mrs Jay's complaint, of that he was certain. It would mean a reprimand and he might even be forced to apologise to the 'miserable old bat'. Tim felt sure the words would stick in his throat, would probably choke him. He imagined the scene as he fell to his knees, gasping for air – they would be sorry then, but it would be too late. As he cycled back to the station he elaborated on the scene, so that somehow Amy could be there and she could utter a strangled cry and run forward and throw herself on to his prostrate body. And weep. Yes, she would weep and would realise how much she would miss him. No, how much she had loved him. It would be very touching and the crowd would have tears in their eyes as they watched. It was a pity, he reflected, that Amy was older than him and an inch taller. Still, no one was perfect and she did have very nice brown eyes. *And* she could cook, of course. His mother had told him how important that was. Looks aren't everything. Tim felt sure he could do a lot worse.

*

'What have you been up to, then?' asked Harry a few days later, as Tim strolled up with his hands in his pockets and a look of studied nonchalance on his face.

'Me?'

'Yes, you. I heard the old man giving you a right ticking-off.'

'Oh, that!' Tim shrugged. 'It was nothing. Mrs Jay came

in yesterday to complain – said I cheeked her. Silly old cow!'
He mimicked Mr Turner's voice and manner: 'It is the duty
of railway officials to be courteous to all members of the
public at all times.'

'And you weren't?'

'I was to her face.'

'Then what happened?'

Harry was tending the station garden, his fingers feeling
gently between the plants, easing out the weeds and pinching
off withered leaves and dead blooms. These he laid on a
sheet of newspaper spread for the purpose, on which a small
digger and a watering-can waited in readiness. While Tim
recounted his unfortunate meeting with Mrs Jay, Harry
worked on, nodding occasionally to show that he was listening although it might appear otherwise. Tim took no
offence; he was used to talking to Harry's back as he crouched over his beloved flowers.

'So what did Mr Turner *say*?' asked Harry when the explanation ended.

'Not a lot.'

'He must have said something.'

Tim took a few springing strides along the platform,
stopped abruptly and swung round on his heel. Sparing him
a quick glance, Harry saw that he was chastened in spite of
his protestations to the contrary and quickly looked back at
his plants as Tim strode back.

'Said it was my last chance,' Tim told him reluctantly.
'He'll make it a report next time, he says. Trust her to come
tale-telling. Nothing better to do with her time, that's her
trouble.' He sighed deeply. 'I hate people like that.' He
looked across at the clock. 'The train'll be here in three
minutes. If the old man catches you weeding when the train
comes in, *you'll* be getting a report as well as me!'

It was Harry's turn to sigh as he pulled himself to his feet
and dusted off the knees of his dark trousers. As Mr Turner
appeared promptly on the opposite platform, his porter and
booking-clerk at once became alert and eager, straightening
caps, tugging at jackets and gazing up the line in the direction
of Tenterden with expressions of unnatural eagerness. The
trail of smoke was already visible and the steady chuff of

70

the engine was audible as the 1.32 'stopper' wound its way past the tall trees of Gazedown woods and on through the land adjoining Bates Manor. The signalman had opened the gates and the train, wreathed in smoke, now drew in to the station with a screeching of metal and a triumphant hiss of steam.

Spotting a face at one of the carriage windows, Harry hurried to open the door; a tall man in ecclesiastical garb alighted and allowed Harry to lift down a bulging carpet bag which had seen better days.

'Thank you, sir,' Harry pocketed the penny and touched his cap to the vicar. Further along the train a man's head appeared and he beckoned to Tim. 'I think you should take a look at this young woman,' he called. 'She's obviously unwell. Very unwell, I would suggest.' His tone was disapproving and Tim, intrigued, went quickly forward.

A young woman lolled in the far corner of the compartment, her eyes closed, both hands clutching her stomach. She was poorly dressed in a faded blue dress and grey shawl and her hat was tipped forward at a rakish angle, effectively hiding her face.

Tim stared at her and she groaned suddenly.

'She keeps on groaning,' said the man. 'She won't answer a civil question – I think she's drunk.'

Tim leaned nearer to the girl.

'Where's she going to?' he asked, in his most professional manner.

'I told you, she won't say. She won't say anything. It really is quite disgraceful that . . .'

The girl gave another groan and sat up so suddenly that her hat fell off. Tim picked it up and offered it to her, but she stared at him vaguely and made no effort to take it. By this time, Harry had joined them and after some discussion it was decided that the young woman should be helped off the train and on to the seat on the platform, where the fresh air might revive her. Harry and Tim took an arm each and they were half-dragging her from the carriage when the stationmaster arrived with the train guard to enquire about the delay. He looked none too pleased when he learned what was happening, not relishing the extra responsibility and anticipating the possibly lengthy report in triplicate which would have to be made concerning the incident.

Before the train could continue, he was obliged to take down a few relevant particulars from the man who had originally reported the girl's condition. When at last the train had gone, he returned his attention to the young woman, who was now sipping water from a glass which Tim was holding to her lips. She was tall and plain, with mousy brown hair, grey eyes and a dimple in her chin. Suddenly she looked up at him, mumbled something and threw up the half-digested remains of her last meal, liberally splattering Tim's trousers and boots.

'Oh, Christ!' he exclaimed, leaping back and stepping heavily on to Harry's foot.

Immediately recovering, the young woman began to giggle and then, unaccountably, to cry.

Harry regarded her helplessly; Tim was more concerned with his uniform and the sour smell emanating from it. The stationmaster cleared his throat.

'Now, that will do,' he addressed the girl sternly. 'There's no need for all that, no need at all. Harry, fetch a bucket of water and wash down the platform. Tim, go round to the house and ask Amy for a cloth and wash yourself down – and tell—'

'But Mr Turner, sir!' Tim protested. 'Can't I go home and change my uniform? I'll never get all this off and it reeks to high heaven!' He held his nose with finger and thumb.

'You can go home later if necessary,' the stationmaster told him. 'Right now you can't be spared. Tell Amy what's happened and send her out to see to the girl. I've no time for all these hysterics; I have a station to run.'

Amy arrived a few minutes later and took the still sobbing girl back to the house, where she talked soothingly to her and made a cup of tea. The girl confided that her name was Clara Midden, but she refused to give her address. Her story was that she had run away from a loutish father a week earlier and had gone to London in search of work. There she had met a woman who offered her a bed for the night, but the woman's husband had tried to take advantage of her.

'I wasn't having that,' she told the astonished Amy, 'so I pinched a pound off him and ran to the station. I thought I'd go to Hastings, because I've never seen the sea and my great-aunt used to live there. Probably still does. Once I was on the train I came over queer . . . and you know the rest.'

Amy thought the story rather improbable, but she made no comment except to ask if Clara was feeling better. The girl nodded and, as if to prove the point, she put on her hat again and stood up.

'That poor chap's trousers!' she said. 'I'm so sorry, but I just couldn't help myself.'

'Don't worry,' said Amy. 'I'm sure my father will send him home to change his clothes as soon as he can.'

'I bet he's mad at me?'

Privately Amy thought so too, but she simply said, 'Oh, not Tim. He's very good-hearted.'

At that moment Tim knocked at the scullery door and came in. 'I'm to go home and change,' he told them. 'Can I borrow your bike again, Amy?'

'Tim Hollis!' she cried. 'You've been using my bike for more than a week! What's wrong with *your* bike?'

'You know it's got a puncture.'

'Well, *mend* it, why don't you?'

Unmoved by her indignation, Tim looked at Clara who said defensively, 'Honestly, I couldn't help myself, but I am sorry. It must've been something I ate. Food poisoning. I feel real ashamed. I expect you think I'm no good, but I felt that ill on the train, I just wanted to die.'

'Where are you going now?' he asked.

'Hastings, I suppose, if my ticket's still good.'

'It is,' he told her, 'for today, that is.'

Amy frowned. 'But what will you do in Hastings?' she asked. 'Have you got any money?'

'What's left of that pound,' said Clara. 'I don't know, really. Pa had an aunt in Hastings as I said, but she might be dead now. I'll think of something; I'll be all right.'

Amy turned to Tim. 'Clara's run away from home,' she explained, tactfully leaving out the rest of the story. 'She's got nowhere to go.'

'I'll be OK,' the girl insisted. 'I'll find myself a job and a room. I'll be fine. Any rate, I'd better be on my way.' She stood up.

'There's no train,' said Tim, 'not till the 5.28.'

He was looking at her thoughtfully. 'Do you have to go to Hastings?' he asked.

'I suppose not — I just thought I would. Why?'

Tim turned to Amy. 'We've got a spare room; at least it's more of a box-room — a bit cramped, I suppose — but it might do.'

There was a long silence while the two girls stared at him and he wondered if he had said something out of place.

'What do you mean?' asked Clara. 'Me come and stay at your house. Like a lodger?'

'If you got a job,' he said cautiously. 'I mean, since my father died things are a bit hard. A few extra bob would help.' He looked at Amy for confirmation that his idea was reasonable and she nodded.

'While your mother's cooking for two, she could cook for three,' she said to Tim. 'You could at least ask her.'

They both looked at Clara, who was smiling delightedly.

'What about your father?' Amy asked her. 'He might come after you.'

'He might,' she said, 'but I don't reckon he will. He's told me lots of times to clear out. We hate each other, always have. He's a right bully, my father. Anyway, even if he did try to find me he'd never find me here, would he?' Her tone grew more defiant. 'Even if he did, I'd never go back. I'd rather starve than live with him again. Look at these!'

She pushed up her sleeve and bared her right arm, which bore several purplish bruises. 'He did that and the other arm's the same! Doesn't know his own strength, that's his trouble. Grabs me by the arms see, and that's what happens.' They watched her silently as she pulled down her sleeve again. 'Look,' she said to Tim, 'tell your ma she can have all that's left of the pound and I'll look for a job. If I can't find one and the pound runs out, I'll move out without no fuss. Cross my heart and hope to die! She can call in a copper if I don't.'

Tim looked at Amy, who nodded. 'Right then,' he smiled at Clara. 'I'll be off home and see what she says.'

A moment later they watched him cycle past the window and then the bell rang upstairs.

'It's my grandfather,' Amy explained. 'Would you like to meet him? He'll tell you his life story, I'm afraid, but he does enjoy a bit of company.'

Clara expressed her willingness and followed Amy up the narrow wooden stairs to the old man's bedroom. Five minutes later Amy left them to it and went downstairs, satisfied that Clara could hold up her own end of the conversation and might even out-talk the garrulous old man!

Tim returned just in time to see in the next train, then reported that his mother would give the girl 'a try' for one month to see if they could all get along. He did not tell Clara that his mother had been very reluctant, that he had talked her into giving the idea a try, or that they had spent half an hour cleaning out the little room and assembling some suitable, if scant, furniture for it. A spare mattress had been laid over a low, makeshift trestle; an old chair had been rescued from the limbo of the garden shed and given a quick brush down to remove the cobwebs; Mrs Hollis had donated her own bedside rug and Tim had contributed a small wooden chest in which Clara could keep her clothes until – hopefully – a small chest of drawers could be borrowed from Tim's aunt who lived nearby. Tim had left his mother frantically polishing and worrying aloud about the state of the curtains.

When Tim went home that evening, Clara went with him on Amy's bicycle; he would ride hers to work the next day and then walk home. Amy watched them go with her fingers crossed behind her back, for she had taken a liking to the girl and hoped things would go well with her.

*

Bates Manor was a large house with six bedrooms, three of which were rarely used as visitors tended to come in twos or fours. All these rooms were situated in one corridor on the first floor, with the master bedroom at the far end next to the servants' stairs. Above them were four small attic rooms, two of which served as bedroom and living-room for Mrs Lester, the cook-housekeeper who had been with the Hatherleys for five years. The furniture in the master

75

bedroom, shared by the master and mistress of the house, was dusted daily and polished twice a week, whereas the carpet was cleaned only once a week. Today, however, Esme was spending the day in bed with 'one of her headaches' and the polishing had been cancelled. Hearing this from the cook, Lorna had understood, for it was a recurrent monthly 'head-ache' and comment on the euphemism was never encouraged by Mrs Lester.

Instead of polishing the master bedroom, she had been instructed to give one of the spare bedrooms 'a bit of a do' and when Gerald entered the room she was standing on a chair, polishing the top half of the large window with a cloth soaked in methylated spirits.

'Good morning, sir,' she said, glancing down and smiling dutifully.

'Good morning, Lorna.'

He stood watching her, blinking repeatedly as her upstretched arms pulled her dress closer to her body and lifted her skirt just a little at the back to reveal a glimpse of bare ankles.

'About time these poor old windows had a clean,' she told him. 'Real dirty they were, but they come up a treat.'

'It's the fires,' he said. 'We had all the rooms in use at Easter. The dust from the fire and the condensation on the panes – it's a fatal combination, you see.'

'I'm sure it is, sir.' She surveyed her handiwork with a critical eye. The difference between the upper and lower window was obvious and Gerald murmured his approval.

'Well,' she said, 'I'd best get myself down and do the bottom one.' She cast a helpless look in his direction and seizing his chance, he rushed forward, put his hands round her waist and helped her off the chair.

'Oh, thank you, sir.'

His eyes were blinking so rapidly that she had to look away for fear of giggling. His hands were still round her waist and she could feel him trembling.

'You're a tiny little thing, Lorna,' he said wistfully. 'Tiny. I like tiny women, you know that? There's something fragile about a tiny woman.' He withdrew his hands and with his fingers formed a circle. 'See that? That's the span of your little waist. I like that, Lorna.'

'I'm glad, sir.'

'Yes, I like it very much.' He stared at her, his hands now clenched in front of him. 'Like an hourglass, Lorna; that's how a woman should be.'

He laughed and Lorna picked up the bottle of methylated spirits and dampened her cloth.

'Lorna . . .' he began, taking hold of her arm and preventing her from reaching the window.

'Lorna, I want to ask you something,' he whispered. 'A little secret between you and me.'

'Sir?' She looked up at him curiously.

He took a deep breath. 'When we're like this, Lorna – together – I want you to call me Gerald. That's all – just call me Gerald when no one is around. Do you see? Will you do that?'

'Ooh sir, I don't know if I should,' she said nervously. 'Suppose someone heard me, when we didn't know. I'd get the sack, sir.'

'You wouldn't, Lorna,' he cried earnestly. 'I promise you, you wouldn't. I wouldn't *let* her sack you. It would just be friendly, you see. Do it now.'

'Do what?'

'Call me Gerald.'

She hesitated, but it seemed a harmless request.

'Gerald,' she said uncertainly.

His hand tightened uncomfortably on her arm. 'No, not like that! Say something with my name in it.'

Lorna frowned slightly. 'Well, Gerald,' she said, 'I think I'd better finish off the window.'

A smile spread across his face and she was surprised how much nicer he looked.

'That's fine,' he enthused. 'But as to the window, why, you can do that later. I've got a better idea – see?' He waved a hand in the direction of the bed only a few feet away from them.

'What?' she cried, instantly alarmed.

'No, no!' he cried hastily. 'I didn't mean *that*. Of course not. I meant just to sit down together, and I'll put my arm around you. No harm in that, is there.'

'But sir, I—'

'Gerald!' he reminded her.

'I mean, Gerald. But we shouldn't, sir – Gerald.' She giggled suddenly. 'Sir Gerald! There, I've knighted you!'

He laughed. 'You could do that, Lorna. You could knight me. Say "Arise, Sir Gerald".' To her dismay, he knelt quickly at her feet, head bowed. 'Go on, girl,' he insisted. 'Tap me on the shoulder and say, "Arise Sir Gerald".'

'All right then – Gerald.' She leaned forward and touched his shoulder, aware of his eager face upturned towards her own. 'Arise, Sir – oh!'

His arms had locked round her knees in a tight grip and his face was now pressed against her thighs. She lost her balance and half-fell, half-stumbled backwards on to the bed, her arms outflung to protect herself. In seconds he had joined her, spreadeagled face down on the bed beside her, one arm thrown across her chest.

'Don't move,' he told her breathlessly. 'Don't struggle. I won't touch you, I swear it!'

She could not see his face, which was pressed into the bedclothes. The bed felt damp and smelt of mildew, she thought, deciding she would drape the covers over the chairs and open the windows to let some fresh air and sunshine into the room. *When* she had finished with her master – or he had finished with her! He was mumbling something into the bedclothes, but his voice was muffled.

'I can't hear you, sir,' she told him sharply.

At once he lifted his head and she saw his face at close quarters, the eyes blinking, the small mouth quivering with excitement.

'I said are you afraid of mice, Lorna?'

'Mice!' Alarmed, she made an effort to sit up.

'No, no, I don't mean a real mouse,' he assured her. 'I mean, if my fingers became a little mouse—' His fingers began to scrabble lightly at her breast like tiny feet. 'Like this, Lorna. Would you mind?'

'I don't know,' she said dubiously.

'You could close your eyes,' he said, 'and pretend it was a naughty little mouse, *exploring*.'

Lorna hesitated.

'There might be a shilling in it for you,' he added.

A shilling! Lorna decided a mouse would be bearable and nodded quickly. At once the fingers began to run all over her neck and face, down to her shoulders.

'Close your eyes,' he told her.

As she did so, she felt him scrambling into a kneeling position and then *two* sets of fingers travelled over her body, across her abdomen, down over her thighs to her ankles. Her employer's voice was now squeaky and mouselike.

'Naughty little mice! What are you doing?' he cried. 'Oh! *This* mouse has found a pretty little ankle!'

Lorna giggled. 'I'm ticklish, sir!' she protested, deciding it was time to put an end to her employer's nonsense.

'Stop it now, you mice,' she said. 'Stop it, or I'll scream!'

At once he leapt from the bed, terrified by her careless words. 'No, Lorna!' he begged. 'Please don't scream. It was just my fun.'

She sat up, straightening her bodice and hair, eyeing him with a mixture of relief and pity. 'He's sad really,' she thought. 'Like a sad little boy.'

'I'm sorry, sir,' she said. 'I wouldn't really scream, only I didn't know where those mice were going next – and you were so strong.'

His expression changed. 'So strong? Was I, Lorna? My poor little girl. I didn't mean to frighten you. But you did like it, didn't you? Just you and me in bed together.'

'*On* the bed!' she corrected him anxiously. 'We weren't *in* it, sir.'

'No, no, of course not.'

He had recovered from his fright and when Lorna held out her hands, he pulled her to her feet.

'This is our little secret, Lorna,' he told her. 'I'll tell no one if you'll tell no one. A pact, eh?'

Lorna nodded.

'Hand on heart?' he insisted, placing his own hand across his chest.

She did the same.

'Our secret,' he declared.

'Our secret.'

He took her hand and had bent his head to kiss it when suddenly, to their mutual horror, a floorboard creaked on

79

the landing. Lorna snatched her hand away as Esme appeared in the open doorway; she knew that her cheeks burned with tell-tale colour and saw Gerald's face grow pale before his wife's suspicious glare.

'I heard voices,' Esme said icily. 'I was trying to read.'

Lorna had never seen her in her negligée and made a mental note that if *she* ever married a wealthy man, she too would wear peach-coloured satin trimmed with delicate coffee-coloured lace.

As Gerald continued to stare at his wife speechlessly, Lorna said, 'I'm sorry if we woke you, ma'am. Mr Hatherley was telling me to . . .' she searched her mind desperately ' . . . to air the bedding. Open the windows and everything.' She sniffed. 'It smells so musty in here.'

'Yes, yes,' stammered Gerald, rallying desperately. 'Very musty. Can't have musty bedrooms, eh? Must get everything spick and span.'

Esme was not deceived and Lorna knew it, but she also knew that her mistress could not prove anything and it would be their combined word against hers. If Gerald betrayed her, he would betray himself. Taking heart, she went on, 'I was just doing the window, ma'am. They clean up really nice, these big windows.'

Esme gave the window a cursory glance and returned to her husband.

'Spick and span,' she repeated. 'Why do we want it spick and span? This room is hardly ever used. We shan't want it before Christmas and it's July now.'

Gerald swallowed hard. 'We might want it,' he said. 'There's your birthday, you see, in less than a month.'

'What has that got to do with it?' She moved forward and ran her finger along the window-sill; as she turned back her eye fell on the crumpled bed, but before she could speak, Gerald said, 'It was going to be a surprise.'

Her attention was momentarily distracted. 'What was? You are talking in riddles, Gerald.'

'Your party, dear,' he invented brilliantly. 'I was going to arrange a surprise party for your birthday. Never mind, Lorna.' He turned to her. 'No need to worry now, the secret's out.' The eye that his wife could not see closed in a wink.

'Oh dear,' said Lorna. 'What a pity! I love surprises.'

Gerald turned back to Esme. 'Poor Lorna,' he said. 'I was telling her to smarten up all the bedrooms without letting you know. Foolish of me, really. She was just saying she was afraid she'd let something slip and then you appeared. Still,' he shrugged. spreading his hands helplessly, 'now that you know, are you pleased, dear?'

After a moment's hesitation Esme's face relaxed into a tight smile. 'Of course I am, Gerald. A party would be fun, I have to admit. It's years since we've given a big one, except at Christmas, of course. How very thoughtful of you, dear. We'll hold it in the Gold Room. It's a good size and we hardly ever use it. Yes, that's a splendid idea – but goodness, there's not a great deal of time,' she said. 'There's always so much to do. Guests to invite, menu to be planned and so many other things besides. The fact is that if one gives a party, it simply has to be a good one.'

'No expense spared,' Gerald told her rashly and then, less rashly, 'It's my present to you.'

Esme's face fell suddenly. 'But the Ballingers are still in India,' she began. 'How frightful – a party won't be the same without them! And when are Moira and Nigel coming home from Scotland?'

'I thought they were back,' he said.

'Are they? Oh, I do hope you're right.' She gave Lorna a brief nod. 'Get on, then, Lorna. And I may need you to put in some extra time if we're going to have a party.'

Lorna smiled eagerly. 'Will we wear the new caps and aprons ma'am, like we did at Christmas?'

Esme laughed. 'Of course you will.' She thought for a moment. 'Now, we can't seat a hundred guests and it will hardly be a party with fewer than that. It will have to be a buffet meal, and you will help carry the food round.'

'A hundred people?' gasped Lorna, seeing from Gerald's expression that he was equally shocked.

'Oh yes!' laughed Esme maliciously. 'Less than a hundred would be quite ridiculous in the Gold Room, wouldn't it, Gerald?'

He hesitated and for one thrilling moment Lorna thought

81

he was going to argue the point, but his courage obviously failed him.

'Of course, dear,' he agreed huskily. 'It's my birthday present to you and it must be perfect. If you say a hundred, so be it.'

They went out of the room together, but not before Lorna had seen the look of undisguised triumph on Esme's face. Esme had seen the rumpled bed and had interpreted the situation correctly. She had said nothing, but she would see to it that her husband paid dearly for his foolishness.

Chapter Five

Mary Leckie stood in the muddy yard with chickens all around her and absent-mindedly scattered handfuls of grain over them. She wore a pair of Jim's old boots under her long skirt and a large sack was tied round her ample waist to serve as an apron. It had rained hard in the night – a summer storm – and the earth in which the hens now strutted had turned into a quagmire, but the late July sun and a light breeze promised to dry the ground before the day was out. Behind Mary in the lean-to shed, her son was splitting logs for the stove with a familiar ringing of metal on wood which barely impinged on her consciousness. Jim was trundling a milk-churn down the drive to the wooden platform he had built in the lane. At 4 in the afternoon he and Don would milk the cows again and the two churns would await collection early next morning. They would be taken to Gazedown Station, whence they would travel to London on the early train.

When she had fed the hens, Mary collected the eggs from the hen-coop, putting them carefully into the ancient basket, then took them back into the kitchen which was in its usual state of cheerful chaos. Unwashed pans and a pile of potato peelings littered the draining-board; the remains of last night's supper were still on the table and a half-plucked chicken sprawled on the dresser. There were feathers everywhere and one had found its way into a large pan of black-currant jam which bubbled gently on the stove, attracting the interest of several flies which buzzed above it.

Humming cheerfully under her breath, Mary dumped the

basket of eggs beside the half-plucked chicken and reached for two large iron frying-pans. It was nearly 9 o'clock in the morning and the Leckie family had been up since 5.30am and had not yet eaten. Breakfast was a major event, as they would not eat again until 7pm or later. Mary began by frying two thick slices of bread and a pound of tomatoes. She took a ham down from its hook over the fire and carved off eight slices, which went into the second frying-pan with a large knob of lard, and put three plates to warm in the wire rack above the stove. Then she pushed the scattered contents of the table into the centre to make room for the coming meal and was brushing crumbs on to the floor as Jim came in, a scowl on his usually good-natured face.

'Bloody heifers!' he said and began to wash his hands in the water in which Mary had peeled last night's potatoes. She knew better than to enquire about the heifers and said nothing.

'What is it?' he asked, drying his hands on the teacloth which hung beneath the sink.

This question posed no problem for his wife, who knew from years of experience that Jim's main concern was always for the meal *after* the one he was about to eat – in this case the evening meal.

'Hunter's pot,' she told him. 'You know: bread, cheese and bacon.'

He grunted non-committally and glanced up as Don came in, silent in stockinged feet, having kicked off his shoes on the doorstep.

'Where's Fred?' he asked his father. 'Can't find the blighter anywhere.'

'Up at the top meadow,' Jim told him, 'fixing that gate. Stan's down at the smithy.'

Mary put the fried bread to keep warm in the oven and began to crack eggs into the pan. 'Sid still not back?'

'No,' her husband snorted. 'Lazy tyke!'

A black cat came out from under the table and rubbed itself lovingly around Mary's ankles. 'Poor old Sid,' she said mildly, discouraging the black cat with the toe of her boot.

'Poor old Sid, my foot!' Jim exploded. 'How long does it

take to recover from a sprained elbow? Anyone would think he'd broken his back, the way he's carrying on.'

Don poured himself a mug of milk and the cat leaped on to his lap and was unceremoniously pushed down again.

'Here you are, Jim.' Mary put a heaped plate in front of her husband. 'Get round that lot!'

'Another slice of fried bread, love, if there is one,' he said automatically.

'Right you are.' No matter how many slices of fried bread she gave him, he would always feel deprived if he did not persuade her to cook him one more.

'Lorna looked in,' said Mary, serving Don. 'She was asking for you.'

'They do,' he grinned, cutting himself a thick slice of bread.

'Hark at him,' said Jim. 'Too modest by far!'

'She's a funny little thing,' said Mary. 'Takes after her mother but pretty in a way, I suppose. Head like a sieve, I reckon. I don't know what you see in her, Don. You could do a lot better for yourself.'

'Such as who?' Her son paused, a forkful of ham halfway to his mouth.

'Such as Amy Turner. There's a really nice girl for you, Don, and her heart's in the right place.'

'Not exactly a ravishing beauty,' Don objected through a mouthful of ham.

Jim snorted. 'Beauty! That's all you lads think about.'

Don grinned. 'Not *all* we think about!' he corrected. 'Anyway, Amy's got her hands full with that family of hers. Marry her – you marry the lot of them.'

No one, it seemed, could argue with that.

Mary picked the feather out of the jam and gave it a stir before sitting down to eat her own breakfast. A companionable silence fell as the plates were slowly emptied, then Mary wiped a last half-slice of bread round the plate and glanced at her son.

'She was on about the Hatherleys,' she told him. 'They're having a party, seemingly, in about three weeks' time. Her birthday present from him. Nearly a hundred people! I wonder how old she is? What wouldn't I give to get a peep at that lot, all waltzing round.'

'All those rich folk and all those diamond necklaces,' said Jim. 'Burglar's paradise, that'll be. They should keep quiet about it – asking for trouble, that is, advertising it like that.'

'How can you keep it quiet?' Mary demanded. 'You've got to order the food and drink and the word's bound to get round. They'll be drinking champagne, I suppose. I wonder what that's like.'

'You'll never know, love,' said Jim. 'We out of bread?'

Grumbling good-naturedly, she produced another loaf from the crock beside the dresser and watched her husband and son cut into it. 'Like ravening wolves', was how she described it later to Amy.

'How does Lorna like working for the Hatherleys?' she asked Don. 'They had trouble with one girl, Florrie what's-her-name. Accused Mr Hatherley of molesting her and he threatened to have her horse-whipped for lying. Nobody did get to the truth of that. She went off to stay with her aunt or someone and it was all hushed up. She was a nice little thing, young Florrie – used to give us a hand with the hay-making. You wouldn't remember, Don; you were only about ten. But they never seem to keep anyone for long.'

'Mr H. is harmless enough,' said Don. 'She says he'd like a bit of slap and tickle, but she won't let him near her. I can believe it, too. *I* can't get near her, so I'm damned sure he can't!'

Jim laughed. 'Like that, is it?'

'I'll say it is!'

Jim leaned forward. 'You should—'

Mary interrupted her husband. 'Don't encourage him, Jim, with silly talk. He's only a boy himself. If he follows your advice, he'll be married before he's twenty!'

'So what's wrong with that?' Jim demanded. 'I was, and I haven't heard you complain. Eighteen you were, and—'

'Now there's no need to go into all that,' Mary said hastily. 'Any more bread, anyone?'

Don looked at her in astonishment. 'Not you two!' he cried. 'Really? Well, I never. Tut, tut! Naughty, naughty.'

Mary adopted a haughty tone of voice. 'We were talking about Lorna,' she reminded them, 'not us.'

'Well, I never!' Don repeated, determined to embarrass them. 'Like that, was it?'

She took a playful swipe at him and he ducked, grinning broadly.

'Lorna can look after herself,' he told them. 'Take my word for it. It's funny, really; she seems to give me the "come on" and then backs off as soon as I make a move. I don't know where I am with her. I don't think she knows what she does want – makes out to be all prim and "must wait for the wedding". Funny creatures, women, if you ask me.' He shook his head. 'No, I don't think Mr H. would get far with Lorna.'

'Well, I just hope you're right,' said Mary. 'If it's a case of his word against hers, he'll be the one that's believed. After all, his brother's a magistrate and they're bound to be on his side.'

She reached for the teapot and filled three large cups 'What must it be like to be married to a man like that? Ugh!' She shuddered realistically. 'Poor woman.'

'Florrie likely led him on,' said Jim, feeling that the honour of the male should be defended. 'Probably no better than she should be.'

'Jim Leckie!' cried his wife. 'What a thing to say! Why should she lead him on and then complain, knowing she'd get the sack for certain? She'd have to be a bit dim to lose herself a good job and Florrie wasn't like that.'

'Well, how would I know that?'

'You should give the benefit of the doubt,' she told him. 'Suppose it was your daughter? You'd be singing a different tune then, I'll warrant.' She snorted indignantly. 'You men are all the same. You all stick together.'

'Well, Lorna's got her head screwed on the right way,' said Don, 'so stop fussing, for Pete's sake. I've told you, if Lorna was giving it away, it'd be to me and I can assure you she's not.'

'Sensible girl,' said Mary, grinning. 'If I'd had her sense I wouldn't have landed myself in this mess, with a hulking great son to wait on hand and foot. Too lazy to pick your clothes up off the floor, too idle to—'

Don winked at his father. 'Sounds familiar,' he said.

'Wonder where I've heard all that before?' He held up his hand and made yapping motions with his finger and thumb. 'You know you love it,' he told Mary, 'so stop nagging. I'm your baby boy, remember? The apple of your eye!'

'Hulking brute,' she said, grinning fondly at her beloved son. 'I wanted a girl – a bit of company.'

There was a knock on the door and Sam Turner came in, Snip at his heels. Jim reached out and ruffled his hair. 'Hullo, young Sam,' he said. 'How's things down at the station?'

'I dunno,' said Sam, 'but I'm getting a ride on the milk train tomorrow with Mr Bell – he's the driver. I'm biking to Tenterden, then riding back. On the footplate, I mean.' He beamed round, bursting with pride. 'I'm going to be an engine-driver if I can. Like grandfather.'

'An engine-driver?' said Don. 'Whatever will your father say to that? Doesn't he want you to be a stationmaster?'

Sam shrugged. 'I dunno, but I'm not,' he told them. 'They're going to let me help clean the engine. Mr Bell's promised on his grandmother's grave and he won't go back on his word; Tim swears he won't. I'm to be there an hour early.'

His eyes shone at the prospect of this forthcoming adventure and Mary laughed.

'So one of these days it'll be you roaring into Gazedown and tooting your whistle? Well, that'll be the day, young Sam! I hope I'm still around to see it. D'you want a slice of bread? They haven't left much else.'

'Yes, please.'

Jim got up. 'Here, have my seat, lad. I've warmed it for you. I must get after old Fred and give him a bit of a hand.'

Sam took his place and was soon biting into a thick slice of bread and jam.

'How's Tim Hollis getting on with his young lady friend?' Mary asked him. 'Clara – is that her name?'

'She's their lodger,' he told her solemnly. 'She's not Tim's lady friend.'

'Oh, the lodger, is she? Sorry, I'm sure. She's definitely staying, then?'

'I dunno.' He shrugged.

'Well, she's been there two weeks or more.'

Sam shrugged again and crammed the last piece of crust into his mouth. 'Amy says, is the chicken ready? We've got company: Mr Allan from The Lodge.'

'Aha!' cried Don. 'Our Amy's got a gentleman caller, has she?'

'I dunno,' said Sam. It was his favourite comment and saved a lot of unnecessary thought.

Reluctantly Don got to his feet. 'Must be nice,' he said to Sam, 'being a woman. They can sit around the house all day making cups of tea while we men have to work and slave!'

Sam grinned but said nothing. When Don had followed his father out of the house the kitchen was quiet for a moment, the silence broken only by the ticking of the clock.

'Tell your sister, Sam, I'll have the bird dressed by mid-morning and I'll pop it round to her,' said Mary. 'Where are you off to today?'

'The pond,' he told her, 'after I've done my errands. There's two parcels and I'm to deliver them so Mr Coombes can get on with the garden. It's the judging soon and he's all in a twitter.'

Mary laughed. 'Poor Mr Coombes!' she said. 'Well, get along now, Sam, and give Amy my message. And you behave yourself tomorrow on that train engine.' She saw him out and then returned to the chaos of her kitchen.

'Sit down all day!' she muttered. 'Blooming sauce!' And chasing the black cat from the dresser, she seized the chicken and sat down with it in her lap. Within seconds her deft fingers were busy once more, pinching and tugging, and the air was brown with floating feathers.

*

When Sam arrived at the loco shed the next morning, the two men already at work were obviously expecting him.

'Is that Sam Turner?' called one of them, a scrawny ginger-haired man. ''Cos if it is, you're five minutes late!'

He and his companion laughed, but not unkindly, as Sam — apologising profusely — jumped from his bicycle and rushed over to join them. Beads of sweat stood out on his forehead and he was gasping for breath.

The older man put a hand on his shoulder. 'Steady on,

young'un,' he said. 'You'll be worn out before you've even *started!* Just you stand there a minute and get your wind. Gordon here's only pulling your leg. I'm Mr Bridges.'

Sam could not wait to get started. The blue engine loomed up in front of him, high as a mountain, but to his eyes ten times more beautiful. Because it was not standing at the platform it appeared much higher and for a moment Sam could do nothing but shake his head in wonder. Then an oily rag was thrust into his hand.

'That's cleaning oil, lad,' he was told, 'and I'll tell you how we do it. Now, you listen hard. There's a lot of loco to clean – tanks and wheels, both sides; boiler, footplate and smokebox.' Sam longed to say, 'I'll do the footplate', but he did not dare, so merely nodded his head to show that he was paying proper attention.

'There's what we call "the works" as well,' his instructor went on. 'There's axles and inside the frames; then there's the dome, chimney, safety-valves and a whole lot of brass fittings. Have you got that, lad?'

Sam nodded, his mind whirling rapturously. While they talked, Gordon was at work on top of the engine cleaning the chimney with a lump of tallow.

'Now, here's all our gear,' Mr Bridges told Sam. 'Wet-washed cloths, rags, a brick swab and two new sponges. They've all got a certain job to do, but don't worry; you'll get the hang of it.'

Five minutes later Sam was cleaning one of the large driving-wheels! His heart thumped with excitement and he wanted to shout with joy. But Mr Bridges and Gordon were not shouting, they were intense and serious and with a supreme effort Sam modelled his features on theirs and for a while the three of them worked in silence. Sam's arm began to ache, but he revelled in the discomfort. If he was going to be an engine-driver like Mr Bell, then he knew he must start at the bottom of the ladder and clean the engines. Determinedly he thrust the rag in and out of the wheel and was thrilled to see the way the metal reacted to his efforts, gleaming in the early morning sunshine. When his right arm ached intolerably, he changed the rag to his left hand and continued, ducking right under the engine where it was dark and cold.

They stopped at last for a ten-minute break. Gordon had brewed a can of hot cocoa on a small spirit lamp and they sipped in companionable silence until Gordon said, 'Why do you want to be a driver, Sam? Why not be a fireman? That's what I'm going to be. I'll get this fire going when we're done, ready for Mr Bell and his mate to take over. Soon I'll be going out firing on the local goods train. Then I'll move on to long-distance goods, then local passenger trains, then expresses. I'd rather be a fireman any day.'

Sam was silenced, his brow furrowed, sorely tempted by this catalogue of delights. He imagined himself with a shovel, hurling coal into the red-hot interior of the firebox. Everything would depend on him! Would he or would he not get up enough steam to pull the train up the hill? He saw the engine-driver turn to him, his face pale. 'Can you do it, Sam?' he would cry and Sam would nod and bend his aching back . . .

'You leave him be, Gordon,' said Mr Bridges, interrupting this delightful daydream. 'Young Sam knows what he's doing. If he wants to be an engine-driver – well, you can't go higher than that.'

From the good-humoured wrangling that followed, Sam learned that Mr Bridges was hoping to become a driver himself.

When the break was over and they returned to work, Sam found himself on the footplate, faced by a bewildering display of tubes, wheels, pipes and levers, many made of brass or copper and all having to be polished to a high degree. Mr Bridges attempted to explain some of the workings, rattling the names off at a careless speed that left Sam impressed but utterly confused.

'These are the driver's running controls and these are the fireman's. This here's the regulator, this the whistle, steam valve for the exhaust, blower . . .'

Sam nodded earnestly, trying hard to take in all the unfamiliar names and phrases. Suppose Mr Bridges asked him a question and he could not answer? The thought terrified him and he concentrated with all his might.

91

'There's a lot more to being an engine-driver than knowing about the loco,' he was told. 'There's all the routes to learn, for a start, then the level crossings, the gradients and the signals. Know any signals, do you?' Sam nodded and opened his mouth, pleased that here at last he could shine, for Bob Hart had taught him about signals. Mr Bridges, however, did not wait for an answer. 'There's the whistle code, too, and the headlamp code. Know those, do you?'

Before Sam could admit that he did not know them all, Gordon shouted to him and it was time to watch him prepare and light the fire. The latter was already glowing by the time Mr Bell finally arrived to make an inspection of their work, to 'oil round' and to compliment the men grudgingly on the results of their labours.

Sam followed Mr Bell round in a seventh heaven of delight and then the fireman arrived to check the water and steam pressure. By the time the engine was ready to move off, he was mentally and physically exhausted, although the best part was yet to come.

The locomotive rattled and bumped her way out of the siding and on to the track where the two goods vans waited to be connected. When all was in order, Sam waved 'Goodbye' to Mr Bridges and Gordon and Mr Bell gave a tug on the whistle cord and they were on their way at last. The rush of cold morning air chilled Sam's back and the heat from the glowing firebox scorched his knees. The roar of the engine deafened him, so that when Mr Bell or the fireman spoke to him he could only nod and smile and pretend to understand. The sturdy locomotive swayed from side to side as it gathered speed and the footplate trembled beneath his feet as the driving wheels turned faster and faster – wheels that he, Sam, had cleaned an hour earlier!

The train ran through the early morning mist; it ran through fields and between raw embankments which were just beginning to grass over; it clattered over bridges and chuffed its plume of smoke between the trees, past isolated cottages and alongside cattle-tracks where the startled cows raised their heads enquiringly. All too soon, for Sam, it began to slow down and drew at last to a juddering halt.

'Gazedown!'

Looking down from the footplate, he saw his father on the platform, his face wreathed in smiles. A few moments more and the milk-churns were on board, then Sam was standing beside his father on the platform watching the departing train with a heart too full for words. When his father asked him if he had enjoyed himself he could only nod his head, his eyes suspiciously bright because suddenly he wanted to tell his mother about it, but she was not there to listen. Fortunately Amy appeared at the window which overlooked the platform and called, 'Breakfast is ready', and somehow that made the moment bearable. Sam gave his father a quick smile and ran along the deserted platform, wondering how long it would be before Mr Bell retired and he could take his place.

Hard work and an early rise had sharpened Sam's appetite and half his breakfast was consumed before he stopped for breath.

'Good fun, was it?' his father asked.

Sam nodded, his eyes gleaming. 'Gordon wants me to be a fireman,' he told them, 'but I said "No".'

'Still going to be a driver then?' asked Amy.

'Yes.' He took a large mouthful of bread and butter and chewed noisily, instinctively aware that on this special day no one would tell him to eat properly or not to talk with his mouth full. 'But it's not easy being a fireman,' he went on. 'It's not just like chucking coal on the fire.'

'Isn't it?' said Amy.

Sam frowned, his expression earnest. 'You have to throw the coal in the right place, you see. The firebox is—' He was going to say 'bloody big' like Gordon, but after a moment's hesitation he changed his mind in case the day wasn't quite special enough. 'It's enormous,' he said, 'and you have to put the coal where it's needed. See, if you're going uphill you need it . . . um . . . well, somewhere, and if you're going downhill you need it somewhere else. At the back or the front or in the middle of the fire-bed.'

'Good gracious me,' said Amy. 'It *isn't* easy, is it?' She glanced at her father, inviting a comment from him also.

'It certainly isn't!' he said obligingly.

Sam stirred his runny yolk with a piece of toast. 'And you

93

can tell a good fireman by his smoke,' he told them. 'No, I mean it. Grey smoke means a good fireman, but black smoke's bad.'

'Bad?' Amy repeated. 'How's that then?'

'Because not enough air is getting through,' he told her earnestly. 'And white smoke!' He grimaced and shook his head. 'Too much air!'

Amy and her father obligingly registered astonishment and Amy 'tutted'. Satisfied with their reaction, Sam again concerned himself with the eating of his breakfast.

'And are you going to get another ride?' Amy asked him.

'One day,' he told her. ' "In the not too distant future". That's what Mr Bell said. Can I go round to Eric's now?'

Amy looked at her father. 'What about your Sunday jobs?' he asked.

Sam's Sunday jobs involved cleaning and polishing all the boots and shoes, filling the coal-scuttle and pumping up water if it was getting low.

Sam squirmed in his seat. 'Can't I do them later on? This afternoon?'

'Remember Mr Allan's coming to lunch,' said Amy, 'and we'll be going for a walk afterwards.'

'I'll miss the walk,' he offered. 'I don't mind.'

He found the Sunday walks extremely boring, with everyone in their best clothes being polite to anyone they met, and talking on and on about the weather and people's rheumatics. Sam would be only too pleased to miss it.

'But I'll want my clean shoes before Mr Allen gets here,' said Amy.

So it was agreed that Sam should clean the boots and shoes before going to Eric's and do the rest of his jobs later on.

*

After lunch Ted Turner settled down for his nap; Thomas went back to the station to finish some paperwork and to chat briefly to Harry Coombes, who was putting in some extra time on the garden. Sam was pumping up water and Amy and Ralph set out for a walk in Gazedown woods.

She was pleased to see him looking so much better; he

94

had obviously enjoyed his meal and had described the half-hour he had spent earlier with the old man as 'very entertaining'. He almost seemed to blossom, she thought, in the warm family atmosphere. What had he said to her, on his previous visit? That he envied her with a family to care for. Perhaps he was lonely, she thought, yet he had chosen to shut himself away in that dark lodge without even a cat for company. Then she remembered that his fiancée had died and a dozen questions sprang to mind, only to be promptly pushed back. Ralph Allan was a very private person and probably would not welcome her enquiries. If he wanted her to know anything about himself, no doubt he would tell her. But if he *did* confide in her, she hoped she could be of some comfort. Perhaps if he talked to her, he might release some of the tension she had detected in his voice. Amy imagined herself as a shoulder for him to cry on and rather liked the idea.

In cheerful silence they trudged over last year's dried leaves. The bluebells had been spectacular, though they were long since over and the starry wood anemones with them, but a few sprawling brambles clutched at them as they passed and here and there a dead branch blocked their path, blown down much earlier by the spring gales. Snip bustled happily beside them, her nose to the ground, investigating every burrow and peering under every tree-root. The day was very warm, but the dense leaves overhead created a cool gloom pierced by an occasional shaft of sunlight in which the midges were beginning to dance, and the air smelt of green leaves and old dank earth.

The silence lengthened. They appeared to have the wood to themselves, apart from the birds and one or two squirrels, and Amy began to wonder uneasily whether Ralph would think she had brought him here to be alone with him, but then dismissed the idea as nonsense. She was surprised, though, to find no one else around. When she and Sam came to the wood, they frequently met other dog-owners exercising their pets, but today there were none.

Amy went cold suddenly at the thought that Ralph might think she had deliberately arranged for Sam to have Sunday jobs still to do, so that he could not accompany them. No, no, she was being silly. Her imagination was running away with her. Ralph Allan could not possibly be considering her in that way; it would never enter his head. She was still trying to convince herself that she was worrying unnecessarily when she tripped and nearly fell, clutching at Ralph's arm to save herself.

'Are you all right?' he asked, steadying her.

Amy nodded. 'I think so. These wretched brambles! I've scratched my ankle, but that's all.'

He knelt to look and exclaimed, 'Oh dear, it's quite a bad scratch and your stocking's torn.'

'It doesn't matter,' she said. 'Really, it's not painful.'

'You could use my handkerchief, it's large and clean.'

She protested that she was fine, although the scratch was beginning to sting and she hoped there would not be enough blood to stain her shoe. Foolishly she had put on the best grey leather pair purchased so long ago for the adventure in London.

'Please,' he insisted, taking out his handkerchief. 'It won't take a moment.' He gave her a shy smile. 'You can do it yourself if you don't trust me.'

Amy gave in gracefully and watched his bent head as he gently tied the makeshift bandage round her ankle. She imagined it took him a long time and was just beginning to wonder if she had misjudged him when he straightened up and she saw that the haunted expression had returned to his eyes. Impulsively, she reached for his hands and held them tightly.

'You were thinking of Lydia,' she said. 'I'm sorry if it brought back sad memories.'

He tried to smile, but his lips trembled. 'It was the laces,' he said. 'Silly, isn't it? You think you are over something – someone – and then a small thing brings it all back. I used to tease her about her shoes, she was always breaking the laces.' He swallowed hard.

'I know how it is,' said Amy gently. 'It's the same for me with my mother – not that she's dead, but she might as well be.' She released his hands. 'I'm sorry, that sounded bitter and I don't mean to be. Like you, I think it's all over, all in the past and then something reminds me. We had a tea-cosy, which my mother had knitted in two colours. Every time we used it, it reminded me that she had gone and I couldn't bear it. I had to give it to Tim for the station office. I can see her now: the two balls of wool on the floor and Snip tangling them up — she was only a puppy then. It all seemed so ordinary and I didn't realise how nice it was that mother was there until she had gone. Then I wanted to say . . .' Tears filled her eyes suddenly, but she went on, 'I wanted to say, "We do all love you and we do appreciate you. Don't go away, it will never be the same without you." '

Looking up then, she saw the compassion in his face and abandoned herself to the tears. 'How can it be?' she sobbed. 'A mother is something special.'

Suddenly his arms were round her and he was holding her close, murmuring soothing unintelligible words of comfort and understanding.

'Oh, Ralph,' she cried helplessly, 'I can't stop. I've waited so long to cry. I'm just . . . oh, Ralph, help me!'

She was dimly aware that he was leading her away from the path and then he was sitting her down on a fallen tree-trunk. He sat beside her and put an arm round her shoulders. 'Perhaps you should talk about it?' he suggested gently. 'I promise I'm a very good listener.'

'But it's all so awful!' she sobbed. 'You won't want to hear it.'

'You mean you don't want to tell it,' he corrected her. 'That's all right. I don't want to pry, but it might help to confide in someone.'

Amy stared up at him through her tears. 'Ralph, you're so kind,' she said gratefully. 'I've never told anyone else. Nobody in Gazedown knows. Papa is so ashamed, although it's not really his fault. It's theirs. *Hers*.'

Ralph waited as she twisted her handkerchief. She was searching for the courage to unburden herself of all the years of pent-up misery, reluctant to face up to the agony she had suppressed for so long. Then, slowly at first, the words began to tumble out.

'I had an uncle, John,' she began. 'He wasn't really an uncle, but Papa's cousin, though his mother died when he was born and so he was brought up as Papa's brother. I

97

loved Uncle John and so did Sam. He was such fun – always laughing and teasing; always hugging us and never too busy to play. He and my aunt had no children of their own.' She frowned at the recollection. 'Papa never hugged us,' she said. 'I suppose he loved us in his own way – I'm sure he did – but he couldn't show it like Uncle John. Strange that he and Papa were brought up together, yet turned out so differently. My mother was the same, very reserved. All the affection in our lives came from Uncle John – and Grandmother, of course. Anyway, everything was happy until Uncle John was widowed and came to stay with us.' She bit her lip and Ralph's arm tightened round her shoulder. Snip paused in his scampering to bark impatiently, eager to continue the walk.

'Not yet, Snip,' Ralph told the little dog. 'Go off and chase something!'

Amy smiled faintly. 'Do you really want to hear all my troubles?' she asked again. 'Maybe they're best forgotten.'

'No,' said Ralph. 'That's not the best way. Please go on.'

Nervously Amy began to tweak the cloth of her skirt. 'Uncle John fell in love with my mother,' she said, 'and she fell for him. It was ridiculous! I couldn't believe it. I kept thinking they would come to their senses, but they didn't; then suddenly, out of the blue, they said they were going away together. My mother begged us to try to understand, but we couldn't; we were so shocked. Poor Papa, he was in a terrible state. We all were. When they left, we stood there, staring at each other. I'll never forget it.'

'Poor Amy.'

She nodded. 'I was due to go to London. I was very bright at school and the headmistress had persuaded my parents to let me train to be a teacher. I had everything ready and had set my heart on going. I felt I had to break away – to try my wings. London *beckoned*.' Ralph nodded and she smiled ruefully. 'I was still desperate to go and Papa wanted me to, so next day he went round to explain things to Grandmother and ask if she would come in every day and look after him and Sam.' She sighed heavily. 'The shock of the news killed her. She just collapsed and died! It was one tragedy on top of another and my whole world seemed to be falling apart.

Then Grandfather took to his bed, vowing that he'd be next. He was lost without Grandmother and I don't think he wanted to go on without her.'

'But he didn't die.'

'No. But he wouldn't get up either, so Papa left him there. The doctor said he was perfectly fit, but Grandfather wouldn't believe it and he's *still* there!'

'And you look after them all. You gave up your big chance.'

'I had to, for Sam's sake. He was so confused and unhappy and I couldn't leave him after everything else that had happened. I wish I could say I did it with a happy heart, but I didn't. I was so disappointed. I was bitter and resentful and I tried hard to hate my mother and Uncle John, but it's not that easy. All this happened in Essex, where we were living at the time. My father had a much bigger station with a large staff, and you can imagine the scandal. Then he started drinking and the Board reprimanded him several times. When my mother finally wrote to say she was expecting Uncle John's child, that was the last straw for Papa. He went to pieces altogether and almost got the sack, but instead they offered him a transfer to a much smaller station.'

'Gazedown?'

Amy nodded. 'It was a terrible blow to him, but he had to accept. He's much better now, thank goodness, but we don't talk about my mother. Sam's forbidden to say anything to the children at school and I just say she's away. People don't like to press the question. I expect they wonder, but I don't care any more. Sam's happy enough and Papa seems to be over it.'

'And you're an intelligent girl with no prospects,' said Ralph. 'That must be terribly frustrating.'

'I try not to think about it,' Amy said. 'Maybe one day I shall get another chance. Maybe when Sam is older . . . I don't know.' She became aware of Snip, who had returned yet again and was staring at them expectantly. With a smile, she stood up abruptly and pulled Ralph to his feet. 'That's the end of my sad tale,' she told him. 'Thank you for listening. I feel much better and I won't cry again, I promise.'

'I shall keep you to that,' he assured her, 'and don't you dare apologise for your tears. They're a vital part of recovery – they told me that in the—'

He stopped abruptly and she glanced at him quickly. 'And I meant to comfort you,' she said, 'because of Lydia. Oh dear, we are a pair!'

Her attempt at laughter was unsuccessful, but Ralph said, 'Let's walk on, shall we? I can't take you home looking like that, with torn stockings and a tearful face. Your father will wonder what I've been doing to you! Come on, give me your hand. I don't want you falling over again.'

Obediently she put her hand in his and to Snip's delight they wandered further into the wood, talking desultorily. Amy told him about her Friday stall and the Leckies' farm and he talked about his problems with the book he was trying to write.

When they finally turned back towards the station, Ralph said, 'May I ask you something personal? It will seem an awful cheek, but I would like to know.'

'Ask me.'

'Have you got a young man, Amy?'

Amy longed to say 'Yes', but she was too honest. 'There is someone I'm fond of,' she said, choosing her words carefully. 'In fact, I'm very fond of him, but he doesn't care for me in that way and he's got a young lady already. You probably know her – it's Lorna Betts.'

Ralph was surprised. 'The girl who works at the Manor, you mean?'

Amy nodded. 'I have to admit,' she said ruefully, 'that when I think of them together, they seem well-suited. His name's Don Leckie; I spoke about the Leckies just now.'

'So you did,' he said. 'And has there ever been anyone else in your life?'

'No. Just Don.'

He gave her hand a little squeeze and said gently, 'Life's never easy, at least not for long. We just have to take the rough with the smooth. It's trite, I know, but true. We have to say to ourselves, "This is a bad bit and I'm unhappy, but it won't last". You mustn't fight too hard against misery –

that exhausts you, you see. It's like grief. Give in to it and work through it.'

Amy looked at him dubiously and he laughed. 'Poor girl,' he said. 'I'm lecturing you like a Dutch uncle. I'm sorry. But I learned a lot in . . .' He stopped again.

Amy asked quietly, 'In where, Ralph?'

'In hospital,' he said.

There was a long silence, then Amy said, 'Do you feel so terrible now that you've told me?'

'I'm not sure. Perhaps not.' He laughed. 'Perhaps this is the day for dragging skeletons out of the cupboards. Well, here's mine, Amy.'

He let go of her hand and reached out both his arms, palms upturned, so that a scar round each wrist was clearly visible. Amy drew in her breath sharply, but he allowed her no time for comment.

'When I lost Lydia, I thought I wanted to die too,' he said simply, 'but I was wrong. After they sewed me up and put me back together again, I was very glad to be still alive. It was worse for my parents, of course; they had to come back from India and have only just returned. They've left me in the care of my brother Elliot; he's two years older than me. We should have been close as boys, but we never were. Chalk and cheese! I was always the quiet one, preferring to be on my own; he's gregarious and great fun, charming company. You'd love Elliot. Everyone does.'

Amy did not know how to answer, so she threw a stick for Snip and they watched the little dog race off after it.

'She won't find it,' said Amy. 'She never does.'

Ralph offered no more information about his family or his past life and Amy let the subject drop. In retrospect, it seemed incredible that they had drawn close enough to have exchanged so many confidences in so short a time.

'Is my face still a mess?' she asked.

'No. It's fine. A nice face.'

They laughed.

'Papa will have a search party out for us,' she said. 'We'll have to look terribly innocent.'

'We *are* terribly innocent,' he reminded her. 'Our consciences are quite clear.'

101

Snip ran ahead, barking shrilly, as soon as the stationmaster's house came into view and Sam ran out to meet them.

'I've had the last slice of cherry cake,' he shouted. 'Papa said I could. I was starving and you were so long.'

Snip leaped up at him and Sam snapped his fingers, encouraging her to jump even higher. 'Oh – and Mrs Hatherley called. She's having a party up at the Manor and she needs some extra girls to hand round plates of things to all the posh guests, and could *you* go, and she'll pay you – and she stinks of perfume! Phew!'

'Sam!' cried Amy, scandalised. 'Don't talk about Mrs Hatherley like that.'

Sam mumbled an apology and ran back into the house, the dog at his heels.

'A party!' said Amy, intrigued. 'What fun! I'll see if I can persuade Papa to let me go. He won't like the idea of me wearing an apron and cap and handing round "things" but I think I'd enjoy it. Do you know anything about a party?'

She thought Ralph looked faintly embarrassed. 'I do, actually,' he said. 'I've been invited and I'm afraid I shall be one of the posh guests!'

Chapter Six

Esme Hatherley sat at her figured-walnut desk with a list of names in front of her, but she was not reading it. She was staring into space and drumming her fingers furiously on a pile of sealed envelopes which she had addressed and stamped. They were invitations to her birthday party, the party that neither she nor Gerald wanted yet which she was determined would be as lavish as possible. She wanted to hurt him as much as she could and his pocket was always a vulnerable spot. The other vulnerable spot she would not touch with a barge-pole, she reflected grimly, not if he were to go on his bended knees and plead with tears in his eyes.

Their standing in the village had never been the same since that stupid business with Florrie. Not that she had welcomed his advances before that occasion – she had never found him attractive as a man, nor even competent as a lover. The affair with Florrie had given her the perfect excuse to reject him permanently.

She dipped her pen in the ink and began to tick off those names with which she had already dealt. 'Ballingers, Williamsons, Doug and Hetty, Elliot and Ralph Allan, Violet Parkinson . . .' Her face was set and there was no joy in the task for her. As a girl she had adored parties and her coming-out ball had been more exciting to her than her wedding day. Certainly, she amended, more exciting than her wedding *night* – a fiasco if ever there was one. The feel of her husband's inexpert fumbling hands, the sight of his rapidly blinking eyes, had reduced her to hysterical laughter which had had a disastrous effect on Gerald's performance as a husband. As a lover, she thought scornfully, he had never even started. Compared with the young captain in the Household Cavalry who had been her companion in bed for most of the year prior to her wedding, Gerald had not even come a poor second. She had apologised for her unseemly hilarity, excusing herself on the grounds of a new bride's nervousness in matters of sex; but when, several nights later, he had finally achieved a certain degree of success, it had been obvious that while he was a virgin she was not and their relationship had suffered accordingly.

'Moira and Nigel . . .' she murmured. 'Invitation sent to the address in Scotland. Harold Cunningham and his ghastly wife – God, how dull that woman is! James and Fiona Walters and her brother Charles; Rex Manners and whoever he cares to bring – either his wife or his current mistress . . .' How many so far? She made it eighteen. Was that all? As her fingers traced the list, her mind went back to the early days of their marriage when at least she and Gerald had pretended to feel some affection for each other. Now they didn't even bother with the occasional endearment; in fact, if one *was* used it was normally a form of sarcasm and said with intent to wound. Whenever Gerald called her 'Dear heart', she knew she would not like what followed.

'Damn you to hell, Gerald Hatherley!' she whispered, wishing that she had not loved her father so desperately. She had married Gerald to please her father although she had never understood why he had favoured the match. Certainly Gerald was a very rich man, but there were others equally wealthy who would have been more to her taste. He had been unable to give her a good reason for his choice, and she had always found that puzzling; Gerald was only fifteen years younger than his future father-in-law and fourteen years older than Esme, but her father had been so emphatic.

'Gerald's a good man,' he had insisted, 'and he'll look after you whatever happens. He has a wise head on his shoulders; he understands.' She had never fathomed his reasoning, but she had agreed. Four months after the wedding, he had been thrown from his horse and killed. If only her father had died four months earlier, she reflected, she would have left Gerald at the altar.

'Damn Gerald,' she muttered, 'and damn Lorna Betts!'

She almost wished she had rejected the offer of the party and sacked Lorna on the spot, but what good would that have done, she asked herself wearily. No, Lorna would have to stay and the wretched party must go ahead as planned.

With a sigh, she took a fresh invitation card from the box and regarded it with a small glow of satisfaction. They were from Harrods, the very best – the most expensive, heavily embossed and edged with gold. Gerald had opened his mouth to complain about the bill, but had hastily closed it again. 'Let him squirm, damn him', she thought bitterly. She could have married her captain in the Household Cavalry – he was a major now, so it was rumoured. But her father would not hear of it and her mother was no help. Poor frail Mama, tucked away in that dreary nursing home.

Esme wrote 'Lawrence and Agnes Cartwright and daughters' – how many did they have now, for God's sake? Was it five or six? The woman was like a rabbit. Hopefully some of them had married by now and flown the nest; they were all as ugly as sin and it was becoming increasingly difficult to find unattached men to partner the single ladies.

'Lucien Berger and friend'. He'd bring another man! She giggled suddenly, then threw down the pen and rose to her feet, moving elegantly even when exasperated.

They needed a secretary almost as much as she needed a personal maid. She had told Gerald so repeatedly. She should not have to slave over the invitations in this ridiculous fashion. What a birthday present! It was simply giving her a lot of extra and unwelcome chores. The menu had still to be finalised with Mrs Lester and Amy and Lorna would never be able to manage on their own. She must contact the girl whom Mrs Betts had mentioned to her: Clara somebody-or-other – staying with Tim Hollis and his mother apparently, and a bit of a mystery. A runaway from London, if Mrs Betts had got her facts right.

Esme walked towards the window, her feet soundless on the thick carpet; as she passed the huge gilt-framed mirror, she glanced at her reflection as she always did. Smooth hair immaculate, complexion clear and peach-toned, slim neck unlined and set off to good effect by the expensive lace frill at

her throat. Beautiful, elegant, sophisticated, she told herself —
but totally unappreciated. Gerald did not value her as he
should, he simply did not deserve her. Esme almost ground
her teeth as a wave of frustration and self-pity washed over
her. Gerald Hatherley, I loathe and despise you, she thought,
but what can I do? A divorce was out of the question — it
would be social suicide.

Standing at the window part of her mind continued to
wrestle with the matter of the invitations while the rest of
her thoughts dwelt longingly upon her fierce need to be loved
and wanted. In spite of her lack of feeling for her husband,
she had been faithful since her marriage, but only because
Gazedown was so depressingly short of men with whom she
could even contemplate an 'affair of the heart'. Unless . . .
she thought of Ralph Allan and hesitated, toying with the
idea. He was younger than she was, but that was no reason to
reject him. He must be reasonably intelligent, she supposed, if
he was writing a book. He seemed to have no female
companion in his life, or if he did she did not come to visit
him. She frowned trying to recall what Mrs Betts had told
her — that he had been engaged, but the girl had died — so
he might well be hungry for affection. With pursed lips she
whispered his name — Ralph Allan. No, just Ralph. He was
presentable, unattached and conveniently near. Good God,
he couldn't be much nearer.

A smile touched her lips as she tried to imagine how it
would be. She, the mature older woman, would sweep away
his inhibitions and show him what passion was all about.
They would meet secretly — no, better still, they would meet
openly, right under Gerald's stupid nose! Her smile broadened. Of course, she had already offered to take him riding,
so she could call round tomorrow morning and suggest a
ride later in the day. She knew how well she looked on a
horse. He would not be able to resist her — few men could,
given the opportunity and encouragement that she would
give Ralph. He might not be as tall as her captain of the
Household Cavalry, but he was just as young and
impressionable. And it would be fun to see how quickly she
could lure him into her bed!

Esme began to feel positively cheerful with the prospect

of a little amusement ahead of her to brighten her dreary life. She went back to the list of invitations with rather more enthusiasm and as she sat down another thought struck her. She had already invited Ralph to the party, so it was all quite perfect. 'Gerald Miles Hatherley,' she muttered vindictively, 'you are about to get what you so richly deserve!'

*

The next morning found Mrs Lester at work in the kitchen of Bates Manor. She glanced up irritably as Izzie came into the room, staggering under the weight of a heavy wooden tray piled with the crockery from the breakfast table. Izzie, the maid-of-all-work, a round-shouldered, grumpy looking girl whose permanently exhausted manner was the result of working from 6 am each morning until 9 o'clock at night with only two hours off, one at 3 o'clock for a late dinner and one at 6 pm for tea. Izzie did the washing-up, carried enormous jugs of hot and cold water up and down stairs, lit fires, black-leaded the vast range in the kitchen and whitened all the steps. She also prepared vegetables, laid and cleared tables and much more; in fact, all the arduous and unpleasant jobs which needed to be done at Bates Manor fell to her lot. Theoretically, a woman came in daily to do the heavy work – scrubbing floors and washing clothes – but she frequently failed to appear and then these jobs increased Izzie's burden. Esme was a difficult employer, quick to criticise and slow to praise, and staff came and went with depressing regularity. The housekeeper had recently left after a series of rows and Mrs Lester, the cook, was trying to do her job as well as her own. Daniel did the gardening and some odd jobs, assisted frequently by his son, Mark. Daniel, Mark and Lorna came in on a daily basis, although Daniel lived in a rent-free cottage nearby provided by the Hatherleys and subsequently found himself 'on call' twenty-four hours a day.

Izzie lowered the tray with a crash that rattled the cups and cursed under her breath.

'I heard that,' Mrs Lester told her. 'Don't you let her ladyship hear you – you know what she's like about bad language.'

107

'Can't think why,' Izzie retorted. 'She uses some terrible language herself when she's in one of her tempers with him.'

'She's entitled to; it's her house, remember. And anyway, you shouldn't listen. It's sneaky.'

'Can't help hearing the way they go on,' said Izzie. 'This morning before he went to London I could hear them rowing in the bedroom when I was half-way down the stairs! Then when he's gone and Mr Allan turns up, she's all smiles and butter wouldn't melt in her mouth!'

Mrs Lester shook her head. 'It's queer, that,' she said. 'Inviting someone to *breakfast*.'

Izzie ran the hot water and said, 'This water's half cold.'

'Top it up, then. There's plenty of hot water left in the big kettle.' The cook chewed the end of her pencil and shook her head again. 'Near on a hundred guests! I don't know how they're all going to fit in and this blooming shopping list's as long as my arm!'

'They've gone riding,' Izzie went on. 'I heard her say she'd found a pair of riding-boots that would fit him, and then I watched them from the landing window when they came out of the stables. Mr Allan was on the master's horse and not looking very happy. Perhaps he'll fall off.' She giggled as she added soda to the water and stirred it with a mop that had seen better days.

'Fall off?' echoed Mrs Lester. 'Why d'you want him to fall off? What's he ever done to you?'

'I didn't say I *wanted* him to fall off – I said perhaps he will. It's not very nice though, is it, sneaking up here when the master's back's turned and then riding his horse?'

Mrs Lester snorted. 'I don't expect he had much choice, poor man, knowing her. She probably said, "You'll come to breakfast and we'll go riding." You know what a bossy madam she is – won't take no for an answer. Lorna says he's quite nice, but a bit too quiet for her. She likes a man with a bit more "go".'

'He's quiet all right,' said Izzie. 'Hardly said a word over breakfast, leastways not while I was serving up. He looked sort of scared.'

'Poor man.'

Mrs Lester scratched the top of her head with the pencil and Izzie glanced at the clock.

'Lorna's late again,' she said. 'I don't know how she has the sauce.' Izzie did not say this with any trace of malice, but with more than a hint of admiration. Compared with her own dreary existence, Lorna seemed to her an exciting creature from another world; she had a mother who owned a shop and a married sister who would soon make her an aunt. Best of all, Lorna had a young man and Izzie loved to hear her talk about them all. Orphaned early in her life, she had none of these riches and treasured the fascinating glimpses into Lorna's life. Added to all this Lorna was pretty, which made her — in Izzie's eyes, at least — a princess, and surely a princess could turn up ten minutes late for work and get away with it.

Mrs Lester was not so generous. 'Ten minutes every day for six days is an hour's work lost,' she stated. 'She takes liberties, that girl does.' She made another note on the paper in front of her and said, 'I hope her ladyship finds another pair of hands. We could do with someone to help clean the house up before the "do" as well as to serve food on the night. Those bedrooms smell real musty and all the windows need cleaning.'

'I could help Lorna,' said Izzie hopefully. 'We could work together. I bet we'd get ever so much work done with two of us at it.'

'I doubt that,' said Mrs Lester. 'You'd talk all the time and get *half* as much done!' She crossed something off the main list and wrote it on a second list. 'I reckon Mrs Betts will be able to retire after this party,' she observed. 'Not that it's all coming from her place — a lot's been ordered from Harrods — but what I call the bread and butter stuff's coming from the shop.'

'I wouldn't half love to go to the party,' said Izzie wistfully.

'What, like Cinderella, you mean?' Mrs Lester smiled. 'I'll wave my wand over you if you like.'

Izzie giggled. 'No fear! Knowing you, you'd get it all wrong and I'd turn into a pumpkin on a white horse.'

'That's all the thanks I get, is it?'

'No offence meant.'

'None taken.' The housekeeper sighed. 'I wonder what they see in quails' eggs – and caviar. Looks terrible, that caviar, all black and funny, but they seem to like it. Salmon mousse, now that *is* nice. Sort of delicate. I haven't made it for years, but you'd like that. Potted shrimps? A bit over-rated, I always think . . . Ah, here she is at last.' She glanced up as Lorna appeared in the doorway. 'Good morning, Miss Betts. Condescended to honour us with your presence, have you, and only a quarter of an hour late?'

'Hullo, all,' said Lorna cheerfully, throwing off her shawl and reaching for her apron and cap. 'Guess who I just saw riding along looking all lovey-dovey?'

'Who?' cried Izzie, beaming at Lorna.

Mrs Lester gave her a withering glance. 'You know very well who, you silly girl – you saw them yourself not ten minutes ago.'

'Oh, them!' Izzie giggled. 'I saw them go off, from the landing. He came to *breakfast*.'

'Breakfast?' said Lorna. 'What's going on? While the cat's away . . . ?'

Izzie laughed. 'Oh Lorna, you are a one!'

But Mrs Lester was not to be diverted so easily. 'You've been late once too often, my girl,' she told Lorna, 'and it's got to stop. All you have to do is set out ten minutes earlier. Now, if it happens once more – just *once* more, mind you – I shall tell the mistress.'

Lorna grinned. 'She's not going to sack me now, is she, with the party coming up?'

'Maybe not, but she might well knock off an hour's money, so you needn't be too smart, miss.' She wagged a forefinger at Lorna to emphasise the seriousness of what she was saying. 'You've had your last chance, Lorna, so you make up your mind to it. No more turning up late and no more back-chat neither. Now, take the tealeaves and do the carpet in the library, the master's study and on the landing.'

'What about the stairs?'

'Leave them for today. There's a lot of shopping to be done for the party, so when you've done the carpets you can take the list round to your ma and then cycle back with some of it. You'll have to make several trips, most likely.'

Lorna brightened at the thought that she would not be confined to housework all day. It also occurred to her that if she was cycling backwards and forwards she might well bump into Don.

Izzie's face had fallen, however, for now she would be deprived of Lorna's company. She put a rasher of left-over cold bacon into her mouth and plunged the dish into the washing-up water. As Lorna passed her with a basin of tea-leaves in her hand, Izzie asked, 'Who was looking lovey-dovey? Him or her?'

'Her, of course!' said Lorna. 'No man in his right mind would fancy that old cow! She was wearing the new hat — the one with the veiling — and looking sideways at him with her eyes all big and girlish. Ugh! I thought that Mr Allan would've had more sense.'

'I would have thought so too,' Izzie agreed quickly, but before she could think of another question Lorna had gone and the kitchen was once more, for Izzie, a quiet and dreary place.

*

Esme laughed lightly as she put out a hand to catch the reins of Ralph's horse.

'Are you sure you're quite happy with Star, Mr Allan?' she said. 'She's being particularly mettlesome this morning, I'm afraid. Gerald doesn't exercise her regularly enough, and when she does get a run she becomes a little over-excited.'

Ralph managed a smile, although in fact he was finding the large roan mare somewhat daunting. As he had told Esme, it was many years since he had last ridden a horse, but she had laughingly assured him she would accept no excuses. They had ridden up the village street (Esme was determined that news of their ride should reach Gerald's ears) and having crossed the main road from Rolvenden to Wittersham, were now riding through the fields on the far side, skirting those with crops and crossing the grazing land any way they chose. The morning was perfect, cloudless but with a breeze. An early morning heat haze had almost dispersed, but still lent a magical quality to the landscape, wreathing in and out of the line of dark elms which were still in shadow and softening the outlines of the farmhouses and oasts which dotted the rolling countryside.

Somewhere a lark sang and the sound of a barking dog was all that disturbed the silence through which they rode.

Esme's mount was a small, high-spirited bay which she rode side-saddle and handled with ease. Despite his reluctance to accompany her on the ride, Ralph was forced to admit that she looked quite perfect in her pale green habit and veiled hat and that she was proving a very charming companion.

'You are doing very well, Mr Allan,' she told him, 'to stay on Star at all. I did have doubts about letting you ride her, but the only other mount we have is poor old Sergeant and he's so old, it would have proved a disappointing ride for you.' She released the rein and they rode along side by side in the shadow of a copse of trees.

'You'll find that it gets easier each time you come out. She'll get to know you and to know who's master.'

She looked straight into his eyes, daring him to say that he had not intended this ride to be the first of several, while Ralph – who had intended to say exactly that – let the words die in his throat. It was hard to refuse this elegant woman who was obviously trying to be kind.

'I'm sorry your husband didn't manage to be with us after all,' he said. 'He's missing some beautiful weather and even more beautiful scenery.'

'Mr Allan!' She gave him a provocative glance. 'I thought you were going to say "even more beautiful company"!'

'Oh – that as well, of course,' he stammered.

Esme leaned sideways and rested her hand fleetingly on his knee.

'Forgive me, I was only teasing you. A married woman gets into these habits. I didn't mean to embarrass you. Yes, it is a shame about Gerald. He was so disappointed, but something came up in London which needed his attention – a board meeting, to be exact – and he had to go. My poor husband "does something in the city", Mr Allan; that sounds much more impressive than it is. He's a consultant to a firm of accountants – a big firm, actually – and a member of the board of one or two other companies. I don't know much about it – I don't feel I have to know. It all sounds so terribly boring.' She raised her hands in a gesture of helplessness. 'Thank goodness I wasn't born a man, Mr Allan,' she went on. 'Being "something in the city" would quite destroy me, I know it would, but there . . . Poor Gerald is *so* generous. He simply lavishes money on me.' She gave Ralph a wry little smile. 'He thinks that's all a woman needs: clothes, jewels, furs. But it's not, of course. I'm afraid we are not the shallow creatures men consider us to be.'

'No, I'm sure you're not,' said Ralph lamely. His companion seemed to be expecting further comment from him, so he added, 'I'm sure you're not at all shallow, Mrs Hatherley.'

The moment he had uttered her name, he knew what would follow. Esme gave another of her soft tinkling laughs and reined in her horse.

'*Mr* Allan and *Mrs* Hatherley!' she cried. 'It really is too absurd, don't you think, for us to go on being so formal with each other? Wouldn't it be much friendlier if you were to call me Esme? I've been told many times that it's a pretty name.'

'It is indeed,' he assured her. She was looking at him with her head tilted to one side and her lips slightly parted. He wished that Star would fidget, so that he need not look at her, but perversely now the horse was docile. 'You must call me Ralph then,' he told her, forcing a smile, then added with an attempt at levity, 'Nobody has told me it's a pretty name, but it's all I have!'

Esme did not laugh but continued to watch him almost quizzically, he thought, and was annoyed to realise how uneasy she made him. Why couldn't he relax and enjoy the ride?

'It's agreed, then,' she said at last, holding out a slim hand in an expensive green kid glove. 'Ralph and Esme.'

They shook hands on it – as though they were celebrating an important event, he thought anxiously, but then chided himself, deciding he was behaving foolishly. The woman was hardly an ogre and he had nothing to fear from her. He was behaving like a silly schoolboy.

'Ralph and Esme,' he repeated and impulsively raised the

slim hand to brush it with his lips. He was not to know that no man had ever failed to do just that when offered Esme's hand, nor that Esme had intended it to happen. She drew back her hand with a gesture of surprise and a hint of alarm in her voice.

'Ralph!'

Taken aback by her reaction, he immediately stammered out an apology, but then she was laughing at him in the nicest way and her horse seemed to move in close until her legs beneath the long green skirt brushed against his as though by accident.

'There I go again,' she protested, 'teasing you. It's too bad – you must forgive me. And there's no need to apologise. A kiss is never an affront, Ralph, or didn't you know that?'

He searched for something to say to remove the tension which had sprung up between them, cursing his stupidity. Kissing her hand! Was he mad? But he *had* done so and could not now insult her by a surly answer to her question. Or perhaps it wasn't a question; perhaps it was a statement. 'A kiss is never an affront.' Oh God! Alarm bells began to ring and his earlier panic returned, but as though sensing this Esme turned her horse away and called back over her shoulder, 'Come on, Ralph. I want to show you the view from the top of the hill.'

He urged Star along the sloping edge of the field, taking care not to trample the barley. When he rejoined her, they looked down over the Weald, over hop-fields, ripening corn and green fields dotted with cows and sheep. Further on were the low softly curving hills and beyond them the blue distance. In spite of himself, Ralph's senses reeled at the timeless beauty of the land laid out before them.

'Ralph,' Esme's voice was low. 'Shall we walk a little? We can tether the horses; they'll be quite safe.'

He turned his head slowly, his reluctance to meet her gaze transparently obvious.

'I won't eat you, I promise,' she said. 'Don't you trust me?'

For a long moment his intense grey eyes were held by hers as Ralph struggled with his instincts. In her own way, this beautiful woman was both dangerous and desirable.

114

Common sense told him that if they walked together they would sit together. She was hungry for love – or she had hinted that she was: 'A woman needs more than clothes, jewels and furs.' And again: 'A kiss is never an affront.'

He swallowed, guessing that she would recognise the tell-tale signs which signalled his nervousness. The seconds ticked by and still she waited – so terribly sure of his answer, he thought. More than anything he longed to be back in the study in The Lodge, alone with his typewriter, his books and his papers – back at The Lodge, where he was safe. But he had only himself to blame for accepting her 'invitation to ride'. The phrase leaped from the depths of his subconscious and startled him. Had he known all along where his accept-ance would lead? Oh God, had he allowed this to happen? Had he led her to believe . . . did he really want this beautiful, eager . . .

'Ralph?' she said softly. 'You've gone off into a daydream. I said shall we walk a little, to give the horses a chance to graze? They're such greedy beasts and they love to snatch leaves from the hedges when they think they shouldn't – you know what they say about forbidden fruits!'

Her voice was so flat now and so natural, her eyes so devoid of seduction that he felt immediately foolish. Mumbling in the affirmative, he slid from his horse, slipped the reins over a convenient fence-post and reached up to help his companion down. But Esme's body was so light, her waist so small between his hands, the subtle perfume of her body so overwhelming, that he cried out in a kind of anguish. Somehow, before he knew what he was doing, his instincts triumphed over common sense and he was pulling her into his arms, whispering her name as he kissed her lips.

But that one kiss was all she allowed him. A frantic, soul-destroying kiss, but enough to form an unspoken bond. Enough to send him back for more another time. Esme, coldly calculating, drew back before it was too late – for both of them.

He began to speak, his voice hoarse, but she laid a gloved finger against his lips to silence him, knowing that if she let him speak he would undo all that she had achieved, whereas if she allowed herself utterance she would shout with

115

triumph. Instead she straightened her hat and tidied her hair, avoiding his eyes, while Ralph stood wordlessly beside her holding the reins of the two horses and struggling to master his emotions.

When she knew that he was once more in control, she smiled in a way which said, 'That shouldn't have happened, but we were both helpless to prevent it. We will not speak of it again. That is the correct thing for us to do.'

He read her accurately and was at once sorry but relieved. He was angry with himself for going so far and absurdly grateful to Esme because she had averted anything worse.

'Ah! There's Mr Leckie,' she said gaily as Jim, accompanied by one of his collies, rounded the corner of the field and waved to them in greeting. 'This is his land,' she explained, 'but of course he allows us to ride through it – hunt through it, too, on occasions.' Calmly, she began to lead her horse back the way they had come and, as she had predicted, the animals paused from time to time to snatch mouthfuls of food.

Making a desperate effort to match Esme's self-control and just for something to say, Ralph remarked, 'I think Star is becoming reconciled to me now.'

Esme turned, her smile deceptively innocent. 'It's just a matter of time,' she told him. 'Everything is just a matter of time.'

Chapter Seven

The next day was Friday. The stationmaster was buttering a slice of toast, but his attention was elsewhere – on the familiar yet unexpected noise he could hear coming from the direction of the station platform. At last he could stand it no longer and got heavily to his feet and crossed to the window. It was already partly open, for the early August sun was hot and shone directly into their kitchen. When he pushed up the window and leaned out, the source of the noise was immediately obvious. Arnold, a broad grin on his face, was standing on the parcels trolley – feet wide apart, legs braced, throwing his heavy body from side to side and making the trolley move. It rolled a few inches to one side and then to the other. Rattle, rattle!

'Arnold!' thundered the stationmaster. 'Stop that at once, do you hear me? Get off that trolley!'

For a moment Arnold froze in pure terror, staring in his direction, then with a long strangled cry he leaped wildly from the trolley and lumbered away down the platform towards the level crossing, glancing back over his shoulder with panic written large on his face, stumbling blindly into anything that lay in his path.

Meanwhile the trolley, given fresh momentum by his jump, careered sideways into a stack of baskets which contained the racing pigeons from a club in Northampton. The trolley stopped, but at the expense of the baskets which tumbled over. One fell on to its side, another was completely upturned; only the third remained upright.

Thomas Turner withdrew his head, his face red and

furious. 'I'll wring that blighter's neck!' he shouted. 'What the hell does he think he's doing? God in heaven!'

'Oh dear, Papa—' Amy began, but he rushed out of the room without even bothering to pull on his jacket, which in itself was a very bad sign.

Sam was now staring excitedly out of the window. 'All the pigeons are tipped over and they're making a terrible noise!' he told his sister gleefully. 'Squawking and fluttering.' He glanced at the clock. 'And that Mr Larkin will be here in seven minutes to let them out!'

'But what happened?'

'Dunno,' said Sam, 'but it looks as though the trolley has run into the pigeon baskets — and Arnold is climbing over the crossing-gate. Mr Hart's yelling at him and so is Papa. I'm going out there.'

'You are *not*,' Amy told him. 'You are going to finish your breakfast.'

'Oh Amy! Just for a minute.'

'No, Sam! Papa will be even angrier if you go out there; you should know that.'

'But Amy, it would only be for a minute.'

It was hard to resist him, but in his own interests she hardened her heart. 'I've said "No", Sam, and I mean it,' she told him with an unconscious echo of her mother. 'So sit back at the table and finish your egg.'

There was a tell-tale creaking of bed-springs from the room above and Amy groaned. 'Now they've woken Grandfather,' she grumbled. 'Bother Arnold and his silly tricks!'

Sam re-seated himself at the table with much noisy scraping of chair-legs on linoleum, but Amy ignored it.

'Won't Papa let Arnold come to the station again?' asked Sam. 'Poor Arnold!'

'I don't know,' said Amy. 'He might when he's cooled down a bit. Anyway, if he doesn't it's Arnold's own silly fault. Whatever got into him, I wonder? He's usually no trouble.'

She put her own head out of the window and reported, 'Papa's put the pigeons back the right way up. Thank goodness Mr Larkin didn't see. He would have been very cross and he might even have put in a report. There's no sign of

Arnold — Papa must have scared the life out of him; you know how timid he is.'

'He's run away, I expect,' said Sam, revelling in the possibility of a drama.

'Oh, don't be so daft! Where would he run to?'

'Gone to join the Foreign Legion!'

Amy laughed. 'I don't think they'd have him. Poor Arnold! Oh well, there's nothing I can do about it. It's Friday and there's Grandfather to see to and then my stall to do. You'll be late for school if you don't go soon, Sam — and wipe the flannel over your face before you go. You've got marmalade all round your mouth — no, not with the back of your hand, Sam! I said the flannel! Here you are.'

She tossed it to him and he licked the marmalade from the back of his hand and dabbed the flannel over his chin.

'Better?' he demanded.

'It'll do, I suppose.' She put a packet of sandwiches into his hands and tried to kiss him, but he wriggled away.

'I'll soon be eleven,' he protested. 'I hate kisses. What's for tea?'

'Cold boiled bacon and fried-up potatoes. Now hurry, Sam, or you'll go in the late book and Papa will blame me.'

He hoisted his school-bag over his shoulder and sauntered out as slowly as he dared. Watching him go, Amy felt the familiar rush of affection and whispered, 'How could you leave him, Ellen Turner? He's growing up and you're missing it all.'

Since her walk with Ralph Allan she had begun to speak occasionally to her absent mother — just a few words here and there, but always by name, never addressing her as 'Mama'. It pleased Amy that she could talk in this way without any bitterness. Once or twice she also allowed herself to consider her mother's present circumstances, to wonder about the new baby and to think about her uncle without hating him. For all this she was sincerely grateful to Ralph, although she had not seen him since that day and so had been unable to put her thanks into words.

The bell jangled from upstairs as she began to clear the table and she called up, 'Coming, Grandfather! I'll only be

119

a moment or two.' Then, putting all thoughts of her mother firmly out of her head, she began the day's work in earnest.

*

Amy was putting the final touches to her stall when Harry Coombes arrived. He greeted her and then looked round the station in surprise.

'No Arnold?' he asked. 'Ill, is he?'

She explained what had happened and, chuckling, the porter went off to have a quick look at his garden before the train arrived. Harry liked to stand on the very edge of the platform to obtain a passenger's eye view of his flower bed and sometimes, when the train was stationary, he would climb briefly into one of the carriages (on the pretext of looking for something or someone) so that he could then look down on the garden from inside.

Amy's stall was nearly ready. She had covered the card-table with a large white cloth which she pinned into place so that on windy days it did not flap about. The table was an old one and not particularly stable, and she did not want it to overturn. On it she had now arranged a jug of marigolds – pale orange, with dark brown centres – a plate containing six rabbit pasties, a jar of her own marmalade, a small basket of dessert gooseberries and a large sultana cake.

It was not always Gazedown people who bought from her stall. A plump woman often alighted from the train and bought a cake, and twice an elderly man had bought the flowers saying that he was visiting his sister who had no garden. A box stood beside the table containing half-a-dozen second-hand books and a small framed picture of a man with a gun gazing out across a moor. Tim Hollis had found these when he and his mother cleaned out the box-room and he had given them to her for the stall; although Amy did not feel at all hopeful about selling them, she had not liked to refuse.

She looked up as her father approached across the track. 'Tim not here yet?' he asked.

Amy shook her head, saying, 'Any minute now, I should think. I expect he's cycling a bit slower today because Clara is coming with him.'

120

'Clara? Is that the girl who was sick on the platform?' His disapproval was evident.

She nodded. 'Yes. She hasn't been able to find a job yet, but she's going to do some temporary work at the Manor. Mrs Hatherley has taken on extra help to get it ready for the ball.'

Amy insisted on calling the forthcoming celebration a 'ball'. To her, a 'party' was for a small group of friends – a hundred guests could only be attending an occasion as lavish as a 'ball'!

A loud tinkling of bicycle bells announced the arrival of Tim and Clara, who appeared breathlessly on the platform on foot a few moments later.

'Where's Arnold?' was Tim's first question and this time it was her father who explained, albeit tersely, the reason for his absence. Tim grimaced, but the stationmaster went straight on before he could comment.

'I want to check last week's freight receipts,' he told Tim. 'It won't tally and I can't see why.'

'Won't tally, sir?'

'No. So if you'd like to come, we've a few spare moments.'

'But I was just going to tell Clara the way to Bates Manor—' Tim began, but already the stationmaster was striding away in the direction of the office with his hands clasped behind his back.

'I'll explain it to Clara,' Amy offered and Tim, after a hasty 'Bye, then,' reluctantly followed Mr Turner along the platform.

After a few general enquiries as to how Clara was settling down with the Hollises, Amy gave the girl clear directions for the Manor.

'And if you see a rather large, scared-looking man,' she added, 'wearing a cardboard badge that says "Station Helper", that will be Arnold. Tell him I said not to be scared, to stay away from the station today but to come to the house tomorrow at 10 o'clock for a reading lesson. That might make him feel a bit better. Whatever actually happened, I'm sure he didn't mean any harm.'

Clara repeated it all and then rode off towards her temporary employment with a cheerful wave. Her money was almost exhausted and she welcomed the chance to earn a few extra shillings. She was also looking forward to seeing the inside of a large house for the first time in her life and, although she had said nothing to anyone else, she secretly harboured the hope that if she showed willing she might be considered for a permanent position. She thought she had been exceptionally fortunate so far, to have found such comfortable lodgings, and she got along reasonably well with Tim's mother. Mrs Hollis, widowed some years earlier, seemed to enjoy having a 'daughter' around the place and since they both made a great fuss of Tim he too considered the experiment a success. However, Clara would have to get permanent work or everything would be spoilt. She could not stay on in her cosy room if she was unable to pay her rent; it would not be fair to accept the Hollis family's hospitality without proper payment. Therefore she approached the job at the Manor with high hopes and kept her fingers firmly crossed as she mounted the steps to the front door and reached up to ring the bell.

*

To Arnold, huddled against the broad trunk of a fallen tree, the minutes became hours and the wood was full of noises. He turned his head repeatedly, looking fearfully in all directions, expecting the stationmaster to appear at any moment and drag him from his hiding-place. What would happen after that was too awful for him to even contemplate, and he struggled to keep his thoughts elsewhere. The fingers of his right hand returned again and again to his badge and he knew that if the stationmaster took it away from him he would die of misery. He had thought of going home to hide under his bed, but that would involve his mother and then she too would get angry and shout at him and that would make him tremble even more. He was still trembling from being shouted at by the stationmaster and Arnold did not like the way the trembling made his teeth knock together. His heart was behaving strangely, too, thumping inside his chest and going faster than usual.

A twig snapped nearby and he bent his head to his knees to make himself smaller.

'Go away,' he whispered.

Looking up cautiously, he saw a squirrel clinging to the side of an oak. For a moment he forgot his terrible predicament and jumped to his feet, a smile lighting up his round moon-like face as an 'Ah!' of pleasure escaped his lips. If only he was a squirrel! Then he would climb high into the trees and the stationmaster would never find him – but then he would not know about 'gee' and 'double-you' and 'when the big hand is on twelve' and he was very proud of knowing that. He watched the squirrel as it darted higher and then leaped effortlessly to the next tree and disappeared from his sight.

'Gone away,' he said listlessly, sinking down into his hiding-place once more. As he did so, the sad and awful thoughts returned. He would never see Tim again, or Harry, or Mr Hart (Mr Hart had shouted at him too) or Amy . . . and he would never see Sandy the cat, or pump water, or hold the shunting horse while Tim raked out the stable. He shook his head slowly as the enormity of the catastrophe dawned on him and two large and tragic tears fell from his eyes. One fell on the back of his left hand and one onto his trousers. He blinked his eyes as hard as he could and forced out a few more tears, considering them carefully for a moment before losing interest in them.

If he didn't go home, he would have no dinner; it was stew or else it was fish, and if was fish then it would be a herring and Arnold loved herrings. He loved stew, too, and sausages and dumplings and 'Spotted Dick' and gravy and Yorkshire pudding and everything. Arnold loved food and was always hungry. The thought of having no dinner made his mouth droop and he put a hand to his stomach protectively.

'Waiting Room starts with a double-you,' he whispered sadly and wondered where the stationmaster was. He imagined that the entire staff of the station had been mobilised to track him down and haul him back for his punishment.

Suddenly, as if a bright light had been switched on inside his head, the idea came to him and it was so tremendous that he gasped aloud. If he *hid* his badge, they could not

123

take it away from him! It was so beautifully simple that he was stunned with surprise at his own cleverness and grinned broadly as he fumbled with the pin of the badge and unfastened it. But where to hide it? Looking round him for a convenient spot, he remembered the squirrel. Squirrels hid their nuts in the ground. Dogs buried their bones in the ground. So he would hide his badge in the ground! Quickly he went down on all fours, scrabbling through the layer of dead leaves to the soft earth beneath, enjoying the moist feel of it and the way it crumbled under his plunging fingers. Pausing briefly to examine his hands, he was pleased to see the line of dark soil under each fingernail. Now he began to enjoy himself, digging deeper and deeper, scattering the earth back over himself, pretending to be a dog. He tried making a 'woofing' noise; it sounded very realistic and he wished he had a tail to wag – a dog wagging its tail always looked so *happy*.

Arnold began to feel happy too as he dug on, 'woofing' quietly to himself. He forgot about the trolley and the pigeon baskets and the stationmaster's terrible shout. He even forgot why he was in the wood. He dug until the hole was nearly two feet deep and then he wrapped his badge tenderly in his handkerchief and laid it in the bottom. It was almost as much fun filling in the hole again. When that was done, he stamped round on it and, feeling particularly clever, scattered some leaves over the top to hide it from prying eyes. Then he realised how hungry he was, so he brushed the earth from his trousers and went home to have his dinner.

*

Late the following evening when Amy knocked at the door of The Lodge, she was puzzled that no one answered. She had already called round twice earlier in the day with the same result, but then she had assumed that Ralph was out. Now, however, she could see the light in the bedroom window although the curtains were closed. She knocked a second time, more loudly than before, and when that produced no response it occurred to her that maybe Ralph had gone out and left the light on to deter burglars. Or had left it on accidentally? Or was ill? She lifted the flap of the letter box, but it opened into a box and not directly on to the hall so she could see nothing. If he *was* ill, she reasoned, he might have been lying in bed all day or maybe for several days. The more she thought about it, the more likely it seemed, so she walked round to the bedroom window again and to her surprise found that the light had now been switched off. So he was in there . . . or somebody was. And he could hardly be sleeping or he could not have switched off the light. Amy hesitated, reluctant to intrude on Ralph's privacy if he did not want to see her but still uneasy about him. She decided to take a chance – if he didn't want to see her, he had only to say so and she would go away. She tapped on the bedroom window and called, 'Ralph? Are you there?'

Silence . . . followed by a crash. Amy ran round to the front door and found it locked, then ran back to the rear door which was also locked. In desperation she clambered in through the kitchen window. She made her way to the bedroom not knowing what to expect, but certainly not anticipating what she did find. Ralph Allan was packing! A small travelling bag stood ready packed beside the chest of drawers, a tea-chest full of books and papers had obviously just toppled from the bed and the contents were scattered on the floor. Ralph himself was staring at her white-faced with an expression of – what was it, she wondered. Guilt? Relief?

'Ralph!' she cried. 'I was afraid – that is, nobody answered when I knocked and I thought you were ill. Ralph, why are you packing?'

'I'm leaving,' he said tersely. 'I don't seem to . . . I can't get on with my work. Too many distractions.'

Amy coloured, assuming he referred to her. 'Oh Ralph, I'm sorry,' she stammered. 'I really didn't mean to be a distraction. Don't go. I'll stay away. I—'

'Not *you*,' he said and bending down, righted the tea-chest and began to hurl the books and papers back into it. Bewildered, Amy watched him.

'I heard the crash,' she went on. 'I thought it was you – that you were ill and had fallen out of bed or something. Ralph, whatever is the matter? You look dreadful. Are you ill? I could fetch the doctor.'

'I didn't sleep last night, I couldn't.' He did not meet her eyes. 'I'm all right.'

'When are you going?' she asked. 'Today? Weren't you going to tell me? Ralph! Please leave those wretched books alone and talk to me properly. I thought we were friends and now suddenly you're packing and you don't even answer the door to me.' Now that she could see that her anxiety was unfounded, she discovered that she was annoyed and for a moment they faced each other: Amy indignant, Ralph defensive.

'I'm sorry,' he said at last. 'I didn't answer the door because I thought you were someone else.'

Amy's eyes widened. 'Who did you think I was? Old Nick?'

'Someone's been . . .' He made a helpless gesture with his hands. 'Someone else kept knocking.'

'Today, you mean? Ralph, that was me too,' she cried, exasperated. 'This is the third time I've been round. What on earth is the matter with you?'

He sat down suddenly on the bedside chair and drew a deep breath.

'I'm really sorry, Amy. Perhaps I was a bit too cautious. It didn't occur to me that it was you and I'm sorry if you were worried. I don't want to talk about it, but I've just *got* to leave here. I can't stay in Gazedown; it's impossible.'

As Amy looked at him, sympathy replaced her earlier emotions. He looked so very defenceless. No, 'defeated' was a better word. She moved across to kneel beside him and looked up into his face.

'Look, Ralph,' she said, 'I can see something's wrong and I can see you're upset. I'd like to help you if there's anything I can do, but if you won't tell me . . .' She broke off, giving a little shrug.

'Oh Amy, I *can't!*' he said with a desperation that startled her. 'I'd like to, but it's so . . . so horrible. I've been such a fool!' He leaped to his feet and began to gather up the books and papers that remained on the floor.

Amy stood up and gently took a folder from his hands.

'Ralph Allan,' she said quietly, 'I don't know you very well, but I like you a lot and I don't care what you've done.

126

You helped me feel so much better about my mother. So I came round to thank you, and now you say you're leaving. Do you expect me to just let you go without even putting up a fight? Whatever has happened will not make the slightest difference to how I feel about you. You are—'

'It will, Amy,' he broke in. 'That's just it. It *will!* I wanted to go with you thinking well of me. I was going to send you a note.'

'I don't want a note!' cried Amy. 'For heaven's sake, Ralph, just *tell* me. I shan't leave this room until you do.'

After a long and tortured silence, Ralph haltingly began to tell her what had happened between himself and Esme Hatherley and Amy listened in shocked silence until he had finished.

'The bitch!' she exclaimed at last. 'I've never used that word in my life before, but there's no other word for it. She's a calculating *bitch!*'

'Maybe, but I should have anticipated what would happen,' he said miserably. 'I did up to a point, but I just couldn't stop myself.'

Amy sat down on the bed looking thoughtful. 'I can see why you're upset,' she said, 'but it isn't all that terrible, is it? I mean, it could have been a lot worse.'

'It nearly *was!*' he cried. 'That's what worries me.'

Suddenly Amy laughed. 'Oh Ralph, you just have to see the funny side of it and then it won't seem nearly so dreadful. You'll have to laugh about it, you really will!'

'It's not a laughing matter from my viewpoint,' he told her. 'How can I face her again? The woman terrifies me! I've been in such a panic all day, thinking it was her knocking. I know it sounds ridiculous, but I don't know how to cope with women like that. She is exactly what you said – calculating. Every word, every look . . .'

'She's horrible,' agreed Amy, 'really horrible, but if you leave Gazedown you're letting her win.'

'Win?' cried Ralph. 'She's already won, hasn't she? I'd call it a major victory!'

Amy laughed again and this time, after a hesitant start, Ralph joined in and soon they were both chuckling.

'If she came in now . . .' gasped Amy, 'she'd wonder what was so funny!'

However, the thought of such an untimely arrival sobered Ralph abruptly and he cast a nervous look in the direction of the door.

'Go and bolt it,' said Amy, wiping her streaming eyes. 'Then we'll know we're safe.'

'Do you mean that?' he asked, but she shook her head.

'But you see,' she said triumphantly, 'it *did* have its funny side. Now does it all look quite so terrible?'

'I don't know,' he replied. 'Maybe not quite so terrible, but pretty frightful just the same.'

'Terrible enough to run away from?'

'It's easy for you . . .'

'I know.' Abandoning her bantering tone, she said, 'Please don't go,' and the phrase rang in her ears the way it had done four years ago when her mother had told them she wanted to leave. 'No,' she amended quickly, 'I've no right to ask you to stay – none at all. Forget I asked you, I'm just being selfish.'

The silence lengthened between them and then Ralph said, 'What a strange thing to say. You're not being selfish.'

'I'm selfish,' she repeated stubbornly. 'I was coming here today to thank you for Sunday – for helping me – but also to offer my services with the book. I was going to ask if I could be your unpaid assistant. I suddenly thought it would be such fun; you said you were finding it difficult to get started and I thought surely there would be some way I could help you. That's why I'm selfish.'

'Good heavens!' exclaimed Ralph. 'What a good idea.'

'Not if you're about to leave Gazedown!'

'No, that's true.' He stared at her.

'Never mind,' said Amy. 'It was just an idea. I was going to suggest an hour a day, maybe. I had it all worked out.' She gazed fixedly at a frayed patch in the carpet.

'I couldn't possibly let you work for nothing,' he protested.

'I told you, I'd enjoy it.'

Ralph said thoughtfully, 'I think it would be fun too. Since we are agreed on that, I accept your offer of help. Now all

I have to do is find a way of keeping Esme at arm's length. That's going to be the problem.'

Amy's head lifted. 'Do you mean you'll stay?'

'You'll have to help me – I shall need moral support.'

'I'll do anything I can,' she assured him earnestly.

'Let's have a cup of tea,' he suggested. 'My grandmother used to say that if only the governments of the world would get together over a cup of tea . . . !'

Over the tea they decided with much hilarity on a plan of action and then wrote it all down on a sheet of paper.

'That's it, then,' said Ralph, nearly an hour later. 'I shall read out the final draft. Ahem, ahem! Unaccustomed as I am to public speaking . . .'

She laughed. 'Get on with it!'

'Right. Number one – tell E. that I've had a letter from my publisher, who has given me a specific publication date for the book, so now I have to work round the clock and therefore have no time *whatsoever* for horse-riding.'

'And all that entails!' Amy giggled.

'Number two – practise looking regretful. Practise saying: "I'm awfully sorry, I'd love to go riding, but I can't possibly " etc. etc. Number three – tell her I've asked Miss Amy Turner to do some secretarial work for me, because I'm so desperately short of time.'

'Which means I'll be here.'

'Right again. Number four – if she ever refers to that stupid kiss—'

'Which she won't, but go on.'

'I look surprised that she even remembers, laugh lightly and say, "That was very foolish of me. I'm sure you've forgiven me by now. It won't happen again." ' He grinned. 'That really is very clever of you, Miss Turner.'

'Don't mention it, Mr Allan.'

She watched him with shining eyes. He looked so much happier than when she had found him packing and now he was going to stay in Gazedown and she was going to be his secretary! *And* Esme Hatherley was going to be put firmly in her place.

'Number five,' Ralph continued, 'the book will be a resounding success and I shall become a millionaire.'

129

'And then you can send the terrible Esme a signed copy,' said Amy, 'to remind her of the one that got away!'

'Miss Turner! You have a wicked tongue!'

They both laughed and very reluctantly Amy stood up. 'I'll have to go,' she said. 'Even secretaries have homes to go to.'

He saw her to the door. 'And you'll come tomorrow about 2 o'clock?'

'On the dot. I shall look forward to it,' she told him.

By the time she had reached the station, Amy was aware that for the first time for years she was ridiculously happy. It was a good feeling.

*

Sam dreamed that he was running through a strange house, flinging open the many doors but finding the rooms bare. He did not know what he was looking for in the large empty house, but he knew he had not found it. He heard his footsteps ringing and echoing on the bare wooden floor as he went faster and faster, in and out. Right through the house he ran and then out of the door into a crowd of people. He began to search amongst them, peering up into their faces but each face was the same. All the people had his grandfather's face and he was shaking his head at each one because he was not looking for Grandfather. He pushed his way out of the crowd and found himself alone in a wide sweeping meadow where there was just one other person. It was a woman and she raised her arm and beckoned to him. Sam began to run towards her and saw that it was his mother, smiling and beckoning to him to join her at the far end of the meadow. The sun was very bright and his mother seemed to be radiating the light. Sam ran as fast as he could, but the nearer he drew to his mother the wearier his legs became, until they were like lead and he could hardly lift one foot in front of the other. His mother waited patiently, but he could not quite reach her . . . and then the dream faded. On waking, Sam could recall every detail of the dream, but he gave it no thought because he had dreamed it all before, many times.

He opened his eyes to find the early morning sun making

130

lace patterns on the ceiling. In the other bed, his grandfather was already awake and smiling at him.

'What time is it?' asked Sam. He knew it must be Saturday or Sunday because it was on those two days that his grandfather woke first. On the other five days, Amy crept into the bedroom without waking the old man to shake Sam out of his sleep and tell him to get up for school.

'It's 8.09 and you were snoring,' Ted told his grandson.

'I was *not*, Grandfather,' Sam protested.

'You were, so. Snoring like a blooming saw-mill. You woke me up, you were snoring so loud. Hee-haw, like a donkey.'

'I was not,' said Sam.

'How do you know, if you were asleep?'

'I just know.'

Sam sat up and stared at the familiar but frail figure of his grandfather and the persistent fear surfaced again.

'Are you going to die, Grandfather?' he asked.

'Some day I'll have to,' said Ted. 'It was the shock, you see. Of your grandmother dying, that is. It knocks all the stuffing out of you, shock does. Like a punch in the belly, shock is.'

'But you won't die yet, will you?'

'Not just yet,' said Ted. 'Leastways, I hope not.'

Sam frowned. 'Why *do* you stay in bed, then, Grandfather? Papa says you're idle, but it's not true, is it? You've got bad legs, haven't you?'

'I have and I haven't, Sam,' said the old man, choosing to ignore the suggestion that he was idle. 'They're not so much bad, as wobbly. They're all right if I lie here resting them, but if I was to try and walk on them, well! It'd be wobble, wobble like a blooming jelly and then down I'd go.'

'What, dead?' cried Sam anxiously.

'No, no,' said Ted. 'I'd just fall down and most likely hurt myself — bang my head or something. You know.'

The boy regarded him earnestly. 'Eric says the old doctor's retired and the new doctor's young and he's called Doctor Brown — and when he went to see Eric's Aunt Agatha he stopped her medicine that she's been having for years and

131

years and said she's got nothing wrong with her heart —
Eric's Aunt Agatha says she's going to report him.'

'Report the doctor? Who to?'

'I dunno. Eric doesn't know either.'

Ted looked at him uneasily. 'Funny sort of doctor,' he
said. Sam shrugged and there was a short silence.

'It's Saturday,' said Ted. 'What are you doing with yourself
today?'

'Dunno'

'Got time for a story?'

Sam grinned. A story meant a stick of barley sugar.

He nodded. The Saturday-morning ritual had been going
on ever since the old man moved into Sam's bedroom and
vaguely Sam acknowledged that the day would come when
he would be too old for it. It might be that he was already
too old for it, but he pretended to himself that he went along
with the little game because not to do so would disappoint
his grandfather. He remembered his noisy, bossy grandmother with affection and he had missed her when she died.
He knew, therefore, that however exasperating his grandfather might be at times, he would die one day and then Sam
would miss him too.

Now Ted was grinning at him. 'It might be in the jug,' he
hinted.

Obediently Sam slid out of bed and pattered over to the
tall rose-patterened jug that stood on the marble-topped
wash-stand. He reached up, found the jug empty and shook
his head.

'No,' he said.

'Oh dear,' said Ted. 'Don't tell me I've forgotten. Now let
me think . . . Where did I put that blooming barley sugar?'
He scratched his head. 'Perhaps it's behind the picture of
your grandmother?'

The picture stood on the chest of drawers and behind it
Sam found the twisted barley-sugar stick, pale amber, with
a thin green peppermint line running through it.

'Thank you, Grandfather.'

He recrossed the room to the old man's bed and allowed
himself to be hugged, giving his grandfather's withered cheek
a hasty kiss in return, thankful that none of his school friends

132

could see this unmanly behaviour. Then he settled himself on the end of Ted's bed, his legs tucked under the patchwork coverlet.

'Let's see,' said Ted. 'There's funny stories, sad stories . . . what shall it be, I wonder . . .'

Sam waited, sucking the brittle sugar carefully so as not to break it. Sucked gently, it would last a long time. He wondered if he and Eric might go fishing later in the day.

'What about an accident?' asked Ted. 'It's a sad thing, but railways and accidents seem to go together. Disasters, they call them in newspapers.'

Or, thought Sam, they might persuade Tim to let them ride the shunting horse. Just one ride each. Or they could go round to the smithy and see the new puppies.

'The Tay Bridge disaster,' repeated Ted. 'That was a dreadful do, that was. A disaster and a half, you could call that. Are you listening, Sam?'

'Yes, Grandfather.' Sam had heard the story so many times he could have recited it word for word – in fact he had done so to Eric. Sam had heard all the stories countless times, but their familiarity was strangely reassuring as though there never could be a time when Grandfather would *not* be telling him one or other of the tales. 'I could write a book,' the old man maintained, 'the things I've heard about the railways.' Sam did not doubt it.

'There's always been accidents,' said Ted, settling into his tale. 'They'll never stop them. If it's not one thing, it's another. There's so many things can go wrong, see? Faults on the track, signal failure, driver's error – not to mention storm and tempest.'

'Storm and tempest. What's that?' Sam asked obligingly.

'The weather, lad, the weather. A storm can blow down a bridge – like it did in '79. Oh, that was a comely-looking bridge, the Tay. Lattice girders on cast-iron columns. Elegant, that's what they called it in the newspapers, and the largest bridge in the world. Bouch, his name was, the fellow who designed it. Timothy Bouch – or was it Thomas? Thomas Bouch, that was it. *Sir* Thomas Bouch, I should say; he was knighted for that blessed bridge and the Queen herself rode over it. Not that it did him much good after the bridge collapsed. Ruined him, poor man. Still, at least he was still alive. Plenty of folks weren't.' He tutted. 'That was some storm – well, they called it a gale in the newspapers. A full gale and pitch-dark. Seventy-five passengers and the train's crew! All lost.' He shook his head lugubriously. 'Everyone on the train died. Or rather "perished" – that's the word they used. A huge section of the bridge was blown into the water and the train fell with it.' He shook his head again and Sam did the same, sucking noisily on his barley sugar. He knew what was coming and he was not disappointed.

Ted brightened slightly. 'But that locomotive lived to tell the tale. A 4–4–0 express, it was, and she lay in the river for three months before they could salvage her. Mind you, she shouldn't have been on that run, but the regular engine had broken down. Later on they put her back to rights and she went back into service, sweet as a whistle. But of course, no one would work her over the Tay – susperstitious, you see.'

Sam removed his barley sugar to check how much of it remained and asked, 'Is she still in service?' knowing full well that she was.

'Of course she is, bless her!' cried Ted. 'She works the expresses on the East Coast.' He shrugged. 'Maybe one day someone'll find the guts to take her over that blooming bridge again. I'd like to see that, I really would.'

Sam gave the story a few moments' consideration. 'You can't blame the loco,' he said. 'It was the bridge's fault.'

''Course it was – and the storm, of course. An extra fierce gust of wind at just the wrong moment! Terrible. It never should have happened, but there you are, it did. Fate, some folks would call it.'

'I'd hate to be drowned,' said Sam. 'I'd never join the Navy. I'd hate to fall over a cliff, too – you'd be thinking about it all the way down. And poison! Aaargh!' He clutched at his stomach and rolled his eyes wildly, but at that moment they heard footsteps on the stairs and as Amy arrived with Snip at her heels and a jug of hot water for the morning ablutions, Saturday began in earnest.

Chapter Eight

Lorna sat on the usual gate at the usual time and waited for Don to put in an appearance. Finding time to meet was not easy. She had her work at Bates Manor and the deliveries she did for her mother. Don had cows to milk and dozens of other jobs to attend to and although his working hours were more flexible than hers, they were also liable to change at a moment's notice whenever there was an emergency such as a calf arriving early or a fox raiding the henhouse. The actual hours they spent together did not amount to many, so the occasions when they were together were more precious than they might otherwise have been.

When they did meet, Don's time was devoted to trying to persuade Lorna to sample some of the more intimate delights of courtship which one or two other girls in Gazedown had already shared with him. Lorna's time was spent trying to wring from him a declaration of intent – did he truly love her and would he marry her? Don let it be understood that when she had given herself to him, he would then seriously consider making the relationship permanent. Lorna, however – aware that his previous conquests had not led to any such permanency – stood out for a proposal before giving in to his other demands. Neither of these points of view were ever openly expressed, but they each knew exactly what the other had in mind and very little progress was being made.

With her sister's example before her, Lorna dug in her heels more deeply as time went on while Don – having invested so much time in Lorna – was reluctant to admit defeat and turn his attention elsewhere. There was nothing new in the situation, it was the age-old dilemma, but some-time, somehow, they both knew it would have to be resolved and as Lorna waited on the gate, she came to a decision. Don Leckie must be made to understand that Lorna Betts was not like his other girl-friends. He must realise that she moved in more exalted circles and was appreciated by older and more discerning men. The only example she could quote as evidence of this was Gerald Hatherley, and the problem was that she had already hinted several times to Don that her employer was 'a bit of a devil'. Somehow she must now find a way to present him in an entirely different light. Don would hardly be impressed by the idea that as a servant at the Manor she was merely the master's plaything. If anything, that idea might lower her in Don's estimation.

Lorna saw him coming and waved her hand but instead of running to meet him as she usually did, she remained perched on the gate, watching his approach. His legs moved easily through the long dry grass, his fair hair was bleached white by the sun, his face was tanned. He wore corduroy knee-breeches, his collarless shirt was open at the neck and his sleeves were loosely rolled above the elbow. He looked so handsome and desirable that for a moment Lorna allowed herself the luxury of a quick glimpse into her secret fantasy in which she waited at the rose-covered door of their own cottage with his son in her arms as Don — her husband — strode up the path towards them at the end of a long day, his face wreathed in smiles. The fantasy faded as he reached the gate and she jumped down and allowed herself to be kissed.

'Hullo, then,' he greeted her.

'Hullo.'

He slipped an arm round her waist and they began to walk up the meadow towards the copse of trees where they would be hidden from prying eyes. It was 5.30, the milking was done and Lorna was not expected home for another half-hour. She had worked right through her lunch time so that she could leave early.

'Miss me, then?' he asked when she did not at once volunteer the information.

'Of course I did,' she replied with only a fractional hesitation. Don gave her a quick look, aware of the subtle change in her behaviour.

'I missed you,' he said and gave her waist a squeeze. 'I thought about you all day. I thought, tonight I'll have her . . . in my arms. It kept me going all through the day, that did. The thought of having you . . . in my arms.'

She smiled sweetly. 'And now you've got me.'

'Only one arm,' he pointed out, 'not both.' He leaned over and kissed her ear, whispering, 'Both arms round that pretty little body! Lovely!'

Don drew back and waited for her to say 'Don'! in a scandalised voice, but instead she gave him a strange look and merely smiled. He had the impression she was considering his behaviour and the idea disturbed him, but then she smiled at him again and he decided he had imagined it.

He let the hand that was round her waist move up until his thumb was under her breast and she made no objection. Taking heart, he kissed her again – this time on the cheek – and as he did so he ran his thumb over her nipple and found it firm under his touch. He stopped walking, pulled her round to face him and kissed her fully on the mouth, allowing both his thumbs to slide up to fondle her breasts. She gave a quick little sigh and closed her eyes and Don's pulse began to race. He was going further and quicker than before – how far could he go in half an hour, he wondered? He was torn between the desire to explore Lorna's body further while she was willing and the desire to be in the seclusion of the copse which was still a few hundred yards away.

'Oh, Lorna!' he whispered, letting his voice drop huskily. 'You do things to me, Lorna; d'you know that? You're wonderful – just touching you like this does things to me.'

Lorna could feel that it did! She drew back gently and disengaged his hands with a show of reluctance, glancing around her nervously as though to see if anyone was watching them. Don seized her hand, deciding to press on to the shelter of the copse. The sun was still very hot and what he had in mind would best be undertaken in the cool shadow of the trees. He had once suffered a sexual disaster, with the sun beating down on his bare back and sweat dripping on to his partner's face; the girl in question had complained and insisted on wiping his face with her cast-off petticoat . . . it had ruined everything.

However, Lorna did not allow herself to be hurried towards the trees but moved languidly, her hand in his, apparently deep in thought.

'Do you know,' she said at last, a dreamy look in her eyes, 'that something happened today which really surprised me. It was so sweet!'

'So sweet?' He was taken aback by the knowledge that her thoughts had wandered from Don Leckie.

'Yes,' she went on, 'I thought it was sweet. Mr Hatherley gave me a rose from the garden – a single red rose on a long stem. Wasn't that sweet of him?'

The lie rolled easily off her tongue; she was surprised how easy it was.

'I wouldn't call it *sweet*, exactly,' said Don. 'More "soft".'

Lorna turned wide surprised eyes towards him. 'Soft? Would you? How funny.'

'Silly old basket.'

She laughed, again that element of consideration in her tone. 'I thought it was rather nice of him. I daren't keep it, of course, in case "her ladyship" saw it and thought I'd picked it, so I stuck it in a bowl of flowers. Huge displays of flowers, they have up there. Really beautiful. She does them all, she's very good with flowers.'

'Nothing else to do all day, I suppose?'

'No, I suppose not.'

Don glanced at her face. Usually by this time she had made several references to marriage, to her sister's coming child, to engagement rings or to bottom drawers. Today she had made none of them. He let go of her hand and slid his arm round her waist, hugging her close.

She smiled brilliantly up at him. 'It surprised me because he's usually so different,' she went on. 'As though all he wants is to get me into bed. As though—'

'He wants to get you into bed!'

'Oh, not *really*, I don't mean, but I've told you what he's like: he wants to touch me and everything. Today he was so

138

different, really quite sweet. Treating me just like a person and not just a girl to be taken advantage of.'

'What do you mean "everything"?' Don demanded. 'What does he want? What does he *get*?'

'Nothing, Don,' she protested. 'Not really.'

They had reached the edge of the copse and in silence he helped her over the stile. 'Silly old basket,' he said again. 'You want to tell him what to do with his rose!'

'Don!' Lorna wrinkled her nose in disgust.

Roughly Don pulled her towards a nearby beech tree and pushed her back against it, pinning her arms against the smooth bark. He always did this and she always responded with feigned alarm and aroused them both.

'You're hurting me,' she protested unconvincingly.

He leaned forward, pressing himself against her, and decided to waste no more time. 'So what are you going to do now?' he demanded. 'You're in my power.' He laughed and she laughed with him, pretending to try to wriggle free. 'I can have my evil way with you!'

'Don! You mustn't!'

Letting go of her arms, he pulled her away from the tree, turned her round and pulled her backwards, holding her against him. His hands moved over her, up and down, further than he had ever dared – or been allowed – to go before.

'Oh, Lorna!' he breathed. 'Let me! Just this once. You'll never regret it, I promise you. Doesn't it feel good? My hands over you like this? Can you feel what else I've got for you? Lorna, please! It will be so good, you'll see. You'll be begging me to do it again. Lorna!'

She began to wriggle in earnest. 'It's all right for you,' she argued. 'You say I'll never regret it, but I might. My sister regretted it, I can tell you. She—'

'To hell with your sister!' he cried. 'It's you I want, not your sister. Lorna, just this once? Just to see if you like it – and then we'll know, won't we?'

She pulled round and faced him, dishevelled and even more desirable.

'Know what?'

'If we're . . . suited. You know – if we like it.'

'Suppose I don't like it?' she asked.

'Well – then we'll know. But we won't know if we don't try. Come here.'

She had stepped back out of reach, but now she put out a hand to fend him off.

'Wait, Don!' she cried. 'If you know you like it and you know I shall like it, why have we got to try it? Can't we just get married and then we can do it all you like. Or at least get engaged to be married. I'd let you do it if we were engaged. I promise I would, Don. I'd like to now, honestly, but I daren't!'

'The others did and we weren't engaged.'

'Well, I'm not them. I'm me.'

She dodged back as he made a sudden lunge towards her and they faced each other – he with mounting anger, she with increasing hope. She had let him go as far as she dared and if he went any further, she knew she would give in. Already her body was racked with exquisite cramps and she did not need Don to convince her that it would, indeed, be 'so good'.

Don also hesitated. She was a pretty little thing and he could do a lot worse, but if he said 'Yes' to an engagement she would have trapped him and he had often boasted that that would never happen to him. He was only nineteen and there were still plenty of girls in the village who would be glad to give themselves to him. He wondered why he had spent so much time on this one. Plenty of pebbles on the beach, that's what they said, and it was true. But this one was very tasty . . . and she was so near and he wondered if he dare throw her down on to the mossy ground and take her. Then, perhaps he would agree to the engagement. He might *have* to agree.

'Lorna!' he whispered, playing for time, agonising over his decision. 'Please say "Yes". I swear to you—'

'Do you love me, Don?' she asked. 'Really love me. Just me and no one else?'

If he said 'Yes', would *she* say 'Yes'? He hesitated a fraction too long and saw her expression change.

'Mr Hatherley was right,' said Lorna, lying desperately. 'He said younger men only wanted a woman for one thing.'

'Oh, he said that, did he?' Don was outraged. 'You two

have got very friendly all of a sudden if he's giving you advice – and roses! I thought you couldn't bear him to even pinch your bottom?'

'Oh, that!' said Lorna. 'That was just fun. I realised today there's more to him than meets the eye. He's got really nice manners.'

'Nice manners, my foot! He didn't have nice manners with poor Florrie Whatnot. He's a nasty piece of work, everyone says so.'

'Well, I don't, because perhaps I know better than everyone else.'

Her expression remained cool and calculating, while Don's face was bright with indignation. Searching his imagination for a trump card, he was suddenly inspired.

'And Amy was right about you,' he cried. 'She certainly was. She warned me, but I wouldn't listen.'

'Amy Turner at the station?' Lorna's confidence crumpled. 'What did she have to say about me? What could she say? She doesn't even know me.'

'She said you'd try anything to get me to the altar.'

Lorna's face paled. 'When was this?' she demanded. 'When did you and Amy Turner get together and talk about me?'

Don threw discretion to the wind. 'About the same time old fumble-fingers was giving you the rose!' he shouted. 'So put that in your pipe and smoke it, Lorna Betts, because you are the meanest girl I've ever met! You think you're so marvellous – that you've got something better than the other girls. Well, let me tell you, you're wrong! There's nothing you've got that I want any more; you can keep your stupid legs crossed for ever, for all I care. Amy Turner is worth two of Lorna Betts, believe me. She's pretty, she's intelligent, she's—'

Goaded beyond endurance by this attack, Lorna stepped forward with eyes blazing and slapped him hard across the face.

'You pig!' she screamed. 'You senseless, horrible, useless pig! Amy Turner's welcome to you – and if she's stupid enough to let you get across her, then she deserves all she gets. Which'll be not much in my opinion. Gerald was

141

right—' She pushed past and began to run away, unaware of her slip.

'Oh, it's *Gerald*, is it?' Don roared after her. 'What happened to "Mr Hatherley"? I bet you've been giving him all he asked for. You're not so pure as you pretend to be, Lorna Betts. Red roses! I'd like to tell him . . .'

His voice trailed off as Lorna disappeared from view, her blonde hair bouncing, her arms waving wildly as she tried to remain on her feet while plunging at speed down the meadow.

' . . . where to put his bloody red rose,' Don finished, exhausted and unhappy. He wished he hadn't made up the bit about Amy – she and Lorna would be working together at Bates Manor on the day of the birthday party and Lorna might tackle her. Oh Lord! Why did he have to let his tongue run away with him? And now he'd upset Lorna and suddenly he realised that he *was* fond of her. Maybe having Lorna as a wife, all to himself, wouldn't be so bad. Maybe that stupid old fool at the Manor would wheedle favours out of her with his smarmy talk and red roses. His throat tightened at the thought that if he ever did marry Lorna, that old fool might have had her first! Would he be able to tell? For sure?

He kicked miserably at a fir-cone and sent it spinning through the trees; then, thrusting his hands into the pockets of his breeches, he let his thoughts revert to Amy Turner. She wasn't bad. Would *she* be willing? He picked up a small branch and snapped it over his thigh, then sent the two halves after the fir-cone.

'Amy Turner,' he whispered, 'your luck is about to change and Lorna Betts can jump in the pond for all I care.'

He was not entirely convinced as he began to make his way back through the meadow, but by the time he reached the farmhouse and pushed open the kitchen door he was quite certain.

*

Lord Stanisbrooke had obviously enjoyed a long and interesting life and the proof of this was in the mass of papers which littered the table and spilled from the shelves. They came in a variety of packages – letters tied with string, bills in a tattered leather case, documents bulging from a large faded blue envelope. Amy counted seven stiff-backed ledgers and there were more papers in a portable writing-desk.

Ralph had already started to sort and label them. There were Lord Stanisbrooke's letters from his two mistresses, from his mother, his son and two daughters, from his accountant, bank manager and solicitor. Sad little notes from an ageing nanny, pensioned off and lonely without him. A scathing school report or two from his preparatory school in Surrey and several more from Winchester. There were bills and final reminders from his tailor, his shoemaker, even his shirtmaker — and others from a variety of tradesmen and workmen. Amy was fascinated. He had bought matching silver lockets for his two young daughters; and for his wife a ring, brooches and a gold chain; his son had been given a gold half-hunter watch as a coming-of-age present; his mother's funeral was paid for in 1842. There were lists of all kinds: party and wedding guests, work to be done on the estate, preparations for a holiday. From various shipping companies there were letters of confirmation about sailings and a last-minute cancellation. Countless personal letters from India and many more which had been sent to him: from the Army had come confirmation of postings, urgent recalls to the regiment, a citation for bravery under fire. There were also a few betting tickets and a receipt for seats at the opera.

Amy looked up at Ralph, who sat on the opposite side of the table. 'The son and daughters,' she said, 'what became of them? Are they still alive? Are there any descendants?'

He shook his head. 'One daughter, Mary, died of consumption at the age of twelve; the other married and died in childbirth — the child, a daughter, was still-born. The son died in India at the age of thirty-seven.'

'How dreadfully sad,' said Amy. 'A whole family gone without trace.'

Ralph laughed. 'Those letters aren't so important. It's the ones which deal with military matters that we have to study.'

'But the personal letters are so fascinating,' Amy protested. 'Of course they matter. If they don't matter, then they jolly well ought to!' The letters from the two daughters were folded and creased and showed, Amy thought, that their father had read and re-read them. From Mary, there was one letter written in a childish, painstaking copperplate: 'Dearest Papa, My breething is so much better. The doctor tells me I will soon be well again. I miss you all so much. It is so cold. We walked on the Downs and I shiverd but when we came back the nurse gave me a mug of hot cocoa . . .' The address was a convalescent home in Bognor Regis.

The photographs were few – the young Nigel Stanisbrooke, aged about sixteen, standing with his parents; another in his cadet's uniform, staring unflinchingly into the lens of the camera; a wedding photograph, his arm resting on the back of the chair in which his young bride sat nervously holding a prayer book and a spray of flowers; his three children and their pet Pekinese dog in the garden of a large country house; an amateur photograph of the youngest daughter's grave, heaped with flowers, the inscription on the back reading: 'My beloved daughter rests here in everlasting peace'. But the portrait of Nigel Stanisbrooke in what might have been his early thirties was the photograph which Amy could not put down. Nigel the man, the real person, stared out at her across the intervening years and almost spoke to her. His dark, humorous eyes held hers with a kind of friendly arrogance so that she longed to speak to him, longed to ask, 'How was it, your life?' and fancied he would tell her all that she could not discover from the papers that surrounded her.

'What is the exact relationship between you and Nigel Stanisbrooke?' she asked Ralph.

He looked up from his ledger. 'Mother and Stanisbrooke's son were cousins. The relationship is really quite slender.' He noticed that she still stared at the faded photograph. 'He was a handsome man.'

Amy nodded and reluctantly put down the likeness. 'It's terrible,' she said. 'I feel like a spy or an eavesdropper. I almost feel sneaky looking at all these things.'

'I know,' said Ralph. 'It's a strange sensation at first, but you get used to it. In the beginning I felt that I was prying and that he would resent my reading everything.'

Amy considered this with her head on one side, then nodded. 'Would they mind, do you think?'

'I don't think so. It's not as though we're writing about them so as to expose them all. We just have to wade through everything in order to get at the background material. Elliot's brief was rather vague, I must admit. I don't really understand the significance of it all.'

There were a few letters written by Nigel Stanisbrooke which presumably had been lent by the recipients for the purposes of the book. One was to his mother, reassuring her that the wound in his leg was not as serious as they had earlier supposed and there would be no need for an amputation. Another was to his wife, sent from Karachi, to tell her that the bungalow was now fit for habitation and suggesting that she set sail as soon as possible to join him. The tone of the letter was at once adoring and masterful and advised her 'not to strike up a conversation with any unsuitable persons on the voyage out'.

Amy was re-reading this letter when there was a knock on the front door and Ralph looked at her in some alarm.

'That will be *her!*' he exclaimed. 'I thought it was too good to last.'

Amy grinned reassuringly. 'Go and greet her and bring her in here,' she told him. 'There's safety in numbers, remember.'

'Oh Lord!' he muttered and did as he was told.

When he came back into the room Esme was with him; she wore a blue travelling suit and looked slightly harassed. On seeing Amy, her smile faltered a little.

'Good afternoon, Mrs Hatherley,' Amy said, rising to her feet with a polite smile. 'How was London today?'

'Oh, hot as usual,' Esme answered. 'It's always such a delight to return to Kent. It may be just as hot here but at least it's green and green is cooling to the eyes.' Her own eyes were taking in the fact that two chairs were drawn up to the table.

Ralph said, 'Meet my new assistant!'

'Oh?' Esme gave Amy a frosty smile. 'Since when have you needed an assistant, Ralph?' The smile she turned on him was several degrees warmer. Ralph launched into his prepared speech. 'Since my publisher brought forward the

145

expected date of publication,' he told her. 'I shall have the devil of a job to get it done in time, so I asked Miss Turner if she would be kind enough to help me. It's an awful cheek, but she said she would be willing to try.'

'I see,' said Esme. 'How exactly can Miss Turner help you?' She put a faint emphasis on the word "help" as though she doubted Amy's ability to help anyone to do anything.

'Why, cataloguing mainly. That's the most time-consuming part of the work,' he told her, 'and single-handed it would take months. Of course, I thought I had months, but now . . .' He shrugged his shoulders.

'We're hoping,' said Amy, 'that two heads are better than one.' Esme looked surprised that Amy had thought fit to comment and chose to ignore her remark.

'I was hoping I might persuade you to ride with me again,' she said to Ralph. 'Tomorrow morning, I thought, about 10 o'clock?'

Ralph's regret sounded genuine even to Amy. 'Oh, really, what an awful shame!' he said. 'Of course I'd love to, but I'm afraid it's quite out of the question now. It really has to be "noses to the grindstone" from now on, but it was awfully kind of you to make the offer. I hope you'll excuse me.'

For a long moment Esme looked at him and Amy saw the suspicion in her eyes, but Ralph was playing his part well – better than Amy had expected in fact, but she guessed that her own presence helped him. It also inhibited Esme.

'Forgive you?' Esme smiled. 'Oh, I don't know about that. I was so looking forward to it. Riding alone is a sad business but there, if you won't come with me . . .' She gave him an appealing look which Amy thought would have melted the heart of most men.

'Not won't,' Ralph corrected her gently. 'Can't. What could I say to my publisher? I haven't finished the manuscript because I was lured away from my work by a beautiful woman. I don't think he'd be very impressed.'

Amy smiled to show how absurd it sounded and Esme was mollified by the compliment.

'Well,' she said, 'if you can't come tomorrow, you can't, but I shall not give up that easily, Ralph. I shall tempt you again, be sure of that.' She laughed to show that she meant it as a joke, but Amy thought how clever she was. Had Ralph been on his own she was quite sure the silvery tongue would have won him over, by fair means or foul.

Gaining courage, Ralph laughed and putting a hand to his heart, said, 'I have been warned.'

'Indeed you have.' Esme gave Amy a moment of her attention, asking, 'And are you finding it interesting work, Miss Turner?'

'Very interesting,' said Amy. 'Quite fascinating, in fact.'

'Oh. You feel you *can* be of some help then?'

'I believe so, yes.'

'Most definitely,' Ralph put in. 'I think we work well together.'

Esme allowed this to pass without comment. She turned to Amy and said, 'Well, I shall see you on the day of my birthday, then. Do be punctual – there will be so much to do. I also have young Clara Midden, of course. She is putting in a few hours beforehand to help Lorna prepare the bedrooms.' She sighed heavily. 'Poor Gerald,' she said. 'He does mean well, I know, and the idea of a party is *so* sweet, but it is giving me so much extra work! Poor lamb, I dare not tell him.' She turned to Ralph. 'You and your brother are coming as my guests, of course, Ralph, but *you* will be my very special guest! I am so looking forward to it.' She sighed theatrically. 'Just between ourselves,' she told him, 'my husband always drinks too much on these occasions and half-way through the evening he takes to his bed and I am left on my own. It will be such a relief to have a reliable escort after he leaves – you can't imagine.'

Amy detected a look of panic in Ralph's expression and said quickly, 'I'm sure it will all go splendidly, Mrs Hatherley. Please don't worry.'

Esme appeared not to have heard. She held out a slim, perfectly gloved hand to Ralph and looked straight into his eyes. 'If we don't manage a ride before then, I shall look forward to your company on my birthday. You promise?'

'Of course,' said Ralph, taking her hand.

She gave him a conspiratorial smile and said softly, 'You're not going to kiss it today?'

147

Ralph managed a light laugh and said, 'Not in front of witnesses!'

Esme laughed also, then turned to Amy. 'Goodbye, Miss Turner. I shall expect to see you promptly at 1 o'clock. There will be so much to do. I shall provide you with apron and cap, of course, but please wear a black dress. You do have one, I hope?'

'Yes, I do. I shall be on time.'

'Good.'

She gave Ralph a warm smile and her eyes were full of promise. 'No, no, I shall see myself out,' she told him.

When they were sure she had really gone, Amy and Ralph eyed each other jubilantly.

'You see!' crowed Amy. 'I told you that you could deal with her. You just have to be firm.'

'And practise beforehand,' he grinned. 'Round one to us, Amy. We ought to celebrate.'

Amy laughed, thinking that Ralph looked like a naughty schoolboy who had played a prank on his schoolmaster.

'I have a bottle of madeira in the cupboard,' he told her. 'A gift from my mother. Suppose we have a glass to cheer us on our way?'

'Just one glass then,' she agreed. 'I'm longing to get back to Lord Stanisbrooke and I want to keep a clear head.'

He fetched the bottle and a few moments later they raised their glasses.

'To Lord Stanisbrooke!' toasted Amy.

'I'll drink to that.'

Having drunk their madeira, they returned with renewed vigour to the work in hand. At ten minutes to four, Amy put down the letter she was reading.

'I shall have to go,' she said. 'I didn't realise how late it is. Sam will be home from school and I'm always there when he comes in.' They stood up and Ralph walked as far as the road with her.

'It's going to be funny,' said Amy. 'You being at the party as a guest and me as a maid. I shall have to call you "Sir".' She laughed.

'I'm dreading it,' he confessed. 'I hate parties. Thank goodness Elliot's coming – and you'll be there, of course. You'll

148

have to keep an eye on me, then if someone who shall be nameless traps me in a dark corner, you can come along with a tray of savouries. I don't like the idea of being her escort . . . or special guest . . . it makes me very nervous. You'll have to give me moral support, Amy; I shall be relying on you.'

'I'll do my best,' Amy assured him.

'And you'll come tomorrow — same time?'

'I hope so, but I can't promise.'

And with that Ralph had to be content. He watched until she was out of sight and thought what a fool Don Leckie was not to appreciate Amy Turner.

'If he doesn't,' he mused, 'I certainly do,' and he went inside and closed the door.

*

Later that evening Amy walked round to Hope's Farm with Snip. She was longing to tell Mary about her work on the book and giving Snip a walk provided a good excuse. There was a light on in the kitchen so she knocked at the door and opened it, as Mary had told her to do, and called out, 'Mary? Are you there? It's Amy.'

The kitchen was deserted, but someone was moving about upstairs. Surprised to see neither Mary nor Jim, she went to the bottom of the stairs and called up.

Don answered, 'I'll be down in a minute. Make yourself at home,' and her heart gave a thump of joy.

He clattered down the bare stairs and came into the kitchen, grinning at her and pointing to a chair. 'There's no extra charge, you can sit down,' he told her and threw himself into a chair opposite hers. Amy sat down and Snip huddled against her legs, aware of the collie outside on the doorstep.

'Where's your mother?'

'Gone out. Pa, too. They've gone over to Wittersham to see my aunt — she's had a fall or something.' He raised his eyebrows comically. 'So we're all alone! Just the two of us. If you want to scream, you'd better start now.'

Amy laughed. 'What have I got to scream about?' she asked him. 'You're not exactly an ogre.'

149

'I might be,' he said, rolling his eyes wickedly. 'I might be tremendously evil — and there again, I might not.'

'I'll risk it,' she said. 'I was only going to tell them about my secretarial work for Ralph. Well, he calls it secretarial but I can't actually type yet although he's going to teach me. He's got a typewriting machine, and it would be a good opportunity to learn.'

She hoped he would be impressed, but if he was he managed to hide the fact most successfully. 'Aha!' he said. 'I've got a rival, have I?'

'Not exactly,' she replied. 'I suppose I'm not really a secretary, more a researcher.'

'And you're researching Mr Allan, are you?' He grinned at her. 'I'm too late, then!'

Amy frowned. 'Too late for what? Did you want to be a researcher?'

'Good lord, no! I like to do my own research.' He hooked his right foot round the leg of one of the chairs and pulled it towards him, then sprawled back to put his feet up on it, boots and all. Amy, out of habit, opened her mouth to remonstrate but then remembered it was not her concern.

'What are you too late for, then?' she asked.

'Why, to woo the stationmaster's daughter,' he told her. 'Life can be very cruel. I give up Lorna Betts and now you tell me that Ralph Allan has pipped me to the post!'

Amy wondered if he were joking about Lorna. It was too much to hope for, but he seemed genuine.

'You and Lorna?' she echoed. 'Aren't you . . . walking out any more, then?'

Don shook his head. 'Never no more!' he said nonchalantly. 'We've had what's known as a lovers' tiff. She flounced off and I came home sulking. It was all terribly sad.' He grinned engagingly.

Amy protested. 'How can it have been sad if you find it all so funny? And what was the tiff about? Or shouldn't I ask?'

'Ask away,' he said with a wave of his hand, 'but wild horses shall not drag the sad story from me. The point is, now that I'm a free man I had it in mind to turn my attentions

150

to Amy Turner, but then you tell me that Ralph Allan has stolen your heart.'

'I did not say any such thing!' she protested. 'I only said I was working for him. That's not the same thing at all. Of course he hasn't stolen my heart; don't be so ridiculous.'

'Cross your heart?'

Amy drew a hand down and across her heart and they laughed.

'Honestly,' Amy told him, 'we're good friends and I like him very much, but that's all. He was in love with someone else and she died. I don't think he's got over it yet.'

'So . . .' he said slowly, 'there's just you and me.'

Amy, hardly able to believe her good fortune, wanted to shout for joy and fling her arms round his neck. Instead she replied, 'I suppose so.'

'I'm serious,' he said and he was no longer teasing. 'I've thought about you a lot since you came to Gazedown. I remember the first time I saw you – when I came down to the station that first week to complain about the missing chicks. You were so serious and you kept on apologising because your father wasn't there to deal with it. I took rather a shine to you then, but . . .'

'But there was Lorna,' Amy interposed.

'Yes.'

'Oh.' The moment that Amy had dreamed about for so long had arrived, but now she could think of nothing to say. She felt breathless with excitement and had to make a conscious effort not to let Don see just how thrilled she really was by the unexpected change of circumstances.

'So here we are,' he said, 'without a chaperon.'

Trying to think of a witty comment and failing, Amy said, 'How dreadful!' and smiled at him to show that she did not mean it. He took his feet off the chair and sat up a little straighter.

'The stationmaster's daughter,' he said softly. 'I wonder if she has ever been kissed?' Amy said nothing. 'I don't suppose you're going to tell me?' he asked.

'No.' It was almost a whisper.

'No, you haven't – or no, you aren't going to tell me?'

He stood up, came round the table and, taking her by the

hands, pulled her to her feet. They stood only inches apart while he waited for her answer.

'No, I'm not going to tell you,' she whispered.

'Then I'll never know if this is your first kiss,' he said. 'What a shame!' He smoothed back her hair, leaned forward and kissed her full on the lips; he saw that she closed her eyes and felt that she held her breath.

'That was very nice,' she said shakily, opening her eyes.

'I thought so too.'

Outside, the collie began to bark furiously and they heard Jim shouting at it to be quiet. Guiltily Amy sat down again and with a muttered curse, Don did the same. When his parents came into the room, they found him looking supremely innocent and Amy with a faint touch of colour in her cheeks. Jim noticed nothing, but Mary read the tell-tale signs and thought with relief that at last her son was showing some intelligence in the selection of a mate.

*

Amy lay in bed that evening and thought confusedly about her day and in particular about the unexpected approach from Don. That was something she had not imagined would ever happen, although she had allowed herself to dream that it might. Instead she had prepared herself for the day when Mary would tell her that Don and Lorna were betrothed and had often rehearsed how she would greet the news, with pretended delight and sincere good wishes for their happiness. If Don had married Lorna, then Amy would have wanted his happiness. Now they had parted and he had turned to her and she knew she should be ecstatically happy the way she had always imagined, yet she had reservations. Her delight was tinged with a suspicion that Don's disenchantment with Lorna might prove to be temporary and that if she allowed herself too much happiness she might later be bitterly disappointed and hurt if the two erstwhile lovers became reconciled. Nevertheless she acknowledged that her attitude was cowardly, that she was very lucky and that she ought to throw herself heart and soul into the relationship, for how else could she give it a fair chance?

The logic of this was apparent but, tossing sleeplessly

in her bed, Amy remained unconvinced. Inevitably she lost patience with herself and decided she did not deserve Don, but quickly abandoned that line of thinking. If only she could be sure of him – but could anyone be sure of anything in this life? Should they be? No, she was asking too much. Life was full of challenges; this was one of them and she must seize it with both hands; she must make the relationship work; she must make Don love her so much that he would never give Lorna another glance.

Smiling into the darkness, Amy felt satisfied that she had come to the right conclusion and allowed herself to recall in great detail all that passed between her and Don before they had been interrupted. He had said he noticed her when she first came to Gazedown, so if he had not already been involved with Lorna he would doubtless have approached her then. She gave a deep sigh of contentment. It was going to work. It was going to be Amy and Don. She murmured his name, then laughed at herself for doing so.

'Amy Turner,' she whispered, 'stop behaving like a love-sick girl! You're twenty years old and ought to know better.'

But she did not stop, because Don Leckie was the first man she had ever loved.

With an effort, she turned her thoughts towards her new work and immediately the image of Lord Stanisbrooke rose so clear and sharp in her mind that she stared at it, astonished. The heavy dark hair was parted in the middle; the large eyes looked out from beneath faintly arched brows with that amused expression which had captivated her earlier in the day; the face was well-shaped, the nose straight, the jaw softened into a curve and the mouth was generous and slightly turned up at the corners. A man who found the world full of fun, she thought enviously. A man who took life as it came, accepted the good along with the bad and found it all marvellous. Perhaps a man who was larger than life itself.

'Nigel Stanisbrooke,' she said, 'I do *wish* I'd known you. I do wish you hadn't died all those years ago.'

Piece by piece she tried to put together all the evidence she had about him from the little she had managed to glean during her work at The Lodge. He was tall, but not thin. A devoted family man? No, he had taken two mistresses. She amended her assessment to 'loved his children and found women attractive and necessary'. He was generous, he had given everyone presents . . . so presumably he was rich and could afford to do so. He was brave – he had been wounded in action and awarded a medal – and had travelled, gambled, gone to the opera. With his wife, Amy wondered, or one of his mistresses? Would he dare be seen at the opera with a lady who was not his wife? Was he that reckless? It seemed possible. Were his mistresses as beautiful as his wife and did she know about them? Perhaps she looked the other way, as many wives did, and continued to enjoy her home and children. Nigel Stanisbrooke's life was like a gigantic jig-saw with a great many of the pieces missing, but she was determined to find out as much as she possibly could. Not just because of Ralph's book, but because she wanted to know all there was to know about the man. No, she confessed, it was more even than that. That was over-simplifying the way she felt.

'I *need* to know him,' she said wonderingly and having established the fact, she at once turned over and within minutes was fast asleep.

Chapter Nine

Mrs Hollis was ironing Tim's shirt and Clara was peeling potatoes when Tim came in from work. He kissed his mother by way of greeting and grinned at Clara.

'Well,' he said, 'Harry's garden didn't win – it can't do, because it hasn't gone forward for the second judging – but he got three handshakes and "A very promising start, Mr Coombes. Keep up the good work." They were only there for two minutes – off the train and straight back on again. Still, it was a bit of excitement.'

'Is he pleased?' asked Mrs Hollis.

'Oh yes. Pleased as Punch although he tried not to show it.'

He took off his uniform jacket and hung it over the back of a handy chair, which had once been his father's, then immersed himself in the evening paper which he had brought home with him. Clara and Mrs Hollis exchanged amused glances and then Clara turned back to the potatoes. The clock on the dresser said 8.15 and the tabby kitten in front of the warm fire blinked lovingly into the glowing grate.

Mrs Hollis was glad Tim had not taken too much notice of Clara. She was really quite fond of the girl and it was fun hearing all the gossip about the big house and the way these rich folk lived, which was all quite extraordinary, but she did hope Clara would not get any silly ideas about Tim. Tim was such a baby, a real innocent and not at all ready to take on the responsibilities of a wife. Perish the thought! Mrs Hollis had not married Tim's father until he was nearly thirty and then he was all at sixes and sevens. He left everything

155

to her – all the major decisions about where to live when they finally left his parents' house, and even what name to give the baby when it arrived. Oh yes, thought Mrs Hollis Tim was his father all over again and she would be looking after him for a long time to come yet, Clara or no Clara. Not that the girl seemed to have any designs on him; they were more like brother and sister, really. Yes, it was nice having Clara and handy her having a bit of work at the big house – thank the Lord her father hadn't come looking for her! The girl was nice enough and had plenty of 'go' in her, Mrs Hollis didn't deny that; it was just that Tim was such a baby and not ready to settle down.

Clara exclaimed, 'These spuds are full of blinking eyes. They've got eyes in the backs of their heads!'

Mrs Hollis nodded. 'I thought so myself. I shall tell Mr Hobbs when I see him. There's so much waste. Who wants to pay for peelings that go straight in the dustbin?'

'You call *that* waste,' said Clara. 'You ought to see what they throw away up at the Manor. Terrible, it is. Izzie says she doesn't like leftovers – Mrs Hatherley, I mean. No good offering *her* shepherd's pie on a Monday. Oh no. It's got to be a completely new menu, duck or salmon or something. The staff eat like lords on what they leave. He's got an appetite like a bird – well, they both have, but hers is a sweet tooth. Almond pastes, she likes; Mrs Lester has to make it into all fancy shapes. He eats a lot of vegetables and as they've got no chickens all the peelings are thrown away.'

Tim put down his paper. 'I keep telling Ma here we should have a few chickens. Suppose we did, would you be able to bring home the peelings?'

Mrs Hollis wrinkled her nose. 'I don't know if I'd like that, Timmy,' she said. 'Boiling up all those scraps – it does smell so.'

'You'd get free eggs though,' he insisted.

His mother shook her head. 'I don't think I'd like it,' she repeated. 'And there's the rats, too. Chickens bring rats.'

Clara shuddered. 'Rats? Ugh!'

'We could keep a dog,' suggested Tim hopefully. 'Terriers make good ratters.'

Mrs Hollis could see things were getting out of hand, so

she changed the subject by saying, 'Tell Timmy about Mrs Hatherley's new gown, Clara. It does sound lovely.'

'It is,' said Clara. 'She was having a fitting and we all took turns to look through the keyhole. Blue satin with chiffon frills at the cuffs and round the neck and tiny artificial flowers sort of looped over the skirt; rosebuds, I think they are. She's going to look lovely even if she is a bit of a tartar. It doesn't bother me though, because I can handle her – she doesn't scare me like she does poor Izzie. Well, a tartar she may be, but she's going to look like a queen in that dress. I think I'll have to marry a rich man.'

Tim appeared to be reading his newspaper. 'He's not listening,' said Clara cheerfully.

Mrs Hollis looked at him fondly and said, 'He's had a hard day.'

'So have I,' Clara reminded her, 'but *I'm* peeling potatoes.'

Tim looked up over his paper. 'I chopped the wood,' he said, 'before I went out this morning.'

'So you did,' said Clara, turning back to Mrs Hollis who was now pressing Tim's uniform with a damp cloth. 'Mr Hatherley had a go at me today – you know, fidgety fingers, but I soon put him in his place. Slapped his hand, I did, then smiled and said, "Naughty!" He had to laugh. Couldn't help himself, could he? I've dealt with plenty like him in my time!'

'Have you?' Mrs Hollis was intrigued.

'Well, my uncle keeps a pub in the Old Kent Road and I helped out sometimes on a Saturday. Have done ever since I was twelve. You get all sorts in there.'

She put the potatoes on to boil and began to prick the sausages; then she prepared the cabbage, talking all the time. 'Poor old Lorna's in the dumps today. I caught her having a quiet sniffle. Had a row with her young man and she says she's "never going to forgive him". I've heard that before, too! The more she says she won't, the more I know she will. It'll be all lovey-dovey again before long. Izzie says she's been getting her bottom drawer together for months and he hasn't even asked her! How silly can you be? No man's going to get me sniffling in corners. My pride wouldn't let me. Plenty more fish in the sea, that's my motto. Anyway,

157

what girl in her right mind wants to get landed with screaming brats before she has to?'

Mrs Hollis thought this talk rather wild and definitely indelicate, but it gave her the chance to say, 'That's what I tell Timmy. Time enough to settle down when you've had your fun; you're only young once.'

Tim looked up suddenly. 'Don't you like kids then?' he asked Clara.

'No, I don't,' said Clara. 'Always bawling and wanting their noses wiped. My sister's got four and she's only been married three years. Mind you, one of them is her husband's by his first wife who died – got a fishbone in her throat and choked to death. Horrible! No, you won't catch any man tying me down before I've seen a bit of life. No fear!'

'Perhaps no one will ask you,' said Tim.

'That'll suit me just fine.'

Mrs Hollis breathed a deep sigh of relief at the news that Clara was not the marrying kind. She really was a very sensible girl, she thought fondly.

*

With two days to go before the birthday party, Esme was growing more badtempered with every hour that passed. She stood on a stool while the dumpy little dressmaker made what she hoped would prove to be the final alterations to the blue gown, but she knew from past experience that no matter how many times it was fitted it would never satisfy Esme Hatherley. Rich women, she thought, were like spoilt children. Always wanted that little bit more, the star on the top of the Christmas tree.

'That's as level as I can possibly make it,' she said at last, straightening up and putting a hand in the middle of her aching back.

'Maybe,' said Esme caustically, 'but *is* it level?' Stepping down, she crossed to the full-length mirror in its heavy gilt frame and looked critically at the hem, turning slowly and then holding out an imperious hand for the small mirror. She tugged and tweaked the heavy blue satin with apparent displeasure and then took a few paces around the room. It rustled softly and the dressmaker thought it looked perfect, clinging to the slim shoulders, just enough movement around the armholes, snug at the waist without a single wrinkle to spoil the sheen of the heavy satin.

Esme returned to the long mirror and said, 'It's stifling me. The waist is too tight.'

'Oh *no*, madam!' The dressmaker's podgy face crumpled with disappointment. 'Oh, don't ask me to alter the waist, madam. It's absolutely right, I promise you. It looks—'

'I tell you it's too tight,' Esme repeated. 'I can hardly take a breath. If I eat so much as a mouthful of food, I shall split the seams.'

'But madam, it will spoil the line.' The dressmaker wrung her hands in desperation, because she knew that if she altered the waist it would not look right and she would have to alter it again and time was short.

Esme hesitated, knowing the waist *was* right, the hem *was* level. She could see nothing wrong with it at all and it suited her wonderfully well, accentuating the colour of her eyes and showing off her figure to perfection. Ignoring the small gestures of agitation which the dressmaker was making, she studied her reflection with deepening enjoyment. There was no point in giving a party if she was going to be outshone by any of the guests, but this dress could not be bettered, she was sure of that. The men's eyes would turn lasciviously in her direction and the women would watch her with envy. And Ralph Allan would be enchanted to be the chosen partner of the most beautiful woman in the room!

'Lucky Ralph Allan,' she said softly and smiled radiantly at herself.

'What did you say, madam?'

'I wasn't speaking to you.'

'Beg pardon, madam. But the gown — what do you think?'

'I don't know what I think yet,' Esme snapped. 'Surely it's obvious that I'm still considering it? When I've reached a conclusion, I shall tell you.'

The dressmaker swallowed nervously and backed away so that Esme could no longer see her in the mirror. Every time she made a dress for this impossible woman she vowed it would be her last, but the money was good and being dressmaker to such a client enhanced her reputation. She must learn not to take any notice. There was nothing really personal in the attacks, she assured herself, it was just the way some rich people liked to treat their inferiors, just part of the scheme of things.

Esme frowned suddenly and snatched up a handful of satin skirt. 'These aren't the flowers I asked for,' she exclaimed. 'They were smaller. These are clumsy-looking things!'

'Oh no, madam!' The dressmaker rushed forward with a sinking heart. 'They are the ones you ordered. Don't you recall, madam, I showed you six lengths: these, the small daisies, the pearly—'

'No, I don't remember,' said Esme. 'Nor do I remember asking for these clodhoppers.'

'But you said the daisies were insignificant, madam. That was the very word you used. "Insignificant". And you thought the pearly strands were ostentatious. Then you said the ivy trails were tinselly—'

'Please!' Esme put her hands over her ears. 'I'm not deaf, you know. Whatever I said or did not say, I'm not entirely happy about these rosebuds. They're too heavy.'

'But, madam—'

Esme held up an imperious hand and the dressmaker choked back the rest of her words, trying desperately to remember that this was not really a personal attack – just the way of a rich spoilt woman with someone for whom she had no regard.

Esme smoothed the skirt and said, 'I think I shall get a second opinion. Go down to the kitchen and tell Mrs Lester to give you a cup of tea and a bun of some kind and send Clara up to me. You can come back in fifteen minutes.'

As soon as the door closed, Esme threw out her arms and whirled round, her eyes gleaming with pleasure and satisfaction as she watched her reflection. 'Oh, Ralph Allan,' she thought, 'you will deny me nothing. Nothing at all. I shall simply crook my finger and you'll come running.'

There was a knock on the door and Clara came in. As soon as she saw Esme, she clapped her hands with delight and let her eyes grow rounder.

'Oh, ma'am, you look beautiful!' she cried. 'A real princess! And it fits you just lovely. Oh, you look a real treat.'

Esme swirled to and fro, showing off both herself and the gown, eagerly lapping up the girl's praises.

'I'm glad you like it,' she told her. 'I am rather pleased with it, I must admit. We've had nothing but problems, but I think it's right now.'

'Right, ma'am?' cried Clara. 'It's not just right, its tremendous! You'll be the belle of the ball in that, I'm quite sure. All the men will be fighting for your dance card!'

Esme decided that what she liked about the girl was her willingness to speak up. Lorna had merely mumbled something inaudible when invited to see the dress and had then agreed with everything she said. Clara had a mind of her own. Not that she was pushy but . . . what was the word? Willing? No, genuine perhaps. And she had enthusiasm. *And* she had put Gerald firmly in his place. Esme had not missed that.

'So you "approve"?' she said, laughing to show that she did not need the approval of a maidservant. 'Perhaps you would like to help me dress on Saturday, instead of Lorna? Poor Lorna is so clumsy – all thumbs. You'd like to? Good. I shall tell her.'

Esme dismissed Clara with a wave of her hand and then prepared to admire herself until the dressmaker returned. She rehearsed her behaviour on the night of the party: how pleased she would be when Ralph arrived and how she would smile at him, her head tilted demurely to one side; she practised accepting his breathless compliments and told him that she hoped he would claim most of her dances; she whispered that the noise of the crowded room was too much for her and asked him to take her outside on to the terrace; she held out her arms as she imagined them dancing together. She had a momentary qualm as she wondered what he would wear – he must do her credit – but then reassured herself that he had had plenty of time to hire a suit if his wardrobe lacked something suitable. She was just about to practise a slight faintness, due to too much dancing whereupon she would ask Ralph to help her as far as her bedroom, when there was another knock at the door and the dressmaker was back. Esme's face changed, her vivacity faded and she held out her arms wearily.

'It will have to do,' she said. 'I have spent enough time on it already. Help me out of it, press it and bring it back tomorrow at 10.30 in the morning.'

*

The letter arrived at the stationmaster's house on the morning of Esme's party. Thomas Turner stared at the envelope for a long time, recognising his wife's handwriting, telling himself he would throw it into the fire unopened. Sam had gone to the pond with Eric and another boy and Amy was up at the Manor, helping to prepare for the evening's festivities. Arnold was upstairs talking to Ted. Thomas sat down at the kitchen table because his legs were trembling.

'Oh, Ellen,' he said, his heart heavy with foreboding. She had written regularly to Sam and Amy and occasionally they wrote back to the latest address in Lewes. Finally he took up a knife, slit the envelope and took out the contents with fingers that shook, finding two sheets of paper apparently torn from a cheap notebook. Unfolding them, he saw that the address had changed yet again. What the hell was John playing at? Couldn't he keep a job – or was he going up in the world? Moving up to better himself?

He began to read the ill-written missive.

Dear Thomas,
    You will be surprised to hear from me but I am at my wits end and dont now which way to turn. To tell you the truth, John has left me. I dont now where he is and he left me no money. Surve you right you will say and I dont blame you, but what else can I do but ask. Not for me but the boy. He has done no wrong to anyone and you might find it in your hart to forgive me. I have been punished for what I did. If you will take me back I will make it up to you, I sware it. We all make mistakes, dont we?
Your unhappy wife Ellen.

Thomas read the letter again and again until he knew it by heart. Each time the picture of his wife, alone and destitute, brought a lump to his throat and he was seized by a desperate longing to hold her in his arms and comfort her. Each time, however, he heard also the whimpering of his brother's child and anger swamped him. There was no way he could have Ellen back without John's child and she would never part with it — not because of John, but because she was too good a mother. If John had gone, then the child had no one but Ellen. Slowly he refolded the letter and put it back in its envelope; then he sat staring at it, remembering what Ellen's desertion had done to him. She had shattered all their lives. He remembered his own crazy drinking, the warnings from the Railway Board, the terrible loss of self-esteem. Because of Ellen, he had been sent to Gazedown with three staff and a shunting horse; because of Ellen his mother had died and his father had taken to his bed; young Sam had wept and Amy had lost her chance to become a teacher. All because she had taken what she called her 'one chance of happiness'. Now it had turned sour on her and she wanted to come back. Not because she had grown tired of John or seen the folly of her ways, but because she had no one else to turn to and nowhere else to go.

'Damn you, Ellen Turner!' he cried. 'Damn you to hell!'

Thomas turned the letter over in his hands, put it to his lips and then dropped it on to the table. Should he show it to Amy and ask her opinion? He thought not. It was unfair to lay such a burden on her young shoulders; she had enough responsibility already: keeping house, working for Mr Allan, helping out at the Manor — not that he approved of *that*. And what if Amy wanted her mother back and he did not? Or he might want Ellen back and Amy might not wish it?

'No, Ellen!' he whispered. 'It won't do.'

Slowly he got to his feet and went upstairs to his father's room, where Arnold was listening to one of Ted's stories. The former jumped up nervously as the stationmaster entered and said, 'I'm only listening to a story. I'm not doing anything.'

He wore a new badge, which Tim had made; it bore the words 'Ass. Porter' which Thomas thought very appropriate.

The old man turned to him as he went into the room. 'I was just telling Arnold,' he began, 'about that terrible business at Armagh. All those young kiddies killed—'

Thomas said brusquely, 'You'd better get along now,

163

Arnold,' and Arnold bolted downstairs like a startled rabbit without saying 'Goodbye' to Ted.

'What's up with you?' the old man protested. 'Arnold's harmless enough. He does love a—'

'Read this,' interrupted Thomas and he tossed the letter on to the bed and sat down on the bedside chair.

'I shall want my specs.'

Thomas found them and waited as his father read the letter. When he had finished there was a prolonged silence.

'Never could spell, that girl,' said Ted at last.

'I'm not interested in the bloody spelling,' cried Thomas. 'What do you think? What am I supposed to say?'

Ted shook his head. 'You're *supposed* to say "Come home, all is forgiven" .' He looked at Thomas over his spectacles and asked, 'Is it?'

'Of course it isn't.' Thomas covered his face with his hands. 'But I miss her.'

'Good riddance to bad rubbish,' stated Ted firmly. 'That girl killed your mother. Oh yes, she did. If it wasn't for her—'

'And John.'

'Aye, her and John. If it wasn't for that pair, your mother'd be alive today. And I wouldn't be in this pickle. Laid up with the shock. She'd be here, perky as a robin, doing her knitting or making a bit of a pie. You miss your wife, do you? Well, I miss mine.' He glared at his son. 'And I'll tell you something – if that woman comes back into this house, I go out. I'll not stop under the same roof with her.'

'Don't talk soft, Pa,' said Thomas, stung out of his stupor. 'You've nowhere to go, so how could you "go out"?'

The old man drew himself up. 'I'd go, lad, don't you worry. I couldn't say a civil word to her, that's why. And if John shows up, I'll break his bloody neck. A right pair of no-goods!'

'I miss John, too,' Thomas confessed. 'We were good friends once.'

'*Were*, lad. Not very friendly to pinch your wife, was it? Pull yourself together, Tom, for God's sake. A right carry-on,' the old man went on. 'John needs a good hiding. That's

164

what he's always needed. Your mother was too soft with him. Always made excuses for him. Your mother—'

Thomas raised his head irritably. 'It's my wife I'm thinking about, not my mother.'

After a long pause Ted asked, 'What would you tell folks here? How would you explain it – her coming back with a kiddie?'

'God knows! It's a bloody mess.'

'Look at it this way,' said Ted. 'I guess you could reckon you've managed without Ellen for the past four years . . . and who's to say, if you took her back, that John wouldn't change his mind and come running after her? Then the fat would be properly in the fire.'

Thomas was silent. 'There's Amy,' he said. 'She ought to go to that college.'

'She seems happy enough.'

'Is she? I don't know. And Sam . . .'

'Nothing wrong with the lad.' The old man looked at his son. 'Never mind them,' he said, 'it's you – what do you want?'

Thomas sighed. 'I keep thinking I'd always blame the child for being John's son,' he said, with a look of deep misery. 'It would be so unfair.'

'Aye, I know.' The old man shrugged. 'Well, that's it, then,' he said.

Thomas nodded. He held out his hand for the letter, tore it in half and without another word, took it downstairs and fed it into the stove. He watched the paper flare briefly, curl and shrivel.

'I'm sorry, Ellen,' he whispered. 'I just haven't got the guts.'

*

By midday Bates Manor was a hive of activity and tempers were already fraying. Mrs Lester, goaded beyond endurance, had had a short sharp row with Esme, as a result of which she had burst into tears and given in her notice on the spot. Only a quiet word from Gerald and the promise of a small rise in salary had persuaded her to stay on and see the day through. Fresh food was being delivered at intervals – rushed

165

down from London on the train – while foodstuffs previously prepared were retrieved from the dark recesses of cold cupboards and the ice-house to be given last-minute decorations. Out of the eighty-nine people Esme had invited, eighteen had reluctantly declined for a variety of reasons, so with only seventy-one guests she had changed her mind at the last minute and decided to seat everyone. Hired trestle tables had been delivered at 11.30 and were being covered with spotless white tablecloths. The accompanying chairs were being dusted off and polished. Esme was everywhere at once, criticising and issuing orders. The florist arrived from London with the flowers and Lorna rushed up and down the stairs keeping her supplied with jugs of water. In the Gold Room – where the guests would gather before supper and later return to dance – the gardener was perched at the top of a ladder draping freshly cut greenery along the tops of the windows.

In the kitchen, Izzie was giving the cutlery a final polish and sulking because she was 'missing all the fun'. Gerald was drifting aimlessly around with a large whisky in one hand, trying to look as though he was enjoying himself and failing miserably.

By 3 o'clock the atmosphere was frantic, by 5 pm it was faintly hysterical. Gerald cornered Lorna on the terrace where she was putting fresh candles into all the lanterns and dug his fingers into her shoulder.

'Lorna,' he hissed. 'I want you to do something for me, later on. About 10 o'clock.'

'What is it, sir?' she asked.

'It's nothing much, Lorna, only you must promise.'

'If you say so, sir.'

'I do say so, Lorna.' He glanced round nervously to make sure they were not being overheard. 'I want you to bring me a drink – a bottle of whisky – to the library. Do you understand? Don't say anything to anyone else; just take a bottle of whisky and bring it on a tray to the library. Bring a couple of glasses – I . . . might have a friend with me. Parties bore me, Lorna, and I like to slip away. With a friend. There's no harm in it, you see. It's our little secret.'

'About 10, sir,' she repeated. 'I'll remember.'

166

'And if I'm not there, just wait for a few minutes. Some idiot might keep me talking. You will remember? You do promise?'

'I promise, sir.'

'Good girl.' He gave her bottom a quick pat and said casually, 'Not very happy at the moment, Lorna?'

'No, sir.'

'Trouble with your young man? Oh, I hear little things here and there. A little bird . . . But don't worry, Lorna, he's not worth worrying about. A pretty girl like you shouldn't waste time on him. They're all the same, these youngsters. Fickle. You're worth something better.'

'Yes, sir,' she said doubtfully, wondering where exactly this was all leading.

'Well, get along then,' he said, 'but remember!' He put a finger to the side of his nose.

'10 o'clock in the library, sir, with a bottle of whisky and two glasses.'

'Good girl.'

Impossible though it had seemed at 7, at eleven minutes to 8 o'clock all the preparations were complete. The tables in the dining-room glittered with glass and silver, the Gold Room was beautifully decorated and the small ensemble (piano, violin and cello) was in its place on the raised platform at one end. The wine waiter who had been specially hired fluttered about importantly with his assistant. In the kitchen the food waited, hidden beneath numerous clean cloths, while Clara, Lorna, Amy and Izzie – immaculate in caps and aprons – were being inspected by Mrs Lester: fingernails, teeth, hair.

The housekeeper peered at Lorna's face. 'Is that paint on your lips? You hussy! Go and wash it off at once. Whatever would the mistress say if she saw you with painted lips?'

Lorna departed, muttering, to remove the offending colour.

The gardener, wearing his one and only uniform jacket, was waiting outside in the drive to direct the carriages round to the stables. Gerald – immaculately dressed, bow-tie perfectly tied – waited on the steps with a welcoming smile ready on his face. Up in her bedroom, Esme gave her reflection a final glance of approval and prepared to descend the broad staircase. It was a pity, she thought, that she could not appear when the entrance hall was full of guests, but protocol demanded that she be at the bottom to greet them as they came in.

Resplendent in black dress and white lace cap and apron, Amy resisted the urge to laugh at herself. She was enjoying everything tremendously, but as the 'witching hour' approached found it increasingly difficult to take it all seriously. She stood with Clara, Lorna and Izzie, waiting to take the guests' cloaks and wraps as they arrived. Izzie was making the most of her moment of glory, for she was destined to return to the kitchen as soon as the first of the plates had been whisked from the tables.

'Ooh, my belly's gone all funny!' she told Amy. 'All shaking like jelly. I can't wait to see the first guest. Oh, don't you wish you were coming instead of being only the maid? Just think of all that food – and dancing with a handsome man! It's like a fairy story.'

'In a way, I suppose it is,' Amy agreed.

Ralph had told her he would arrive about 8.15 and she had laughingly promised to drop him a curtsy and take his coat. She had also undertaken to keep an eye on him during the evening and to rescue him from Esme if the need arose.

Then Esme appeared on the stairs and they all turned to gasp with delight, except for Clara who had helped her into her finery and suffered the lash of her tongue when the blue satin shoes pinched and her tiara would not stay in place without extra hairpins.

Even Gerald was impressed with her appearance and he went forward, hands outstretched to meet her.

'Darling Esme, you look breathtaking,' he told her loudly, taking her hand and kissing it.

She smiled dazzlingly while whispering, 'Gerald, your hands are sweating. For God's sake wipe them!'

At that moment the first carriage rolled up to the steps and an elderly couple alighted from it with some difficulty. Gerald greeted them and brought them up to his wife.

'Stella!' cried Esme. 'And Frederick! How simply splendid

168

of you to come all this way!' She kissed the withered cheeks and Clara moved forward to help them off with their wraps.

As the carriage rolled away a gleaming brougham took its place and the greetings were repeated with cries of, 'Happy Birthday, Esme dear!' and 'Oh good heavens! A gift! How very kind.'

Now it was Amy's turn to take coat and cape and carry them to the cloakroom. Meanwhile the other guests were being offered champagne as they entered the Gold Room, where soft music created a soothing background for their conversation.

For the next half-hour there was a wild flurry of activity as a constant stream of horse-drawn vehicles wheeled up to the front steps, the horses tossing their heads and jingling their harnesses, the female occupants of each carriage descending the steps in a rustle of silks and satins, the men immaculate in dress suits and crisp white shirts. Amy saw more pince-nez and monocles than ever before in her life and the air was heady with attar of roses, lavender water and the pungent smell of expensive cigars. Gerald played out his role as delighted host with considerable assurance and Amy guessed that there had been many such occasions in the past. Esme was in her element: kissing friends, accepting birthday presents and receiving compliments on her appearance with exactly the right mixture of delight and modesty.

As Clara passed Amy she whispered, 'I wish I was a burglar! I'd make a blooming fortune!'

Lorna gave Izzie a nudge and said, 'Don't gawp like that. You have to look as though we do this all the time,' as she hurried briskly on her way. Izzie closed her mouth, wondering if she dare carry her tray of champagne to a dark corner and try a sip.

In the Gold Room the music was now a little louder as the hum of conversation increased and the guests stood around commenting on the delightful floral decorations.

When Ralph Allen arrived he was not alone; he came up the steps and into the entrance hall with a tall, dark-haired companion and Amy, catching sight of him, was momentarily rooted to the spot. She gave an audible gasp and the greeting she had rehearsed for Ralph's benefit died on her lips.

169

At that moment Gerald went forward, shook both men warmly by the hand and spoke to Ralph's companion.

'Splendid of you to come all this way,' he said. 'Keep your brother out of mischief, eh? I'm glad my wife had the good sense to invite you!'

He looked round and caught Amy's eye and she hurried forward to take the men's hats. She managed to give Ralph a dazed smile as she bobbed a curtsy, but the look she gave Elliot was one of shocked incredulity.

Ralph was saying to her, 'This is my brother, Elliot, who is responsible for my being here in Gazedown; he arranged for me to have The Lodge.'

Elliot held out his hand and Amy took it, but still she could not manage more than a shaky, 'Pleased to meet you.'

The dark, humorous eyes which looked into hers were so familiar that she felt she was greeting an old friend. The lean figure, thick dark hair, full but sensitive mouth, all belonged to Lord Stanisbrooke! When Elliot smiled at her confusion, the smile itself was exactly as she had imagined it would be.

Ralph laughed. 'Good heavens, you've struck my secretary dumb, Elliot. That's quite an achievement!'

Amy managed to laugh, but her mind was racing. Of course, the two men were distantly related to Nigel Stanisbrooke, but even allowing for that fact the likeness was startling. Even the moustache was the same, she thought, recognising too the long, well-shaped fingers of the hand that had rested along the back of the chair in the photograph.

'I'm sorry,' she stammered. 'I'm just so amazed . . .' She turned to Ralph. 'Can't you see the likeness between your brother and Lord Stanisbrooke?'

Surprised, Ralph looked at his brother. 'I suppose there is a similarity,' he said. 'How odd – I've never noticed it before.'

'A chip off the old block!' said Elliot, laughing delightedly and throwing back his head with such obvious enjoyment that several people turned towards him and smiled too, although unaware of the joke.

Amy nodded, beginning to recover her composure. 'I didn't mean to stare,' she told Elliot. 'Do please forgive me.'

'My dear, I love to be stared at by pretty girls,' he declared,

170

whereupon Ralph said, 'I *told* you he was a charmer, Amy,' and Elliot laughed again.

This time Esme turned sharply to see what she was missing and gave Amy a frosty look, saying 'See to the next guest, please, Amy.' She then turned to welcome Ralph and Elliot. 'Ralph! How sweet of you to come so early – and your brother. How nice to meet you again, Mr Allan. How is London? As marvellous as ever?'

She offered an arm each to Ralph and Elliot and led them into the Gold Room, smiling radiantly and looking up at each in turn.

When at last the meal was announced, all the guests drifted into the dining-room as slowly as they could, pretending well-mannered indifference to the prospect of food, but once they were there an immediate hunt was on until everyone had found his or her appointed place at the table. Esme sat at one end of the main table with Ralph and Elliot on either side of her, while Gerald sat at the opposite end. Grace was said and then the wine waiters moved in unobtrusively to fill the glasses and the various cold collations were served.

Amy, Lorna and Clara were rushed off their feet and Izzie returned to the kitchen, there to bemoan her bad luck and make a start on washing the first of the glasses. Mrs Lester – her face set in an expression of deep suffering – paid her no attention, being far too concerned with her own problems to heed those of anyone else. Dish after dish was sent into the dining-room as others were emptied and brought out.

'Strewth!' Mrs Lester exclaimed as Lorna rushed in with another empty dish. 'They must have been starving themselves for a week! It's a wonder they haven't scraped the blooming pattern off the plates.'

Izzie looked round from the steaming sink. 'I hope they're going to leave *something*,' she said pointedly. 'I'm starving – I don't know about them!'

Mrs Lester said, 'Yes, well . . .' and felt rather guilty because, being under so much pressure, she had not found time to provide any lunch for the staff, but had assured them that they could eat their fill of delicious leftovers later on.

Passing Amy in the hall, Clara said, 'How on earth are they going to dance after all that food!'

171

Lorna was keeping her eye on the clock, remembering Gerald's instructions with regard to the library. She wondered who his 'special friend' would turn out to be; she dared not ask anyone for Gerald had warned her it was a secret. She certainly could not confide in Clara for she had not forgiven her for being chosen to help Esme dress and Amy, it seemed, had now taken Don's eye so she could not look upon her as an ally. Izzie was too likely to blurt everything out.

It was almost 10 o'clock before the guests began to leave the dining-room, the ladies wandering off in search of the powder room while some of the men, already a little the worse for drink, headed out into the kindly darkness to take a quick turn in the fresh air.

The ensemble struck up a vigorous polka amidst cries of amused protest that no one could move a step but the pianist – a middle-aged man with unfashionably long hair – persisted with his lively melody in the belief that it would draw the guests back into the Gold Room. When this object had been achieved, he switched the tempo to something more sedate. At once Esme turned to find her husband, so that they could start the dancing, but he was nowhere to be seen. After a perfunctory search for the benefit of the guests, she threw up her hands despairingly.

'We must make a start!' she cried gaily. 'I shall find myself another partner; Gerald will understand.'

Her gaze flitted amongst the faces until she saw Ralph talking to an elderly man.

'Ralph,' she cried. 'Our author! Who better to partner me for the first dance. No, no, I shall take no excuses!'

Triumphantly she led him into the centre of the room and a ripple of applause broke out as Ralph bowed and Esme curtsied and they began to move together along the floor in the familiar pattern of the two-step. After a few moments several other couples joined them and then the room became a swirling mass of colour as they swayed and dipped to the music while upstairs Gerald waited in the library, his eyes blinking, his fingers on the desk rapping out the rhythm of the dance.

Chapter Ten

Lorna made her way upstairs, balancing the tray which carried a bottle of Johnnie Walker whisky and two cut-glass tumblers.

She knocked on the library door and Gerald opened it within seconds. As she held out the tray, preparing to relinquish it, she tried to peer into the gloom to catch a glimpse of the 'friend'. To her surprise, however, Gerald said, 'Bring it in and put it down on the table, there's a good girl,' and when she went into the room there was no one else there. Hearing a faint click, she turned to see Gerald holding up the key to the door.

'I thought you said . . .' she began.

Gerald giggled. 'It's you, you silly thing, Lorna. *You* are the friend! I thought – since you've been such a good girl – that you and I would have a little drink together. You would like that, wouldn't you?'

'Whisky, sir?' said Lorna, alarmed. 'I can't drink that stuff. Ma would kill me if I drank whisky.'

'No, no, Lorna.' He came forward dangling the key skittishly in front of her eyes. 'I've brought up some champagne! The whisky was just to fool any nosey-parkers.'

Lorna's eyes widened. Champagne! Surely her mother could not object to champagne? 'Oh sir – Gerald, I mean. Champagne for me? Oh, do you think I should? I mean, I've never tasted it before.' She imagined herself telling Don Leckie about the night she had drunk champagne. That would show how much the master of Bates Manor respected her; that would make Don realise the kind of girl she was.

'Here it is,' he told her, pulling a few leather-bound books from the bookshelf and drawing out a bottle of champagne. 'It'll make a bit of a "pop", but no one will hear over the noise downstairs.' He set the bottle down on the desk and produced two glasses from a drawer somewhere beneath it. 'Just you and I, Lorna, eh? A little treat for us – no harm in that, is there?'

'No, Gerald. I don't suppose so.'

The truth was that Lorna did not *want* to suppose so; she was anticipating her first-ever glass of champagne with a mixture of awe and delighted apprehension. Champagne was a wildly exciting drink, a madly sophisticated drink, the drink of duchesses and earls and suchlike.

'Is it very . . .' she searched for the word and said, 'fizzy?'

'Of course it is, my funny little Lorna.' Gerald giggled again. 'The bubbles will nip your nose and explode inside your head. You'll feel wonderful, light as air!'

She watched, fascinated, as he eased the cork and gave a little shriek when it came out.

'Oh sir! It went right up to the ceiling!'

With trembling hands Gerald filled the glasses and handed one to her. Then he raised the other to his lips.

'To you and me, Lorna,' he toasted.

'You and me, sir,' she echoed.

He did not bother to correct her use of 'sir', but watched as she sipped the clear gold liquid. Then, discovering that she liked it, she gulped it all down with childish eagerness, her eyes screwed up in a kind of ecstasy and both hands clasped round the glass.

'Oo-er!' she said, gasping and spluttering. 'That was really lovely, Gerald. Thank you ever so.' She put down the glass and wiped her mouth with the edge of her apron. 'It *was* fizzy – it nearly made me cough.'

He immediately refilled her glass, but she did not notice that he had scarcely touched his own.

'Another one?' she said dubiously. 'Should I?'

'It's not very strong, Lorna,' he told her quickly. 'Here, I'll sit down on this chair and you sit on my lap and sip it slowly. There's no hurry, you see. You sit on my lap, and if it makes you cough I'll pat you on the back. That would be cosy and friendly, wouldn't it?' He patted his lap and Lorna decided to humour him. Two glasses of champagne! What would Don say to that?

'Oh, Gerald, you're tickling me,' she protested half-heartedly as she finished the second glass.

'It's not me,' he laughed with mock innocence. 'It's that mouse again! He likes to scamper round your sweet little waist and under those dear little breasts. Lorna, my little mouse wants to scamper inside your collar – you wouldn't mind that, would you?'

'I don't know, sir,' said Lorna. She too felt very excited, her head was delightfully light and she wanted to smile all the time. She wriggled round to face him. 'Maybe if I could have just one more glass of that champagne . . .'

This seemed to her a very daring and cunning suggestion, but she felt daring and cunning . . . and giggly. She hiccupped as she watched Gerald pour a third glass and could feel his knees trembling.

As she sipped her fourth glass Gerald began to unpin her apron top and then to unbutton her bodice and by this time it seemed a very reasonable thing for him to be doing. In fact, in her inebriated state, it seemed the *only* thing for him to be doing.

'Sir!' she cried. 'Look! I've drunk more than half the bottle!'

'It's all for you, Lorna,' he said hoarsely, sliding his fingers inside her bodice and wriggling them under the top of her stays. 'The whole bottle is for you,' he repeated, 'because you're a lovely, lovely little thing—'

His gasp of pleasure as he reached her nipple was matched by her own; she was at once in a state of acute arousal – astonished, dismayed, deliriously happy.

'Oh, you darling mouse!' she whispered.

She was aware that Gerald had refilled her glass for – what was it – the fourth or fifth time? She had lost count. Now he was forcing it to her lips and making her drink, and she was not protesting. The glass clinked against her teeth and the sparkling liquid rushed down her throat.

Groaning, she turned so that he could reach her more easily. Then both his hands were exploring beneath her stays

175

and sending waves of pleasure through her whole body. She could feel it in her stiffened legs and arched feet.

'On the floor!' he whispered urgently. 'Before you fall. On the floor, Lorna.'

Obediently, with a dazed laugh, she slipped on to her hands and knees and then before she knew it, he had thrown up her black skirt and she was giggling and her head was so light that it seemed to float, yet so heavy she felt she could not support it and allowed herself to crumple on to the floor, face down. Hiccupping, she felt his hands tugging at her limbs, pulling her over so that she lay on her back staring up at the ceiling which whirled pleasantly above her. This was exactly what she had been waiting for; she had longed for Don to 'pleasure' her but he had always taken her resistance at face value. Foolish Don, she thought. If only he had persevered, if only he had given her champagne! A woman could do anything after a few glasses of champagne. If only he had known that . . . but what did it matter? Someone was finally unlocking the desire in her body and she no longer cared who it was.

'Oh, you are naughty . . .' she murmured happily as she felt him tug at her drawers. His hands slid up her legs and rolled down her black stockings.

'Do you like it, Lorna?' he demanded hoarsely. 'Tell me and I'll make it even more beautiful.'

Suddenly all the breath was knocked out of her as Gerald threw himself on top of her. She wondered fleetingly if she ought to let him do that, but it didn't seem terribly important. What he was doing thrilled her from her head to her toes and she knew that the ending would be wonderful. Suddenly, shudderingly it was all over and as they clung together, Lorna giggled helplessly while tears of joy ran down Gerald's face.

*

By 11 o'clock the dancing was in full swing as the most popular ladies were whisked around the floor. Their unfortunate sisters who were less in demand watched enviously and talked and laughed in brittle voices to hide their disappointment, fanning themselves furiously to pretend that they were too hot to dance and glad of the chance to relax. Amy, tray in hand, paused in the doorway to survey the dancers and make sure that Ralph was still in evidence amongst them. He was dancing with Esme and seemed to be enjoying himself. Either he *was* enjoying himself, she thought, or he was acting most convincingly. She thought they made a very handsome couple and was sure that many other people watching them would think the same.

Mr Hatherley was nowhere to be seen, she noted, and neither was Lorna – but that was none of her business really, except that she and Clara were having to do Lorna's share of the work and Clara was already grumbling.

'Ralph seems to be quite happy,' said Elliot, appearing beside her with a glass of champagne in his hand. 'I don't think you need worry about him.'

'I'm not worrying about him,' she protested.

'Then why are you watching him like the proverbial hawk?' he asked, his tone teasing.

Amy laughed. 'I kind of promised to keep an eye on him,' she explained. 'But are you happy? You should be dancing. Look at all those poor ladies waiting for a partner!'

'I have been dancing,' he protested, 'and I'm worn to a shadow. Let me see, there was a two-step with the rather weighty Lady Morgan; a gavotte with the very shy Isobel Something; the Lancers with a dreary girl whose name began with "P" – Penelope or Pamela I think it was; a waltz with another of Esme's distant cousins . . . the list is endless!'

'I'm sorry,' said Amy. 'I hadn't noticed.'

'Then I'm forgiven for snatching a brief respite?'

'Totally.'

He laughed. 'May I say how well your uniform becomes you? You should seriously consider becoming a full-time maid.'

'Just so that I can wear the uniform?' She shook her head. 'I don't think so. It's very hard work – and I shouldn't be standing about talking with the guests.' She looked round guiltily. 'We've been told "not to mingle and not to encourage undue familiarity".'

Elliot rolled his eyes expressively. 'So if I pinch your arm, or any other part of you . . .'

Amy smiled. 'Then I must discourage you with "a look" and move away! I've been practising the look all day, I may add. I hope I've got it right.'

He laughed delightedly. 'I'm terribly tempted to try it,' he told her. 'I'm curious to see how you look when you're discouraging unwelcome advances!'

'I'm just as curious as you,' Amy confessed. 'I don't think I've ever had to repel any unwanted attention.'

'What a modest young woman,' he said. 'May I have the honour of this dance?'

The suddenness of his request startled her. 'Dance with you?' she stammered. 'Oh no! I daren't. Really . . . but thank you for asking.'

Aware of his dark eyes, she felt the colour rising in her face. How marvellous it would have been to accept his invitation, almost like dancing with Lord Stanisbrooke!

'It would be my pleasure,' he insisted, 'and I doubt if "her ladyship" would even notice. She has eyes for no one but Ralph.'

'But I'm afraid everyone else would notice,' she told him, 'and it would certainly be mentioned. She would probably send me packing without any wages.'

'What a shame!'

Was he mocking her, Amy wondered.

'I've been considering,' he said, abruptly changing the subject again. 'I think perhaps we should commission Ralph to write that book. That way we could make him an advance and he could afford to take on a paid assistant. Don't look so horrified, Amy. I mean *you*!'

She did not bother to hide her relief. 'I thought you were proposing to do me out of my job,' she told him, 'though Ralph is already intending to pay me.'

'But that would be out of his own pocket,' explained Elliot. 'You ought to be paid properly for your work. Would you be able to manage more hours, do you think? There is really a great deal of work to be done and if we commissioned the book we would want it within a reasonable time.'

'I don't know,' said Amy. 'Perhaps Ralph would rather not be hurried. Shouldn't we ask him first?'

Elliot smiled, approving her concern for his brother. 'Of course we will,' he said, 'but I didn't want to suggest it if you were not able to give him more of your time, because he obviously wants you as his assistant.' He smiled engagingly. 'I wish you would dance with me,' he said. 'We could find a broom cupboard and dance in there, if you would feel safer.' He joined in her laughter, then took hold of her hand and led her out of the room. 'We'll find somewhere quiet,' he assured her. They went through the entrance hall and into the shadows of the passage which led to the kitchen. 'This will do,' he said.

'Oh dear,' said Amy nervously. 'Now we can't hear the music properly — and I can't dance very well.'

'*I* can hear it perfectly,' he assured her, 'and you will dance well with me.' Taking her into his arms he began to dance, humming the slow waltz under his breath, his eyes gleaming with amusement. To Amy's surprise, after the first few stumbling steps she found she could follow him quite easily, as he had promised, and she was able to relax and enjoy herself. His arms held her firmly but gently and the movement of his body guided her own; she was very aware of the closeness of their bodies and the fact that they were alone. She felt protected by the circle of his arms and yet vulnerable to discovery by disapproving glances, and the combination of these two conflicting emotions was strangely exhilarating. Closing her eyes, she surrendered herself to the excitement and was therefore unprepared for Elliot's kiss. She felt his lips brush her hair and looked up in alarm. At once he released her and held up a placating hand.

'Forgive me,' he said. 'Please forgive me. I thought I could get away with it. Your eyes were closed and I thought "she won't notice" but you did.'

Amy stared up at him speechlessly and he went on, 'I've never kissed a parlourmaid before! I couldn't resist it — and now I suppose you'll give me the "discouraging look" and move away, as laid down in the Hatherley rule book.'

She had to laugh at the expression on his face. 'How can I?' she asked. 'I know you won't take me seriously. I pity any real parlourmaid who falls into your clutches.'

'Then you aren't angry?'

179

'I don't know,' she confessed. 'Perhaps I should be, but it was a nice kiss and I did enjoy the dance.'

'So did I.'

At that moment the kitchen door opened and Clara rushed into the passageway with a tray of clean glasses.

'Amy!' she cried. 'You're missing all the excitement – or perhaps you're not!' She grinned at Elliot. 'Mrs Lester's hopping mad because Lorna's vanished and the wine waiter wants a word with the master and *he's* vanished.' She lowered her voice. 'If you ask me, they've vanished together! So if Mrs Lester finds you here and not collecting glasses, she'll probably start foaming at the mouth!'

'Thanks for the warning,' said Amy with a nervous glance in the direction of the kitchen.

'It was my fault,' said Elliot, 'and now I must let you get on with your work, Amy. But you do forgive me?'

'Of course I do,' she replied. 'Only please, do go back to the dancing before – oh no!'

Clara's jaw dropped and they all stared. Lorna, giggling helplessly, was making her way along the passage from the direction of the main stairs. Her hair and clothing were dishevelled and she clung to the wall as she moved unsteadily towards them.

'Lorna Betts!' gasped Clara. 'You're pickled!'

Lorna hiccupped loudly, put a hand to her mouth, giggled and said, 'Pardon, I'm sure,' then clutched at the wall again, swaying desperately.

Elliot rushed forward to catch her as she almost fell and she stared blearily up into his face.

'D'you know what?' she demanded with another hiccup. 'Do you – do you know what?'

Elliot held her upright as her knees buckled suddenly, but she burbled on happily. 'Do you know what?' she repeated, forming the words with difficulty. 'I'll tell you what. I'll tell you because . . .' She stopped and turned her head to peer up into Elliot's face. 'Well, whoever you are, I'll tell you – I'll tell you all. I liked it. You know that? I really, truly liked it.' Her head lolled forward and for a moment she appeared incapable of speech.

'We'll have to get her home,' said Amy. 'Poor girl — she is in a state. We daren't let anyone see her like this.'

'Don't let her near the kitchen,' said Clara. 'Mrs Lester will kill her!'

Lorna's head snapped back suddenly and she smiled, her eyes half-closed in pleasure as the memories flooded back. 'I really truly did,' she told them. 'No, I mean it. I was . . . I was surprised. Yes, that's what I was. Surprised. Because, you know — because I liked it.'

Clara rolled her eyes expressively. 'I should think you *did* like it,' she declared, thinking that Lorna was refering to the alcohol. 'You must have drunk about a gallon of whatever it was. You're well and truly tipsy, Miss Betts. Lordy! What *are* we going to do with her?'

Before anyone could answer this question, there were footsteps and the master of the house appeared at the far end of the passage. There was a moment's shocked silence as they all stared at him.

'Ah, there she is,' said Gerald. 'I've been looking for her; I've just been told what a state she's in. Good heavens! What has she been drinking? She'll have to go home at once.'

Amy said, 'Shall I take her, sir? I know where she lives.'

To her surprise, he shook his head emphatically. 'I'll take her myself. Can't spare two of you with the party in full swing. I'll walk her home. It's not far and she might come round in the fresh air.'

As Lorna opened her mouth to speak, he said sharply, 'Hold your tongue, you silly girl! You're in enough trouble already.' He glanced at Elliot. 'Staff! They're such a responsibility. I don't think her mother's going to be too pleased, but there you are.' He sighed heavily. 'I'll take her out through the kitchen — don't want anyone to see her like this. Well, don't stand there gaping, Clara; they'll be wanting to refill those glasses. Oh, and Amy, if you can find my wife — she's not in the Gold Room — you might tell her the Langhams are going home, they have such a long drive. She'll want to say "Goodbye" to them.' Gerald's words reminded Amy that for the moment she had forgotten all about her promise to Ralph. As Clara and Elliot returned to the Gold Room and Lorna was dragged away in the direction of the kitchen, Amy sped up the stairs. If Ralph and Esme were nowhere to be seen, they must be either on the terrace amongst the other partygoers or else upstairs. At least she now had a valid excuse for interrupting them.

Knocking on the bedroom door, she waited for a 'Come in' and then opened it to find Esme sitting on the edge of the bed with a hand to her forehead, while Ralph stood beside her looking distinctly nervous. Esme looked up irritably, annoyed by the interruption.

Avoiding Ralph's eyes, Amy began to gabble her hastily amended message. 'I'm sorry to intrude, ma'am, but the master says to tell you that the Langhams are leaving early because of the long drive home and they specially want to say "Goodbye" to you if you could spare them a few minutes.'

Esme muttered something under her breath, then she said, 'I have this terrible headache and Mr Allan has kindly brought me to my bedroom – I need my smelling-salts, Amy.'

'Yes, ma'am, but the Langhams—'

'Surely Gerald can say "Goodbye" for me,' she said pettishly.

'No, ma'am,' said Amy as firmly as she dared, 'he can't. Lorna Betts is unwell and he's taken her home.'

Startled out of her headache, Esme stared at Amy. 'Taken Lorna Betts home himself?'

'Yes, ma'am. I did offer, but he said he couldn't spare two of us. The Langhams, ma'am? Shall I tell them you'll be down?'

Ralph, who had been silent this far, suddenly found his voice. 'It might be a good idea if you sat outside on the terrace,' he suggested to Esme. 'When you've made your farewells, that is. The fresh air would very likely ease the pain in your head.' He managed to wink at Amy over Esme's bent head.

'Oh yes, it would, ma'am,' said Amy. 'And I could bring out your smelling-salts. It's beautifully cool on the terrace; quite a few people are sitting outside.'

They both waited and for a long moment it seemed that Esme would argue the point, but at last she rose to her feet with a very bad grace.

'I can't think,' she said, 'why these wretched people bothered to come to the party at all if they have to leave so ridiculously early.' She put a hand on Ralph's arm for support and Amy held the door open for them. 'And don't forget my salts, Amy. They're on my dressing-table.'

'No, ma'am. I'll bring them down right away.'

Amy followed them down the stairs, clutching the bottle of smelling-salts. One to us! she thought triumphantly and found it difficult to keep her face straight.

Chapter Eleven

The signal-box at Gazedown, situated between the level crossing and the platform, was a sturdy affair. The base was built of brick and above that the signal-box itself was of wood construction with large windows on the three sides which faced the station and track, it was topped by a steeply pitched slate roof. At the end facing the station there was a door which led out on to a small wooden platform, from which steps led down to the ground. The name GAZEDOWN was painted on a board which ran along the side of the signal-box. To outsiders the interior appeared cramped but to Bob Hart, the signalman, it was 'comfortable', even 'cosy'. As well as the row of highly polished levers, there was a shelf for the block bells, a small stove, a cupboard, a box of coal, a chair and a small table. Another shelf held various books in which messages and train movements were logged. A large clock in a wooden case held centre place in the one wall which was not glazed.

Ten days after the party at the Manor, Bob Hart was enjoying his breakfast – a few early mushrooms gathered on his way to work, an egg, bacon and a slice of fried bread. The milk train had gone through and the first 'stopper' was twenty minutes away. Sunlight streamed through the windows, and the signalman had already removed his jacket which was now hanging over the back of his chair. A checked duster, the signalman's badge of office, was tucked into Bob's right-hand trouser pocket and would be used to hold the highly polished levers whenever they were 'pulled off'.

Bob Hart was thirty-four years old and plump; he had the

air and manners of a much older, wiser man and his life revolved around the railway. He had a timid wife and a shrewish widowed mother-in-law who lived with them, and his happiest hours were those spent in his signal-box. He had no children and did not want any, but he did not dislike Sam Turner and on this particular morning had promised that he could bring a friend to see inside the signal-box.

'But only one,' he had warned. In his experience, boys had too many arms and legs and he had expensive and delicate instruments entrusted to his safe-keeping. He pushed the last mouthful of fried bread around the plate to soak up the egg yolk and bacon fat, then put it into his mouth with a contented sigh. It was Bob's firm belief that no man could do a good day's work without a full stomach.

He glanced at the clock and saying, 'By golly, they'll be here directly!' he pushed his breakfast things to one side to be dealt with later. Taking off his round, metal-rimmed spectacles, he gave them a quick polish with the corner of the duster and then settled them firmly back on his nose. His slightly protuberant eyes were blue and his hair was a soft brown cut short around the ears. He was, in most respects, a mild little man with no vices.

From his vantage point he spotted Sam and another boy hurrying along the station platform, deep in conversation, and as he watched he saw Arnold lumber into view and call out to them.

'Oh no!' muttered Bob to himself. 'Not Arnold – I'm not having him up here.'

Although he would never have admitted it, Bob was very nervous in Arnold's company. He found him unpredictable and the thought of such a small brain in such a large frame frightened him.

'No, no,' he repeated firmly. 'Not Arnold.'

But Sam and Eric were now climbing the steps to tap on the door and the signalman opened it to them, pretending not to see Arnold who was loitering hopefully below them.

'Good morning, Mr Hart,' chorused the two boys. Bob's opinion of boys in general rose marginally. He did like youngsters to show a little respect.

'Good morning, Sam,' he answered. 'And who's this?'

'It's Eric, sir,' said Sam. 'He's my friend at school.'

'Eric, eh? Well, pleased to meet you, Eric. Come in, both of you.'

Out of the corner of his eye, Bob saw that Arnold had now reached the bottom of the steps and before he closed the door he waved his hand with a dismissive gesture.

Sam said hesitantly, 'Arnold wanted to come up and I said I'd ask you.'

'Oh, dear me no,' replied Bob. 'Too crowded already, I'm afraid.' He called down the steps. 'Sorry, Arnold. No room for anyone else, so off you go – there's a good lad.'

Arnold hesitated, his disappointment obvious, but Bob closed the door and turned to Sam and Eric.

'Well,' he said proudly, 'this is the signal-box. Here is where it all happens – where all the important decisions are made.' He rubbed his hands together briefly. 'Let's see now, you've never seen inside a signal-box before?'

'Eric hasn't,' said Sam, 'but I saw one at our other station.'

'I see.' Bob addressed himself to Eric. 'Well, Eric, I'll tell you what's what and then if you've got any questions you can ask me.' He waved a small plump hand towards the gleaming levers. 'This is called the frame and these are the levers. Got that?'

Both boys nodded earnestly.

'Right then, what happens is this,' Bob began. 'Say there's a train at Tenterden and it wants to come through Gazedown and then on to Wittersham. Tenterden's signalman gives me a ring and asks if my section of the line is clear. That's the block system, you see: we never let a train leave one block until we know the next block is clear. That way, you don't get one train crashing into another like they often did in the old days. They worked on a time interval system then and always kept three minutes between trains. Trouble was, you could let train number one through your section and then three minutes later let train number two through. But—' he rolled his eyes expressively, 'who's to say the number one train hadn't broken down and was still on the next section of line?'

'Ker-runch!' said Eric, wide-eyed.

'Exactly,' Bob agreed solemnly. 'So these days that can't

happen. Same as signals and points. Nowadays they work together, so the signal only says a train can move on to another track when the points are set correctly. In the old days you could signal a train to move across, only to find they'd forgotten to alter the points so it couldn't. Oh no, we've got a much safer railway than our fathers had, believe me. They've worked it all out.'

He smiled at Eric. 'You going to be a railway man, then like young Sam here? He's going to be an engine-driver, or so he tells me.'

'I *am*,' Sam protested. 'It's definite.'

There was a gentle tap at the signal-box door and as they turned it opened slowly and Arnold peered in.

Bob's smile faded abruptly. 'Now you get along, Arnold!' he shouted. 'I've told you there's no room for anyone else.'

Sam and Eric exchanged looks and Sam ventured, 'Couldn't he just watch from the doorway?'

'No, he couldn't.'

Sulkily Arnold began to rattle the door handle and Bob's expression changed from irritation to alarm.

'Do you hear me, Arnold?' he cried. 'You can't come in, so you just get along. Clear off!'

He went up to the door and waved his arms threateningly until Arnold backed away down the steps, mumbling to himself.

'He shouldn't be encouraged on the station,' said Bob defensively. 'A man like that – he could do anything. He could cause damage to railway property. I've nothing against him but we all know he's not right in the head and he could do some damage; he can't be trusted.'

The boys remained silent and the signalman swallowed. 'Now where was I?' he said, his voice as normal as he could make it.

'About the signals and points,' said Sam.

'Oh, yes.' Bob took a deep breath. 'Well, the signalman at Tenterden gives me a "ting-ting" and asks me if he can send a train through. I say "yes" and then I give Wittersham a ring and clear the road with them.'

Sam nodded and Eric asked, 'Have you ever had an accident, Mr Hart, on your stretch of road?'

The signalman shook his head emphatically. 'No, I haven't and I hope to God I never do,' he said. 'Signalman's nightmare, that is. Mind you, I expect you've heard the old superstition about the rooks?'

Dutifully both boys shook their heads.

'You haven't? Well, I'm blowed!' Bob's good humour was at once restored. 'Well, they say that rooks are the ghosts of dead gangers – the men who built the railways – and they warn railwaymen of faults in the track by putting a small stone on the appropriate sleeper.'

'Rooks do?' cried Eric. 'Oo-er!' He shuddered.

'I've never heard that,' said Sam. 'Rooks are really ghosts? I'll tell Grandfather that.'

'You do that,' said Bob.

At that moment there was a shout from below the signalbox and then Arnold clattered up the steps once more in a state of obvious excitement. Bob rushed to the door to head him off but having attracted their attention, Arnold clattered down the steps again. Bob, Eric and Sam went out on to the small wooden platform to see what was happening and found Arnold pointing to the word GAZEDOWN, a look of great excitement on his face.

'I've found another one!' he told them. 'Another gee.' He stabbed his finger against the first letter of the name and said loudly, 'Gentlemen starts with a gee!'

Eric giggled and Bob snorted with disgust, but Sam leaned over and smiled. 'It is a "G", Arnold,' he explained, 'but it's not for Gentlemen, it's for Gazedown. The name of the station, Gazedown, starts with a "G" too.'

Arnold's smile widened. 'Gazedown starts with a gee two,' he repeated. 'This is a gee two?'

'Really!' muttered Bob. 'I don't know why you waste your time with him. He gives me the creeps and that's the truth.'

'Not a gee two,' said Sam, realising the way Arnold's mind was working. 'I mean, it's another "G". Oh dear – look, Amy will tell you, Arnold. You go and see Amy.'

Arnold needed no second bidding but rushed off and Bob, Sam and Eric turned their attention once more to the intricacies of the signal-box. They saw the next train through the station and out again before Bob decided they had taken up enough of his time, whereupon they departed with many thanks. The signalman watched them go and shook his head.

'Boys!' he muttered. 'Nice enough lads, I suppose, but that Arnold, he's a different kettle of fish. I must have another word with the stationmaster about him. He's getting out of hand, if you ask me, and I smell trouble.'

*

Gerald Hatherley stood at the window of his study and stared across the lawn towards the shrubbery and beyond that to the trees. He held a pair of binoculars in his hands, but was not using them. In fact, he was seeing nothing at all, for his eyes were unfocused and today he was not concerned with the various birds which made their homes in the Manor grounds: he was thinking about Lorna Betts and his heart was heavy. After the débâcle at the party, Esme had given her the sack and Gerald missed her. The whole affair had turned exceedingly sour and he did not know what to do about it.

Mrs Betts had sent them a very unpleasant letter, complaining about Lorna's condition when she arrived home after the party and suggesting that one of the guests had obviously fed the champagne to her since she would never have taken it without someone's encouragement. So obviously, Gerald surmised, Lorna had not told her mother the full story of what had taken place in the library, but he did not know the reason for this omission. Was she protecting him or was she unable to remember what had happened? Did she even know he had seduced her? He wanted to believe that she did know and that she cared for him enough to remain silent. Or, better still, had enjoyed it so much that she would welcome the opportunity to repeat the experience. The problem was how to ascertain the exact situation now that Lorna was no longer employed at Bates Manor.

He dared not send her a message, for who could he trust? Not Clara, he decided. She had been offered – and had promptly accepted – Lorna's position as housemaid-cum-parlourmaid. Izzie, then? No, she was a foolish girl and would be sure to tell someone that he was contacting Lorna. Sighing heavily, he raised the binoculars to his eyes and

189

lowered them almost immediately. Birds had ceased to interest him since the night of the party. For Gerald it had not been the sordid seduction of a servant, but a wonderful experience to be cherished deep in his heart. He could recall so clearly the sight, feel and smell of Lorna's yielding body. For the first time for many years he had experienced the shared joys of sexual excitement and release and he was deeply grateful to Lorna. He wanted her to know how much it had meant to him to give and receive so rapturously; to know that he was not a failure as a man in spite of Esme's protestations to the contrary. After many years of suppressed yearnings he had finally succeeded as a lover and his self-confidence was renewed. Even if Lorna never again surrendered herself to him, he wanted to reward her for that one glorious occasion.

In his wildest imaginings he set her up in a little love-nest – he could easily afford to do so – and visited her regularly, showering her with presents and revelling in that warm young body which she offered so generously. Because Lorna had enjoyed it! That, for Gerald, was the icing on the cake. She had had a young man, a good-looking young man, but she had never allowed *him* what she had allowed Gerald Hatherley, who was plain, balding and middle-aged! And she had cried aloud with the pleasure he had given her. Yes, he was a success as a man where Lorna Betts was concerned, he felt sure of that. But was it just the champagne? Would it ever be the same again? Would she be prepared to even try?

'Oh Lorna! Lorna!' he whispered. 'I'm in love with you, Lorna Betts. Perhaps I'm mad, foolish, ridiculous, but I can't help myself. Oh, my lovely, my sweet Lorna, what am I going to do about you?'

Turning from the window, he threw the binoculars into the nearest armchair and began to pace up and down the study. If only Esme would leave him or even die, but it seemed unlikely that she would do either. How he hated her beautiful, untouchable body. How he loathed her cold eyes and hard voice. Esme had everything in life while the girl had nothing, but Lorna was warm and natural and Gerald was infatuated – no, he amended hastily – he was in love with her.

'I'm forty-two years old,' he reminded himself, 'and God willing, I shall live another thirty years. But not if I stay with Esme for she will shrivel me into old age before my time.'

He smiled, vaguely pleased with the notion. Yes, Esme would shrivel him! Lorna would fulfil him and give him back all those lost years.

'Oh Lorna!' he whispered in an agony of frustration and despair. 'What am I going to do?'

*

Amy, darning Sam's socks, waited until he had gone to bed before approaching her father on the subject of her work for Ralph Allan. True to his promise, Elliot had discussed the possibility of commissioning the biography and Ralph, after some initial reluctance, had agreed to the idea. Within days the wheels had been set in motion and Elliot's editorial director had given his approval to the scheme. However, nothing had been put in writing yet because Ralph did not wish to commit himself unless Amy was able to put in extra time on the project. He had no wish to employ anyone else as his assistant and certainly did not want to be faced with a fixed date for completion of the manuscript if he was going to have to work unaided.

Now Amy explained the proposal to her father, who listened attentively until she had finished.

'They must think very highly of you,' he said slowly, 'and I can see it's an opportunity that doesn't come every day of the week. The trouble is, Amy, how will we manage without you? We can't leave your grandfather alone all day and there's all the cooking and cleaning . . .'

'I've thought of that,' said Amy, 'and I could go round there in the morning for an hour or two and then again in the evenings after I've washed up the tea-things – about 6.30. Sam's old enough now to put himself to bed.'

Her father looked doubtful. 'I don't know about evenings,' he said. 'Just you and Mr Allan? People might talk.'

'But Papa, how could they?' she protested. 'It would be a business arrangement, not a social visit. And the money

191

would be very useful. I could give you something for my keep and maybe save a little.'

'It's still not proper, is it?' he said. 'The two of you together in that lonely place?'

'But Papa, you've met Ralph and you know he is honest — and surely you trust *me*? How could you worry about that side of it? I'm not a child.'

Her father was silent — not because he was considering Ralph and Amy, as she imagined, but because he was wondering about his decision not to allow Ellen back. If his wife had resumed her 'rightful' place in the family, Amy would be able to go to The Lodge during the daytime and no tongues could wag. Perhaps, he thought for the hundredth time, he had been wrong to listen to his father's arguments, although the old man was right in one respect: Ellen's infidelity had certainly brought about his mother's death. And how would he explain her sudden appearance in Gazedown with the child? Also, he liked to think that what remained of the family was happy and contented — except, of course, that poor Amy was wasting her undoubted talents. Not that there was anything out of the ordinary about her predicament, for a great many women still died in childbirth and it always fell to the lot of the eldest unmarried daughter to take her mother's place in the home.

Amy, watching him anxiously, finally broke the long silence.

'I've been thinking about Grandfather,' she said. 'Do you think we could afford to ask the new doctor to visit him? Maybe we shouldn't let him lie in bed all day, the way he does. Oh, I know he's happy enough, but is there really anything wrong with him, Papa? If he would just get up for a few hours after dinner,' she suggested, 'then I could spend the afternoon at The Lodge instead of the evenings. Grandfather would be around when Sam comes home, to give him a bit of bread and jam until I get back and cook the tea. I don't want to be unkind, Papa, but I would so much like to take on this work if I possibly can.'

'I know, Amy,' he said, 'and I would like you to do it, but I don't think you should rush into these things.'

'Papa,' cried Amy, 'Ralph wants an answer *now* because

192

Elliot is waiting to draw up the contract. Can't I tell him "yes"? Then if Grandfather can't – or won't – get up, I'll go round in the evenings and I simply don't care about the wagging tongues, but I must give them a firm answer. It's business, Papa, and they won't wait for ever.'

Her father frowned unhappily. '*You* may not care about the gossip, but I do. I have a responsible position to maintain in Gazedown and it won't look good if the Company gets to hear that my daughter is the subject of unpleasant gossip.'

'But they won't gossip!' cried Amy. 'Who will know, for a start?'

Wearily her father shook his head. 'Everyone will know before the first week is out – you know that as well as I do.'

Amy's eyes flashed angrily. 'Well, I shall know I have nothing to be ashamed of!'

'Some folk won't want to believe that, Amy. People love a bit of scandal; it's human nature.'

She jumped to her feet and threw down the socks. 'Well, then, damn them all!' she cried. 'And damn Gazedown!'

'*Amy!*'

Two spots of colour burned in her cheeks as she rushed on. 'This is my chance, Papa, and I'm going to take it,' she cried. 'I've looked after you all for the past four years without a word of complaint. I don't think you even knew what it meant to me to lose that college place. Now this is my *second* chance – perhaps my last. I lost the first one when Mama left us and I'm not going to lose this one.'

Thomas Turner stared at his daughter in dismay. It was not at all like her to make so much fuss and it made him feel uneasy.

'It's all very well saying you're going to do it,' he began, 'but do be sensible, Amy.'

'No!' cried Amy. 'I don't want to be sensible. I don't want to stay in my quiet little rut while life goes by. I think I've done my duty by you all and it's not as though I'm planning to run off and leave you.' Like your wife did, she thought bitterly. 'I just want a chance to use my brain. Everyone told me I was clever when I was at school; you used to boast about me then. So if I've got ability, why shouldn't I make some use of it? You ought to be encouraging me, Papa.'

'But do be sensible, Amy—'

Amy sucked in her breath sharply and her voice rose. 'Don't keep telling me to be sensible, Papa. I don't want to be sensible, I want to be selfish for a change. What happens to me when you don't need me? When Grandfather is dead and Sam grown up and left home? It will be too late then for me to try to break away. I want to go to London. Or Paris. Or even Rome! Can't you understand, Papa? I want a different kind of life.'

Her father's face hardened. 'A different kind of life? What's that supposed to mean? What's wrong with your life here? You've a roof over your head and shoes to your feet and you come and go as you please. You've never complained before.'

Amy swallowed. She had not meant to say so much, but the words had tumbled out and it was too late now to take them back. She was committed.

'I'm not complaining now,' she said. 'All I'm saying is that if I sit back and do nothing for the next ten years, I shall never be able to make anything of my life. I'll stay in Gazedown—'

'What's wrong with Gazedown?' her father demanded. 'Not good enough for you? Is that it?'

Amy's eyes flashed. 'No, that *isn't* it! You're twisting my words, Papa, you know you are. Look, there is a whole world outside Gazedown and I'd like to know more about it.'

'What about your friends in Gazedown?'

'I'll make new friends.'

'London's a big city.'

'I'd like to see it for myself.'

'I don't want you to go.'

'Why not?'

Thomas stared at the stranger who had once been his daughter . . . his reliable, sensible daughter.

'If your mother could hear you now . . .' he began.

Amy's eyes flashed anew. 'If she hadn't walked out on us, I wouldn't *be* here now,' she snapped. 'I'd be a fully qualified teacher earning my own living. I might be in London; I'd certainly be making a new life for myself. It's her fault I'm having to beg for this chance, so don't you dare bring her into it!' Her face was flushed and her hands were clenched. 'I deserve my chance,' she repeated doggedly, 'and I mean to take it. I shall ask the doctor to call on Grandfather with or without your permission, and I shall pay for it out of my Friday stall money. If the doctor says he can get up, I'll go to The Lodge in the afternoons. If he doesn't, I shall go in the evenings.'

She sat down abruptly and snatched up her darning. The clock ticked loudly in the brittle silence and she felt her heart racing. For a long time her father said nothing and Amy could not bring herself to glance up at him. Never before in her whole life had she spoken to him like that. She had never spoken to anyone with such passion and she was shocked by her own temerity. Her hands shook as she tried to guide the needle through the matted wool of the heel.

The silence lengthened uncomfortably and Amy wished she had not spoken so harshly of her mother. She had not wanted to hurt him.

Suddenly her father stood up and went outside into the garden. When he came back some minutes later he sat down heavily, picked up his newspaper and rustled it irritably.

'I'll call in the doctor first thing in the morning,' he said at last.

Amy resisted the impulse to throw herself at his feet; instead she glanced up and said quietly, 'Thank you, Papa.'

Relief flooded her whole being and she drew in her breath in a long sigh. She was going to have her chance.

*

Resentment showed in every toss of Lorna Betts' pretty blonde head and every movement of her plump body as she measured sugar into pounds in the brass scale pan and carefully tipped it into sugar bags made of coarse blue paper. She hated working in the shop and she hated being under her mother's eye from dawn until dusk. She had no freedom and no wages. Mrs Betts, furious at her daughter's dismissal from Bates Manor, would give her only a token payment for her labours in the shop – a few shillings that amounted to less than pocket money. Also the work was boring in the extreme – she was sure her mother saved her the most unpleasant tasks – sweeping out the stock-room, checking the incoming deliveries, weighing up currants, dusting the shelves and rearranging the shop window. She was not even allowed to serve in the shop in case curious customers tried to wheedle out of her the sordid details of 'that night'.

Lorna had told her mother several lies the morning after the party when she was again able to speak coherently. In the cold light of day, she had decided not to reveal to anyone what had actually taken place in the library. Her story, finally elicited from her by a sound slapping, was that, one of the guests had insisted that she accompany him upstairs to the library and had then fed her glasses of champagne. He had kissed her mouth and fondled her breasts and then left her in order to return to the celebrations below. Lorna insisted that she did not know the name of this unscrupulous beast and would not recognise him again if she saw him. Then, according to her story, Gerald Hatherley had discovered her in a state of inebriation and had kindly brought her home. He had not stayed to discuss the matter with Mrs Betts because, obviously, he could not be away from his guests for too long.

Mrs Betts had found the story unconvincing and the next morning had intended to escort her daughter back to the Manor to demand an explanation from the Hatherleys, but a letter had then arrived from Esme dismissing Lorna from her employ without a reference. Lorna then refused to go with her mother to the Manor, so Mrs Betts had gone alone and tackled Gerald and Esme face to face, demanding to know the name of the scoundrel who had brought about Lorna's downfall. To her dismay, Esme (who did most of the talking) declared that to her knowledge no one had taken advantage of the girl, that the story was a pack of lies to cover the fact that Lorna had helped herself to the champagne. Esme then added that if Mrs Betts pursued the matter, she herself would report Lorna's *theft* of the champagne to the local police sergeant.

Baffled and temporarily defeated, Mrs Betts had been forced to withdraw, but she had made it clear to Lorna on her return home that she was far from satisfied and that she would find out the truth if it killed her. Lorna hoped that it would. In the clear light of the following day she had wondered what to do for the best, because she remembered quite clearly what had really happened and could not bring herself to regret a single moment of it.

As she scooped yet more sugar into the scale pan, she decided that somehow she must go to see her sister in Robertsbridge. She would tell her the whole story and ask her advice. Janet would not betray her, she was sure of that, because at the time of Janet's own fall from grace Lorna had taken her side against their mother at the cost of more than one box round the ears. Janet's baby was due in a few months' time and Mrs Betts would be going over to 'lend a hand' immediately it arrived; meanwhile she was visiting her daughter about once a week. Lorna felt it would be prudent to see Janet before her mother did and suddenly she made up her mind to slip away from the sugar while her mother was occupied with a customer and travel to Robertsbridge on the next train.

*

Janet had married a man called Daniel Hubbard who worked in a draper's shop and they lived in the small attic flat over the premises. This comprised a bedroom and a kitchen-cum-living room, but although the accommodation was rather cramped it had two advantages – the rent was very low and Daniel was never late for work.

When Lorna arrived unannounced at the kitchen door Janet was slumped in one chair with her feet propped on another one. She was already very large and the midwife had hinted at twins, but there was no history of them on either side of the family so Janet had chosen to ignore the possibility.

'Who is it?' she called, reluctant to get to her feet.

'Me, Lorna.'

'Lorna? Good God!'

Janet knew her sister well enough to be sure that she would not arrive in Robertsbridge unexpectedly unless something was wrong. Lowering her feet carefully to the ground, she called, 'It's not Ma, is it? Not another fall?'

'No!'

197

'Come in then, it's not locked.'

Lorna let herself into the room and after a brief greeting, the two girls eyed each other warily.

'Strewth!' exclaimed Lorna. 'You look like a blooming whale!'

'Thank's very much!' said Janet. 'I'm beginning to feel like one. Lord knows what I shall look like by January. But pull up that stool for my feet and you can have the chair!' She watched as Lorna settled herself on the rickety chair and then said, 'I'll be glad when it's all over!'

'Mm.' Lorna was non-committal, awed by her sister's bulk and somewhat slovenly appearance. A year earlier she had been trim and vivacious and had boasted *two* suitors, Daniel and the Gazedown man.

'How's Daniel?' she asked.

'Daniel?' Janet snorted. 'He's fine. It's me that's carrying the baby, not him.'

'Don't you love him any more?' Lorna asked wistfully.

''Course I do. What's that got to do with it?'

'I don't know. You look so . . .' she faltered.

'So awful?' Janet pushed back a stray lock of hair. 'So will you when you're expecting. But you haven't come here just to tell me how awful I look.'

'I'm sorry. I didn't mean . . .'

'I know you didn't.' Janet's eyes narrowed. 'There's nothing wrong, is there, between you and Don? Like this, I mean.' She patted her swollen abdomen.

'Don?' echoed Lorna. 'No, I almost wish there was. The truth is that we've sort of parted. He wanted to and I wouldn't – you know how it is.'

Janet laughed ruefully. 'I know how it was when Daniel wanted to and I *would*!' It's a blooming rush up the aisle, that's how it is, and then months of looking like a pudding.' She sighed and then asked, 'Does Ma know you're here?'

Lorna shook her head.

'Oh dear!' said Janet. 'You'd better start at the beginning – or do you want a cup of tea?'

'No, thanks. I'll have to catch the next train back. There'll be hell to pay when she finds I've gone.' She took a deep breath. 'It's like this . . .'

198

Lorna then launched into a detailed account of what had happened on the night of the ball and Janet listened in growing astonishment.

'What I really want to know,' said Lorna at the end of the recital, 'is . . . could I be like you? I mean, is what we did what you and Daniel did? Exactly, I mean?'

'*Exactly*,' said Janet, her voice heavy with meaning.

'Oh Lord!'

The two sisters stared helplessly at each other.

'I don't think I could bear it,' said Lorna.

'You won't have much choice,' Janet remarked tartly.

'Oh Lord!' she smiled faintly. 'The funny thing is that I'm not mad at him. Not a bit. He's a funny old codger, I know, but there's something rather sweet about him.'

'Sweet!' cried Janet. 'Him?'

Lorna nodded. 'Him,' she said. 'I know it sounds daft but he was like a little kid, all excited and then so grateful. He was crying.'

Janet was not impressed. 'He wasn't playing a violin as well, was he?' she asked. 'Honestly, Lorna, you must be mad!'

'You did it with Daniel.'

'Yes, but he's my own age and I knew we could get married if anything went wrong, which it did. Your old chap's not going to marry you, is he?'

'He's not old,' said Lorna crossly. 'At least, not really old.'

'Well,' said Janet, 'all I can say is we must hope for the best. Hope nothing happened. I mean, hope you're *not* going to have a baby. You haven't missed your monthlies?'

'No. There's another week yet.'

'Well, pray like mad, Lorna – and for Pete's sake don't let him do it again. Do you hear me? Whatever he says, whatever he promises you, don't do it again. Once, you just might get away with it. Twice, I doubt it.' She looked at her sister curiously. 'Don't you wish it was Don who'd done it?'

'Not really.'

Suddenly Janet clapped her hands. 'I've got it!' she cried. 'Lorna Betts, your sister is a genius! Listen, if you find you *are* going to have a baby, all you have to do is make up your quarrel with Don and let *him* do it.'

'But . . . ?' Lorna looked at her blankly.

'Because then, after you've done it with Don, you say, "Oh dear, I'm going to have a baby," and Don marries you because he thinks the baby's his. He'll never know — and you do like him, don't you?'

'Of course I do.'

'You sound a bit unsure.'

'Well, I do, but — oh Janet, I couldn't do that. It wouldn't be fair.'

'But Don would never know unless you were daft enough to tell him.'

'Not unfair to Don,' said Lorna. 'I meant it wouldn't be fair to Gerald.'

Janet's mouth dropped open with shock. 'For God's sake, Lorna, you wouldn't tell *him?*'

Lorna looked unhappy. 'I don't know. I don't know what I'd do. He'd be so excited.'

'Lorna!' shouted Janet. 'I think I'm hearing things! Now you listen to me. You do not tell Gerald Hatherley if you're expecting a baby, because he can't marry you and if word gets round, neither will anyone else! Use your head, for heaven's sake. Don will marry you if he thinks it's his and then you'll all live happily ever after.'

'I don't know . . .' began Lorna.

Janet looked at her helplessly, then uttered a gasp of triumph. 'I've an even better idea!' she said. 'You go round and make up with Don and let him do it *before* you know if you're in the family way. Then you won't know whose baby it is, so you needn't feel guilty or sorry for old what-not up at the Manor.'

Lorna's eyes gleamed briefly, then she shook her head.

'But if I'm not having Gerald's baby,' she said, 'why go and let myself in for Don's when I don't need to marry anyone?'

There was a long silence as the logic of this registered with Janet.

'And anyway,' Lorna continued, 'Don's taken up with the stationmaster's daughter. She's a bit older than him and a bit toffee-nosed, but she's a nice enough girl.'

'Is she likely to be letting him have his oats?' asked Janet.

Lorna pursed her lips thoughtfully. 'I can't imagine it,' she said at last. 'But they might. She might be desperate – she's twenty, if she's a day.'

'Well, you'll have to win him back, and quick. Go round there, be all sorry and lovey-dovey. You can if you put your mind to it.'

'I don't know what to do,' said Lorna, 'I really don't.' She sighed. 'You know what I'd really like to do? I'd like to march up to that old cow, Esme Hatherley, and say, "I'm having your husband's baby." I'd just like to see the look on her face! Do you know, she never lets him touch her? He told me so. Never! That's why they've never had a family. I think it's downright cruel.'

Janet groaned. 'I never thought I'd hear a sister of mine talking so daft,' she declared. 'Never mind him and never mind her. You just do what's best for *you*, Lorna Betts. And if you take my advice, you'll do it before next week!'

Chapter Twelve

Breakfast at Bates Manor on the days when Gerald was not going up to London was a formal affair, with the parlour-maid in attendance. Gerald sat at one end of the table and Esme sat about a yard away, further down the table on his right-hand side. On this particular morning – ten days after Esme's birthday – they sat in silence, ignoring each other. Clara presided over the teapot and over the range of dishes set out on the sideboard – bacon, scrambled eggs, kidneys, porridge and stewed prunes. There was always toast, butter, home-made marmalade and cherry jam.

Gerald chewed his way mournfully through a slice of toast and marmalade while Esme toyed with the bacon and scrambled eggs she had asked for.

'More tea, Clara, please,' she ordered suddenly. 'A fresh pot.'

'But, ma'am, I've only just—' Clara recollected herself quickly. 'A fresh pot of tea? Certainly, ma'am.' She seized the teapot which was still half-full of freshly made tea and hurried out of the room, closing the door carefully behind her.

'I like that girl,' said Esme, breaking the long silence. 'She's learning quickly. Much better than that dreadful Betts girl, don't you think, Gerald?'

Gerald continued to stare at the tablecloth immediately beyond his plate and said, 'I really couldn't say. The household staff are your province, Esme.'

'Then I can assure you she is,' she told him. 'Altogether

quicker, more polite and knows her place. She's very good with my hair, too. The Betts girl was so heavy-handed.'

'Was she?'

Esme's eyes narrowed as her husband continued to avoid her eyes. 'Yes, she was,' she said sharply. 'The only thing that bothers me about Clara is her background. Somewhere she has a rather unpleasant father from whom she has run away – a brute, from what I hear. I should not care to deal with him, if he should ever come looking for his daughter.'

'I'm sure you would be more than a match for him, Esme,' said Gerald, his tone flat and unprovocative.

'What does that mean exactly, Gerald?' she demanded.

He shrugged. 'Exactly what it says, dear heart. A few well-chosen phrases from you should send him off with his tail between his legs.'

'If that is supposed to be a compliment, Gerald, I don't care for it.'

'Please yourself, Esme. You always do.'

'I have to,' she said spitefully. 'No one else does.'

Finally Gerald glanced up at her. 'You might consider young Mr Allan,' he suggested. 'He seems very *pliable*.'

Esme's face crimsoned. She had not been aware that her husband had noticed her attempts to woo the young writer, although she had intended that he should.

'At least I don't interfere with the servants!' she cried.

'Not yet,' he agreed.

Esme drew a deep breath. 'You really are quite despicable, Gerald,' she told him.

'Am I, Esme?'

His tone continued unruffled, almost indifferent, while Esme was becoming agitated. That would not do at all. Normally it was Esme goading Gerald; now he was goading her.

She began to breathe in and out deeply, carefully, in an effort to regain her composure. Gerald was in a strange mood and at the back of her mind warning bells rang. She knew she ought to step warily, but some demon within her persisted in forcing a confrontation.

'This so-called marriage of ours is a sham,' she stated suddenly.

'I believe it always has been,' he answered calmly. 'Perhaps you had not noticed before?'

'You can't pretend you love me, Gerald.'

'No, I'm afraid I can't.'

The words shocked her. She had known this for years and had not cared, but she had never asked him directly and he had never admitted it. Now he looked up at her and said sadly, 'It's mutual, I fear, and will never be otherwise. Why talk about it?'

She stared at him and swallowed the sudden lump in her throat, thinking: Why is the truth — this particular truth — so painful? She did not love him and never had, so how could she expect him to love her? The relationship was hollow, devoid of joy and understanding, empty even of caring. Their marriage was merely one long pretence, a day-to-day charade — he playing the role of husband, she that of wife, but both totally blind to the other's needs. They had wealth, status, health, they were envied by many and yet in reality theirs was a bleak loveless existence, in which she laughed at his tragedies and he gloated over her failures.

Suddenly overwhelmed by the magnitude of their personal disaster, Esme covered her face with her hands so that Gerald should not see the icy fear that gripped her. What have we done, she wondered? How has it happened? She dared not ask who was to blame. She was appalled to feel a sudden rush of scalding tears and could not allow her husband to witness — and personally enjoy — this unexpected display of weakness. Jumping up from the table, she ran out of the room, almost colliding with Clara who was returning with the fresh pot of tea she had asked for.

Upstairs in her dressing-room, Esme fought to keep back the flood of tears that threatened to overwhelm her and when she heard a tap at the door, she snatched up a clean handkerchief and covered her eyes. It was Clara who came into the room unbidden, her expression full of concern.

'Ma'am?' she said softly. 'I thought you looked a bit upset and might need me.'

'Need you?' The voice, shaky and thin, shocked Clara. 'Need you? No, I don't *need* anybody.' She began to tremble and the tears ran down her cheeks as she struggled to repeat that she needed no one – no one at all.

'We all need someone, ma'am,' said Clara. 'Someone to turn to when things go wrong; that's only human. Would you like me to brush your hair, ma'am? That's what I used to do for my ma when she was feeling a bit low. Very soothing, it is.'

'No, I don't need . . .' sobbed Esme. 'I don't—'

To her dismay the trembling was spreading to her limbs and she could hear her teeth chattering. She was becoming hysterical and wanted to be alone, but this wretched girl would not leave her. Instead, Clara calmly searched among the bottles and phials on the dressing-table until she found the sal volatile; she handed this to Esme, who clutched at it desperately and unscrewed the top with feverish haste.

'You breathe in a bit of that, ma'am,' said Clara, 'while I brush your hair. I'll pin it up again afterwards. You'll be surprised how much better you'll feel in a few moments.'

With deft movements Clara unpinned Esme's long fair hair and began to brush it with smooth even strokes. It was, as she had promised, extremely soothing: each brush-stroke like a caress. Esme inhaled the sal volatile and at once her head cleared, and the terrible panic began to fade.

She had been so right to take on this girl in Lorna's place, she thought, and the fact that she had made a wise decision restored a little of her shattered confidence.

Once her equilibrium had been recovered Esme was able to lean back and close her eyes and turn her thoughts to the more pressing question of Ralph Allan. He was the most probable source of affection, she felt. He had kissed her and she knew he had wanted her body. In his eyes she was desirable and for that reason she could not let him slip away. If only that stupid Turner girl from the station had not come blundering into the bedroom on the night of the party, they would have become lovers. And if only that had happened Ralph Allan would be hers, she told herself, because she knew how to please a man. He could stay on at The Lodge and they would be everything to each other. He needed love and affection, and so did she; they would make each other happy, she was sure of it. If she could make Ralph fall in love with her, then the rest of her life would be tolerable.

Clara, watching her mistress in the mirror, was busy with her own plans as her hands wielded Esme's hairbrush. She had decided that a permanent place in the Hatherley household was what she wanted. Parlourmaid and *confidante* – that is how she saw herself. Admittedly, she did not like the woman whose hair she brushed so tenderly; in her eyes, Esme Hatherley was a spoilt brat whom she knew could be a dangerous enemy – the speed with which Lorna had left the household was proof of that. However, Clara did not intend to earn Esme's enmity – quite the opposite, in fact. She meant to become indispensable to the mistress of Bates Manor because that way power lay. Clara had given her future a great deal of thought and had come to several conclusions. First and foremost was her decision not to marry. What she knew of men and their habits did not inspire her, nor did she have any maternal yearnings. She wanted to live in a grand house and eat good food and wear clean clothes. Above all, she wanted security – to know that she had a roof over her head – and was prepared to work hard and scheme hard to achieve her ambition. Yes, she thought gleefully, the position of parlourmaid and *confidante* would suit her very well. Clara Midden had moved into Bates Manor and she was determined that no one would ever move her out again.

*

The evening of that same day found Amy and Mary Leckie deep in conversation in the farmhouse kitchen. Father and son had gone down to The Harrow for a mug or two of beer and a game of shove-ha'penny. Mary, a pair of ancient spectacles perched on her nose, was labelling the results of the previous day's honey extraction, with much licking of the pencil. A row of twenty-three jars of honey awaited their respective labels.

'So,' Amy concluded breathlessly, 'tomorrow is the big day! Doctor Brown is coming at eleven and if he is as forceful as everyone says, we just might have Grandfather on his feet again.'

206

Mary grinned. 'And about time too, if you ask me! And then you'll be a working woman, a researcher. It sounds too good to be true, but I'll keep my fingers crossed for you.'

'Oh, Mary!' said Amy, 'if it all goes wrong, I think I shall die!'

'You said just now that you'll do it anyway.'

'I know I did,' said Amy. 'I told Papa that, too, but I'm not terribly sure I could go through with it. To be gossiped about, I mean. I wouldn't mind for myself, but Papa has been through so much in the past few years.'

She hesitated, aware of Mary's curiosity with regard to her past life, about which Amy had told her very little.

'When my mother left us, Papa had a lot of troubles,' she said carefully. 'He was confused and ill and his work suffered.'

'Understandably,' said Mary kindly.

Amy nodded. 'And now he has this chance to make good at Gazedown,' she went on. 'I wouldn't want to be the one who spoils it for him. Gossip about me would reflect on him — he's quite right about that and I don't think I could be that selfish.'

Mary peered at her over the spectacles. 'You'll have to try, then, Amy,' she told her. 'Everyone else is being selfish. Look at your Grandfather — lazy old devil!'

'Until tomorrow!' laughed Amy.

'You hope!'

'I don't only hope, I pray!' said Amy. 'God must be getting bored with the same old prayer floating up from my bedroom.'

Mary stuck on another label and said, 'You can take a jar of this.'

'Thank you,' said Amy, 'but you must let me pay you.'

'A present from me to you.'

'But, Mary—'

'No buts. If I can't give my future daughter-in-law a jar of honey . . .' She paused, taking a sly look at the startled expression on Amy's face. 'Take no notice of me,' she laughed. 'I'm only teasing. But that's not to say I wouldn't be pleased if you and Don . . . oh, Amy, you do *like* him, don't you?'

'Of course I do,' Amy stammered.

'I mean, you won't be so wrapped up in your important work that you don't have time for "stepping out"?'

Amy managed what she hoped was a little laugh. 'Of course not. And I do like Don very much.'

Mary leaned forward, her expression earnest.

'He's very keen on you,' she said, 'I can tell that. I was so pleased when he broke up with that Betts girl. I don't like the mother, that's the truth of it. Very wicked tongue, that Mrs Betts – and that ridiculous sun-bonnet! Not to mention her Janet, who's no better than she should be – baby due before long, so I hear. No, I reckon you and Don would make a real go of things. I know he's got faults, Amy, but so have we all. No respect for his elders and won't change his socks, but at heart he's a good lad and he works hard. And you and me – well, we get along fine. I wouldn't interfere I swear, not like some mothers-in-law. What do you say, Amy? What are you laughing at?'

Amy was still laughing when the door opened and the menfolk came clattering into the room with the collie sneaking in behind them. Jim sent the dog out again and closed the door.

Greetings were exchanged and Jim put a handful of coins on the table. 'Sold three rabbits,' he said. 'Put it in the roof fund, Mary.'

Don explained to Amy that the tiled roof immediately over his bedroom was beginning to leak and would soon have to be repaired.

'And a pricey old job that'll be,' added Jim. 'So we're saving up for it. All contributions gratefully received!'

He threw himself into a chair but Don remained standing. 'If you're off now, Amy,' he said, 'I'll walk you home.'

Before she could answer Jim said, 'Of course she's not off now, Don. Don't be so cheeky!' He turned to Amy. 'You stay as long as you like, lass. Take no notice of him. He's got no manners, no charm.'

''Course he's got charm,' declared Mary. 'He just keeps it for the cows and pigs. I've heard him with those cows – talk about buttering them up!' She stuck on another label and went on, 'Amy's just been telling me about her new job –

an official job with proper wages and everything. Assistant researcher, that's what she is. You tell them, Amy.'

Willingly, Amy launched into an account of her change in fortunes and Don and Jim listened attentively.

'Well,' said Jim when she had finished, 'sounds very high-flown to me. You *are* going up in the world, Amy Turner, and good luck to you. Don't forget all your old friends, when you're famous, will you?'

They all laughed as Amy protested, 'It's only for a few months, maybe a year at the most, and it won't be me that's famous, it will be Ralph Allan. At least, I hope he will be if that's what he wants. If the book's a success I suppose he might be a bit famous, but I don't really know much about it.'

However, Don refused to be impressed. 'It sounds stuffy old work to me,' he said, 'fishing into someone's bills and letters. I don't know what you see in it.'

'But it's not stuffy,' Amy told him eagerly. 'It's exciting in a way that I can't really explain. I don't think even Ralph understands how I feel about it. It's like . . .' She searched for a way to explain how she felt about Nigel Stanisbrooke.

'It's like bringing the man back to life again. All that he did when he was alive, all his thoughts and hopes and fears . . . they don't matter any more — until we read about him. Then it all comes back — all of his life — giving him a chance to be known and understood all over again. It's as though—'

Don held up his hand, grinning. 'As I said before, Amy, if you're off now I'll walk you home.'

'Don Leckie!' she cried, exasperated. 'You've got no soul!' But she got to her feet, smiling. 'I can see you won't be rushing to the bookshops,' she said, winking at Mary. 'I'll work on him,' she promised. 'I might even convert him.'

'Stranger things have happened,' agreed Mary. 'I don't know where we went wrong with him — he's nothing but a lout.'

Don was unperturbed by his mother's words. 'I'm a nice lout, though,' he said. 'A lovable and handsome lout!'

'You're just a lout,' said Jim, grinning at his son. 'Get out of here. And Amy — you pop in any time, lass. You're always welcome.'

Mary saw them to the door. 'And good luck for tomorrow when the doctor comes,' she said. 'I'd like to be a fly on the wall!'

The door closed behind them and Amy and Don walked in silence for a few minutes; then Amy stumbled slightly and Don put an arm round her. When they were out of sight of the farmhouse, he pulled her gently round to face him and kissed her nose.

'I've missed you,' he said. 'You haven't been round lately.'

'I've been too busy,' she lied. The truth was that she had been reluctant to risk a disappointment, unable to believe that Don and Lorna would not soon be reconciled after their lovers' tiff.

He kissed her again, putting his arms around her and holding her close. 'Do you think I'm a lout?' he asked.

'No, of course not!' she said. 'That was only in fun – and anyway, I didn't say it. It was your mother.'

'I don't really think the work sounds stuffy. I'm just jealous.'

'Of me?' gasped Amy, 'but, Don—'

'Not of you, you cuckoo! Of *him!* You and Ralph Allan cooped up together for hours on end. I told you before, it's not decent.' He kissed her mouth, a long slow kiss.

Amy gave herself up to the luxury of his caress, but when it ended she protested. 'Don! I can't think straight when you're kissing me like that.'

'That's the idea,' he told her.

'But I need to think,' she told him. 'I need to convince you Ralph Allan and I are nothing more than friends – well,' she amended, 'perhaps close friends, but not in a romantic way and no matter how many hours we spend at The Lodge, we will still be no more than two close friends working together. You'll have to trust me, Don.'

He slipped an arm round her waist and they walked into the lane in the direction of the station. Suddenly he said, 'Lorna came up to the cowshed this afternoon, just as I finished milking. She wanted to put things right between us.'

Amy's heart skipped a beat but she said nothing, trying to hide her dismay and glad of the darkness. It was no more than she had expected, she told herself.

210

'I told her I was seeing you now,' he said. 'I said we were courting.'

'Courting!' Amy stopped abruptly, startled. '*Are* we courting, Don? I mean, well it's a bit sudden, isn't it? Courting sounds so serious.'

Don said, 'I'm courting. Aren't you?'

'I suppose so.' She laughed nervously. 'Yes, I suppose we are.'

'You are a strange girl, Amy.'

She opened her mouth to say that Ralph Allan shared his opinion, but then thought better of it.

'I'm courting you, Amy Turner,' he said, 'and it is serious. Are you serious?'

'Yes, I am.'

'That's what I told Lorna.' He seemed relieved. 'She was in a funny sort of mood. I've never seen her like that before, sort of . . . amorous – I think that's the word. She wanted to do all the things lovers do, that she would never agree to do before. I couldn't make her out at all. When I said I wasn't interested any more, she got all upset and cried.'

Amy felt terrible. Sorry for the girl's humiliation but glad, for her own peace of mind, that Don had refused Lorna's advances. She began to wonder exactly what it was that Don had wanted the other girl to do and whether he would want *her* to do it – and whether she, too, would be reluctant. Courting, she concluded uneasily, was not as easy as it sounded.

'Lorna has lost her job at the Manor,' she volunteered. 'I expect she's feeling upset about that.'

'So I heard. Funny do, that. I couldn't make it out.'

'Nor could we. Clara Midden's got her job now.'

He nodded, then laughed. 'Why are we talking about all these other people?' he asked. 'We should be talking about us – now that we've agreed we're courting. I suppose you'll be inviting me to meet your father?'

Amy was amused. 'But you've already met him.'

'Not as a prospective son-in-law.'

His words made her uneasy. It was all happening so fast, she thought, feeling vulnerable and unprepared. Did she actually want to marry Don Leckie? True, she had admired him from afar and had thought about him in a romantic way ever since their first meeting, but now that her dream was about to become a reality, she was not so sure. He was younger than her and he did seem rather immature . . .

'A penny for them,' he said.

She hoped desperately that she did not sound as guilty as she felt. 'I don't know what I'm thinking,' she hedged clumsily.

Did she really want to take Don home to her family as her prospective husband? Once she had done so, she would feel committed. Mary and Jim would be pleased and everyone would congratulate them – and what about her work with Ralph? Would that have to stop?

'Think about me, then,' suggested Don.

The moon was very bright as he led her into the shade of a large sycamore tree where they could not easily be seen if anyone should pass by. Don kissed her again, with his left hand held firmly behind her head. His right hand began gently to explore her back, moving up across her shoulders and then down to her waist and below, then sliding up to fondle her breast. The left hand came down, too, and Amy was speechless, astonished at how easily it had happened. New sensations swept through her as his fingers explored her body through the thin stuff of her bodice.

'Oh Don, please!' she begged desperately, moving out of reach and holding out her hands to ward him off. 'I don't mean I don't like it, I do. So much, I can't tell you. But it's all happening so fast.' Her voice shook. Was this what Don had wanted from Lorna, she wondered frantically, or would he want more? Had she already allowed him to go too far on their first walk? She cursed her lack of experience and hoped he would not guess she had never been courted before. Perhaps he was already comparing her with Lorna? Perhaps he was laughing at her. Here she was, older than he was and knowing next to nothing about love. She felt stupid and ill at ease.

'Perhaps I should go home,' she said wretchedly. 'I'm sorry . . .' Then to her relief she saw that he was smiling. 'Ma's right, I am a lout,' he said contritely. 'Forgive me, will

you? I was in too much of a hurry and now you're upset.
I'm sorry, Amy.'

'There's nothing to be sorry about,' she stammered gratefully. 'It's me; I didn't know quite what to expect. You were
very sweet and it was quite wonderful. You could never be
a lout, Don – you're really a very nice man.'

Impulsively, she put her arms round him and hugged him.
'I think,' she said, 'that I could very easily learn to love you.'

'So long as I don't rush you,' he suggested. 'Is that it?'

'Something like that,' she confessed. 'Does it sound
stupid?'

'No,' he considered, his head on one side. 'I'd say it sounds
reasonable. But you did like it?'

'Oh yes!'

He leaned forward and whispered, 'Has anyone ever told
you, Miss Turner, that you have a very nice body?'

'No,' she whispered back.

'Then let me be the first.'

'Thank you, Mr Leckie.'

'I shall probably mention it again sometime,' he told her.
'Help you get used to the idea.' They looked wordlessly at
each other for a moment, then clung together.

'I'm supposed to be walking you home,' he reminded her
when they finally drew apart. 'Should we do that?'

'Perhaps we should.'

'I might even hold your hand.'

'That would be very nice,' she agreed.

They had almost reached the level crossing gate when Amy
asked, 'Am I really a strange girl, Don?'

'Of course you're not. A little bit different, perhaps, a bit
special. I'll have to remember that.'

She was still worried. 'But different in a nice way?'

'In the nicest possible way,' he said as he kissed her again.

*

Promptly at 11 o'clock a dog-cart drew up at the level
crossing gate and Doctor Brown jumped down. Seeing
Arnold wandering aimlessly along the track, he beckoned to
him, gave him a penny and told him to look after the horse
until he returned. Ignoring Arnold's protests, he strode cheer-

213

fully along the platform, crossed over and was soon wielding the small brass knocker against the door of the stationmaster's house. Amy let him in and began to explain the situation, but he interrupted her.

'I know it all,' he said briskly. 'You told me when you called on me yesterday. I'll find my own way up.'

Before Amy could remonstrate, he was half-way up the stairs and she called up after him. 'The door on the right, doctor.'

'Splendid!' he answered, then beat a quick tattoo on the appropriate bedroom door with his knuckles before bounding inside.

Sitting up in bed, Ted Turner eyed the new doctor with considerable alarm. He had prepared a brief but pathetic speech with which to convince him of his frailty, if not the actual imminence of his demise. Now the well-rehearsed phrases deserted him as he eyed Doctor Brown with trepidation. Young by comparison with his predecessor, he was in fact nearing forty. He was tall and thin, with a ruddy face, small twinkling grey eyes and a shapeless mass of frizzy hair which had once been dark but was rapidly turning grey. He seemed to be endowed with an excess of energy and every move he made was expansive, giving the impression of a man about to perform a tremendous feat of physical activity – a man who might achieve success in the sporting world as a hurdler or a pole-vaulter.

Now he dropped his medical bag on to the floor and stood in the middle of the room with hands on hips, surveying the old man with a look of incredulity.

'Good God, man!' he bellowed. 'What has she done to you, eh? Left you to rot in this God-forsaken room away from the rest of the world? It's disgraceful, that's what it is! Show me a man confined to his bed and I'll show you a man with one foot in his grave. Oh yes, one foot in his grave. Trying to kill you off, is she? Women are the very devil. You have a bit of a seizure and all they can think of is to bundle you into bed. Quite ridiculous! Life goes on, Mr Turner. But never mind, we'll soon put a stop to all this nonsense.'

'It wasn't a seizure, doctor,' Ted ventured. 'Leastways, not exactly.'

Ignoring him, Doctor Brown approached the bed at a great pace and before the old man knew what was happening, had tugged off the bedclothes and was examining the bony legs that protruded from the flannel nightshirt.

'Look at these poor specimens!' cried the doctor, shaking his head in apparent disbelief. 'Puny little fellows, but can you wonder? No exercise, poor things. Oh, Mr Turner, what have they done to you, eh?'

Utterly confused by this unexpected attack, Ted said cautiously, 'It's my legs, you see, doctor,' and tried desperately to remember his speech.

'Your legs, man? I can see it's your legs. Stuck in bed all day, it's a wonder the poor useless things haven't dropped off from lack of use. Let's see how you can bend it – ah, there's hope there yet. And the other one. Good, very good!' He dived back across the room, seized his bag and began to rummage around in it.

Ted took advantage of the silence to say, 'It was the shock of my wife going – just knocked the stuffing out of me.'

Doctor Brown paused in his rummaging and looked up sympathetically.

'Oh, it does, doesn't it,' he agreed. 'Mine went, you know, three years ago. Drowned bathing in the river Thames. Knocked the stuffing right out of me, I can tell you, but I picked myself up and dusted myself down. I didn't let them stick me in a bed away from the fresh air. You a gardening man, Mr Turner?'

'I – well – that is, I used to have an allotment,' Ted admitted, wondering if this was a trick question.

The doctor beamed. 'Absolutely splendid! Get back to it, man. Nothing like fresh vegetables. Tennis? Cycling?'

'Er – no,' Ted stammered. 'I don't think—'

The doctor beamed again. 'Splendid exercise, tennis,' he told Ted. 'It's becoming very fashionable and you're never too old to start. Now don't tell me how old you are, let me guess. Sixty? Sixty-one?'

'I'm seventy-three,' said Ted, a quiver of self-pity in his voice.

'Better and better!' cried Doctor Brown. 'I always think

215

sixty is a dangerous age for a man. Get past sixty and you could go on forever.'

He began a thorough examination of his patient: checking his pulse, temperature and reflexes and peering into his eyes, ears and throat, all the while keeping up a tirade of encouragement and assurances of a full and energetic future.

Finally, he snapped his bag shut with a satisfied air and sat down on the corner of the bed. Drawing a prescription pad and pencil from his pocket, he scribbled on the top sheet, then tore it off and with a small nod handed it to Ted.

'I shall need my specs,' said Ted nervously.

Doctor Brown tweaked the paper from his fingers and read out in a loud voice, 'Fresh air and exercise. To be taken daily from nine until eight!' He smiled radiantly, shook Ted's hand vigorously and returned the prescription to him.

'You're fit as a fiddle, man,' he told him. 'Fight back, Mr Turner! I'm on your side.'

As he went out of the bedroom he began to bellow instructions to Amy while Ted, in a state of shock, listened incredulously.

'Get him up, woman!' cried the doctor. 'It's a damn disgrace to keep a man like Mr Turner cooped up like a chicken. He's a damned sight fitter than you or me and he'll probably live to be a hundred. Get him out of bed this very minute and back into the big wide world. He's going to grow you some vegetables and he might even take up tennis. Anything's possible! The world's his oyster. That'll be two shillings, but I'll send in the bill at the end of the month. Yes, vegetables! There's nothing quite like a freshly pulled carrot, I always say. You get him up at once. Marvellous old man! No telling what he may be able to do!'

Ted heard Amy start to ask something, but the front door banged and after that the gate. Then he heard the doctor shouting cheerfully to Arnold. There was a clatter of hooves and a rattle of wheels and then silence.

Ted put a shaking hand to his head as Amy came up the stairs, knowing with a terrible certainty that his life would never be the same again.

Before he could collect his wits, Amy had bundled him into long-johns, trousers and shirt and he found himself sitting in a chair by the window while she stripped his bed and proceeded to drag the mattress downstairs and out into the sunshine. Doctor Brown had told her it was to be aired in the sun, she told her grandfather. She then brought him up a mug of sweet, hot tea and when he had drunk it (making it last as long as possible), she helped him to make his way downstairs and into the rocking-chair which had once been his favourite. Humming cheerfully, she then left him to get used to the idea of being downstairs while she busied herself with preparations for the evening meal.

'He blamed me,' she told the old man, with pretended indignation. 'Said I'd mollycoddled you and I ought to be ashamed of myself. Gave me a real talking-to, he did.'

Ted grunted non-committally and eyed his worn slippers with disfavour. 'I shall need some new slippers,' he announced, determined not to give in too easily.

Amy smiled cheerfully. 'I was thinking the same thing,' she said.

'And the knees of those trousers are going a bit thin.'

'I'll put on some leather patches for you.'

'Hmm.'

When Sam came in and found his grandfather downstairs, his excitement was infectious and before Ted understood what was happening, he found himself agreeing that the next day he would try to mend the door of the rabbit-hutch. He went to bed early that night, tired out by his unexpected exertions, and slept better than he had done for several years.

The next day Amy had him up and downstairs by 10 o'clock and by half-past twelve the rabbit-hutch was as good as new. By the end of the week he could hardly remember what it was like to lie in bed all day, whiling away the hours and hoping for visitors. He even cut back a few rose bushes and, with Sam's help, prepared a small strip of soil and planted a row of cabbages. The old man made several references to 'when I'm gone' and 'until my strength runs out', but after a while he found it all a bit pointless. It *was* more fun being mobile once more. The station staff and passing footplate men made quite a fuss of him and Ted began to see himself as a bit of a hero, snatched from the jaws of death and restored to the land of the living. Amy was pleased to see that, for the time being at least, her grandfather was reasonably content.

*

Outside The Lodge, Gazedown slumbered in the late after-noon sun as the last of the grain – the oats and barley – was harvested and the loaded wagons rumbled their way towards their respective farms. It had been a good summer, with rain at night and plenty of sunshine during the days. On the outskirts of the village the hop-picking would continue for another fortnight and apples were still being gathered. The countryside was changing colour from summer to autumn now and the yellowing leaves were beginning to fall, blown into small drifts by the occasional breeze. Berries were every-where in the hedgerows, red-orange hips and haws and a few early blackberries. In the meadows, there were mushrooms to be found and the children foraged on their way home from school for hazelnuts and conkers. Gnats were flying and the sun was dipping low in the west, sending long shadows across the village, as inside The Lodge Ralph and Amy came reluctantly to the end of their first 'official' week's work on the biography. The laborious process of sorting and filing was well under way and a growing pile of numbered folders gave mute testimony to their hard work. Amy, slowly mastering the intricacies of Ralph's typewriting machine, was compiling a list of the folders and their contents for easy reference in the future. Ralph was still reading and sorting the vast accumulation of material, from time to time looking up worriedly and shaking his head.

Amy smiled suddenly and glanced up, fidgeting with a stray wisp of hair which persistently fell across her face.

'I'm beginning to understand the man,' she said slowly. 'Nigel Stanisbrooke, I mean. I feel that I know him quite well; he's almost part of the family! But what has occurred to me is the absence of a personal diary. I mean, it seems odd that neither he nor his wife kept a diary. In fact I suspect they did, but if so then where are they? Do you think the family are withholding them? Do you think there *is* a diary and maybe they felt it contained matters that were not for publi-cation? I know we don't really need them, but I would so love to read them, just for my own satisfaction. I feel I shall never get the whole picture without them.' She shrugged. 'Could we make some enquiries?' she suggested. 'Dare we ask if there is any more material that hasn't been given to us?'

Ralph looked thoughtful. 'We could try,' he said, 'if you really think it's worth it. I could write to the remaining members of the family – or maybe Elliot could approach them. He'd probably have more luck – he could charm the birds out of the trees if he wanted to!'

Amy was surprised by Ralph's mention of his brother and quickly lowered her eyes. She had not seen Elliot since the birthday party but now, unbidden, she remembered the brief dance they had shared and felt again his kiss. It had startled her then and now it shook her with an intensity which was almost frightening. She had tried so hard to put the incident out of her mind. For him, she was sure, it had been an impulsive gesture of no significance at all. It was ridiculous for her to exaggerate it into more than the mildest flirtation – the party spirit, perhaps. Since that evening she had neither heard from him nor expected to, and had tried assiduously to forget all about it. To allow herself to feel attracted to a man like Elliot – a man who could 'charm the birds from the trees' – would be to court disaster and Amy liked to believe that she was too level-headed to do anything so foolish.

'Amy?' said Ralph.

'I'm sorry.' With an effort, she put Elliot out of her mind.

'You were miles away,' he told her. 'I was saying that maybe Elliot could get hold of the diaries, if there are any.'

'Oh, that would be marvellous!' cried Amy. 'If we had his wife's diaries . . . I'd love to see him through her eyes! There are bound to be references to him. Or,' her eyes gleamed hopefully, 'the diary of one of his mistresses! Or both! No, that's being too greedy, isn't it? We could never be that lucky. But if only we could!' She laughed. 'I know what you're going to say: that I'm becoming obsessed with the Stanisbrookes! It's true – I think about them when I go to bed at night and again first thing in the morning.'

He laughed at her excitement. 'I'll talk to Elliot on Sunday,' he promised. 'He's coming down again, so he tells me. Keeping an eye on the masterpiece, he says. I wish he wouldn't call it that; it makes me so nervous.'

'Don't let it worry you,' said Amy. 'Let's make up our minds to enjoy ourselves. I'm having a wonderful time! I feel such a fraud, taking money for enjoying myself.'

'Which reminds me,' said Ralph, taking a small brown envelope from his pocket, 'the assistant researcher's first week's salary!'

'Oh, how lovely!' She took the envelope and pressed it melodramatically to her heart. 'Thank you, Ralph.'

He stood up. 'Don't thank me, thank Elliot. It was his idea. Well, I suppose we must leave it all until next week. I must say we've covered a great deal of ground; it's quite surprising.'

'Two heads, . . . ' Amy began.

'Are much better than one,' he finished. 'And your grand-father – is he still managing?'

'Of course he is,' said Amy. 'I shall be eternally grateful to that doctor. Grandfather grumbles a bit now and then, but no one pays much attention. I think he's actually quite enjoying himself, pottering about and being noticed. The train drivers all wave to him if he's on the platform and he has a laugh and a joke with them. Arnold's in his element too, because Grandfather has plenty of time for him.' She smiled. 'If ever you are taken ill, call in Doctor Brown. I shouldn't think he ever loses a patient! He simply wouldn't allow it! Well, I must go. Have a nice weekend – I'm sure you will if your brother is coming down.'

'You too, Amy.' He grinned. 'Don't work too hard!'

'I don't mind the housework any more,' she told him, 'because I know that when Monday afternoon comes I shall be back here with you and Nigel Stanisbrooke.'

As she walked home her mind was busy, piecing together the jigsaw that was Lord Stanisbrooke's life. As Ralph had said, they now knew what he did, and when. Nigel Edward, born in England in March 1816, he was the first child of Sarah Ann and Henry Miles Stanisbrooke who had four other children, three of whom later died. They were a wealthy land-owning family who had early connections with India, where Henry Miles was a Colonel in the British Army.

Did poor Sarah Ann travel home alone so that she could have the child in England, wondered Amy. Did the family remain at home in the big house while father finished his 'tour of duty' or whatever it was called? There had been a nanny too, one Mary Myers, who joined the household early in 1816 and stayed until all the children had fled the nest or died. Poor Mary Myers, who forty-five years later wrote: 'I pray for you every night, my dearest Nigel, and I read your letters over and over. I have a box full and never tire of them. They were such happy days. You were such a loving child, always my favourite . . . '

He had been sent away to a school in Surrey at the age of eleven and Amy tried to imagine him parting with his mother or nanny as he climbed into the carriage, trying to be brave but inside feeling sick with fear at what lay ahead. Eleven years old — about Sam's age, she reflected. Did the young Nigel Stanisbrooke like the school? Was he happy there, or was he bullied by the older boys? Her thoughts sped ahead. And how and where did the older Nigel take a mistress? No, *two* mistresses! Were they married women or did he set them up in separate establishments? Were they English? Deep in thought, she was startled when someone materialised beside her.

'Don!' she cried. 'You made me jump.'

She allowed herself to be kissed and found herself returning the kiss with enthusiasm. It was very pleasant to feel a pair of strong, warm arms around her and to smell the faint tang of Don's body.

'How did it go?' he asked. 'The first official week? Ma said you were looking forward to it.' He fell into step beside her, his arm draped casually but possessively around her waist.

'I enjoyed it,' she told him. 'I was just thinking it through in my mind.'

'I thought you were thinking about me!' he exclaimed, feigning disappointment.

Remembering that he had confessed to a feeling of jealousy that she was to spend so much time with Ralph, Amy said quickly, 'I have been thinking about you. In fact, I found it hard to keep my mind on my work at times.'

221

She could see the answer pleased him as he squeezed her waist and said, 'Nice thoughts, I hope? No doubts?'

'No doubts,' she said, with a prickle of conscience.

He kissed her again. 'Have you told Ralph yet — about us? So that he doesn't go getting any fancy ideas?'

'I have hinted,' she told him carefully, 'but don't want to alarm him. He might assume I'm going to give up my work and I've only just started. He's not terribly confident at the moment, and I don't want him to think I would leave him in the lurch.'

'What do you mean, not confident? What's wrong with him?'

'Nothing's wrong with him!' Her indignation was clear and at once she regretted her swift reaction. 'It's just that there's a lot of work to be done and he's still feeling his way towards it. It's difficult to explain to someone who—'

'To a farmer's boy, you mean!' he interrupted, sounding hurt.

Amy looked at him in surprise. 'I was going to say "to someone who isn't familiar with the problem",' she explained. 'I'm beginning to know the man, but Ralph isn't yet. Perhaps it's because I'm a woman, I don't know. I just think he's relying on me quite a lot at present, and I don't want him to imagine that I might suddenly give up.'

Don's face had settled into an aggrieved expression. 'Well, I hope it's not going to take too long,' he said. 'I don't want to share you with anyone else.'

'Don, please!' she protested. 'You're not sharing me, I just work with him.' She stopped walking and faced him squarely. 'I said before that we have to get this clear between us, Don, otherwise we shall have this conversation again and again. Ralph and I are fond of each other, but only like brother and sister, whereas you and I are . . .' She searched for the right words.

'Courting?' he suggested hopefully.

She relaxed into laughter. 'Courting,' she agreed. 'Now kiss me again and tell me you trust me.'

'I trust you,' he said, kissing her, then added mischievously, 'but I don't trust him!'

'Don Leckie!' cried Amy, exasperated. 'Maybe I don't trust

Lorna Betts, but I don't throw a tantrum every time she appears on your horizon. Oh Don, I think right now I'm getting too happy! There's you and the job and Grandfather's up and about again. It all seems too good to be true.'

As he looked at her, Don saw for the very first time that Amy Turner could be beautiful. Her expression was radiant, her gold-brown eyes glowed with excitement. He felt a strange misgiving, a nagging doubt that this glowing woman could ever really love him; he felt inadequate and the emotion was a novel one.

Amy saw the doubt in his eyes. 'What is it?' she asked gently.

'Nothing.' He swallowed, but his mouth was dry. 'At least – Amy, you will love me, won't you?'

'Of course I will! Oh Don, I'm sure I will,' she said, dismayed in her turn. 'It will work out for us,' she added wistfully, 'but we must give each other time. We have to get to know each other. Am I disappointing you, is that it?'

'No, but maybe I'm not the sort of man—' he stopped.

Amy laughed a trifle shakily. 'Suppose I make my confession,' she said. 'I've never had a young man and never been courted before. I was only sixteen when my mother went away and since then – well, Papa was ill for a long time and there was simply no time in my life for courting. Maybe I seem cold, but I don't mean to be. I'm sure Lorna was a different kettle of fish but I'm trying hard, Don, to get it right. So there it is. My guilty secret is out,' she concluded tremulously.

She saw that his expression had changed to one of relief. With a whoop of joy he caught hold of her and swung her off the ground, then hugged her fiercely.

'It will work!' he told her. 'My little Amy is a virgin and that makes everything marvellous. You might be older than me, you might even be cleverer, but I shall teach you about love. Don't worry, Amy, it's going to be just fine.'

Don felt a new fierce wave of affection for her and all his doubts fled. 'I love you, Amy Turner,' he whispered. 'Say you love me too.'

'I love you, Don,' she answered.

And there was new hope in both their hearts as they kissed again.

Chapter Thirteen

The down platform at Gazedown came alive at 5.23 in readiness for the train due in at 5.27. It was Friday and Amy's stall was well-stocked in the hope of a little trade. She had agreed to work with Ralph for four afternoons – from 2 until 5 o'clock on Mondays to Thursdays. On Fridays she caught up on the household chores and prepared her stall. Today she was reluctant to admit to herself how much she had mised her session at The Lodge, but she had busied herself with ironing, scrubbed the kitchen table and floor and made a week's supply of cakes. Her stall now contained a freshly made coconut cake, a basket of hazelnuts, another of mushrooms and two bunches of pink roses. Clara stood with Amy, and the two girls chattered cheerfully, exchanging news and gossip. Friday was Clara's half-day; she also had one full day off every two weeks or could, if she preferred, have two full days once in four weeks.

Harry had torn himself away from the station garden – where he had been whitewashing the edging stones to good effect – and was now talking earnestly to Ted Turner. Tim was striding up and down the platform with his hat at a rakish angle, attempting to impress Clara with his efficiency. Arnold was sitting cross-legged on the trolley, staring at the clock and muttering loudly about the fact that the big hand was on the twelve – which it was not.

The stationmaster was not present. He had taken the whole day off in order to call personally on several firms in the area with a view to persuading them to 'send their goods by rail' at the very competitive prices he could offer them.

This form of canvassing was a very important part of his job and one in which he took pleasure and pride. He knew that the railway gave a good, quick service and he could put the Company's case with confidence.

Bob Hart descended from the signal-box to close the gates, the train was signalled and soon appeared amongst the trees, its whistle sounding, a plume of smoke drifting lazily behind the gleaming blue locomotive. Mr Bell waved and the fireman gave the 'thumbs-up' sign as the train drew into the station. Harry ambled forward to open the carriage door and help the Reverent Ambrose Stokes to alight, while further along, Gerald Hatherley stepped down and gave up his ticket to Tim. To Amy's delight, a woman passenger briefly left the train to purchase a bunch of roses and the coconut cake. The vicar bought the mushrooms, then delayed his departure in order to congratulate Ted Turner on his amazing recovery and to tell Arnold to remind Sam that choir practice the following day would begin promptly at 10 o'clock. The various groups of people on the platform gradually merged into one, for the afternoon was warm and no one was in any hurry.

Except for Gerald Hatherley. He hurried out of the station unnoticed and was turning left into the lane when Lorna Betts ran up to him breathlessly, one hand held to her side.

'Oh sir! I mean, Gerald. Thank goodness I've caught you! I must speak to you, but no one must see. Through here, sir. Quickly!'

For a moment he stared at her, speechless with joy at her unexpected appearance. His senses swam deliriously at the sight of the blonde head and comely young shape, and it was all he could do not to seize her in his arms. He could not imagine what she wanted so urgently, but he did not care as he followed her obediently through a hole in the opposite hedge and into the field beside the pond.

'My dear Lorna!' he whispered, almost tearfully. 'Oh, my very dear girl! Let me just look at you. It's been so long and I've missed you so terribly.' He reached out. 'Let me kiss you. Please, *please* let me kiss you. Just one little kiss!'

The one little kiss became a flurry of kisses and Lorna,

225

aroused by his obvious passion, had to take herself strictly in hand.

'Gerald, stop it a moment,' she gasped, holding him at arm's length. 'I've got something to tell you – something awful!'

Her words sobered him instantly and he looked at her with foreboding. 'You've told your mother!' he guessed. 'Oh, Lorna—'

'No, sir. No, Gerald,' she assured him. ''Course I haven't! I never told anyone what happened; I said it was someone else got me tiddly.'

'Oh, good girl!'

'But Gerald – oh, you mustn't be angry with me, Gerald, because you did make me drunk although I did like it – we both did, didn't we?'

'Yes, yes.' His eyes began to blink. 'But what is this awful something?'

'It's about me and you, sir. It's about what we did – well, can't you guess?'

'No. No, I can't.' He looked bewildered. Like a small bewildered child, she thought compassionately, and did not want to burden him with the truth. But there was no other way out.

'It was what you did to me, Gerald,' she said. 'It's going to be a baby. I mean, I've missed my "you-know-whats" sir, and it must have been you because there wasn't anyone else.'

Gerald was frowning, trying to make head or tail of the girl's blathering. Her "you-know-whats"? A baby? Realisation, when it finally struck him, came like a blinding ray of pure delight. A baby! He, Gerald Hatherley, had got this beautiful golden girl with child! Tears filled his eyes.

'Lorna! My sweet little Lorna! A child,' he murmured. 'How wonderful.'

'Wonderful?' cried Lorna. 'It's not wonderful, sir, it's terrible. What am I going to do? I can't have a baby, I don't *want* a baby. I'm not even married – and it makes you fat and ugly!' She burst into tears at the thought of her sister Janet. 'Ma's going to kill me when she knows. She will, sir – Gerald, I mean. She'll wallop me, I know she will. You'll have to tell me what to do, because I don't know; I really don't!'

Gerald took her into his arms, but she continued to sob wildly. 'I've got no job neither, sir, and it's all your fault, but I did like it. It was lovely, what we did, but now I wish we hadn't! Oh cuddle me, sir. I'm so scared, I feel cold and shivery.'

The whistle of the departing train alerted Gerald to the fact that shortly the vicar would be making his way along the lane and might possibly overhear them. He therefore urged the weeping Lorna further into the field, past the pond and into the shelter of the small hazel copse.

Lorna continued to cry, assuring him that her mother would drag the truth from her when she saw her red eyes and would no doubt turn her out of the house to fend for herself. Or she might storm up to the Manor, or even to the police station! Gerald did his best to calm her fears, promising that as soon as she stopped crying he would be able to think of a way out of the 'little difficulty'. When at last she did stop, he made her sit down with him on the grass while he outlined his hazy plans.

'You must have the child, Lorna,' he told her. 'It will be our own little son. You see that? I've always wanted a son and with Esme it wasn't possible. Not my fault, you know, Lorna. Well, of course you know! I could have given her a child, but she wouldn't let me near her. You see? What could I do with a woman like that? No, you must have the child and I will make you a handsome – yes, I mean it, a *very* handsome – allowance.'

'But my ma—' Lorna protested.

'I will speak to your mother,' he promised.

'You don't know her like I do,' said Lorna doubtfully. 'She'll tear you to shreds, sir.'

'Gerald,' he reminded her with a broad smile. 'You can't keep calling me sir, if you're having my child. Now can you?'

Lorna managed a watery smile. 'You are kind, Gerald,' she said. 'I thought you'd be cross with me.'

'Cross with you? Good heavens no!' He leaned forward and brushed her hair back from her face with trembling fingers. 'Listen to me, Lorna,' he said. 'You are a good girl

227

and everything will be fine. You must do as I say and no one will be cross with you. I won't let anyone hurt you — you see?'

'Yes, sir. But where will I live? What will your wife say?'

'Ah!' His face darkened. 'That is one of the problems, but I shall think of something. I've got money, you see, Lorna, and that does help; it smoothes out the wrinkles, as they say. Yes, somehow I will make everything all right, so now you can go home — but you must say nothing to anyone until I tell you to. Are you well? Can you feel anything?'

'Not yet, I can't.'

'You shall have the best doctor, Lorna, I promise you. The best of everything. And we shall have a dear little son. How do you feel about that, eh? You do like children?'

'Oh yes, sir.' She was recovering now from her outburst. 'I would like a son — I mean, it would be fun, wouldn't it? And I don't really want to get rid of it.'

Gerald's face crumpled with horror. 'Get rid of it!' he choked. 'Oh, my dear God! Never, never say that again, Lorna. Do you hear me? Never even *think* such a dreadful thing!'

'I wouldn't. I'm sorry.' Impulsively she threw her arms round his neck and hugged him. 'And thank you for not being cross with me. It was fun, wasn't it? That night, I mean, with the champagne and everything!'

For a moment neither spoke as the same idea entered both their heads. Lorna found her voice first. 'I suppose it wouldn't matter now,' she said cautiously, 'since it's already happened.'

Gerald's voice came huskily. 'I suppose not. But there's no champagne.'

Lorne put her head on one side and a pert smile played around her lips. 'You're my champagne,' she declared and began to unbutton her bodice.

*

Just as their love-making reached and passed its climax, a sixth sense made Lorna open her eyes. Her frightened gasp made Gerald's blood run cold and he rolled sideways and

228

scrambled to his knees to find Arnold only yards away, grinning down at them.

'I know,' Arnold told them triumphantly. 'I know what you're doing – it's the bees. Tim told me. You're doing the bees.'

Gerald, struggling to fasten his clothes, groaned aloud but Lorna, after her initial fright, began to giggle. Seeing that she laughed, Arnold laughed also, his face wild with excitement.

Mopping his face with a handkerchief, Gerald stumbled to his feet and pulled a still giggling Lorna upright.

'Doing the bees!' echoed Lorna, now helpless with laughter. 'Oh Gerald, I like that. I really do. Doing the bees!' She staggered to the nearest tree and leaned against it, while tears of laughter streamed down her face.

'It's nothing to laugh at,' Gerald mumbled, disconcerted. 'Where on earth did he spring from, dratted idiot?'

Lorna's shoulders still shook. 'Arnold's no bother,' she said at last. 'He's harmless, poor lad. Look, give me a sixpence and I'll send him off.'

She went up to Arnold, who stopped laughing abruptly and frowned with concentration as she held up the silver coin.

'For you, Arnold,' she said. 'A sixpence! But first you must listen to me.'

He nodded his head furiously.

'What we did – what you saw, Arnold – that's a big, big secret,' she told him. 'Do you understand? You mustn't tell a soul. Not your mother. Not anyone at the railway station. No one! This sixpence is for you to help you remember our secret. Understand?'

Arnold pursued his lips thoughtfully and then sighed deeply.

'Look,' said Lorna patiently, 'you know what a secret is, don't you. A secret is something you mustn't tell. So *you* mustn't tell the secret about what we did – the bees.'

'The bees!' he cried, beaming once more.

'A secret,' said Lorna.

'A secret,' he agreed.

'Good. Here's the sixpence!' She put it into his large,

sweaty hand. 'If you tell, then I shall come and take it back. Got it?'

They watched him lumber away through the trees and then Lorna turned to Gerald with a gleam in her eyes.

'I've got an idea,' she said. 'Why don't I meet you here tomorrow? We could do the bees again!'

*

Forty miles from Gazedown a woman trudged along the roadside. She was thin and her face was grey with exhaustion. Her left hand carried a carpet-bag and the right held the hand of a very small boy who was crying fretfully. It was nearly dusk and they had been on the road since early that morning. The date was the nineteenth of September, but the woman did not know that; she had long since lost touch with the days of the week. She knew only that they were walking towards the east because the sun was going down behind them, and that if they kept going east for enough days they would eventually – with God's help – reach Gazedown.

Ellen stopped to change the bag into her right hand and obligingly the boy moved round to her left side. Holding up his arms appealingly, he said, 'Carry me,' but dropped them again without waiting for the shake of her head. He knew she could not carry him; they had walked for days and she had never carried him. She took up the weight of the carpet-bag and, taking his hand again, said, 'Come on, little lad,' and he glanced hopefully into her face. Sometimes, though rarely, she smiled at him and then he felt happy.

Ellen guessed that they had about two more hours of daylight. If they had not managed to secure a ride by dusk, they would be forced to stop and find somewhere to stay for the night. She had a few shillings left, no more, but people were kindly and might let the two of them sleep in a barn or outhouse with a blanket to cover them. Hearing the clatter of hooves and rumble of wheels behind her, she turned to see a farm cart approaching and raised her hand beseechingly. To her delight the driver reined in the large grey cob, but when she explained their predicament he could not help as he was on his way home barely half a mile away. He could offer her shelter, but Ellen thanked him and decided to try to travel a few more miles before the daylight faded. The next driver, a carrier, cursed her impudence. The third was a doctor on his rounds.

Finally, however, her luck changed when a brougham stopped, containing an elderly woman by the name of Eleanor Hobbs. She was returning home from her annual holiday and invited them most courteously to share the carriage with her for the remaining eleven miles. She then offered them a bed for the night in the rambling old house where she lived alone.

Ellen lay in the bed and listened to her son breathing beside her, the son Toby that John had given her. John, who had been all the world to her, who had seduced her with laughter and the promise of happiness, who had later taken a younger woman into his bed and then gone away to a new life in America.

She wanted to hate him, but her heart still ached at the thought of him and she cherished the few years they had had together. It was still difficult for her to believe that John had gone from her life for ever, but she told herself that all joys had to be paid for, especially stolen joys. She had snatched her brief happiness at the expense of others and it was only right that she should suffer in her turn, yet Ellen acknowledged in her nightly soul-searching that if she could turn back the clock – knowing the ultimate outcome of her adventure – she would do the same again. But although she was prepared to pay the price herself, she was not prepared to see her son suffer and for that reason alone was prepared to throw herself on her husband's mercy and beg for another chance. He had not answered her letter, but she had made up her mind to go to him anyway and make one last appeal. If he refused to take them in, she would accept his decision without argument and move on, taking her son with her; she would not embarrass the family by staying in or even near Gazedown.

Every night before she fell into an exhausted sleep, Ellen rehearsed what she would say and tried to imagine the very worst that could happen. Tom would laugh at her, Amy would despise her, Sam – perhaps he would not even recognise her. She did not deserve their forgiveness and could not expect their love, but if they did take her back she would spend the rest of her life trying to make amends for the heartache she had caused them. In her more hopeful moments she imagined herself caring for the family again with infinite patience, gradually winning back their love and respect. And surely they would find it in their hearts to love little Toby? He was an appealing child with a sturdy frame, John's curly black hair and her own bright blue eyes. Would Sam like the idea of a brother? Most boys did – but most boys' mothers stayed at home to care for them.

'Dear God,' Ellen prayed earnestly. 'Forgive me for what I have done. Forgive me for loving John.' She wanted to say, 'Forgive him for leaving me,' but the words stuck in her throat. Instead she said, 'Help me if you can and I will serve you all my days.'

There were so few miles to travel. Soon she would be there and it would be up to Tom to decide what to do. She allowed her eyes to close, then opened them sharply.

'And God bless Eleanor Hobbs,' she said before sinking into an exhausted sleep.

*

Choir practice was held in the vicarage in the room referred to as the 'morning room' by Mrs Jay and 'the parlour' by the vicar himself. Once it had been held in the hall adjacent to the church and music had been provided by an ancient harmonium played by the Reverend Stokes. One day, however, the harmonium had failed to produce its full range of notes and it was discovered that some creature – presumably a rat – had gnawed through vital parts of the instrument's interior. No one had been found who could undertake the repair work; everyone approached had insisted that the harmonium should be pensioned off and a new one bought to replace it. The fact that all the church's funds at that time were earmarked for the preservation of the main window made that impossible, so the choir practices had been reluctantly transferred to the largest room in the vicarage.

This room also boasted an upright piano which belonged to Mrs Jay and had been given to her by her father when she reached the age of twenty-one; in fact she had been known to play it on rare occasions. She had not been at all pleased at Ambrose's suggestion that he should make use of it for the choir practices, but since she was a widow and dependent on her brother for a roof over her head, she had felt unable to refuse.

Instead, she complained bitterly and regularly about the footmarks, the noise, the pile of coats in the hall, the fact that she could not use the morning room between 10 and 11 o'clock and the need to expend precious coal to warm the room in winter. She did not complain about the choir practice as such and frequently pointed this out to her brother.

This particular Saturday was no different. She opened the door to Albert Stokes, the carrier, and said, 'Wipe your feet, please,' without adding any kind of greeting.

'Morning, Mrs Jay!' he responded cheerfully, ignoring her rudeness which he secretly put down to her having no man of her own to keep her in her place. Albert sang baritone and had a strong, thought untrained, voice. Before she could close the door Fred Evans, the retired postman, made his way up the steps. He had once been a very good tenor, but now he was way past his best although no one would ever tell him so. Eric and Sam were chasing each other along the path and Mrs Jay, ignoring Fred, cried, 'Boys! Behave yourselves. This is a house of God, remember.'

'I thought it was a house of Vicar,' muttered Eric, which Sam found hilarious, and caused them both to collapse in helpless merriment.

However, Mrs Jay did not intend to allow such frivolity within her home and she barred the doorway with her arm.

'*When* you have pulled yourselves together,' she said, her tone positively withering, and waited until they had composed their faces before letting them pass into the dim hallway.

There were no women singers, not because the vicar had any objection to them but because only three had volunteered to join and that had unbalanced the choir. They now had six boys and four men, one of whom was a rather sickly youth who suffered from poor health and an over-anxious mother and missed quite a few practices as well as some of

233

the services. Making up the four with Albert and Fred was Harry Coombes, who hated singing but had a splendid bass voice. The vicar had persisted valiantly in the face of Harry's steadfast refusals and at last – in God's name – had prevailed, but Harry was always last to arrive and first to leave. He came direct from and returned straight to his allotment, and as Mrs Jay made him leave his muddy boots on a sheet of newspaper inside the front door, he had to stand in his socks throughout the practice.

When everyone had assembled, Mrs Jay informed her brother and he hurried briskly into the room, polishing his spectacles on a duster and smiling at all and sundry. He put on the spectacles, folded the duster carefully and put it on the table, then rubbed his hands together.

'Well, here we all are again,' he said. 'And only one more practice before Harvest Festival! I know it's all going to go splendidly, with His help,' he cast his eyes upwards, 'but we do have a lot of work to do, so let's get started. Number 73 in the little green book. Once through all together, I think, then we'll try the tenors on their own.'

There was a great rustle as ten little green books were opened at the appropriate page. Then the vicar sat down at the piano while the choir arranged itself nearby, faces turned dutifully towards him. As soon as they began to sing, Eric pinched Sam's bottom and Sam kicked Eric's ankle, whereupon the sickly youth tapped each one on the shoulder and 'tutted'.

All is safely gathered in
Ere the winter storms begin . . .

The room had a high ceiling with large windows, but the spacious effect was markedly reduced by the choice of colour scheme. Dark green velvet chairs sat upon an even darker green carpet square which was bounded on all sides by dark brown, highly polished floorboards. The walls were a paler green picked out in cream, but the lighter area was reduced by six large oil paintings in heavy gilt frames. There were large ferns in pots, too, and an aspidistra on a pedestal which took pride of place in the main window bay. The mantlepiece

was crammed with knick-knacks – pewter jugs, ivory eleph-
ants, china vases and brass candlesticks – all of which
belonged to Mrs Jay who was an avid collector.

. . . Raise the song of harvest home.

As the last note faded, the sickly youth began to cough and
under cover of the sound Sam dropped a marble on to the
floor. Encouraging it with the toe of his boot to roll towards
the piano, he nudged Eric at the same time so that he should
share in the joke. Meanwhile the vicar turned from the piano
and beamed at his choristers.

'Splendid!' he said. 'What a beautiful hymn this is; it has
always been one of my favourites. Now it's—' he consulted
a small notebook, '—first verse unison, second verse tenors,
third verse unison, fourth—'

At that moment Harry Coombes leaned back on his stockinged feet to whisper something to Fred Evans and stepped
painfully on to Sam's marble. His foot shot from under him,
his arms went up in an effort not to overbalance and the
little green book flew out of his hand and landed on the
mantelpiece. Somehow this dislodged a small china
shepherdess, which promptly fell into the hearth and broke
into several pieces.

There was a stunned silence from which the vicar was the
first to recover.

'Oh dear, dear me!' he said in a scared voice, because he
would have to suffer his sister's wrath long after the real
culprit had been forgotten.

Harry Coombes protested, 'But dammit, it wasn't my
fault. I slipped on something and whatever it was it went
under the bookcase.'

The sickly youth stopped coughing, rushed forward and
fell on his knees; within seconds he was holding up Sam's
marble between a disapproving finger and thumb. Meanwhile the retired postman picked up the broken shepherdess
and handed it to the vicar without a word.

'Oh dear, dear me!' said the vicar again. 'This really is too
bad. My sister will be most upset; she was very fond of her
little shepherdess.'

Harry Coombes caught his eye and said firmly, 'Don't go blaming me, vicar. All I did was slip on that there marble.' He remembered Mrs Jay's rout of Tim Hollis and had no intention of risking a similar encounter. 'All I did was try to save myself. I'm sorry, but you can't go blaming me.'

The sickly youth held up the marble and asked, 'Who owns this, then?' Sam and Eric stared at each other in a deafening silence until at last all faces were turned towards them. Sam's heart sank.

'Well?' said the vicar helpfully. 'Is anyone going to confess?'

Sam and Eric now stared at their respective boots, and the vicar cleared his throat. 'We all do wrong at times,' he declared. 'We all give in to temptation. Sin is not new to the world, and there are few of us who do not succumb *at times* to the snares of the devil. All we can do is to confess our wrongdoing and ask His forgiveness.'

Sam was prepared to ask for His forgiveness – it was the idea of asking Mrs Jay's forgiveness that held no appeal – but Eric was digging him with his elbow and he knew it was only a matter of time.

''Smine,' he mumbled loudly.

'Ahah!' said the vicar in a voice which held no surprise. 'Sam Turner – you are the culprit, are you?'

Sam nodded and added unwisely, 'Can I have my marble back, please?'

The sickly youth said. 'Well, really!'

The vicar raised his eyebrows. 'When you have apologised to my sister,' he said, 'I will return the marble.'

Sam also had heard about Mrs Jay from Tim Hollis and, like Harry Coombes, had no wish to face a verbal lashing. So he said sullenly, 'I don't want it back then.'

Poor Harry Coombes was now in something of a spot, having indirectly brought the stationmaster's son into conflict with authority. Although it was undeniably Sam's fault initially, Harry felt that as a grown man and a member of the station staff, he ought somehow to be able to avert what looked like a social disaster. The trouble was, he could not think how to go about it. If only he had had his shoes on, the marble wouldn't have hurt so much and then he wouldn't have nearly fallen and then the hymn-book would never have left his hand. Therefore he told himself, Mrs Jay herself was partly to blame for making him take his shoes off, but no one was going to consider that a very convincing argument.

'I expect,' Harry said hopefully, 'the lad's a bit shy. Of course he's sorry, aren't you, Sam?'

Sam's lips remained tightly closed, however.

'Well, Sam?' prompted the vicar.

Sam raised his head and looked round at the circle of faces: Harry's imploring,' the vicar's hopeful, the sickly youth's horribly and undeniably triumphant; and it came to him very clearly that the real choice lay between apologising to Mrs Jay or receiving a good hiding from his father when he found out what had happened. He opted for the latter and, with a strangled cry of relief, elbowed his way through the affronted choir and bolted for the front door.

*

Mrs Edwina Jay was one of the people who had objected to the notion of a railway running through Gazedown from the very beginning and now, as she stared at the shattered remnants of her shepherdess, she knew she had been right. The station and track were a blot on the landscape and would never be anything else. The level crossing gates were an inconvenience, repeatedly closing off the road to people with horse-drawn vehicles who had every right to use it. The trains were noisy and had ruined the tranquillity of the village with their shunting, braking and whistling, not to mention the disgusting smoke which belched from their funnels or chimneys or whatever they called them. The staff, too, had proved intolerable. Young Hollis was cheeky – he had called her 'a miserable old bat' – and Sam Turner was constantly into mischief according to the headmistress of the school. The daughter, Amy Turner, was always sneaking round to the fellow in The Lodge and now Harry Coombes, the porter – abetted by the stationmaster's son – had wantonly smashed one of her favourite pieces of china: the shepherdess her grandfather had given her when she was seven, to celebrate his appointment as master of the local workhouse. It really was the last straw.

237

Edwina and Ambrose had been brought up by their grand-parents. To Edwina the gaunt figure and austere behaviour of her grandfather remained with her into adulthood as an example of the perfect man. As workhouse master, he had been feared by many and respected by few, but Edwina had admired him greatly. It was a disappointment to her that her brother Ambrose did not resemble him in any way, being withdrawn and shy and lacking entirely what Edwina considered to be the strong moral fibre of her grandfather. To her intense chagrin, he grew up to be weak-willed and much too tolerant of other people's failings; without realising it, she tried to compensate for this by becoming excessively strict and repressive in her own life so that now sister and brother were poles apart and each disapproved silently – or not so silently – of the other.

Now Harry repeated, 'I really am sorry, Mrs Jay, but it's one of those things. A little accident that—'

Edwina's eyes flashed dangerously. 'An *accident?*' she said. 'From what my brother tells me, I deduce that it was an act of pure carelessness on your part and pure nastiness on the part of the Turner boy. I see no way at all in which the damage to my shepherdess can be considered an accident.'

Harry shook his head regretfully and decided not to argue the point. He had hoped to leave Sam out of it, but the vicar had insisted on telling the whole truth.

'If you'd let me take those pieces home,' he began, 'I reckon I could put that back together so as you'd—'

'Let you take this home?' Edwina demanded with an incredulous toss of her head. 'Most certainly not, Mr Coombes. I don't know how you dare suggest such a thing. I should have thought you had done quite enough harm already and I shall certainly not entrust the fragments into your obviously inept care. No, I shall have it replaced by the finest workman I can find and I will then send you the bill. You may be sure it will not be cheap and if you decide to ask Mr Turner for a contribution on behalf of his son, that is your business. I shall of course report the whole matter to Mr Turner and in fact I may even write directly to the Railway Company authorities, telling them exactly what I think of each member of the Gazedown Station staff. Oh

238

yes!' she cried malevolently, seeing the dismay in Harry's eyes. 'The very highest authority. Tell that to your stationmaster, Mr Coombes.' She pulled herself up to her considerable height and folded her arms. 'Unlike some people, *I* am not a person to be trifled with and if I see evil flourishing in the world, I do my best to pluck it out.' The last line had been one of her grandfather's favourite remarks and she could still see him, erect and strong (and taller than ever in his stovepipe hat) castigating the workhouse immates for various misdemeanours which had been brought to his attention.

Harry Coombes twisted his hands together awkwardly, aware that the incident was rapidly getting out of all proportion. He could not decide whether to get out of her sight before anything worse was mooted or stay and try to appease her.

He blurted out, 'I've *said* how sorry I am and I really do believe it was an accident in that no one meant any harm — that is, no one meant to break anything, especially one of your little treasures . . .'

His voice faltered as Edwina stiffened perceptibly and he felt at once that he had made a mistake by attempting the appeasement. Nevertheless he stammered on, 'That really was a pretty little thing, Mrs Jay, I've thought so many times, and if only you'd allow me I could mend it. Not that I mind if you must send it elsewhere, but if it was to turn out very expensive I don't quite see how I could — that is, we could — repay you the money—'

'Weekly instalments, Mr Coombes,' she snapped, 'for as long as it takes!'

She saw herself aged eleven at her grandfather's death-bed, the shepherdess clutched in her shaking hands and Ambrose beside her, older but even more frightened than she was. He had grasped at the big brass bed-knob for support and Edwina remembered the dull marks of his fingerprints when he took his hand away to join in their grandmother's prayer. In death the workhouse master had looked grimmer than ever, his jaw set firmly.

'Yes, weekly instalments,' she repeated, deciding to seek out the most expensive repairer in London. That would serve as a lesson both to Harry and the Turners.

'And I doubt if we shall see you here again,' she added. 'I shall speak to my brother; I'm sure he can find a replacement for you. I do think the members of a church choir should behave with a *minimum* of decorum and that is apparently more than we can expect from you. Good morning, Mr Coombes. We have nothing more to say to each other.'

'But Mrs Jay,' he began, 'the vicar won't like that, not one bit. That is, he's most insistent I should be in the choir. It was him what—'

Edwina favoured him with one of her most icy stares. 'Are you still here, Mr Coombes?' she demanded.

Harry took the hint and Edwina watched him go with a heart full of bitterness towards the station, its staff and the Turner family in particular. Somehow, she vowed, she would make them suffer. But how?

*

The following Monday, Sam came home from school whistling cheerfully. He had recovered his spirits after the good hiding his father had given him on Sunday and thought it well worthwhile to be out of the choir. He could easily survive the so-called disgrace and he now had every Saturday morning free, while poor old Eric did not. Harry Coombes had also left the choir at Edwina Jay's insistence, but much to the vicar's dismay. All in all, Sam felt that the incident of the marble had proved very beneficial to all concerned, although there were rumours that his pocket money might well be withheld at some future time in order to go towards the cost of the repair. Sam would worry about that when the time came. He swung his school-bag round over his head as he strolled up the lane and then threw it over the level crossing gate while he climbed over. Bob Hart opened the window of his signal-box and shouted to him to, 'Get the hell down off there,' but by that time Sam was already on the other side, grinning broadly and picking up his bag.

He made his way along the platform exchanging greetings. His father was in the booking-office checking the ledgers and filling in forms. Amy was still at The Lodge and his grandfather was helping Harry with the station garden. Tim was surreptitiously reading the *Daily Mail* and supervising

Arnold, who was cleaning the windows of the waiting-room and considering himself most fortunate to be accorded such a treat.

Still swinging his bag, Sam made his way across the track and over the grass towards the house, where he would pour himself a glass of milk and cut himself a large slice of bread on which to spread butter and honey as thickly as he could. Suddenly he became aware of an unfamiliar creaking and saw a small boy swinging to and fro on the gate which led to the house. The boy stopped swinging when he saw Sam and the two of them regarded each other over the gate.

'Hullo, then,' said Sam.

The boy's eyes widened but he said nothing and Sam's gaze travelled along the path to a woman who sat on the step, leaning against the side of the porch. She had a bulging carpet-bag on the step beside her and Sam assumed she was a gipsy.

'Can I come in?' Sam asked the boy with a smile. 'I live here.'

As the other child made no answer, Sam pushed open the gate with the little boy still clinging to it and began to walk up the path. There was something vaguely familiar about the carpet-bag . . . and something odd about the woman. She seemed to be laughing or else crying, for her head was hidden in her hands and her shoulders were shaking. Suddenly she looked up, rubbing at her eyes with a handkerchief and Sam's mind began to play tricks on him. He *knew* this bedraggled woman! It looked like his mother, but that could not be possible for she had gone away long since and was never coming back and now he had Amy instead. Sam vaguely remembered his mother – there was a photograph of her in his father's room – and she was not at all like a gipsy. She did not sit around on doorsteps crying her eyes out and whispering 'Sam' over and over. As he stared down at her, the small boy abandoned the gate and ran to stand beside his mother and two pairs of bright blue eyes stared up into his.

'Ma?' he said dubiously, but that seemed to make her cry harder than ever and she clutched the child to her and hid her face against him.

Sam could not bear the sight of so much grief and he tore his gaze from them and stared fixedly down at the ground, hoping she would stop crying. The boy turned his head towards Sam, who was beginning to think that this woman *was* his mother and that the boy with the black curls must be Uncle John's son – but if that was so, where was Uncle John and why were they sitting on the doorstep and did anybody else know they were here?

'Is it you, Ma?' he asked, wondering what he ought to do if she said, 'Yes'.

'Yes, it's me, Sam.'

She had said it! Then immediately, she cried, 'Oh, say you love me, Sam!' and began to sob again. Hastily, Sam took a step backwards while he pondered this new problem. Grown-ups never asked him whether or not he loved them; it was simply something they did not do. The little boy pulled himself free and ran back to the gate where he began to swing to and fro while the gate creaked in protest.

'Toby!' called his mother.

So the boy's name was Toby – a nice name, thought Sam. He glanced back towards the station and the lane, but there was still no sign of Uncle John which was a shame because he liked Uncle John even though nobody else did – at least, not any more, although Sam could vaguely remember a time when they were all happy together. He could just remember that Uncle John had had a wife of his own who always smelled of lavender water, but she had died. People were always dying. It occurred to him that he was hungry and that there would be bread, butter and honey on the kitchen table, but if his mother was going to stay on the front step crying, he would have to go round to the back door and get in that way. We wondered suddenly what Grandfather would say, because he would keep telling Sam that his mother was a 'wrong 'un' and 'good riddance to her', only here she was again.

'Sam,' said Ellen, controlling her tears with an effort, 'I'm so sorry, Sam. And you've grown so big!'

Sam nodded, but now there was a funny shaky feeling in his stomach and he did wish she would get up off the step because she didn't look quite right there.

'Are you going to stay?' he asked her.

'I don't know, Sam,' she said. 'I'll have to – well, we'll maybe talk about it.'

As though reading his thoughts, she now pulled herself to her feet and brushed herself down, trying ineffectually to smarten her clothes a little and tidying her hair.

'How do I look?' she asked him and her lips trembled.

Sam's funny feeling became an ache. He dropped his school-bag and moved towards her and then she was hugging him and even kissing the top of his head and he didn't really mind. He didn't *care* that she was saying the silly things grown-ups always seemed to say, because he was so glad to see her again and now that he'd got used to her he could see she wasn't at all like a gipsy – just like his mother, only rather tired and sad. After a few moments he heard the gate stop creaking and then two small arms went round Sam's legs as Toby tried to join in the hugging. Sam turned and kneeling, put his arms round Toby and hugged him.

Then he stood up and said, 'Want a twister, Toby?' and taking his hands, swung him round so that his feet came off the ground while the little boy squealed with excitement. As Sam swung Toby he felt very old and wise and rather like an uncle, because once upon a time Uncle John used to swing *him* round. When the twister ended he said, 'I'd better go and fetch Pa,' and his mother replied, 'I suppose so. Yes,' and looked unhappy again.

Chapter Fourteen

When Sam entered the booking-office he found his father perched on a high stool trying to add up a column of figures. There was no one else present.

Sam said, 'I think you'd better come, Pa. Ma's come home.'

It was just as well they were alone because Sam had to repeat it twice in a much louder voice before his father finally heard him. Then his face turned very pale and his fingers shook so much that the pencil fell from them and rolled across the table and on to the floor.

'Come home?' he whispered. 'She's come home? *Here*, you mean?'

Sam said, 'Yes, here,' and retrieved the pencil. He was sorry for his father, because he suspected that now *he* had a funny shaky feeling in his stomach. 'Ma and Toby, they're both home,' he explained and added, 'Ma keeps crying.'

'Ellen!' whispered his father. 'Here! Oh, dear God!' He looked round the tiny booking-office as though he had never seen it before.

'Toby?' he said.

Sam nodded. He was secretly glad to see how shocked his father was because of yesterday's good hiding, but he knew that was a mean way to think.

'Where—?' asked his father helplessly.

'At the house. On the step.'

'Oh, my God!' He stood up and then sat down again, putting a hand to his head.

'Does your grandfather know?' he asked Sam hoarsely.

'No.'

'And Amy?'

'No.'

'Dear God!'

Sam waited. The large ginger cat strolled in at the door and when he bent to stroke it, the cat broke into loud purring, like a small motor starting up. For a long time Sam waited, while his father came to terms with the knowledge that his wife and his brother's child were waiting on the front step of his house.

At last his father stood up again. 'You stay here,' he told Sam. 'I'll go and talk to her. And don't tell anyone, not *anyone*, that she's here. You understand?' Sam nodded.

'Oh my God!' his father said again and then he was gone.

Sam began to enjoy himself as best he could, although he did wish he could have something to eat. He looked in the biscuit tin where the staff biscuits were kept, but there were only three left and that was one each and someone would be sure to notice if he took one . . . He took one anyway. Then he played around with the official rubber stamp, stamping 'Gazedown Station' all over the underneath of the table top where no one would ever see it and once on the last page of a very thick ledger where no one would see it for a very long time – by which date he hoped to be an engine driver. He pasted a few scraps of paper together with the 'Gloy', looked at all the tickets and then at all the money in the till, which reminded him about Mrs Jay and the future threat to his pocket money.

It occurred to Sam that if his mother went away again he might go with her and then he wouldn't need to worry about Mrs Jay or school or anything else.

Eventually Tim put his head in at the door and asked, 'Where's your father?'

'Dunno,' said Sam, avoiding his eyes.

He spent the next ten minutes weighing things on the large parcels scales: ledgers, parcels, his shoes, himself. Having played with the large ball of station string, he then fiddled with the pens until he dropped one and broke the nib and was forced to put it in the table drawer out of sight.

After what seemed like hours, his father came in; his face was more red than white.

'Go to The Lodge,' he said, 'and fetch Amy home. Tell her Ellen's here. And run all the way! Then you can take Toby to see the shunting horse.'

'Pa?'

'What is it?'

'If Ma goes away again, can I go with her?'

'No, you can't, dammit!'

Sam heard him calling his grandfather and could imagine how it would be with all of them talking at once and crying and shouting and nobody listening to anyone else. He was glad he and Toby were going to the stable; he had done his part and was glad to be out of it.

*

All the way home Amy was rehearsing what she would say to her mother when she saw her. 'Hullo, Mama' would be quite inadequate. 'It's been such a long time' would sound like a reproach. What about 'I hope you're home for good'? Did she hope that? They had managed; they had adjusted their lives and they did not need her. Amy was now mistress of the household and wondered whether she wanted to relinquish that position. When her mother left them she had been sixteen years old, nearly seventeen – a young woman physically but still a child at heart. The intervening years had turned her into a woman and the two women might not like each other.

She glanced down at Sam who was walking and running beside her, trying to keep up with her longer stride.

'So what happened,' she asked, 'to Uncle John?'

'Dunno,' said Sam, kicking at a pebble to show how little he cared about it all.

'Did he leave her?'

'I told you, I don't know,' repeated Sam.

'You could have asked,' said Amy unreasonably.

'You ask, then.'

Amy felt a little of her original bitterness returning. If Uncle John had left, then her mother was returning for the wrong reasons. She was not coming back because she realised how foolish or wrong she had been, or because she missed them all, but because she had no man to support her and nowhere else to go; she was making use of them.

She shook her head without realising that she did so.

'What?' asked Sam.

'Nothing,' Amy snapped. 'Can't you see I'm thinking?'

'Well, don't blame me,' he said, his tone injured. 'I didn't ask her to come back.'

'Nobody did,' said Amy. 'And stop scuffing your boots. I've told you before about that.'

Sam relapsed into an aggrieved silence. Then, to try to annoy her, he said cheerfully, 'Toby's nice. I'm going to show him the shunting horse. Pa said.'

'Papa, not Pa,' she corrected automatically. 'I don't know what your grandfather will have to say. Do *you* want her to stay?' He shrugged. 'Do you, Sam?'

'I suppose so,' he mumbled. 'Do you?'

'I don't know, I can't think straight. She ought to have written or something.'

*

Her father was in the front garden looking for them and he was holding Toby by the hand. He gave Sam a penny to buy two chocolate bars and when the boys had gone Amy and her father exchanged worried looks.

'Don't ask me, Amy,' he said. 'It's beyond me. Your grandfather's been carrying on alarming, so I brought the boy out. What a thing to happen – who'd have thought it!' He broke off, aware that he at least had had prior warning but had chosen to ignore it. If only he had answered Ellen's letter! But then she would not be here now, in his kitchen, and deep in his heart he knew that he was pleased to see her and wanted her to stay. How, though, to explain her sudden reappearance, to reconcile his father, to tolerate the presence of John's child?

Amy said, 'Sam told me she looked "odd".'

'She's very thin. Exhausted. They've walked nearly seventy miles.' He spoke flatly, hiding his admiration for Ellen's courage; courage born of desperation, maybe, but courage none the less.

'Have they eaten?' Amy hid her feelings in practicalities.

247

'No.' He looked stricken. 'I never thought,' he said. 'I should have offered – Amy, she looks so terrible! So old and so ill! Do you want her to stay?'

Amy hardened her heart. 'Don't make me decide, Papa,' she said. 'She's your wife.' Then she took a deep breath to calm the nerves fluttering in her stomach and walked into the house.

In the kitchen Ted Turner sat in the rocking-chair, a sullen expression on his face, his mouth firmly shut. Ellen sat at the table resting her folded arms on the surface, her head on her arms, but as Amy entered the room she looked up and rose to her feet. In spite of all Amy's intentions to the contrary, she found herself staring at the unkempt woman who faced her – shocked, unable to take her eyes from Ellen's face. She saw the untidy, unwashed hair, the tear-stained face and swollen eyes, the gaunt cheekbones and the scrawny neck, but these things did not shock her. What shocked her was the realisation that this woman was virtually a stranger to her; it was not her mother, although it *was* Ellen Turner. The bond of mother and daughter no longer existed and Amy was struck by a searing sense of loss. Even after Ellen had left them, in their thoughts she had still been their absent mother; but now, to Amy, this woman was simply Ellen Turner, her father's wife.

Staring in turn at her daughter, Ellen saw a young woman she did not know. She had left a gawky sixteen-year-old girl, with childish sulky moods and airs and graces. In her absence, Amy had blossomed into an attractive woman with calm brown eyes and a confident manner. As they stared at each other, each knew intuitively that the old relationship was dead and that wishing it otherwise would be quite useless. If there was ever again to be a bond between them, it could only be one of friendship – a deep and lasting friendship, but never more than that.

'Amy . . .' Ellen whispered helplessly and Amy saw the threat of fresh tears in her eyes. Quickly she stepped forward and took hold of her mother's hand.

'You'll be thirsty,' she said tactfully. 'I'll make a pot of tea.' As she busied herself, Ellen sank down again on to the chair and Tom stood in the middle of the room, not taking his eyes from his wife's face.

Ted Turner said belligerently, 'That's right, Amy. Wait on her hand and foot. She only killed your grandmother, that's all, but you go right ahead and—'

Amy spun on her heel. 'That's enough!' she said sharply. 'We can still be civilised.'

The old man banged his fist on the table and roared, 'Civilised? Was it civilised to run off with that bloody no-good John? Was that civilised?'

'That was four years ago,' said Amy, setting out cups and saucers with hands that shook slightly.

'Years ago, was it?' he shouted. 'Well, Sarah died four years ago, but she's still bloody well dead!'

Ellen began to cry again. 'I know . . .' she sobbed, 'but God knows I didn't mean to hurt anyone.'

'But you did hurt someone,' roared Ted, 'and I won't share a roof with Sarah's murderer. Aye, murderer! You might just as well have stabbed her to death—'

'Don't!' sobbed Ellen. 'Don't say such things. I'm so terribly sorry, but I can't bring her back.'

Amy asked calmly, 'Will you have a cup of tea, Papa?'

He nodded vaguely. 'Don't take on so, Ellen,' he said.

'Grandfather? A cup of tea?' In the face of so much passion Amy was struggling to keep her emotions under control, believing that at least one person should remain calm. In the few minutes she had been in the house it had become clear to her that no one would be willing to make the final decision – whether she liked it or not, she would have to make it herself. She guessed her father wanted Ellen to stay, but did not see how this could be achieved; her grandfather would continue to oppose such an arrangement with every breath in his body; Sam would accept his mother's return and would welcome Toby. Ellen wanted to be allowed to stay . . .

'Where's John?' she asked suddenly. For the first time ever, she did not give him the courtesy of his title as uncle, although she did not really know why; it was not intentional.

Ellen shook her head helplessly, unable to speak.

'Apparently he's gone to America,' said Thomas, 'with

someone called Nettie Barlow – and he won't be coming back.'

Ellen wiped her eyes on the handkerchief her husband had lent her and said, '*Netta* Barlow.'

'What?'

'It's Netta, not Nettie.'

'Netta?' growled the old man. 'What sort of name is that, for God's sake? I'll give him Netta if ever I set eyes on him again!'

No one disputed this. Amy poured the tea and handed it round, then fetched a caraway cake from the cupboard and, thankful that it had risen well, cut a large slice for Ellen.

Her mother said, 'Toby's very hungry . . .'

'He's had some chocolate,' said Thomas. 'Don't worry.'

Everyone accepted a slice of caraway cake and briefly they sat together in silence, eating cake and drinking tea.

Amy was thinking: 'If we send them away, we will never forgive ourselves. They will just have to stay and somehow we shall have to face up to all the problems.'

She swallowed the mouthful of cake she was eating and said, '*I* think Mama and Toby should stay. What do you think, Papa?'

There was another long silence. 'Yes,' he said at last, trying to hide his relief. 'I think they should.'

'Oh, Tom!' cried Ellen.

'What about me?' shouted Ted, jumping to his feet. 'Isn't anybody going to ask me?'

'No,' said Amy firmly, 'because this is Papa's house and his word is final. And please don't get too excited, Grandfather. We don't want another tragedy.'

Her words stopped him in mid-sentence as the full impact of her meaning sank in. Her words, though harsh, had an immediate sobering effect on him. He started to speak, changed his mind and sank down again into his chair.

It was still not over, of course, for they had yet to decide how they would explain Ellen's return. After discussing various ideas, they agreed on a basic story. This was that Ellen had been staying in Devonshire nursing her dying aunt and had kept their youngest child with her. Now the aunt had died and she was free to return home. No one in Gazedown knew exactly how long she had been away from the family, only that she had been absent since they moved to Kent. In response to any questions as to why no one had ever mentioned Ellen or the ailing aunt, they would say that Thomas Turner had not approved of his wife going, but that Ellen had insisted because the aunt had no one else left in the world. Her departure had thus caused a family rift and they had not wished to discuss it. The aunt had been suffering from an unnamed wasting disease – never properly diagnosed – and had taken longer to die than anyone expected.

'A tough old bird, our Aunt Emma,' commented Amy with a faint smile.

Toby was also a problem. He must be told that Thomas was his new 'Papa', and if he made unfortunate references in public to his 'other Papa', they would cover up the slip by a second story. This was that Ellen had left to care for the aunt while Toby was too young to remember his own father – that is, Thomas Turner – and had persisted in calling the aunt's next-door neighbour 'Papa', much to the amusement of all concerned.

These two stories were not watertight, but in the absence of anything better Amy thought they would suffice. Hopefully, no one would ask questions that were too direct.

It seemed, then, that the worst was over. Amy sent Ellen upstairs to rest on the bed while she prepared to stretch the supper to serve two extra mouths. Ted Turner stumped off, muttering morosely but bearing in mind Amy's hint about his health. Eventually Sam returned with Toby and received the news that his mother was staying with a laconic 'Oh, is she?' adding, 'Is Toby staying too?'

Amy could see that Sam was pleased and because he thought he was too old for hugs and kisses, she gave him a conspiratorial wink to let him know that everything was going to be all right. Then, while Toby amused himself with one of Sam's old wooden engines, she explained the stories they had created to explain Ellen's and Toby's return. She thought that, as the youngest member of the family, Sam was most likely to be 'interrogated' and satisfied herself that he understood the need for the white lies and was fully conversant with them.

'So now you've got a brother,' she told him. 'Lucky old you!'

'He kept running away,' said Sam, intrigued. 'When we were in the stable yard. He wanted me to chase him and when I did he laughed; he thought it was a game.'

Amy smiled. 'I expect he likes having a big brother.'

'He doesn't say much,' said Sam, 'just runs away laughing.'

'Perhaps he's shy,' suggested Amy, peeling a few extra potatoes to go with the stew and deciding to make a jam tart for pudding, since it was rather a special occasion and Ellen and Toby looked as though they needed fattening up.

Sam frowned suddenly. 'He's pulling the wheel off!' he hissed. 'Off my engine!'

'Little boys always do things like that,' Amy told him. 'You were always pulling the wheels off that engine and Papa was always having to fix them back on again.'

'Was he?' asked Sam. 'Was I?'

'Yes and yes,' Amy smiled.

Toby gave an extra large tug and the wheel came off in his hand. After a moment's consternation, he turned to Sam and held the wheel up for him to see.

'Wheel's tum off,' he said solemnly.

Sam looked at Amy. 'He said "tum off",' he grinned, then turning back to the little boy said, 'Yes, it has.'

'Tum off,' repeated Toby sadly, pushing the wheel against the engine in a vain bid to replace it. 'Wheel's tum off!'

'He means the wheel's *come* off,' said Sam. 'He can't say "come".'

'He's very young,' Amy pointed out.

Sam sighed noisily and said, 'Do you want me to mend it, Toby? No! No! It's no good doing that – that won't mend it.' He took the offending wheel. 'Look, we'll have to find a hammer and then I'll mend it for you. Come on, Toby. I'll take the wheel and you bring the engine. All right? There's a hammer in the garden shed.'

As Amy watched them go out together, there was a lump in her throat and tears in her eyes, because suddenly she knew that Sam and Toby would make it all possible.

252

Chapter Fifteen

Esme screwed up a second sheet of notepaper and tossed it angrily into the waste-paper basket.

'It really is quite intolerable!' she muttered.

Clara, dusting the bookshelf on the far side of the room, reflected that the letter in the plain brown envelope obviously contained some news which had badly upset the mistress of Bates Manor. She was dusting the small study while Esme was working there because Esme had asked her to do so, and that was because Esme seemed to need her company. Since the day when Clara had first brushed Esme's hair, Esme and Gerald had not spoken to each other except to exchange the barest courtesies: a 'Good morning' if they met at the breakfast table, or an 'Excuse me' if they passed on the stairs.

Esme picked up the offending letter and read it again, her face set in an expression of extreme distaste.

Dear Madam,

You obviously do not know what is going on in your own property or you would take steps to put a stop to it. I refer to The Lodge, where a certain young woman who should know better is spending too much of her time unchaperoned in the company of a certain young man. The young woman sneaks down there day after day as bold as brass, and without any care for the moral tone of this village. One shudders to imagine what they do together, shut away from the eyes of the world and from God's sight, but in my opinion — and, I'm sure, that of any other right-minded women — it should be stopped. This kind of unpleasantness, if unchecked, could easily undermine the values of other young people in Gazedown and I am sure you will wish to take some action. I have assumed that you know the identity of the young woman in question, but in case you do not it is Amy Turner, the stationmaster's daughter. I have felt it my duty to bring this distasteful matter to your attention and trust you will appreciate that my motives are entirely honourable although I prefer to sign myself,

Anonymous

Esme had tried unsuccessfully to deduce the identity of the writer. The letter was grammatical, the spelling was correct and the handwriting was well-shaped and entirely legible, which eliminated quite a few people from the list of possibles. The notepaper itself was of reasonable quality, although the brown paper envelope in which it had been sent was fairly flimsy. It was obviously written by a woman, unless the phrase 'other right-minded women' was intended to mislead her. She thought perhaps it might have been written by Ivy Peck.

'Despicable!' Esme said aloud. 'Quite despicable.'

'What's that then, ma'am?' Clara asked dutifully.

'This letter.' Esme waved it in the air. 'A poison-pen letter.'

'Poison? Oh, do be careful, ma'am!' cried Clara, trying not to over-act but pretending ignorance so that Esme might enlighten her further.

Esme threw down the letter again. 'It's not poisonous, Clara,' she said. 'It's the contents which are poisonous. A poison-pen letter is written, in my opinion, by someone with an unhealthy mind. And, of course, such letters are never signed.'

Clara had stopped dusting and, genuinely curious, moved towards the desk at which Esme was sitting. 'Oh that's terrible, ma'am,' she said. 'Wicked! Oh, I don't know how anyone could. I'm sure you've done nothing wrong, ma'am,' she added ingenuously.

Esme gave her a sharp look and said, 'Not me, you stupid girl! It's about someone else. It doesn't matter; just get on with your work.'

'Yes, ma'am.' Clara managed to convey that she was hurt but then added, 'It's not about me, is it, ma'am?'

'Of course it's not. Please don't be silly, Clara. If it was, you would have heard about it before now.'

Clara returned to her dusting, still curious but pleased with the little exchange between maid and mistress. She did not want Esme to realise how shrewd she was and frequently feigned ignorance so that Esme would feel secure in her superiority. However, she was fully aware of the undercurrents present between Esme and Gerald and half aware of the reasons behind them. She was beginning to judge Esme's moods from the expression on her face or the tone of her voice and found she could exploit this in small ways — making the remarks that Esme needed to hear exactly when she needed to hear them. Humouring her, in fact.

Esme, unaware that she was being humoured, was upset by the letter on three counts. She was annoyed that anyone should dare to suggest that she was allowing The Lodge to be used for improper purposes; she was angry that Amy Turner should be spending so much time there; and she was furious that Ralph Allan obviously preferred Amy's company to her own. Now she knew why he had turned down her recent invitations — to go riding, to accompany her to London to the opera and to attend the preview of an art exhibition. Of course, the girl was supposedly helping him with his work whenever she could spare the time, but every afternoon? Esme did not for one moment stop to wonder whether or not the sender of the letter had given accurate information. In her mind, it all added up to the fact that some kind of relationship was developing between Ralph and the stationmaster's daughter.

Determined to put a stop to this, Esme was now trying to compose a letter to Ralph in which she was forceful enough to ensure his cooperation but not so forceful that she sounded jealous or shrewish. The tone must be more in sorrow than in anger, she knew, if it was to have any effect on Ralph Allan.

She had made three false starts to this letter, but now she dipped her pen into the inkwell and started again.

My dear Ralph.

    This letter is very difficult for me, but I'm sure you will understand what prompts me to write it.

She crossed out 'it', and wrote 'what prompts me to write to you in this way.' Then she continued:

> I have had a serious complaint from someone in the village regarding Amy Turner who, she suggests, frequently calls at The Lodge and is obviously making herself a nuisance to you. I think perhaps it was a mistake on your part to encourage her originally, although I'm sure you acted only out of kindness. In the circumstances, I should appreciate it if you would put an end to her visits.

After a few moments she went on:

> If you feel unable to deal with the matter yourself, I will speak to the girl on your behalf. I am truly sorry to have to write to you in this vein, but naturally I cannot tolerate unsavoury gossip and am acting promptly in the hope that I can prevent the matter from coming to my husband's attention.

That, she thought, was an implied threat, but so much the better. Hopefully it would appear that she felt obliged to write as firmly as she did in order to prevent an even more drastic response from Gerald. She re-wrote the letter, signed it, 'Regretfully, Esme', put it in an envelope and sealed it. Having considered for a moment, she then wrote 'By Hand' on the envelope.

    'Clara, stop fidgeting round me and take this letter to The Lodge,' she ordered. 'See that you give it into Mr Allan's own hands. If anyone else is there, ask to speak to Mr Allan himself. You understand? If there is no one in, bring it back to me.'

    'Yes, ma'am,' said Clara, 'I understand.' She held out her hand for the letter, but Esme still held it.

    'Despicable,' said Esme, shaking her head. 'What sort of mind does a person have to write a poison-pen letter? But there you are, people do.'

    'Yes, ma'am.'

'Well, get along and remember what I say. Give it directly to Mr Allan or bring it back.' She handed over the letter and Clara nodded.

When she had gone, Esme went to the window to watch the figure of the maid as she walked along the drive and into the shadow of the trees.

'That will cook your goose, Amy Turner!' she muttered. 'And damn good riddance too. Perhaps that will teach you to know your place!'

Was there really anything between Ralph Allan and the stationmaster's daughter, she wondered uneasily. No, she did not believe for a moment that there was. Amy Turner was nothing: a silly little social climber. Well, she would soon find herself at the bottom of the ladder again and serve her right. Turning to the mirror, Esme smoothed back her hair, admiring the lines and colour of her face and the way the turquoise earrings matched her eyes. Using the backs of her fingers, she patted the flesh underneath her jaw and then examined the corners of her eyes for crows' feet. Finding none, she smiled at her reflection and said softly, 'Goodbye, Amy Turner', hoping that by now Clara had reached The Lodge and was delivering the bombshell.

Esme's smile deepened and she crossed to the desk, picked up the anonymous letter and put it briefly to her lips. 'Thank you, whoever you are,' she whispered. 'Now perhaps Ralph Allan will start to see things *my* way!'

Now that that little problem had been settled, Esme's day stretched ahead of her until 6.30, when she was expecting friends to arrive for dinner at 7.30, followed by a game of bridge. She wondered how much longer she and Gerald could maintain the pretence that everything between them was normal; how long before their friends put two and two together to make four.

Tonight she would dress in her finery and her conversation would sparkle. Gerald would look distinguished and everyone would laugh politely at his jokes as they always did. She would force down good food and wine feeling that it choked her, and find the bridge a colossal bore. She would not enjoy a moment of it, yet would dread their guests' departure because then there would be no one to pretend for and she and Gerald would go their separate ways, preparing for bed with barely a glance at the partner who had shared that bed for so long. They would lie well apart, trying not to touch each other, but they would both be wide awake, thinking and hating.

As Esme waited at the window for Clara to reappear, she thought about her and congratulated herself for engaging the girl on a permanent basis. Clara was malleable and very promising. Yes, mused Esme, Clara was a 'find' and she would make sure that she stayed. Perhaps she would give her the old blue silk dress; presumably the girl could sew and would be able to alter it to fit. And if she continued to work well and remained polite and anxious to please, perhaps a small increase in salary at Christmas? Esme decided she would drop a hint to that effect, anyway; it would do no harm. Standing at the window, she became aware suddenly of the rest of the house — uninhabited and silent except in the kitchen, where Mrs Lester and Izzie were preparing the next meal. Esme felt suddenly small, insignificant and of no interest to anyone. No one really cared whether she was happy or sad, well or ill and if she died tomorrow, who would grieve for her? A wave of self-pity brought the prickle of tears to her eyes, but she blinked them back. She would not give way, she told herself. She, Esme Hatherley, would fight for what she wanted. Damn Gerald! Damn the empty house and her empty life! Once she had wanted children, or at least she had expected to have children, but not any more. Now it was too late and she had no one to love her. If only Gerald would die, she thought, and leave me a rich widow. Then I would marry Ralph Allan, life would be full and I would be happy. I would make him happy, too . . .

Just then Clara reappeared, hurrying along the drive, and a few minutes later she was running up the stairs and into the room.

'Well?' Esme asked.

'He was there, ma'am,' gasped Clara breathlessly, holding her side, 'I put the letter right into his hand.'

'What did he say?'

'He gave me threepence, ma'am, and I said "Is there any answer, sir?" '

'Good girl!' said Esme.

'But he said, "Not now" and then he shut the door.'

'Was she there?' asked Esme.

'Who, ma'am?' responded Clara innocently.

'It doesn't matter,' said Esme. 'Thank you, Clara; that will be all. Oh, I wondered if you could make use of an old dress of mine. Can you sew?'

'Oh yes, ma'am. At least, I can do alterations.'

'It's the blue silk with the pearl buttons which is in the brown trunk in the attic. You can take it; do what you like with it.'

Clara's enthusiasm was not totally feigned. A blue silk dress! 'Thank you very much indeed, ma'am,' she cried. 'That *is* kind of you!'

'I'm glad you're pleased. Now you'd better go back downstairs. No doubt Mrs Lester wants you to set the table. And, Clara . . .'

'Yes, ma'am?'

'What I told you about the poison-pen letter was in strictest confidence. You understand?'

'Yes, ma'am.'

'Good. Then off you go.'

She really was a very nice girl, thought Esme, then promptly forgot her as she tried to imagine Ralph's consternation when he opened and read her letter.

*

Amy looked up from her work as Ralph returned with a letter in his hand.

'I thought it was the dreaded Esme,' he said, 'but it's a letter from her instead.'

'Probably a proposal,' suggested Amy with an attempt at humour.

She rubbed her eyes tiredly and put a hand to her aching head. Since her mother's return, life at home had been much more difficult than she had expected and Amy was not sleeping well. Her grandfather's continuing hostility towards Ellen was making even a pretence of normality impossible.

Amy's role seemed to be that of perpetual peacemaker and she tired of the daily battles which had to be smoothed out if life was to be tolerable. She tried to believe that with time all the problems would be resolved, but it was hard not to feel depressed. Her father looked pale and wretched, although he made an attempt to pretend things were better than they really were. He had crossed swords with Ted on several occasions and the latter was sulky and spiteful by turns.

Amy's salvation was in her work and the hours she spent at The Lodge were the only relief she had from the tensions and frictions of home. She had confided in Ralph, who understood her problems and made no reference to the deterioration in her work. She had been making good progress with the typewriter, but recently had found it difficult to concentrate.

Ralph glanced at her now as he began to unfold the letter and thought she looked exhausted and unhappy. Then as he began to read, his face darkened with shock.

'Dear God!' he exclaimed. 'I just can't believe this! It's – it's so unfair! Amy, I'm so sorry . . .'

She looked at him in alarm. 'What's unfair, Ralph? And what are you sorry about? What on earth is the matter?'

'This!' he cried. 'God! What have we done to deserve this? Amy, this is all my fault. I should have realised . . . oh, you'd better read it for yourself.'

Amy took the letter from his trembling fingers and began to read what Esme had written. Her own colour faded as she drew in her breath sharply.

'That is really horrible!' cried Ralph. 'Horrible and despicable – and Esme had no right to be influenced by whoever it was. She should have come down to see me personally, to ask me if it was true.'

Amy had risen to her feet as she read the letter, but now she handed it back to him and sat down wearily. This was the end to all her hopes; it was the final blow. Someone's malicious tongue was going to spoil everything.

Dully she said, 'She's jealous; Esme's jealous of me and she's taking this chance to get rid of me – to push me out of your life.'

Ralph was re-reading the letter and when he had finished

it for the second time, he screwed it up into a ball and hurled it across the room.

'Hell and damnation!' he cried. 'What the hell can I say to you, Amy? How can I apologise?' He faced her, miserable and angry. 'I wouldn't have had this happen for the world – and to you, of all people. You're as straight and honest as the day is long!'

'It's not your fault,' she said. 'Don't blame yourself, Ralph; it's other people and their nasty minds.' Her distress deepened as a new thought struck her. 'My father! He'll be so worried. As if we didn't have enough problems to deal with! I wonder if I can possibly keep it from him.'

'Not if you have to give up the work,' said Ralph. 'How would you explain that? Oh, this is impossible. I shall have to go up there and sort things out. I'm sure I told Esme that you are officially working for me now.'

'She believes it because she wants to,' said Amy wearily, 'and because it discredits me. She's clever and calculating – it could be one of her tricks to get you up to the Manor.'

'You may be right,' he said thoughtfully.

'Then I suppose whoever it is with the nasty mind will write to Gerald Hatherley about Ralph Allan sneaking up to the Manor while he's away in London! Ugh! The whole thing is so vile. Ralph, we must take time to calm down and think carefully. We mustn't fly into a panic—'

'We already have!' he said with a half-hearted attempt at a smile.

'Well, let's calm down now,' said Amy. 'If she's expecting you to rush up there, we must disappoint her and think of some way round it. Don't ask me how, but we must try.'

'I blame myself,' he said wretchedly.

Amy took a deep breath and tried to think rationally. 'We both underestimated village gossip,' she said. 'I should have known, but it's too late to keep blaming ourselves. That won't help. Do sit down, Ralph; you look as awful as I feel.'

He sat down opposite her at the table. 'Who on earth could it be?' he whispered. 'We shall never know, but we shall look at people and wonder about them.'

Amy retrieved the letter and smoothed it out thoughtfully.

'Maybe there never was a letter,' she said slowly. 'Maybe Esme made it up, to give herself an excuse to get rid of me.'

'I don't know whether that makes it better or worse,' said Ralph.

Amy shrugged. 'Worse, if Esme is really that devious, but better if no one in the village really is accusing us. It's six of one and half a dozen of the other, I suppose. Oh, poor Ralph, don't look so upset. That's exactly what she wants, isn't it? To demoralise us. To make us give up. I think we need to show her that we're not a bit demoralised, even if we are.'

Ralph covered his face with his hands without answering and Amy forgot her own distress as her heart went out to him. He was not a fighter, she knew that. The thought of facing up to Esme must be terrifying.

'Maybe you need not go to see her,' she suggested slowly. 'Wait a while. Let me think this out, Ralph. Maybe it would be better just to write a brief note saying . . .' She stared at the crumpled letter, deep in thought. 'Maybe you could say you're sorry that she has been upset by such a silly letter but that as you have told her, I am now your official assistant and my salary is paid by the publishers.' They stared at each other with growing hope and Amy rushed on eagerly, 'You could add that since there's no truth whatsoever in the rumour, you think the best thing we can all do is to ignore it. You needn't even answer straight away. Show her how unconcerned we are and sent it tomorrow.'

Slowly Ralph uncovered his face. 'I'm going to London tomorrow,' he reminded her, 'to meet the daughter of Lord Stanisbrooke's first mistress: Elliot's big discovery!'

That name again, thought Amy with a flash of longing. Why on earth did his image persist when she had tried so hard to forget him? Elliot Allan was not for her and probably she would never see him again, yet she kept on hoping. Occasionally Ralph would mention him and she envied the easy relationship that existed between them. On very rare occasions she ventured a remark about Elliot; then Ralph would elaborate and she would learn a little more about the man who had come into her life so unexpectedly – and who was looming so large in her thoughts. London was so far away. If only she had gone to college and if only she was teaching in London . . . but then she would never have met him! Fate could be very unkind, she decided.

With an effort she recalled what Ralph had said about his forthcoming trip to London. 'Better and better!' she told him. 'Waylay Clara on her way to the Manor and give her the letter to deliver to Esme. By the time she's read it and decided what to do about it, you'll be on your way to London. If she comes rushing down to The Lodge, she'll find me here working alone.'

'But then you'll be in the firing line,' Ralph protested.

'I don't mind,' said Amy. 'I can be all innocent and terribly surprised that she's taking it all so seriously.' Her eyes gleamed suddenly. 'I could even say that we had a good laugh about it. Surely she couldn't persist in the face of so much indifference. What do you think, Ralph?' she asked.

'Amy Turner,' he said, 'have I told you lately that you are a genius?'

'Not lately, no,' she said, with a faint smile.

'Well, take it from me,' he said. 'You are!'

*

The next train would take Ralph to Cannon Street, where Elliot would meet him. He waited on the platform for it to arrive, glancing nervously round in case Esme, having read his letter, should already be in pursuit. The only other prospective passenger was the Reverend Ambrose Stokes who was talking to Harry Coombes, although Ellen was at the far end of the platform with Toby who was waiting to see the train.

Tim Hollis was in the booking-office, his lips pursed into a tuneless whistle. Mr Hatherley would be getting off the incoming train and that was beginning to arouse Tim's interest. He had noticed that the master of Bates Manor had been going to London much more frequently than before, and now always came home on an earlier train. Tim had also noticed that Lorna Betts was often to be glimpsed in the vicinity of the level crossing about this time, but he had not been able to make a positive connection between the two – at least, not one that made any sense to him.

Arnold was also on the platform waiting for the train to arrive, but he was not talking to anyone nor telling anyone about 'gee' or 'double-you'. He was sitting cross-legged on the trolley, in a deep sulk. Earlier he had knocked over a tin of dark red paint which Tim had been using to repaint the waiting-room window-frame. The station master had shouted at him again and had called him 'a useless idiot'. When Mr Turner had gone, Tim had tried to cheer him up by explaining about the stationmaster's wife having come home with their youngest son Toby, who was a bit of a handful. All this, Tim had explained, had made Mr Turner very moody, and that was why he had shouted at Arnold. However, Arnold was not at all mollified by Tim's explanation and had taken himself off to the trolley to brood on his troubles. He was still sitting there when the train was signalled and did not even move when, with an exciting release of white steam and a screeching of brakes, it rolled alongside the platform. As it did so, several things happened in quick succession. Young Toby hurtled across the platform, laughing, and Ellen ran after him, shouting to him to keep back from the edge. Forgetting his sulks, Arnold jumped to his feet in excitement and inadvertently set the trolley in motion. The sudden movement threw him off the trolley and he landed awkwardly, sprawling on his back. The trolley, however, moved on, gathering speed. Suddenly it became obvious to the horrified watchers that it was heading for Toby and would knock him under the approaching train.

For a moment everyone seemed to freeze, then Ellen screamed as Ralph — nearest to the boy — threw himself across the few yards which separated them and somehow managed to catch hold of him. With a superhuman effort he threw Toby back from the edge towards his mother, but as he did so the trolley hit him and knocked him into the path of the train. There was nothing anyone could do to save him. In a hopeless attempt to stop the train, the driver flung the controls into reverse, but the heavy blue locomotive rolled on as Ralph disappeared from view and his agonised scream was drowned by the hiss of smoke and the crash and clatter of wheels and couplings as the train finally shuddered to a halt.

264

Ellen, sobbing, was shaking Toby. The vicar ran forward
– his lips moving in a muttered prayer – to stare down under
the train, fearful of what he would see. Harry Coombes, a
hand to his heart, joined him, his face white and shocked.
Mr Bell and the fireman both jumped from the engine and
ran back along the platform, their faces pale.

'It happened so fast!' cried Mr Bell. 'There was no time.
Christ Almighty! It just happened so *fast!*'

Arnold was picking himself up, unaware of the tragedy
which he had provoked. On the opposite platform, Tim
stared trance-like at the crumpled figure which he could just
make out between the wheels of the train.

'He's there! Down there!' he shouted, pointing, as he
caught sight of Harry's face in the gap between the first and
second carriage. 'I'll fetch Mr Turner!'

Astonished that his trembling legs could still carry him, he
raced away in the direction of the signal-box where he had
last seen the stationmaster talking with Bob Hart.

Ellen had been told by Harry to take Toby back to the
house and to stay away from the scene of the accident, and
this she was glad to do. Meanwhile the vicar was kneeling
at the edge of the platform trying to determine whether or
not Ralph Allan was still alive. His stomach churned as he
saw the bloodied stump of a leg and the prayer that formed
in his mind faded when it reached his lips. Gerald Hatherley
joined him, lips trembling.

Apparently lifeless, Ralph lay with one arm thrown over
his face. His hair was matted and blood was spattered on
the gravel around his head. No one, the vicar thought, could
have survived such injuries. It might be better for him if he
were already dead. Harry was running along the platform,
begging the curious passengers to stay where they were,
arguing with a belligerent red-haired man who wanted to
get out to see what 'the bloody fuss' was about.

At last the stationmaster appeared, having sent Tim in
search of Doctor Brown. Meanwhile, he decided they must
try to lift Ralph clear and apply a tourniquet to his leg before
he bled to death. Fortunately, the railway had trained him
well for just such an emergency and Harry ran for the first-
aid box with the feeling that if anyone could save Ralph's

life, it would be Mr Turner. It was awkward work, clambering under the train in a limited space, but their task was made easier by the fact that Ralph was still unconscious. He had suffered a severe blow to the top of his head, his right shoulder was crushed and his left leg was severed just below the knee.

The vicar left the rescue to the members of the railway staff and concerned himself with placating the passengers in Harry's place. After the train had been uncoupled and the rear half shunted backwards, the stationmaster, Mr Bell, Gerald and the fireman finally managed to lift Ralph clear. They laid him on the platform. As the tourniquet was being applied, a woman passenger threw down her coat to serve as a cushion under Ralph's head but at that moment, to everyone's heartfelt relief, the doctor arrived. He at once took charge of the injured man and organised his removal to the nearest hospital. Ralph Allen, he told them, was alive but only just, and he did not hold out much hope for his eventual recovery.

*

When Gerald arrived at their usual meeting place amongst the trees, he found Lorna standing with her hands on her hips glaring down at Arnold who sat with his back against a tree, sucking his thumb. His broad face was blotched, his eyes were red from past tears and fresh ones hovered in his round blue eyes. His expression was one of deep despair.

Lorna turned to greet Gerald. 'I can't get rid of him,' she said furiously. 'He won't budge. Everywhere I go, he follows me! Grizzling and carrying on about a trolley or some such. I can't make head or tail of it. I've told him to go home, but he won't.'

Gerald beckoned her away from Arnold and she followed him, puzzled by his manner.

'There's been an accident,' he told her, his voice low. He gave her a brief outline and her eyes widened.

'Poor Mr Allan!' she cried. 'Is he going to die?'

'That is possible, I'm afraid. It's all most unfortunate and there will have to be an enquiry and so on. Naturally the stationmaster is very distressed about it. He gave me all the

266

facts because I am Mr Allan's landlord and I shall have to get in touch with his next of kin, which is his brother. I must telephone Elliot right away. So, I'm afraid, my dear little Lorna, that fate is not on our side today.'

He leaned forward to kiss her, but at that moment Arnold lumbered up and stood staring at them, sniffing loudly and muttering to himself about the trolley and the fact that the stationmaster had shouted at him again.

Gerald and Lorna gazed at him. 'Poor Arnold,' whispered Lorna. 'He didn't mean to do it, he wouldn't hurt a fly. Do you think he knows about Mr Allan?'

Gerald shrugged. 'No one person was to blame,' he said, 'from what I can understand. It was just an unfortunate combination of circumstances.' He sighed deeply. 'And I was so looking forward to our time together – just the *three* of us!'

Lorna said wryly, 'Four, with Arnold!'

'I live for our meetings,' he whispered. 'You know that, don't you?'

She nodded, then a thought struck her. 'But if you go home now, she'll want to know why you came back early.'

'I'll say I was unwell; stomach pains.'

'It's terrible,' said Lorna. 'Poor Mr Allan, I mean.'

'And poor us!'

'And us, of course.'

Arnold was still watching them, although they kept their voices as low as possible. Lorna said kindly, 'Well, you'd better go home now, Arnold. I think your ma must be looking for you.'

A frown settled over his face. 'No, she's not,' he said. 'She's not looking for me, she never looks for me. My ma *never* looks for me.'

'Oh, all right then, she's not,' Lorna said hastily, lowering her voice again to say, 'I just wanted a quick kiss and a bit of a cuddle if we can't "do the bees".'

Arnold's innocent phrase had become a personal joke between them now, but Gerald did not smile. He fumbled in his pocket for a penny and held it out to Arnold.

'Here,' he said. 'Go and buy some sweeties.'

But Arnold did not want to be alone with his fears. If he

was alone and defenceless, the stationmaster might appear and shout at him again. He felt safer in someone else's company. He knew these two people did not want him around, but he was reluctant to go and so he stubbornly shook his head, refusing the money.

'He called me names!' he said suddenly, remembering the earlier disaster with the pot of paint. 'He shouldn't have done that; my ma will get on to him for calling me names.' He knew that as a boy his mother had defended him against the jibes of the other children. 'It's not nice to call people names.'

'No, it's not,' Lorna agreed helplessly. 'Who called you names?'

'*He* did.' Overcome by yet another painful memory, Arnold sat down on the ground and began to cry again.

'I shall have to go,' said Gerald. 'We're never going to get rid of him and it will look odd if I don't get home soon after the train arrived. I have a note of Elliot Allan's telephone number somewhere; he left it in case of emergencies when he first arranged the lease of The Lodge. I didn't expect to need it, but I shall find it.'

'Maybe *she'll* have telephoned him,' said Lorna. She hated saying 'your wife' and did not even use Esme's christian name. 'I wish you didn't have to go.'

'She won't know yet,' he said. 'And I must go — without even a kiss or a squeeze of my lovely little Lorna.' He eyed her lovingly, his eyes blinking. 'And you are still quite well? And quite sure about you-know-what?'

'Quite sure, sir — I mean Gerald.' She laughed at the slip. 'I still forget sometimes.'

Gerald looked around them. 'We can't both leave together,' he decided. 'If I go first, will you be all right with him?' He glanced towards Arnold, who was still snivelling quietly to himself.

''Course I will. I'll just walk a little way with you.' She slipped her hand into his and said, 'I don't know why we worry. He saw us doing it once, remember?'

'I do, but I hope *he* doesn't,' said Gerald. 'Just move away slowly and he might not notice.'

'Will he get into trouble about the accident?'

Gerald shook his head. 'I doubt it. He's not responsible for his actions. He's been banned from the station, though and he's not to set foot on railway property again, ever. He won't like that.'

They were edging away from the trees as gently as possible, leaving Arnold behind.

Lorna said, 'Well, if he can't go to the station any more, he'll hang around here. We'll have to find somewhere else to meet.'

'I've been thinking about that, Lorna,' he said. 'There's no time to talk now, but we must settle things between us somehow. I've been giving it a lot of thought.'

Just then he stepped on a dry twig. It snapped under his weight and Arnold was on his feet in a flash and lumbering after them, panic in his eyes.

Lorna looked at him and shook her head. 'What a mess you are, Arnold,' she told him kindly. She turned to Gerald. 'Try giving him a penny again,' she said. 'I'll go with him to the shop and buy him a stick of barley sugar. You can sneak off in the other direction.'

He agreed reluctantly. 'And you will remember your promise?' he urged. 'Don't tell anybody anything until I tell you to – certainly not your mother; she'll have you jumping off the table or whatever outlandish things these girls do.' He put two fingers to his lips and threw her a kiss which she returned.

A large grin spread over Arnold's face. 'Kiss her!' he cried. 'Give her a proper kiss!'

With a muttered oath, Gerald hurried away and Lorna turned to Arnold.

'Kiss me?' she repeated, with mock indignation. 'Arnold! What a thing to say! Me kiss Mr Hatherley? Certainly not! Now, do you want a barley sugar stick? I'll come with you as far as the shop. And wipe your nose. You look terrible, you really do. You'll find a hanky if you look – your ma always gives you a hanky. That's it, I told you so.'

Bullying and coaxing, she got Arnold looking more presentable and then led him off to the shop. She wondered what Gerald had in mind for the future. Whatever it was, she would agree and she would fight her mother if she had to. She was growing fond of the man she had once dubbed 'a dry old stick'. Fond of him and sorry for him. She could not imagine what the future might hold, but for the moment she was happy.

Chapter Sixteen

Ralph hovered between life and death and in rare lucid moments he knew that he did so. In between these rare moments, his world was a dark confusion over which he had no control. He was content that it should be that way, for he felt so weary that the effort needed to resolve the confusion was quite beyond him. He was aware that he lay on his back – that much was clear – but he could not see through the darkness that enveloped him and so he did not know where it was that he lay. He was not too cold, nor too hot. Sometimes he felt severe pain in his chest or legs, sometimes in his head. Then he would hear himself groan, or perhaps it was a cry for help. He was not sure, because for much of the time he could not hear either. When he did hear, there were voices and occasionally he thought someone touched his hand, moving his fingers into a fist and then releasing them, but he was never quite certain. Once he thought he felt the bed move as though it were on wheels, but perhaps he imagined that.

Although Ralph did not see and rarely heard, his dreams were very vivid – if they were dreams. In one of his lucid moments he wondered whether they were dreams or memories, but he had no way of knowing and it did not seem to matter. Nothing mattered any more and that pleased him. Once he caught a glimpse of his mother walking ahead of him; then she turned back, waiting for him to catch her up, holding out her hand and smiling down at him the way she did, her eyes full of humour and that special tenderness. The bungalow was there, too, nestled into the hill bleached white by the fierce Indian sun. The sun was warm across his back as he ran towards the bungalow, but then it seemed to retreat from him so that he could never quite reach it. He could never go inside.

He saw a pair of grey gloves and took them in his hands, smelling the faint tang of kid leather and counting the tiny buttons. Then Elliot was there, nearly eight years old, wrestling with him on the beach among the sand dunes. They were wrestling in fun, not hurting each other; Elliot was laughing and his dark eyes gleamed with excitement. Ralph loved Elliot as he had never loved anyone else and Elliot loved him in return. Elliot was his hero, his protector. He wanted to be like Elliot. No, he wanted to *be* Elliot.

There was a girl in one of his dreams, a girl with smooth hair and gold-brown eyes. When he saw her she gave him a pie she had made and he thanked her for it, and whenever he glimpsed her he heard the whistle of a train and then saw a small boy running – a boy with curly black hair.

Not all the dreams were pleasant. One of them made him cry – at least, he thought he cried. It seemed his eyes were wet with tears, but he could not be sure of anything in the dark confusion. He thought he cried when he sat in his locked room and turned on the gas. He could smell the gas and hear the banging on the door, and when they broke down his door and dragged him out of the room into the corridor he thought he had tears on his cheeks. He only knew he was unhappy and he wanted to die. Perhaps now he *would* die. Perhaps he could slip away in the darkness and no one would stop him. Ralph hoped very much that that would happen. He tried to pray; he tried to say, 'Please God, let me die', but he could not feel whether or not his lips moved and he did not hear himself speak the words.

The dreams or memories came and went and in between there was pain and silence and darkness. Ralph Allan hovered between life and death and hoped to die.

Ralph's bed was number 14 in a row of eighteen which stood along one side of the vast ward. The bed-frame was of white-painted metal and had wooden side supports, presumably to prevent him from rolling out although in his present state that seemed unlikely. His face was white beneath the heavy bandages that bound his head and his arms with their long slim hands lay across the blankets. His eyes were closed and his face was expressionless.

Amy thought, with a chill of dread, 'He's so still. He might well be dead already. How would anyone know?' She longed to take his hand and talk him back to consciousness, but instead she stood passively beside Elliot. His face was drawn and she knew that his concern for his brother was painfully real. They were together on one side of the bed, facing Sister Martin who stood opposite them – a tall, thin woman with iron-grey hair and an abrupt manner. She seemed highly efficient and an iron disciplinarian, and the nurses treated her with a respect amounting almost to awe. Amy felt a certain wariness in her dealings with her and left most of the questions to Elliot, who appeared completely unaffected by Sister Martin's cold tone and impersonal manner. She certainly did not believe in mincing words.

'His own doctor's diagnosis is probably correct,' she told them. 'The chances of a full recovery are very slim, especially with his history. Will-power is so important.' Her voice was brisk, her face expressionless. 'The surgeon has done all he can for the time being – all he dare do, in fact – but the pressure of the brain remains unaltered. Later, he may try another operation. We don't know yet if that will be advisable.'

'When would the surgeon take that decision?' Elliot asked her. 'Would there need to be a general improvement before it was safe to operate again?'

'No, Mr Allan, quite the reverse in fact. If there is no general improvement, the surgeon may decide another operation is your brother's only chance.'

Amy looked with compassion at the still figure in the bed and plucked up courage to ask, 'Is he in a coma, Sister?'

'No, he is not.' Sister Martin's shrewd grey eyes regarded her coldly. 'He is unconscious for much of the time, but he does respond occasionally. It is early days yet. You are a member of his family, I presume?'

'Er . . . no,' Amy stammered. 'I'm a close friend—'

Elliot interrupted to say, 'Miss Turner and my brother are – were involved on a project together.'

273

The sister's lips tightened as though this information did not impress her. 'We do have certain rules,' she said. 'Only next of kin are allowed to visit seriously ill patients. It's for the patient's own good.'

'I understand,' said Amy. 'I'm sorry, I didn't know. I was so anxious . . .'

Sister Martin straightened her shoulders. 'If all the anxious friends and colleagues visited our patients, the hospital would be hopelessly crowded,' she told Amy. 'But since you are already here, I will make an exception on this one occasion.'

'Thank you, Sister.'

Elliot intervened, 'And Ralph's leg, Sister. What is the exact situation there?'

'We have had to amputate above the knee,' she stated. 'The surgeon had hoped to save the knee-cap, but it was out of the question.' She took the chart from the end of the bed and glanced at it for corroboration of her statement. 'The damage was too extensive. I'm afraid, too, there are now signs of an infection. We are doing our best to reduce it naturally, but it is always a danger.'

Elliot nodded. 'Does he know we're here?' he asked. 'If I speak to him . . . ?'

'Most unlikely,' she said. 'There really is nothing you can do, but you are welcome to sit with him during the official visiting times. 6 o'clock until 7 weekdays; 1 o'clock until 2 on Sundays. Now if there are no more questions, I have other people needing my attention. Good-day to you both.'

Amy and Elliot stayed for the remainder of the visiting period, though they could do nothing but look helplessly at Ralph and it was a relief when the clamouring bell sent all the visitors out of the ward.

*

Cannon Street Station, where they waited for Amy's train home, was a colourful, noisy place and she was glad to have something to look at which would take her mind off the reason for her presence in London. The vast roof was of iron and glass and the walls were covered with posters advertising all manner of items for purchase — Lamplough's Pynetic Saline to cure headaches and biliousness; Keating's Cough

274

Lozenges; Dr Collis Browne's famous Chlorodyne and Ede's Patent Eye Liquid. Cooks, the travel firm, were offering tours from their office at Ludgate Circus and Thurstons were encouraging sales of their billiard balls!

Against this urgent commercial backdrop hundreds of people milled around, waiting for their trains to be signalled so that they could make their respective ways to the correct platforms. Amongst the crowds of travellers the station staff, resplendent in their uniforms, moved briskly (or not so briskly) about their work. Porters wheeled trolleys loaded with tin or leather trunks, carpetbags and well corded boxes. Ticket collectors dispensed information about departure times and platform numbers. A disembodied voice over the loudspeaker announced the name of a lost boy: 'aged about four and gives his name as Billy', and asked his parents to collect him. An amateur photographer was taking photographs of train engines and two dogs, fighting half-heartedly, were being belaboured by an elderly woman who wielded a rolled umbrella with surprising energy. Everywhere people embraced in fervent farewells. Well-dressed women swept through the crowd clutching small dogs and hat-boxes, while their maids followed laden with bundles and bags of all shapes and sizes. A group of men stood around the small bookstall and urchin boys hovered hopefully near the fruit barrow.

The iron seats were full of anxious women with infants on their laps and wide-eyed toddlers at their feet. Over it all was the rumble of the approaching trains, the grinding of brakes and the rush and roar of escaping steam and smoke. Carriage doors slammed and there was a constant movement of feet and the ever-present hum of excited voices.

'What did the Sister mean,' Amy asked Elliot, 'about Ralph's history? I didn't understand at all.'

Elliot hesitated briefly and his brown eyes darkened as he considered his answer.

'Ralph has a history of . . .' He shrugged helplessly. 'Well, I don't know how to soften the truth. He has what the doctor calls a self-destructive wish — that is, he has tried to take his own life. He—'

Amy interrupted him. 'Oh, that's not quite fair, Elliot! He

was terribly shocked then by the death of his fiancée. Surely that's understandable?'

'I'm afraid it's not as simple as that,' Elliot told her with obvious reluctance. 'That was understandable to some extent, although most people would not go so far in the same circumstances. But I'm afraid that was not the first time it had happened.'

'Oh, no!' Her eyes widened in dismay.

He nodded. 'Twice before, to be exact. Once when he was at college; he tried to gas himself and they only just found him in time. Once when he was only fifteen; he just swam out to sea, knowing he would never swim back. He wasn't a strong swimmer and the sea was quite rough. My uncle was nearly drowned saving him.'

'But why, Elliot?' cried Amy. 'Why doesn't he want to live?'

Elliot shrugged. 'No one knows,' he said. 'The doctors don't understand enough about these things. Our family doctor is a very good man who has known Ralph all his life – brought him into the world, in fact, and knows him as well as any doctor could know a patient. He warned my father after the swimming episode that Ralph would probably try again. He said that people with this awful urge to die usually keep trying until they succeed.'

'How terrible! If only I'd known,' she cried.

'You couldn't have helped him more than you did,' Elliot told her. 'And it was best for him that no one knew. Except me, that is. Ralph wanted to go to Italy after his fiancée died, but I didn't think he should be so far away, so I persuaded him to come to Gazedown where I could keep an eye on him. I also talked him into the book, partly because I thought it would keep his mind occupied and partly because it gave me an excuse to telephone him and to come down to Gazedown. He was getting on very well, actually, with your company to keep him cheerful.'

Amy said slowly, 'So is that why you asked me to put in more hours on the book, so that he would have company for longer periods?'

Elliot looked a little shamefaced. 'Oh dear, you've tumbled to it!' he said. 'Yes, it was mainly for that reason, but also because earlier on Ralph was not making much progress and had written a rather despairing letter suggesting he had no real talent for the work and wanted to give up. I didn't want that to happen. I hoped that at Gazedown he might find some peace of mind and that with your help, we might avert another disaster.'

Amy shook her head. 'And then this had to happen. Why is life so very unfair?'

'Because it is,' said Elliot. 'We know it is, yet still we kick against the pricks.'

'So the Sister at the hospital knew about the suicide attempts?'

'Yes. Our family doctor, Doctor Haddon, came up yesterday to talk to the consultant, and thought it right to put them in the picture about Ralph's background.' He sighed. 'To recover from this sort of major tragedy, you *must* have the will to live. Ralph hasn't got it, which is why they don't hold out much hope.'

'But if he was going to kill himself sometime—' She stopped, biting her lip, unwilling to put her thoughts into words.

'Yes,' said Elliot, 'I know. I've been thinking the same thing and hating myself for doing so. If he didn't want to live when he was whole and healthy, would he want to live with all the problems he will have to face if he recovers? I don't think so, Amy. I love him, we're very close, but' – he shook his head – 'I'm not sure I want him to regain consciousness. It sounds terrible, but I'm trying to be honest and I'm putting myself in his shoes.'

Amy swallowed. 'I feel so helpless!' she whispered. 'Just to wait for him to die seems so feeble and yet, after what you've told me . . .'

He took her hands in his and squeezed them gently. 'Poor Amy,' he said. 'So many worries of your own and now I've shared my problems with you. Do you forgive me?'

'Of course I do!' she told him. 'I'm glad I understand.'

'You mentioned your father,' he said. 'Is he in serious trouble over the accident?'

Amy sighed. 'There's certain to be an official enquiry. He's very upset and worried and my mother blames herself because it was really Toby's fault. If he hadn't run on along the platform, none of this would have happened.'

'And if Arnold hadn't been on the trolley . . . Amy, no one is to blame. It was an accident, an act of God even.'

Amy's eyes flashed. 'Then it was very mean of Him!' she cried.

Elliot threw back his head and laughed. 'Oh, Amy Turner!' he said. 'You are wonderful! I can just imagine you giving Him a good dressingdown in your prayers tonight.'

'It's good to see you laugh,' she said, strangely comforted. 'It's such a nightmare at the moment. Everything is going wrong just when I thought it was all going right. But that's selfish, I know.'

Her train was announced as she was speaking and Elliot walked with her to the correct platform where the train now waited. He found her a seat by the window in a first-class carriage; as the daughter of a railwayman, she was allowed concessionary travel.

She lowered the window and leaned out. 'You needn't wait,' she told him.

'But of course I will,' he insisted with a smile. 'I want to see you safely on your way. I'm feeling like a Dutch uncle today, so you must bear with me.'

'Yes, uncle!' she mocked, then her expression changed suddenly. 'About the book, Elliot,' she said. 'Do you want me to carry on with the research?'

He hesitated. 'Why not?' he said at last. 'For the time being, at least. If you want to, that is.'

'I think I do,' said Amy, 'although I may feel differently when I go to The Lodge and Ralph—' She broke off.

'Try it,' he told her, 'and see how you feel. I shall write a letter to Esme Hatherley – I can be very persuasive when I put my mind to it – and I shall point out that the book is commissioned and that you are still one of our employees.'

While she still hesitated, there was a great slamming of doors and the whistle blew.

'Oh, we're going!' cried Amy. 'Thank you for everything, Elliot. And do please let me know how Ralph gets on. I must know. I shall pray for him.'

The train gave a shuddering lurch and began to move,

slowly, accompanied by loud bursts of steam and clanking metal.

Elliot ran along the platform, pushing through the crowds to keep up with the train. 'I'll be down to see how you're getting on!' he told her. 'With the book, I mean. And, Amy—'

'Yes.'

'Try to keep cheerful – it's the only way.'

'I'll remember – oh, Elliot, do be careful.'

He slowed down, breathlessly, and waved his hand.

'Goodbye, Elliot!'

'It's not goodbye,' he shouted. 'It's *au revoir!*'

'*Au revoir*, then,' she agreed, watching him until he was lost among the crowds.

Then she settled back in her seat and tried to make some kind of order from the chaos of her thoughts. Ralph was going to die, she *knew* it. There was nothing she or anyone else could do to save him because he didn't want to be saved. Her heart ached for the slight figure lying so still in the hospital bed. Elliot had said she had helped Ralph and she took comfort from his words; she certainly hoped she had eased his loneliness. Poor Ralph. It was sad that they would share no more hours at The Lodge – and sad, too, that now the book would never be finished.

But had Elliot ever intended that it should, she wondered, or had it been merely a ploy to keep Ralph usefully occupied? The thought made her sick at heart. Without the book her life stretched before her, aimless and uninspired. The project had meant so much to her and now it would never see the light of day. Lord Stanisbrooke would never live again but would remain a frail ghost, lost amidst the shadows of the past. She sighed deeply and stared out at the passing houses, seeing nothing. And Elliot . . . She would not see him again, if Ralph died, he would gather up the papers and books and take them back to London. She supposed she would stay in Gazedown and marry Don Leckie. Yes, Don Leckie would make her a good husband and Mary would be pleased. She must marry Don and forget Elliot Allan and the book and all her fantasies of a new life. 'Keep your feet on the ground, Amy Turner,' she told herself and made up her mind to try.

*

Further along the train, but in another first-class compartment, Gerald Hatherley was apparently doing *The Times* crossword. His pencil hovered over the folded newspaper and the blunt end of it was occasionally pressed into the small dimple in his chin. His expression was one of intense concentration and once or twice he entered a word. He did not want to do the crossword, but still less did he wish to be engaged in conversation with the man who sat opposite him. Pretending to do the crossword was the only way he could think of to discourage the fellow without being rude. True, the man would get out at Tonbridge, but Gerald did not wish to wait that long for he was eager to be alone with his thoughts in order to perfect the plan he had devised for dealing with the future of Lorna and his child.

Gerald had given the matter hours of thought and had rejected several earlier plans for one reason or another. The final plan, he felt, was almost perfect and he hoped to convince Lorna that this was so before they both attempted to convince her mother. In Gerald's opinion, the only flaw in his plan was that it denied him paternity and that saddened him. He would have liked the whole of Gazedown to know that he was the father of Lorna Betts' child and that he and Lorna were lovers. He would have liked everyone in the *country* to know, but it was simply not sensible for anything to become public and he had finally accepted the fact, though not without much heart-searching. The main priority was to ensure that Lorna lived somewhere close at hand so that he could visit her and the child whenever he chose.

To his astonishment, Lorna continued to enjoy their stolen moments together – she actually enjoyed him! His heart leaped at the very idea that in spite of his unassuming appearance, his foolish blinking eyes and his fumbling passion, Lorna found him attractive. A young girl with softly rounded arms and peachy skin found *him*, Gerald Hatherley, attractive! Not only that, but she was carrying his child!

To Gerald, Lorna was the most wonderful thing that had ever happened to him, and he was determined to fight for her with whatever weapons he could muster. The only weapon that promised to succeed was cunning, and Gerald had dreamed up a most devious plan: they would pretend that on the night of Esme's birthday party one of the guests had given her champagne to drink and then, when she was helplessly drunk, had seduced her. Lorna would be very vague about this man and it would obviously be impossible to line up all the male guests in an identification parade, so they would never discover his identity. Very properly, Lorna would confide the details of her seduction to Gerald, her former employer, complaining that she dare not tell her mother. Gerald, full of remorse, would then break the news to Mrs Betts, apologise on behalf of the unknown guest responsible for the child and offer to make reparation by setting up Lorna in a cottage on the estate. Esme would then have to be told and would be forced to agree to Gerald's plans because if she did not, Mrs Betts would inform Gazedown in no uncertain terms that her daughter had been *raped* by one of the Hatherleys' friends – in which case the occupants of Bates Manor would never survive the ensuing scandal.

Once Lorna was installed in the cottage which Gerald would furnish for her, she and the boy would flourish and as benefactor, he could visit her quite openly, since in the eyes of the village he would be entirely innocent of any wrongdoing.

Gerald had allowed his fantasies to go on even further, imagining that at some future date his wife would die and he would be free to marry again. By that time the boy would look upon him as a father and Lorna would welcome him as a husband. Meanwhile he would buy them presents and take them on outings – all in an apparent attempt to compensate Lorna for the grave wrong she had suffered at the hands of his anonymous 'friend' while under his roof. The more he thought about the plan the more he liked it, and the more eager he was to put it into operation. This eagerness was being frustrated, however, by the fact that he had been unable to meet Lorna. Since the accident at the station Arnold was at a loose end and was frequently to be found by the pond or in the copse, making it impossible for them to meet. Another complication had arisen in the form of Lorna's sister, who had taken a nasty fall and was threatening to lose her unborn child, therefore Mrs Betts had rushed to be with her and Lorna had been forced to take over in the shop. In these circumstances, Gerald had not yet managed to contact Lorna and arrange a new meeting place.

With a sigh, he entered in the answer to one of the crossword clues, but this proved to be a mistake for the man opposite immediately leaned forward.

'Got one, have you?' he asked Gerald.

'I beg your pardon?'

'I say, have you got one?'

'Yes, I have.' Gerald spoke in a discouraging tone but the man appeared not to notice.

'Not nine down is it, by any chance?' the man smiled. He was middle-aged, with a distinct smell of mothballs about him.

Gerald cursed inwardly. 'No, it's not,' he said shortly.

'It is *The Times* crossword you're doing?'

'Yes.'

'Damned tricky today,' the man persisted. 'I see you're not getting many of them either.'

'No.'

Gerald looked at him with distaste and longed to say, 'No, I'm too busy thinking about my young and very pregnant mistress,' but of course that was out of the question. A pity! He felt a sudden compassion for the man opposite, who did not look at all the sort of man who might have a desirable young woman waiting to share his bed. Probably married to a dowdy wife with whom he was thoroughly bored.

Feeling generous, Gerald said, 'I did number nine earlier as it happens. I think it's a quote from Macbeth. I put "Courage".'

' "Courage"?' He looked baffled. 'How's that then?'

'Lady Macbeth says, "But screw your *courage* to the sticking-place and we'll not fail." '

'Does she?' He laughed. 'Well, I'm much obliged. Never been my strong point, Shakespeare.' He wrote in the word carefully and said, 'Ah, that helps with four across.'

Gerald said hastily. 'I couldn't get four across.' Then without knowing why, he added, 'Married, are you? Any family?'

The man looked surprised at the question. 'I am and I'm

not,' he said. 'My wife died four years ago and left me three daughters to bring up. My sister moved in with us, bless her.'

Gerald nodded smugly. Just as he'd thought. No *sons*.

'And you?' the man asked.

Gerald had not anticipated that he would be put to the test and now he could not bring himself to admit that his wife was childless.

'I've just married for the second time,' he said. 'My wife's expecting a boy — at least,' he corrected himself quickly, 'we hope it will be a boy. That is — she is convinced it will be. You know how these young women are!' He stressed the word 'young' and fancied the man looked at him with envy, but then the train was slowing down at Tonbridge and the man was preparing to leave the train.

'Well, it's cheerio, then,' he said to Gerald. 'I shall look out for you if ever I'm stuck with the crossword.'

Gerald smiled. 'By all means,' he said.

'And take care of that wife of yours. I lost my wife in that way. Three months into the fourth child and she had a haemorrhage. Nothing anyone could do — lost mother and child. But that's the way it goes sometimes.'

He left the train with a cheery wave, unaware that his careless words had struck a chill into Gerald's heart. What would he do, how could he bear it if his wonderful little Lorna should die in childbirth?

'No!' he cried aloud. 'Dear God, no!'

A stout woman, climbing into the carriage, looked at him suspiciously and decided to find a seat elsewhere. Unaware of her existence, Gerald sat on in solitary splendour, in a state of abject terror as the train once more lurched into motion. He must take steps to safeguard Lorna and the child and he must do so now before it was too late.

*

The next day, as Amy let herself in at the back door, Ellen was adding the dumplings to the mutton stew; one quick glance at her face told Amy that she was no happier and the rest of the Turner family appeared to be equally gloomy. Her father was sitting at the table reading a letter; her grandfather, a sullen look on his face, was repairing the clock. Toby was sitting beside Sam on the floor looking at an old railway magazine, but both boys looked rather subdued.

Ellen looked up, her face showing signs of recent tears.

'Hullo, Amy dear,' she said, smiling briefly. 'You're just in time. Ten minutes or so for the dumplings and it'll be ready.'

'Lovely,' said Amy, her voice artificially brightening. 'I'm so hungry, I could eat a horse.'

Sam glanced up. 'Perhaps it *is* a horse,' he said. 'Perhaps it's horse stew with dumplings. Yummy!' He gave Toby a playful poke in the ribs. 'Hear that, Toby?' he asked him. 'Gee-gee stew. Would you like that?'

'Gee-gee,' said Toby obligingly, but without much enthusiasm.

'He does like it,' said Sam. 'Two helpings of gee-gee stew, please, Ma.'

'Mama,' his father corrected him. 'How many times do you have to be told, Sam?'

Ted Turner dropped a screw and said, 'God dammit! Sam, see if you can find a small brass screw about so big . . .' He held up finger and thumb to show the size. 'Your eyes are better than mine, leastways I should hope so. Mine have really gone to pot since your grandmother died.'

This last reference to his wife's death was one of many such reminders he gave to his daughter-in-law, underlying the reason for his intransigent attitude towards her. The state of hostility existing between them did nothing to lighten an already difficult situation. Amy and her father had both remonstrated with him to no avail, while Ellen was constantly forced to bite her tongue and ignore his remarks.

Amy had been forced – albeit grudgingly – to admire her mother's self-control and had to admit that she was finding it pleasant to have another woman to talk to. They talked as equals, there being no suggestion of mother and daughter, and Amy was gradually beginning to realise that Ellen had her good points – a fact she had tried to forget. The years away had changed her mother in subtle ways – she was more tolerant and less abrasive now, but she smiled rarely. If she still grieved for John, she kept it to herself, but Amy knew that she often cried when she was alone. On the sole occasion when Ellen had gone to the village shop, Amy had accompanied her to give moral support. Ellen had not asked for it, but Amy had sensed her mother's anxiety and had made the offer. She also supported her mother against Ted's jibes, but on this occasion Thomas himself was roused to protest. He looked up sharply and said, 'That'll do, for God's sake. Dig, dig! I'm getting a bit sick of it!'

The old man muttered something that no one could hear, while Ellen flashed her husband a grateful look and for a moment their eyes met. Amy thought she detected a spark of mutual sympathy and wondered if perhaps the old man's unrelenting attitude towards Ellen might be encouraging her husband's protective instinct instead of alienating him as Ted obviously intended.

Sam began to hunt for the missing screw and Amy went upstairs to take off her jacket and hat and wash her hands. When she came down again, the family were gathered round the table and Ellen was ladling out the stew.

'Yum, yum!' said Sam. 'Gee-gee stew.'

'That's enough, Sam,' said his father, who was in no mood to be amused by such nonsense. 'Let's have a bit of quiet.'

'Gee-gee!' said Toby solemnly and Sam found this very funny, stuffing a grubby handkerchief into his mouth and rocking with silent laughter.

Amy sat down between Toby and Sam. Her father sat between Ellen and the old man, the latter still muttering resentfully to himself in a way that was intended to irritate as many people as possible. If everyone ignored him, then he had failed, but if just one member of the family took him to task he felt he had scored. His resentment at Ellen's return was no longer so openly expressed, but he intended to make sure that no one was left in any doubt as to his feelings on the matter. Nothing, he told himself, would ever reconcile him to the reappearance of 'that woman' in their lives. He was, however, quite taken with young Toby and although he paid the boy as little attention as possible, his genuine fondness for children was making this increasingly difficult. In another year or two, he reckoned, Toby would be able to appreciate some of his reminiscences – the prospect was a tempting one.

Amy smiled at her father as she sat down. 'How are things, Papa?' she asked. 'Was the letter good or bad?'

He brightened a little. 'Ah, that letter was good news. A party of amateur photographers have booked an excursion from London on the first Sunday in November. It's a block booking for about twenty-five people.'

'From London to Gazedown?' she asked. 'Good heavens!'

He smiled briefly. 'I thought that,' he told her, 'but apparently one of the members knows the area and has recommended it. They want to visit the old chapel at Bates Manor, the church and the woods. They're going to picnic in the woods at midday, but ask me if I can arrange for the local pub to provide an evening meal, so I'll have to pop down to The Four Bells later and see what can be arranged.'

'I suppose I could put the Friday stall out,' suggested Amy. She glanced at her mother. 'What do you think?'

'I could bake some buns for it,' volunteered Ellen.

Sam said, 'A Friday stall on a Sunday! That's funny, Toby, isn't it.'

'That's funny,' echoed Toby with his mouth full of potato.

'Don't talk with your mouth full,' Ellen told him. 'What else could we sell?'

They all began to eat as they discussed the forthcoming excursion and then the talk turned to Amy's day.

'It was fine,' she told them. 'I did a lot of work, but of course it's not the same without poor Ralph – not so much fun. We used to talk things over and I suppose in a way we inspired each other. Still, it was very interesting. Elliot has sent down a diary which belonged to one of Lord Stanisbrooke's mistresses and it's fascinating. It seems she was the governess. He also sent me five letters which were written to the other mistress, who was an actress! Ralph would have been so thrilled. Oh, and Esme Hatherley came by to ask after Ralph. She said she feels she ought to visit him in hospital, but she has a horror of hospitals and can't face it. Anyway, she's not a relative, so they wouldn't allow her in. She said she's written to him.'

Thomas stared at her over a forkful of mutton. 'I thought he was still unconscious.'

'He is,' said Amy. 'I told her that, but she said the nurses could read it to him!'

'Read a letter to an unconscious man?' Her father tapped his forehead. 'Sounds a bit funny up here.'

Amy frowned. 'Actually, now I think about it, she does look a little odd. I can't quite put my finger on it but she seemed . . . well, I don't know quite how she seemed, but not quite herself. Maybe a bit vague.' She shrugged. 'Clara said she was terribly upset when she heard of the accident – almost hysterical. Clara had to get her the smelling-salts.'

Her father shook his head. 'It's a terrible business,' he said. 'I sometimes feel we shall never hear the end of it.'

'Have they set a date for the hearing?' asked Amy.

'Yes,' he told her, 'Friday week. I've sent in my report and the police have several eyewitness accounts. Harry and Tim had to go down to the police station in Tenterden today to answer a lot of questions. Hundreds of questions, so Harry says.'

'Never mind,' said Amy. 'It was an accident and they'll have to come to that conclusion.'

'I'm not so sure,' he said wearily.

Ellen looked up. 'Amy's right, Tom,' she said. 'They'll have to.'

'They might allege negligence on the part of the station staff,' he said, 'because Arnold shouldn't have been on that damned trolley in the first place. I've told him so many times. He shouldn't have been on the station at all, come to that.' He laid down his knife and fork, his food only half-eaten.

Ellen and Amy exchanged anxious looks and Amy said quickly, 'Well, don't let's go over it all again now, Papa. All we can do is wait and see. I'm sure it will turn out better than you expect.'

Her father reached out and patted her hand. 'I know you mean well, Amy,' he said. 'I just wish I had your confidence.'

Chapter Seventeen

Rodney Midden, known to his cronies as Rod, was a large man with bright red hair which curled untidily round his bright red face, the latter the result of hundreds of broken veins brought about by heavy and regular consumption of gin. Once – in his youth – he had been good-looking in a coarse way, with a large raw-boned face and a muscular body of which he was very proud. Now, at the age of thirty-seven, his muscles were already turning to fat and his blue eyes were often blurred by drink. He had always been a loud-mouthed braggart and a liar and, whenever the opportunity presented itself, a cheat as well. He was not bright, but had survived thus far in an unfriendly world and intended to do so for many more years. He had worked at a number of jobs, rarely keeping any of them for more than a year or two and his most recent job – unloading beer barrels – had just ended after a row with his employer. He was therefore free to continue to search for his daughter, Clara. Clara's account of her background, as told on the occasion of her undignified arrival at Gazedown Station, had not been entirely accurate, as Amy had suspected at the time. If anyone had asked Rodney for an account of his daughter's defection, his account would also have been distorted. The truth lay somewhere between the two.

Clara was the oldest child of a family of four, none of whom was born in wedlock; when she reached the age of fourteen and began to look like a young woman instead of a child, Rodney Midden had begun to take more than a fatherly interest in her. Clara's mother had objected and after

288

a particularly violent quarrel, had threatened to leave him. Rodney promptly told her to go and to take all the children except Clara. When she refused, he left home himself and for nearly five weeks the family survived on charity.

When Rodney finally returned, his desperate wife was so thankful that she was forced to overlook his advances towards Clara, advising her daughter that 'all men like a bit now and again and it doesn't do no real harm'. She begged Clara not to deny him in case he left them all again. Clara found she could just tolerate her father's kisses and his rough careless fingers, but when at last he stripped and tried to rape her, she resisted fiercely and a wild and bloody battle ensued. This so alarmed the neighbours that the police were called to the house where they found Clara in a state of shock, with multiple bruises to her face and body. Rodney Midden had disappeared and his wife's version of the affray was suitably modified since she did not relish the idea of a jailbird for a husband. The sexual assault therefore went unrecorded.

Rodney returned home at the end of the week fully intending to repeat the experience, for his daughter's resistance had excited him and he was now confident of his wife's connivance. Clara, however, had other ideas. She stole his wallet, which contained nearly four pounds, and fled the house. Once it was obvious that she was not coming back, Rodney made up his mind to find her when the opportunity presented itself; losing his job now gave him plenty of spare time.

It seemed likely to Rodney Midden that his daughter would make her way to Hastings, because his uncle and aunt had once kept a boarding house there. On his first journey down to the resort he had been delayed at Gazedown by an accident. This, his second attempt, met with no such delays and he passed the station with his bottle of gin raised to his lips, unaware that his missing daughter was only yards away, enjoying a brief conversation with Tim Hollis in the booking-office as she collected a small parcel from Harrods destined for Bates Manor. Rodney told himself he would find the little bitch and drag her back home. Then he'd keep her under lock and key; there would be no more running away and no denying him. The world owed him a bit of fun and she was his daughter, after all. *And* she'd robbed him of his money! Oh yes, she owed him now, he told himself truculently and he'd make damned sure she paid him. As the train gave a jerk, he put the bottle back in his jacket pocket and patted it lovingly. It might take a week or so, but there was nothing to keep him from his search and he'd find the little hussy if it was the last thing he did.

Hastings was not at its best, he discovered, as he made his way along the sea-front with his jacket collar turned up against the sea mist. He remembered coming down for the day when he was a boy of six or seven to visit his uncle and aunt, who had what they liked to call a small guest-house. Ada had married wisely – an elderly widower with no family who had later died and left her the business. 'Sun Lea' was the name of the house and when at last Rodney stood outside it, gaping up at the peeling façade, he had momentary doubts about the wisdom of calling. He had stolen a silver teaspoon from them on his last visit, and wondered if the theft had ever been laid at his door. Probably not, he thought, and even if it had, the old girl must be nearly seventy now if she was a day and no doubt her memory was failing.

He went past the rusty railings, up the crumbling steps and rang the bell. There was a yellowing cardboard square wedged into the upper half of the window advertising VACANCIES and an aspidistra in an earthenware pot took up most of the lower half. The door opened and an elderly woman stared at him suspiciously. She was small and wiry and her fine white hair was tied up in curling rags. The summer season was over and she was not expecting callers.

'What do you want?' she snapped.

Rodney smiled. 'You don't remember me, Aunt Ada? I'm Alf's boy, Rodney.'

Her eyes widened when at last the name registered. 'Alf's boy?' she gasped. 'Well, I never! I'd never have recognised you. Alf's boy! Well, I'm blowed. Sidney, did you say?'

'No, Rodney.'

She nodded as she repeated the name and he thought, 'Ask me in then, for Christ's sake, Auntie!' but went on smiling. Slowly she put up a hand to her curling rags and then glanced down at her apron and worn blue slippers. 'Oh dear, look at me!' she exclaimed. 'All at sixes and sevens. So it's Rodney, is it? Alf's boy.'

'That's it.' Still she made no effort to open the door and he did hope she had not remembered the teaspoon.

'I've got a bit of a problem,' he told her, 'and you might be able to help me. It's my eldest girl, Clara, poor lass. Got in a bit of trouble with a lad who lives nearby.' He shook his head. 'Well, you know what young people are like these days.'

'Not really, dear. No, I don't,' she said. 'The Lord never did bless us with any family. Well, your uncle was already getting on a bit when I married him, him being so much older than me. Poor old—'

Rodney interrupted hastily. 'The point is, Aunt Ada, the silly girl's run off – ashamed like, I suppose – and she's taken ten pounds out of my wallet . . .'

'Ten pounds? My, you're doing well for yourself, Rodney.'

He shrugged as though the money itself was of no interest. 'What worries me,' he went on, 'is what will happen to her when the money's all gone. I thought she might find her way down here to you, you see, because she always had a fancy to come and see you and have a quick paddle in the sea.'

The old woman's expression changed to one of alarm. 'Oh dear,' she said, 'that would never do. I couldn't possibly – I mean, if she's in that condition . . .'

'Exactly,' said Rodney. 'I don't want you worried, so I thought if I give you fair warning, then if she does turn up you could drop me a line and I'll come and fetch her home.' He allowed himself a sad smile. 'We all miss her, you see, and her poor mother's out of her mind with worry.'

Nervously his aunt looked up and down the street as though she expected the girl to materialise suddenly.

'Yes, yes,' she agreed. 'Of course I will, Rodney, I'll write you if I see her.'

'You might see her around the town,' he said, 'even if she doesn't actually call on you.'

'I might, dear, yes.'

'And you will write to me?'

'Of course I will, dear. Poor soul! She must be in a state.

A girl needs her mother at a time like that.' She shook her head mournfully. 'In the family way. Oh dear me. What a silly girl.'

Rodney shrugged and pulled the collar of his coat closer around his neck. 'I thought,' he suggested, 'that you might ask me in for a quick cuppa?'

The door moved imperceptibly as the old lady's hand went once more to her curlers. 'I would,' she said, 'but I'm just getting ready to go out.'

'Not just a quick one?' he asked, his smile wavering. He wished he'd taken all the spoons. Serve the silly old cow right!

'Some other time perhaps,' she said vaguely. 'I always go out on Tuesdays to my friend round the corner. Arthritis, poor old soul, and she does so rely on me to do a few bits of shopping for her.' She began to close the door. 'But it's been nice to see you—'

Rodney's smile disappeared. He took a scrap of paper from his pocket and thrust it into her hand.

'Here,' he said, 'it's my address in case you see my daughter. Clara, her name is. Can you remember that?'

She peered shortsightedly at the address and nodded.

'I'll remember. Yes, I'll let you know if she turns up. And remember me to your mother and father. Well, are they?'

'Both dead,' he told her with satisfaction.

'Dead, are they? Oh, that's right, so they are. My memory's not what it used to be, what with one thing and another. Well, we all have to go when we're called.'

Rodney made one last effort. 'But you will remember to write to me if you see her – oh, and don't let her know.'

'Yes, dear. I'll remember. Now you must excuse me.'

The door closed gently but firmly in his face and he cursed her as hard as he dared before turning away. Not even a cup of tea or a biscuit, the miserable old cow!

He shivered and stood for a moment, undecided what to do next. Then he began to walk back along the road towards the shops. The gin wouldn't last much longer and he must find a public house. A drink and a pie to warm him up, then he'd wander around the town for a while, looking for his daughter. The thought of what he would do to her when he got her home again gave him new heart and, with a quick swig from his bottle, he squared his broad shoulders and quickened his pace as he set off once more along the sea-front.

*

The following day, which was Wednesday, another parcel for Bates Manor arrived at the station; this time Amy offered to take it, as she was going to The Lodge anyway and it only meant walking on an extra quarter of a mile along the drive.

When she knocked at the kitchen door, Izzie opened it and Mrs Lester called to her to 'Come on in'.

'Another parcel from Harrods,' said Amy, placing it on the kitchen table.

To her surprise, Mrs Lester and Izzie exchanged startled looks. 'Not more stuff for her face!' whispered Izzie. 'That's the third lot since the accident.'

The cook, her hands on her hips, shook her head in disbelief and then turned to Amy.

'Ever since poor Mr Allan's accident, the mistress has gone mad for creams and lotions and I don't know what!' she explained. 'She must be spending a fortune. Lord only knows why, she's got a perfect skin already. I don't know what's got into her.'

Izzie sat down again and resumed her work – she was polishing the candlesticks – while Mrs Lester picked up the parcel and shook it enquiringly, close to her ear.

'Yes, I reckon that's what it is,' she said. 'Lordy, what a to-do that was when the master told her about the accident – screamed, she did! Terrible it was to hear, and then she put her hands over her ears. The door was open a bit and I could see right in. I was on my way up with the menus, you see, and I got to the door just in time to hear her. "No!" she screamed. "I don't want to hear it!" and she didn't stop screaming until he slapped her round the face.'

'Mr Hatherley slapped her?' exclaimed Amy.

'Oh yes. A real hard slap. "Stop that", he told her, "Get a hold of yourself."'

Izzie sighed. 'I wish I'd seen it,' she said enviously. 'I never see nothing, stuck in this blooming kitchen.'

293

Mrs Lester ignored her. ' "Don't tell me any more," Mrs Hatherley kept saying. "I can't bear it!" Crying she was, and then after he slapped her she was sort of laughing.' The housekeeper shuddered. 'Sent shivers down my back, it did, I can tell you. Clara gave her smelling-salts, but we had to fetch the doctor in the end. Couldn't do anything with her; she just sat on the floor and kept rocking to and fro. It was horrible. And the master was upset, too — you could see. And he's been so moody. I don't know what's got into them lately, the pair of them.' She sighed. 'Sometimes he's all miserable and snappy and the next minute he's grinning to himself like a blinking schoolboy. You know, cat's got the cream — that sort of look!'

Izzie regarded her stained fingers with distaste. 'I'd like to have seen her sitting on the floor,' she said. 'Rocking backwards and forwards. I miss everything, I do. It's not fair.'

Just then Clara came into the kitchen and she and Amy greeted one another.

'The mistress saw you from the window,' Clara told Amy. 'She wants you to bring the parcel up.'

Half-way up the stairs, she turned to Amy and whispered, 'I expect she'll ask you about Ralph Allan. Try not to make it sound too awful. The doctor says she's to be kept calm at all costs. He's given her a sleeping draught to make her sleep, but her nerves are very bad and she spends haalf the day in bed.'

Clara led the way up the broad staircase and along the landing to Esme's bedroom. She went in first and said brightly, 'Here's Amy Turner, ma'am,' and Amy followed her into the room. What she saw shocked and distressed her.

Esme was sitting up in bed, propped up on pillows, her long fair hair flowing loose around her head and shoulders. Her face was thinner than Amy remembered; her eyes were large and there were dark circles under them. She was wearing a pale blue satin nightdress and a matching woollen bed-jacket with a collar of pale blue feathers. Around her on the bed were various bottles and jars and she was rubbing something into her hands with great concentration. She looked up at Amy, but did not smile. Instead, she held up her hands for her visitor's inspection.

'I've never found anything better for the hands than glycerine and honey,' she said. 'It's old-fashioned, but it's still the best. Harrods make an excellent version of it – a very refined version – and I've never used anything else.'

Amy nodded, trying not to let her dismay show on her face. 'I'm sure it's very good,' she agreed.

Esme examined her hands, then nodded in satisfaction. 'Let me have it,' she told Amy, holding out her hands for the latest parcel.

Amy handed it to her and she and Clara watched as Esme tore at the wrapping impatiently. She stopped suddenly and looked up at Amy.

'The doctor has confined me to my bed,' she said with a shrug. 'So here I am, a virtual prisoner in my own bedroom. I told him I wanted to go to London to visit Mr Allan, but he wouldn't hear of it. It was the shock. He's very worried about me.'

She glanced at Clara for confirmation and she nodded and said, 'Oh yes, he is, ma'am. We all are.'

Esme tugged impatiently at the expensive wrappings, then threw them on to the floor beside the bed. The box, made of cedarwood, was filled with crumpled red velvet.

'I may be unwell,' she said to no one in particular, 'but I don't have to let myself go. I don't have to neglect my looks . . . Ah! Just what I wanted.' She drew out a small cut-glass bottle, snatched off the stopper and inhaled deeply.

'Wonderful!' she breathed and, replacing the stopper, plunged her hand into the box and drew out a round opaque pot with a silver lid.

'Now what was this?' she murmured and, finding a receipt, scanned the list anxiously. 'Ah yes. For the throat!'

She touched her own throat with a tentative stroking motion, as though to ascertain the texture of her skin. Unscrewing the silver top, she dipped her fingers into the pink contents, but when her hand was almost at her throat she hesitated and glanced towards Amy again.

'How is he?' she asked. 'Making good progress?'

'I believe so,' said Amy, colouring slightly at the lie.

'Good!' said Esme. 'I shall visit him as soon as I am allowed up. I have written to him several times – just to let him know he is not forgotten — and I have sent a basket of fruit. My husband is going to the hospital at the end of the week and will give me a progress report.' She began to apply the pink cream to her neck with slow, careful movements. 'I feel, in the circumstances, I have done all I can. Poor Mr Allan! Or perhaps I should call him Ralph; he asked me to do so. Gerald and I both liked him — *like* him, I mean — enormously. A very talented young man.'

Amy said, 'Yes, he is.'

'And you are carrying on the good work in his absence, I understand?'

'That's right.'

'I have had a letter from Elliot Allan,' Esme told her. 'A charming letter. I simply could not refuse him when he asked if you could continue there alone.'

'We're all most grateful to you,' said Amy.

Esme finished applying the cream to her neck and then picked up a small hand-mirror backed with tortoiseshell. She examined herself critically for a moment, turning her head from side to side as though she had forgotten that Amy and Clara were still in the room. At last she gave a long shuddering sigh and beckoned to Clara, telling her to clear the bed as she wanted to sleep.

Amy hesitated, then moved towards the door. 'I must be getting along then,' she said.

Esme was pulling off the fluffy blue bed-jacket and did not glance up. 'Give him my kindest regards,' she said. 'Tell him I shall look forward to his return. We'll celebrate with a bottle of our best champagne. Poor Mr Allan! Poor dear Ralph.'

Amy could bear it no longer. She slipped quietly out of the room and closed the door behind her.

*

Lorna was very fond of her sister Janet and very sorry that she was ill and might lose the baby, but on the other hand she herself had problems of her own and did not enjoy being forced to act as full time shopkeeper. The work was hard, the hours were long and she found most of the customers either boring or irritating. She weighed sugar, cut lard and measured out dried dates until she hated the sight of it all. She unpacked boxes, filled shelves, checked the till (which was never right), swept the floor and did her best to deal with telephone queries from the wholesalers about currants and sides of bacon. Lorna found the work distasteful and wondered how her mother could put up with the succession of people who came in for six eggs and then expected to take up ten minutes of her time in silly chit-chat. The only customers for whom she had any sympathy were the school-children who came in with farthings and half-pennies to spend when the day's lessons were over. These she watched benevolently as they tried to decide between liquorice wheels, vanilla drops, barley sugars, sticks of chocolate, butter nuggets or almond rock.

But by far the worst part of it all was not being able to see Gerald, who did such exciting things to her body and who had promised her such a glittering future. Lorna really missed him. She felt that she really loved him – and she was going to have his baby! She felt very contented when she thought how kind fate had been to her, with the exception of Janet's recent trouble. When there were no customers she indulged her fantasies to the full and saw herself as the envy of all as she pushed her handsome son through the streets of Gazedown in his handsome pram. He would be a mystery child, the adored and pampered offspring of an unnamed father. She had no idea how this would all come about, but Gerald had promised and she had complete faith in his ability to make her dreams come true.

She looked at the clock on the wall and, seeing that it was five minutes past one o'clock, hurriedly crossed the shop to the door and turned the key in the lock. Lunch-time closing was from 1 until 2 o'clock. She was humming cheerfully as she recrossed the shop and made her way back behind the counter and through into their own living quarters. What did she want to eat, she wondered? She had hoped to develop a pregnant woman's craving for pickles or raw suet, but so far her appetite seemed little changed. She longed, too, to see even the slightest swelling of her body, but it remained obstinately flat. She hoped Janet would keep her child because then, when Lorna's son was born, the two sisters

297

could visit each other and compare notes on how fast the children were growing and how many teeth they had and that would be such fun. Naturally, Lorna's baby would have better clothes and a better crib, but she would not be smug and she would not in any way suggest that the clothes or crib of Janet's baby were in any way inferior.

A sudden and disturbing thought struck her. Janet would no doubt have a second and third child. How could she, Lorna, possibly manage that? One accidental pregnancy was excusable, even romantic, but a second one would create terrible difficulties, particularly if Gerald was her most frequent caller, which he obviously would be.

'Oh, Gerald!' she wailed. 'How shall we manage it? I don't want our son to be an only child.'

Deciding to eat a slice of ham, she buttered two thick slices of bread and made a sandwich, spreading it thickly with mustard. Then she went back into the shop and stood at the door while she ate it. She had just swallowed the last mouthful and was wiping the crumbs from her mouth when she heard the sound of hoofbeats and Gerald's brougham appeared at the end of the road. To her astonishment, he drove up to the shop. He had come courting in broad daylight! With a cry of delight, she unlocked the door and let him in. The master of Bates Manor was in a state of great excitement and Lorna hustled him through into the passage behind the shop where there were no doors or windows and they could embrace without being seen by anyone. She flung her arms round his neck and his arms went round her waist.

'Oh Gerald, my funny, my dear Gerald!' she cried happily.

'Oh Lorna! My sweet little Lorna,' he gasped. 'I've missed you so much. It's been such agony.'

They kissed passionately.

'I've missed you, too. Oh Gerald, let me look at you. Oh, kiss me. Hold me.'

'And you are well, Lorna? And still . . . you know?'

'Still that!' She laughed. 'Yes, I'm still having our baby. Oh, that wretched Arnold. Always hanging round the copse – *our* copse!'

'And now your mother has to go to your sister!' cried Gerald. 'Fate can be so cruel. But not for much longer, my sweet little girl. Listen, I've worked it all out. Even about Arnold. I've got him a temporary job, Lorna – one that will keep him busy all day and away from the copse.'

'A job? Arnold?' she exclaimed. 'But what sort of job could Arnold possibly manage?'

He grinned like a naughty schoolboy. 'I've fixed it up with Jake Drury, who's going to do the work on the cottage.'

Lorna gave a squeal of excitement. 'Our cottage, do you mean?'

'*Our* cottage! I've promised him the contract if he'll agree to take Arnold on, at a very low wage of course. He can fetch and carry for the men, run errands, clean the brushes, weed the garden, unblock the gutters. He's not entirely useless and it will keep him out of mischief.'

'Oh Gerald, you are clever,' breathed Lorna. 'Arnold will be like a dog with two tails! A real job! He'll be so proud.'

'And we'll be able to meet in the copse,' he said slyly, giving her bottom a playful pinch.

'Gerald Hatherley!' she cried. 'You are cunning!'

They hugged again, then Gerald went on, 'But I must tell you the plan for you and me – and the boy – so that as soon as your mother gets back we can tell her—'

'And your wife?'

'Yes, her too. Oh, my darling girl, I've missed you so! I've wanted you so much.'

The clung together in the dim, narrow passageway while, in fits and starts, Gerald carefully outlined his plan which Lorna thought quite brilliant.

'And just in case,' he told her breathlessly, 'anything should happen to me—'

'Oh, *don't!*' she cried.

'Well, it won't, of course, but I am older than you and so just in case, I've made provision in my will for you both—'

'Don't talk about it!' she cried. 'It's unlucky to talk like that. Nothing must happen to you. Oh, please Gerald, say it won't. I want you to live for years and years.'

'I will, little girl. Of course I will. You've given me something to live for.' He kissed her nose, her eyes, her ears. 'Still, we won't talk about that. So you like the plan? You agree?'

'It's wonderful. I can't wait.'

'And now, about the cottage, Lorna. I've put the work in hand. It's to be redecorated inside and out and we'll choose the furniture together. Our own little nest. I'm not dreaming, am I, Lorna?'

'No, no, sir!'

They both laughed at the slip which, as it grew less frequent, caused them more amusement. Then Lorna whispered, 'Do you think we could go upstairs? To the bedroom? You've got me all excited.'

She saw the longing in his eyes.

'I know. Oh, I wish we could,' he cried, 'but if someone came . . . no, we daren't risk it. It would ruin all our plans. And the brougham is standing right outside. That's risky enough, though at least I can pretend I was bringing down the order, but if someone comes and it takes you ages to get downstairs and I'm nowhere to be seen . . . oh no, my little Lorna, we daren't. I must go before I weaken and change my mind. But say that you love me.'

'I do love you, Gerald! You're a darling, funny old thing and I love you.' She clung to him, pressing her head against his chest. 'Do you love me?'

'Of course I do! I adore you. We're such fools!'

'But happy fools!'

'Yes, yes, we are. And soon we'll be even happier.'

He pulled himself free, turned back for one last fervent embrace, and then was gone.

Lorna watched the carriage until it was out of sight and then, filled with elation, danced round the empty shop, drumming her feet on the bare boards and snapping her fingers. After that she went out to the kitchen and helped herself to a pickled onion. And then another . . .

*

Rose Cottage stood just over half a mile from Bates Manor at the edge of the estate, on the side furthermost from the station. It was a simple building of brick construction which had been built in 1817 as a home for the gardener and his family. Now it had been untenanted for nearly seven years and all Gerald's attempts to sell it had fortunately failed. Orange lichen grew on the slate roof, the chimney-stack

300

leaned, the guttering hung loose in places and the window and door-frames were quietly rotting. Climbing plants and a film of green mould combined to obscure the windows, while the brick pathway which extended from the gate to the front door was hidden by moss and weeds.

Three men stood on this path. Gerald Hatherley was telling the builder, Jake Drury, what he wanted done in the way of repairs, while Arnold was standing beside Jake listening to the conversation with an expression of deep earnestness.

Arnold's mother had been delighted with Mr Drury's unexpected offer of employment and his own enthusiasm was unbounded. Before, at the station, he had been an unpaid, unsung 'Ass. Porter', but now he was one of Mr Drury's paid workmen. He had insisted on starting work only an hour after Mr Drury had offered him the job and the good-natured builder had found him something to do in the workshop, sweeping the sawdust into sacks.

'Going to put it on the market, are you?' Mr Drury asked, referring to the cottage.

Gerald shrugged. 'Can't make up my mind,' he said. 'I might, I might not. I just can't let it deteriorate any longer, or it'll be a complete write-off.'

'Right off!' muttered Arnold to himself. 'Right off!' It sounded important and he wanted to remember all the important things so that he could tell his mother when he got home.

Mr Drury said, 'It's pretty far gone already. Chimney needs repointing and the flashing's probably gone. New gutters all round?'

'Oh yes, I think so,' Gerald agreed. 'New window frames and door jambs too.'

Frowning with the effort of concentration, Arnold repeated, 'Jams', and began to hope that there would not be too many important things to remember. He caught Mr Drury's eye and nodded, then he folded his arms the way Jake had folded his and wondered if he dared ask his mother if he could smoke a pipe like his employer's. He muttered, 'Right off and jams.' Panic raced through him. That was two of the important things, but had he forgotten one of them! He stepped back a little and tried to remember. He knew he would not forget 'Right off', because it sounded like 'Right away' which they used to shout at the station, and he would remember 'Jams' because his mother made them, but what was the other word he had heard? It came to him suddenly.

'Flashing!' He shouted it out in his relief and both Mr Hatherley and Mr Drury turned to look at him. 'And jams,' he told them proudly, 'and right off.'

Mr Drury looked somewhat puzzled. 'You'll get the hang of it, Arnold,' he said and then the two older men continued their discussion. They agreed that all the outside repairs would be done first and then they would turn their attention to the inside.

'Well,' said Gerald, 'since we have a little time in hand now, we can take a quick look around inside to satisfy ourselves that there are no major problems.'

The front door opened into a sizeable hallway – 'Wasted space,' Mr Drury told Gerald with a shake of his head.

From this hall one room opened off on each side. On the right there was a kitchen with a sooty ceiling, a rusty range, a copper and a large walk-in larder. On the left of the hall was a general purpose living-room with a window-seat and a large frayed carpet. Upstairs they inspected the two bedrooms and then returned to the hall.

'It'll need a damp course,' said Gerald. 'I want it to be really comfortable.'

The builder looked at him in surprise and Gerald amended hastily, 'That is, habitable.' He cleared his throat nervously. 'Well, I've told you what I'm prepared to spend. Are you still confident you can do the work for that amount of money?'

Mr Drury removed his pipe and 'tutted' dubiously, but they both knew that his answer would be in the affirmative. He desperately needed the work and Gerald Hatherley knew that he did.

'It'll be tight,' said Mr Drury reluctantly. 'Very tight indeed. I won't pretend otherwise, but yes, I'll do it. There's my hand on it.'

The two men shook hands briefly and Arnold beamed at them, proud to be present at such an exciting moment. He thought Mr Drury was a very nice man – much nicer than

302

the stationmaster, he decided, and almost as nice as Harry Coombes or Tim Hollis. Arnold made up his mind to work really hard at his job and then Mr Drury would never shout at him. And he would ask his mother about the pipe as soon as he got home.

*

As days passed and Elliot's visits to the hospital continued, the ward became a more familiar and less depressing place. Today, as he pushed open the swing doors, the smell of carbolic soap and the rustle of starched aprons no longer registered in his mind. He smiled at one of the ward-maids and greeted some of the patients whom he recognised, knowing by the position of their beds whether they were improving or getting worse. Those who were very ill were nearest to the nurses' desk, while those on the way to recovery were furthest away. He strode along the ward on his long legs, refusing to tiptoe as so many people did. Some of the visitors frowned at his retreating back as he passed, but the patients themselves smiled and were pleased to see him for he made them laugh with his outrageous remarks and breezy laughter. 'Like a dose of salts' was how one of the men described him. Even the attitude of the nurses had softened towards Elliot and they now enjoyed his light-hearted banter instead of constantly struggling to retain their dignity.

This time he stopped beside an elderly gentleman whose chest and left arm were swathed in bandages.

'Ah!' he said. 'Nurse's pet! You've got more bandages than anyone else – it's a sure sign! They'll be winking at you before you know it and what will your wife have to say then?'

The old man roused himself from his gloomy thoughts to say, 'I shudder to think!' and to smile at the idea of being winked at by the nurses. No one had ever winked at him, so far as he could remember.

'I scalded myself,' he told Elliot. 'At work. Industrial accident. That's what I am; an industrial accident.'

Elliot stabbed a slim forefinger in his direction and said,

'You do what the doctors tell you and you'll soon get out of here. And eat up all your greens.'

'My greens?' he protested.

'Your greens,' repeated Elliot. 'If you don't eat your greens, you won't grow big and strong. That's what my mother used to tell me!'

As Elliot walked on the old man turned to his neighbour in the next bed. 'Won't grow big and strong?' he said. 'But I'm sixty-one!'

His neighbour laughed. 'He's only jossing you,' he said. 'He likes to joke a bit.' He lowered his voice. 'That's his brother, the one that fell under the train, that never speaks. Must be sad for him, day after day, just sitting there by his brother's bed.'

Elliot had now stopped beside a young man in his early twenties who, with a wicked look in his eye, was whispering in the visitor's ear. Suddenly Elliot threw back his head and roared with laughter so that all heads turned towards him.

'D'you get it?' cried the young man eagerly.

'Disgusting!' Elliot declared. 'I must remember that one.'

The young patient grinned weakly. He had lost a leg with gangrene and was in danger of losing the other one. 'My cousin tells me them,' he said. 'He works in a bicycle factory and they have all these jokes going round.'

Elliot stopped twice more, delaying the moment when he would see Ralph, who was lying exactly as he had done on the previous day's visit — eyes closed, hands relaxed and idle, mouth and jaw slack. The only difference was in the angle of his head. Sometimes the nurses had turned his head to the left and sometimes to the right. Only the slight rise and fall of the bedclothes over his chest hinted at life. When he reached Ralph, Elliot raised one of the limp hands, clasped it to him briefly and then carefully replaced it on the blanket.

'It's me,' he said softly. 'Elliot. Maybe you can't hear me, but I'm here.' He swallowed and blinked his eyes. All the false cheerfulness had faded and his expression was sombre as he pulled up a chair and sat down beside the bed. Then he drew an envelope from his pocket, from which he took a small gold cross on a chain.

'It's from Amy,' he told the silent Ralph. 'She's not allowed to visit, but she sends her love and she wanted you to have this. It's the gold cross she used to wear round her neck — do you remember it? Here, hold it for a while.'

With infinite tenderness he opened the fingers of Ralph's right hand and dropped the cross into the palm. Then he closed the fingers round it and held the hot hand between his cool ones.

'She misses you,' he said. 'We both do.'

For a while he sat there, with so much to say and no way to reach the lonely figure in the bed. Suddenly he became aware of a shuffling behind him and turned to see a wizened old man approaching. He wore a hospital dressing-gown and his worn felt slippers were on the wrong feet.

'Your brother, is it?' the old man asked wheezily.

'That's right.'

'He's quiet enough now . . . but last night!' The old man rolled his eyes. 'What a to-do that was!'

Elliot frowned. 'A to-do?' he echoed. 'Why, what happened last night?'

'Why, he started hollering, that's what happened!' the old man explained. 'Woke me up, he did, though mind you I never do take my sleeping draught. Ugh! Terrible stuff! I pour it down the back of the bed when they're not looking. Yes, hollered right out, but I couldn't catch what he said. You should have seen the nurse come running!'

'My brother!' cried Elliot, turning back to look at Ralph. 'Are you sure it was this man who hollered?'

'*Course* I'm sure,' the old man insisted. 'The sister will tell you when she comes back. Hollered right out, he did. Gave me a right fright, I can tell you.'

'Did he say anything?'

'I told you, I couldn't catch it.' The old man coughed and then rubbed his watery eyes. 'Pretended he'd woke me up, I did, and asked for a cup of cocoa. Oh, I do like a drop of cocoa — nice and strong with plenty of sugar.'

'Did the nurse understand what he said?'

'Shouldn't think so. Leastways, if she did she didn't let on. "Go back to sleep, Mr Arbutt" was all I got. No cocoa, no nothing.'

Elliot stared at Ralph and for a moment felt wildly

hopeful. If the old man was right, then perhaps Ralph was going to regain consciousness.

'Thank you for telling me,' he said. 'I'll speak to the Sister about it.'

However Mr Arbutt was warming to his theme, encouraged by Elliot's reaction to his news.

'Hollered right out,' he repeated, 'and I nearly jumped out of my skin. Gone midnight, it was, and everyone snoring. Hollers out, he does, and then sits bolt upright and—'

In his excitement, Elliot grabbed the other's arm. 'He sat up?' he cried. 'Ralph *sat up*? Please, Mr Arbutt. Think carefully . . .'

But now the old man had seen the Sister striding towards them between the rows of beds and tugging his arm from Elliot's grasp, he began to shuffle away down the ward.

Sister Martin then gave Elliot a more accurate description of what had taken place during the night. Ralph had not stirred from his prone position, but he had called out. He had not 'hollered' at any time, but he had muttered and murmured loudly enough to attract the attention of the night nurse.

'I'm afraid, though,' she told him, 'that he was delirious due to a high temperature and was not regaining consciousness. The night nurse managed to reduce his temperature a little, but he is still very hot and the delirium may recur tonight. I'm sorry if Mr Arbutt raised your hopes unduly; I shall have a word with him about it.'

'It doesn't matter,' said Elliot, although in fact he was profoundly disappointed. 'The old chap meant no harm. Did my brother say anything that made any sense?'

She shook her head. 'I'm afraid not, Mr Allan. Not to us, anyway. Mostly it was just the usual confusion of words and phrases. There was one word he seemed to repeat, but we couldn't understand it. It began with "L". It could have been a name.'

'Lydia!' said Elliot. 'Could it have been "Lydia" I wonder. That was his fiancée's name.'

'It's possible,' said the Sister. 'He could have been calling her name. He said "Mama", of course, but most people call for their mother when they're delirious – oh, and there was something that sounded like "brook", as in stream. I really think that's all, Mr Allan, and I do hope you won't raise your hopes too much. A high temperature in these cases is not a good sign, I'm afraid. I am being quite frank with you, because you asked me to be so. His condition was stable until last night but now, because of the fluctuation in temperature, it gives cause for some concern.'

'I see.' Elliot nodded and turned back to the bed to hide the extent of his disappointment. 'If he were suddenly to take a turn for the worse, you would notify me at once, I hope? I would come as quickly as possible.'

'Of course.'

'At any time of the day or night.'

'We will certainly notify you, Mr Allan. I'm sorry I can't hold out any hope for you but as I've said before, with your brother's history I fear it is only a matter of time . . . and, Mr Allan . . .' Her tone changed slightly.

'Yes, Sister,' he said, his heart heavy with dread.

'I believe his time may be running out faster than we think.'

·

Chapter Eighteen

Ellen Turner lay in the double bed beside her husband and stared up into the darkness. From time to time the moon appeared from behind the racing clouds and lit the small room, casting long shadows. Outside, the door of the lean-to creaked on its hinges, straining at the ill-fitting latch, while downstairs in the kitchen Snip barked sharply at a fancied footstep. In the next room the old man snored erratically, but somehow the two boys slept through the noise. Above them a bedspring creaked as Amy turned restlessly. Ellen thought about them all and about the husband who had taken her back into his life.

Amy, her first-born, had given them so much joy and even now, twenty years later, Ellen could still recall the pride in Tom's voice and the expression on his face as they stood beside the font at their daughter's christening. He had been so proud of his little girl and had loved her in his own way, she was sure of that, but he had never found it easy to show his love. Small wonder, she thought, for his own parents had rarely if ever shown either of their sons the affection they deserved. Yet somehow John had grown into a cheerful, outgoing man while Thomas had learned, by his parents' example, to hide his emotions. In the early days Ellen had tried to make up to Tom by holding his hand or putting an arm around his shoulders, but this had embarrassed him in front of his parents and she had soon given up. For nine long years, after Amy's birth, it seemed they would never have a second child and this had grieved them both although Tom, longing for a son, had suffered most deeply at what he thought of as his 'failure'. When Sam was born his delight had been heart-warming, though even to the long-awaited son he could not show his feelings, but maintained a distance between them, an invisible barrier. It was left to John to bring into Amy's and Sam's lives the warmth and fun that was lacking. Aware of what was happening, Tom had remained an austere father figure while John became the adored uncle.

Powerless to reverse the trend, Ellen had watched her husband withdraw into a protective shell. She tried many times to talk to him about the problem, but the discussions always ended in an argument and the resulting bitterness drove a wedge between husband and wife. When, after the death of his wife, John moved in to share their home, she too had enjoyed her brother-in-law's charm and finally the inevitable happened – she and John had fallen in love. At least she believed that they had done so and at the time John believed it also. Only later did he suggest that what he had felt for her was no more than infatuation and that was two years after the birth of Toby, when the young Netta had entered their lives with such disastrous results. Disastrous, that is, for Ellen. John had declared himself truly in love for the first time in his life and had taken a new chance of happiness with her. Ellen had suffered then what Thomas had suffered earlier – rejection, humiliation and an over-whelming sense of loss. Seeing young Toby's distress had brought home to her the anguish that Sam and Amy must have experienced because of her own departure from their lives.

Now, as she lay sleepless beside her husband, she tried to come to terms with the inescapable facts of their relationship. For her, John was the only man she would ever love in the fullest sense of the word, because with him her world was complete and without him it would always be empty. Tom, on the other hand, would never love anyone else but Ellen and he had behaved magnificently towards her by taking her and her illegitimate son into his home once more. She owed him a debt of gratitude which she could never repay, but she would do her utmost to make him happy until the day she died. Not, she reflected bitterly, that she had had much

309

success so far, for now Toby had unwittingly brought about a serious accident for which Tom, as stationmaster, would be held responsible. The hearing was set for the following day at 9.30 am.

Tom lay beside her silent and still, but she knew he was wide awake just as he knew that she was. She searched her mind for a way to express all the grief in her heart but even if she found one, how would it help him? She needed somehow to give him courage and confidence, but she doubted he would even let her try. However, she could lie there no longer without making the attempt and timidly she put out a hand to touch his unresponsive shoulder.

'Tom? Are you awake, dear?'

'Mm?' He pretended, unconvincingly, to rouse from sleep. 'What's up?' He made no move to turn towards her.

'I don't like you lying there, worrying,' she began clumsily. 'I thought that if we talked—'

'I was asleep,' he told her, his tone brusque and defensive.

'Were you, Tom? I'm sorry,' she said. 'Then it's me that's awake and miserable.'

'What have you got to be miserable about?' he asked. 'I'm the one whose head is on the block, not you. Let me do the worrying.'

Ellen was silent, counting to ten, telling herself not to react crossly, urging herself to understand how he felt, to remain sympathetic and not to take offence at his words. 'I have sworn to try and make him happy,' she reminded herself silently. 'I have sworn to accept all the rebuffs as part of my punishment.'

'I'd just like to help you,' she said gently. 'Comfort you, maybe.'

'I don't need comforting,' he told her. 'Comforting is not going to help me tomorrow morning when I stand up there before judge and jury and try to—'

'It's only an enquiry,' she said, 'not a court of law, Tom. You're not a criminal, for heaven's sake!'

He turned over angrily. 'It may be *only* an enquiry to you, but it's a damn sight more than that to me.'

'I didn't mean it that way, Tom,' she protested. 'I meant, don't let things get out of proportion.'

310

As soon as the words were out she knew they would be misinterpreted. Perhaps, she thought wearily, he needed to argue, to relieve some of his pent-up emotions. Perhaps her role was that of whipping-boy. It was not what she had intended. She had meant to take him in her arms and be loving and gentle. She had wanted to make him forget his problems, if only for a few moments. Since her return he had been polite, even friendly, but they had not been lovers. Once, when she had tried unsuccessfully to rouse him, he had told her in an agony of despair that the image of her with John would not leave him.

'Out of proportion!' he repeated grimly, keeping his voice down with an effort. 'A man loses a leg and probably his life on *my* platform at *my* station because *my* son—' He hesitated, then substituted, '—your son, I should say, is where he shouldn't be and that bloody Arnold is where he shouldn't be and it's all my responsibility! And you think I'm getting it all out of proportion? My God, Ellen, I sometimes think—'

'Tom, please!' she begged. 'You know I didn't mean it like that. I just want to help you; I want to be of some use. Can't you see that? Can't you understand that I hate to see you so . . .' she searched for the right word, ' . . . so alone in all this. Let me share it with you, Tom.'

She slid her arm across his body. 'Let me just hold you, Tom,' she said. 'Let's just be friendly. I know a lot of the blame is mine because of Toby and that's hard for me to bear. Can you imagine how guilty I feel? For that poor Mr Allan and for you. I need some comfort, Tom. Can't we please try to help each other?'

After a long moment his arms slid round her, albeit grudgingly, but he did not kiss her nor did he speak reassuringly.

'You have no idea what this enquiry will do to me if I am found guilty of negligence,' he went on. 'It won't be the first time either. While you were away—' He broke off and she knew with a sickening lurch of fright that he was going to talk about the subject which had so far remained forbidden between them.

Ellen had never asked why the family had moved to Gaze-down or why her husband now controlled such a small and insignificant station. Once she had tried to talk to Amy about what had happened, but Amy had not been prepared to discuss it. Sam, with obvious reluctance, had said, 'Pa got ill or something and everything went wrong', and had then refused to answer any more questions. Now Ellen lay with her eyes closed as her husband's words poured out, describing in bitter and graphic detail the catalogue of disasters which had followed her departure. Tears rolled down her face as the full extent of her husband's tragedy was revealed to her and she lay beside him in despairing misery, aware that having once caused him so much harm she had now returned to cause him more. He never could forgive her, she thought, and she had no right to expect that he would. She had ruined his life and she must pay for her selfishness for as long as she lived.

'So now you see,' he told her, 'that Gazedown was my last chance. If I am censured over this, it will be the final blot on my copybook and I shall be forced to leave the railway service for ever. I don't rate my chances high, Ellen, so you may wish you had stayed on your own or looked for another man. You're still an attractive woman.'

'I don't want another man,' she sobbed, although in fact she did. She wanted John; she wanted him to scoop her up in his arms, laughing and loving, and carry her away from this nightmare of despair. 'Oh, John,' she cried silently, 'I love you still. If only I could hate you, it would be so much easier to bear.'

Tom patted her back awkwardly as her sobs grew more violent.

'I'm sorry,' he said. 'Perhaps I shouldn't have told you. It's all over now, that part of it, and we're together again. It doesn't matter — sometimes I think that nothing matters any more.'

'But it does matter,' she cried brokenly. 'I wanted to know what had happened, but now I do and it's so terrible — oh, Tom! What are we going to do?'

'Do?' he asked. 'How do you mean?'

She clung to him, beside herself with grief, the tears streaming down her face. 'What are we going to do without love, Tom?' she cried. 'Without love and without hope! It's

312

all so grey and terrible – I can't bear it for you or for myself. I'm such a coward, Tom. Help me, for God's sake.'

'We'll manage,' he declared, but without much conviction. 'We shall have to make do somehow for the children's sake. They deserve a better time. Amy's been marvellous – it's such a shame about the book. She was so thrilled and now I don't suppose it will ever be finished.'

'And that's my fault, too,' sobbed Ellen. 'It should be me at the enquiry – not you, Tom. Would they let me speak? Would they let me explain?' Her voice rose querulously.

'Hush!' he exclaimed. 'You'll wake everyone up. It's no good taking on so, Ellen. Tears won't help us. There's nothing we can do except wait and pray. I'll answer their questions and I'll tell the truth. After that, it's up to the Board; we're in their hands. They say Stephens is a very fair man; presumably he'll be there.' He sighed deeply. 'If the worst happens, we shall have to move on again, that's all, and make another start somewhere else. I'll find work of some kind; we won't starve.'

Ellen found a handkerchief under the pillow and blew her nose. 'I could find work,' she told him eagerly. 'I could take in washing or serve in a shop. I can turn my hand to most things. Or sewing! I can sew, Tom. I could take in mending. I'd do it willingly, Tom. I'd be glad to.'

'So far,' said Tom slowly, 'it isn't a fatality.'

'Isn't a fatality?' She stared at him uncomprehendingly. 'What isn't a fatality?'

'The accident,' said Thomas. 'Poor Allan is still alive and that will help. If he were dead, it would be classed as a fatal accident. If he died tonight . . . oh God! What am I saying? The poor devil's lost a leg and will most likely die and all I'm worrying about is my bloody job! How selfish can you be?'

'Don't be too hard on yourself, Tom,' Ellen told him. 'We're all only human and we all make mistakes and do things we regret or that make us ashamed.' She was calmer now. 'We had a sampler on the parlour wall when I was a child. "Love One Another", it said. I think "Forgive One Another" would be better.'

'Forgiving's not so difficult,' he said sadly. 'It's the forgetting that's difficult. You can forgive till you're blue in the face, but you can't make yourself forget.'

'No,' said Ellen, thinking of John, 'you can't.' She wondered whether to suggest that she made some cocoa, but Tom's arms were round her and he was *talking* to her and she was reluctant to break the spell.

'I sometimes think,' he went on, 'that I've never been really happy in my whole life. Even at the best times there's always been something to spoil it – to take the edge off it.' He sighed again. 'I suppose it's the same for everybody.'

'Maybe it is,' said Ellen. She turned her head and kissed his shoulder. 'Maybe we all expect too much from life and then we're disappointed. I don't know.'

The silence between them lengthened, but it was not uncomfortable. Thomas said suddenly, 'You always wanted John; I knew that even when I asked you to marry me, but he was already engaged and I thought I could make you love me.'

The accusation, if that was what it was, shocked her.

'I don't—' she stammered. 'That is, I didn't know . . .'

He gave a short laugh. 'Oh, you didn't know it at the time,' he told her. 'John didn't realise either. Nobody did but me. I suppose I should have talked to you about it, but I was afraid. I wanted you so much I didn't dare risk losing you. You need someone like John. I'm not really the man for you, but I did my best.'

Ellen, choked with emotion, could not speak.

'I should never have taken John in when he was left on his own,' he said, speaking to himself rather than to her. 'It was a stupid thing to do – a stupid risk to take. Almost at once I realised it was a mistake, but by then it was too late. He'd moved in and I couldn't say, "My wife's always loved you, John." I knew what might happen and it did.'

Ellen propped herself up on one elbow and tried to read the expression on her husband's face. 'You mean you thought we might fall in love and yet you still invited him to live with us?'

'I don't really know,' he replied. 'Maybe I hoped that after all those years you'd have grown fond of me and maybe . . .'

He shrugged. 'I knew the risk I was taking,' he said, 'and I lost.'

'We both lost!' she said wonderingly. 'Did I really love John all those years ago? Are you so sure?'

'Oh yes,' he said. 'There's no doubt in my mind. I'm surprised at John. He's a fool. He's lost you and he's lost his son. Toby's a nice child.'

'Oh, Tom!' she whispered. 'You deserve someone who adores you.'

'I wanted you,' he told her, 'and I still do.'

'I don't know what to say.'

'Then don't say anything, love.'

Neither of them spoke again for a long time, but they both knew that the worst was over.

Ellen asked, 'Do you fancy a cup of cocoa or anything?'

'I know what I *do* fancy,' he said shakily. 'And I think we've waited long enough.'

'Oh, Tom, I think so too,' whispered Ellen.

*

Amy put up a hand to her hat, which was threatening to blow away as she searched for Don amongst the crowds that thronged the market. The cattle market, held every Tuesday, was a noisy bustling place and Amy, visiting it for the first time, found it exhilarating. Pigs squealed and jostled in their temporary pens, grunting occasionally with ecstasy as a child or a farmer's wife paused to reach down and scratch their bristled backs. The gates clattered open and shut as sheep were herded from their wagons to the pens. Some came by rail, others still made the journey from farm to market in horse-drawn wagons. Once in the pens they huddled together in one corner, regardless of how much space was available to them, bleating anxiously and surveying with large, vacant eyes the farmers who felt their thick fleeces or leaned over to examine their hooves.

Further on, the cattle bellowed incessantly and tossed their heads, constantly shifting their position, while their eyes rolled wildly and saliva dripped from their large, lolling tongues. Farmers and stockmen were everywhere in earnest groups, discussing the quality of their own and other people's animals or standing pensively alone, considering the current market price. Behind the sheep, chickens squawked indignantly as the baskets which imprisoned them were tossed from seller to purchaser with scant regard for their complaining occupants. Some were being sold as 'layers', others for the table and the latter, when purchased, fell quickly silent as a quick twist from experienced hands put an end to their discomfort.

An elderly man sold live rabbits from a hutch mounted on a barrow; his podgy wife, sitting beside him on a rickety stool, sold snared rabbits which hung upside down in stiff rows from a large wooden frame. A basket of kittens attracted a crowd of admiring and hopeful children and several litters of puppies had the same instant appeal for the younger members of the crowd. A dozen or so horses were being paraded in an open space – a piebald cob, a chestnut gelding, a pair of diminutive Shetland ponies. Amy stopped to watch, admiring the high-spirited gait of the gelding and the thick coats of the ponies. Beside her a little girl tugged at her father's hand and assured him desperately that the ponies looked like brother and sister and should not be separated, suggesting hopefully that they should buy them both!

Goats were on sale, too, milling about excitedly in their corner. They were all sizes and colours: white, black, brown or a patchwork of all three. A small boy with tears in his eyes crouched beside one of the white nanny-goats, who fretted at the end of her short chain. A pet being sold, thought Amy with compassion, pausing to give the boy a cheerful smile which did nothing to lessen his unhappiness. There were creamy ferrets for sale, cage-birds of every hue, even goldfish, and a young man in a large straw hat sat cross-legged on the ground and did a roaring trade in white mice.

Amy, resplendent in a new blue jacket (bought with the first of what she called her 'book money') had arranged to meet Don at the market. After his business was concluded, they would repair to a public house for a hot pie and a mug of beer – or in Amy's case, a bottle of stout which Don had promised her would 'bring a bit of colour to her cheeks'.

316

She had accepted the invitation with some misgivings but Don had insisted that if she was to become Mrs Leckie, farmer's wife, the sooner she got used to the rough and tumble of market day the better for all concerned. She would also, he pointed out, meet some of his friends.

However, the plan seemed about to misfire for Amy could not find him and as time passed she was becoming flustered. Buffeted by the crowd, blown by the wind and half-dazed by the noises and smells of the market, she began to think she would never find him. She could not even remember which public house he had mentioned.

'Oh, you'll find me,' he had told her airily. 'I'll be the good-looking one!'

Her mouth twitched into a brief smile as she recalled his words, but then a burly woman with a huge basket on her arm pushed past, almost knocking her over. She put out both hands to steady herself against the metal rails and came face to face with an unhappy Friesian cow, whose agitated head caught her a juddering blow on the chin. Amy gasped in dismay as the cow's large mouth then brushed against her new jacket, smearing it with a generous helping of saliva. To add insult to injury, a beefy young man on the far side of the pen apparently found her discomfiture highly amusing and burst into loud guffaws, while digging his elbow into his companion's side so that that gentleman – a slightly older man – could also share the joke. While Amy was rubbing her jacket and searching for a sufficiently scathing comment, the wind caught her hat and that went flying off to disappear amongst the crowd. Her heavy brown hair, released from the confines of the hat, slipped free of its pins and fell around her shoulders at the mercy of the wind.

Amy knew in her heart that the only way to deal with the situation was to share in the laughter at her predicament, but she could not do so. The men's boorish amusement at her expense offended her and she was grieved at the loss of her hat and upset about the jacket. She had tried hard to look attractive so that Don would be proud of her, and now she felt utterly demoralised by the knowledge that when he introduced her to his friends she would look a mess. She felt at a distinct disadvantage in the unfamiliar environment, but at least her smart appearance had given a small boost to her confidence. Now she felt ridiculously vulnerable and wished most heartily that she had gone to The Lodge as usual to carry on with her work.

Ignoring the two men opposite, Amy took out her handkerchief and tried to smarten up her jacket, while trying unsuccessfully to restrain her hair with her other hand. She longed to escape to a more congenial atmosphere; she did not belong here, she thought miserably, and unless Don appeared within the next five minutes she would turn her back on the market and her 'intended' and make her way back to the station. Or perhaps she would move up into the town, buy herself a cup of tea and then look at the shops. She would not stay in this noisy, smelly place, she told herself, where good manners seemed to have gone out of fashion.

The more she rubbed at her jacket the worse it looked, and she was finally forced to give up the hopeless task. She would look a wreck and Don would have to put up with it, she decided. Looking round her, she saw that by far the majority of people were men and thought ruefully that obviously most of the farmers' wives knew better than to set foot in such a place. The future Mrs Leckie had learned the hard way, but she would not make the same mistake twice.

Pinning up her hair as best she could, she straightened her shoulders and began to push a way through the crowd once more. Suddenly she saw a blond head in front of her but having fought her way towards it she discovered that the man was not Don and disappointment only fuelled her wrath. It was all Don's fault, she reasoned. If he had suggested a proper meeting place, none of this would have happened. Suddenly she saw an upturned crate – if she stood on it, she would get a better view. This proved to be a mistake, however, for the moment she stepped up on to it a wag in the crowd cried, 'Hullo! Going to give a speech, are you, missus?' and grinning faces turned towards her, enjoying her embarrassment. Swallowing furiously, Amy stepped down without taking time to look for Don.

Damn them, she thought angrily, yet at the same time she

318

blamed herself for letting them upset her. It was all so foolish and probably they meant no disrespect, but—

'Amy! I'm over here!'

Don's voice broke into her thoughts and she glanced round in relief. Her relief, however, was short-lived, for he was making his way towards her accompanied by the two men who had enjoyed her earlier misfortune. Amy's heart sank. 'Not those two, please, Don!' she begged silently. 'Don't let those two ill-mannered wretches be your friends.' But it seemed they were.

Don came up to her with a large grin on his face. 'Someone pulled you through a hedge backwards?' he joked, giving her a hasty peck on the side of her face. 'Where's your hat?' Before Amy could answer, he rushed straight into the introductions.

'Paul Bailey, Les Davis, Amy Turner.'

Try as she would, Amy could not manage anything remotely resembling a polite smile.

'We've already met,' she said coldly.

The two men looked somewhat abashed, she noted with satisfaction; the younger man, Les Davis, said, 'We sort of bumped into each other.'

Don nodded cheerfully, and said, 'That's good! So what d'you think of her, eh?' He put an arm round her waist and pulled her towards him. 'Amy Turner, soon to be Mrs Donald Leckie. Not bad, eh?'

In spite of her dishevelled appearance, Don was obviously very proud of her, but Amy was in no mood to be judged by Les and Paul. How could he humiliate her further by asking his two cronies for an opinion, as though she was merely another animal on sale in the market? Amy wanted to wring his neck with her bare hands. The older man, Paul, winked broadly and said, 'Very nice bit of horseflesh, Don. Knocks my old missus into a cocked hat, I'll tell you!'

Don laughed with pleasure at the 'compliment' as Les added, 'I reckon you've got a bargain there, boy, so let's go and celebrate. Pub's been open too long already and I've a thirst on me a yard long. A pint of best bitter would go down very nicely – and one for the lady, of course.'

Don laughed. 'A pint and a pie! Let's make a move then, before the others have downed the lot.'

As they all moved off, Don said to Amy, 'What kept you, love? I was nearly giving up on you.' He raised a hand by way of greeting as a farmer passed them carrying a brace of pheasants and said, 'Hello there, Charlie!'

'Nothing kept me,' Amy told him curtly. 'I just couldn't find you in the crowd.'

'I told you, I'd be the good-looking one!' he joked.

'There were so many good-looking ones,' she retorted.

He gave her a puzzled look. 'Anything wrong?' he asked, lowering his voice.

'Wrong?' echoed Amy. 'No, I'm having a wonderful time. Looking forward to lunch with your two charming friends.'

'There is something wrong,' he insisted. 'What's up, then?'

His concern, so obviously genuine, brought a sudden lump to Amy's throat and she knew that if she tried to explain she would burst into tears. It would all sound so ridiculous, he would laugh at her and rightly so.

'Nothing's up,' she said with a shake of her head. 'Don't keep on about it.'

He shrugged and then laughed aloud at one of Paul's coarse comments and Amy's anger faded into despair as she followed the three men into the public bar of the Three Tuns. She could not imagine that she would ever fit comfortably into Don's way of life, although presumably she would have to try. He was an attractive man and would make a good husband for the right woman. But was *she* the right woman? As they searched for seats she thought of Mary and Jim Leckie. Mary seemed happy enough with her lot and Don was not so very different from his father. Perhaps it was only a matter of time. Perhaps she was too sensitive and would learn to take it all in her stride. Perhaps – she became aware that Don was shouting from the bar.

'Amy! I said steak or ham pie?'

'Sorry. Er – steak, please.'

Paul came back from the bar carrying two dripping mugs of best bitter. As he reached the table he accidentally stepped on the paw of a black and white collie which was lying on the floor minding his own business. The dog yelped and Paul, startled, spilled the beer on to the table.

Cursing under his breath, he scooped the spilt liquid from the table to the floor with the side of his hand. It splashed on to the floor, spattering the skirt of a woman who sat with the dog. She glared at him and said, 'Watch what you're doing, can't you?' but Paul ignored her and perched himself precariously on a very small stool.

He raised his glass and took several large gulps of the dark liquid, smacked his lips appreciatively as he grinned at Amy.

'So you and Don are going to name the day?'

'Yes.'

'Good luck to you, then. You'll need it, by Christ you will!' He took another mouthful. 'It's not easy.'

Amy eyed him with distaste but said nothing and then Les and Don joined them, distributing the pies and the rest of the drinks. For a moment all three men attended to their beers, and Amy bit into her pie as the pint of stout they had brought her looked rather daunting.

'I'm just telling Amy here that marriage isn't easy,' said Paul. 'Not all it's cracked up to be. Not in my opinion, anyway.'

Don laughed. 'Depends who you marry,' he said. 'I reckon I've made the right choice.'

'Oh, you have,' said Paul. 'It's me that's picked a wrong-un.'

All three men seemed to find this very amusing and Amy smiled obligingly, wondering if they would dismiss her in an equally disparaging way at some date in the not-too-distant future. She felt sorry for Paul's absent wife, yet curious too. In what way she wondered, was the unfortunate wife a 'wrong-un' in her husband's eyes?

The meal proceeded with boisterous conversation from the men and a few comments from Amy. Try as she would she could not think of anything witty or intelligent — or even interesting — to contribute, and hoped that Don was not too disappointed. Not that they seemed to notice her reticence, engrossed as they were in their own affairs, exchanging greetings from time to time with people who passed them and returning at regular intervals to the bar to refill their pint mugs.

Amy found the stout too bitter for her liking, but she persevered without comment, aware that if she gave up and declared herself beaten it would provide the men with further opportunity for ribald comment. The talk turned from the falling price of sheep to the shortage of winter foodstuff; it touched on a suspected outbreak of foot-and-mouth in the North of England and moved to a rumour that more Californian hops were going to be allowed into the country untaxed. From the conversation, Amy learned that Paul – who farmed at Wittersham – ran only sheep, while Les in Peasmarch grew hops and kept a few cows and pigs. If she had been in a happier mood she might have found it instructive, but instead she sat at the table forcing stout down her unwilling throat and feeling out of place and unloved, perversely surrounded by dozens of people who were obviously thoroughly at home and enjoying themselves immensely.

She was quite unprepared for the sudden glimpse of Elliot's dark head as he made his way towards the door of the Three Tuns. She guessed that he was looking for her and for a moment her heart leapt joyfully at the prospect of some company she could appreciate, but then as he hesitated in the doorway, she saw the expression on his face.

'Excuse me!' she cried, jumping to her feet. 'I've seen someone I know – I must go.' She was edging her way out as Don put a restraining hand on her arm.

'Who is it?' he asked.

'Ralph's brother, Elliot,' she told him. 'I think it's bad news—'

His hand tightened on her arm, but she pulled herself free and when Elliot caught sight of her he turned and waited for her outside the door. For a moment neither spoke, then he took her arm and led her away to a less crowded part of the street where they could talk more easily. He looked very pale and his face was drawn.

'I went to your home,' he said. 'They told me I'd probably find you here. Oh Amy, I'm afraid—' He broke off.

'It's Ralph, isn't it?' Amy whispered. 'Tell me.'

The brown eyes that looked into hers were dark with grief.

'He died early this morning. I was there,' he said quietly. 'I held him in my arms.'

Although Amy had been expecting it the news still shocked her and she felt as though she was drowning in sorrow. She gave a deep sigh of anguish and her eyes filled with tears.

'Ralph!' she whispered. 'Oh, poor, dear Ralph!'

'He didn't regain consciousness, Amy,' Elliot said gently, tears glistening in his own eyes as he spoke. 'One minute he was breathing and the next he had slipped away.'

'I can't believe it,' she said dully. 'I know it's happened, but I can't believe we shall never see him again. And poor you! You've lost your brother. I'm so dreadfully sorry.' Her voice began to tremble and the first tears splashed down her cheeks. 'Oh, poor Ralph!' she cried. 'He had such a sad life and now it's all over.'

Elliot pulled her towards him and held her close as her tears flowed, shaking her slim body with their ferocity. For a while he let her cry, his own tears too imminent to allow him any words, but eventually he tried to comfort her, stroking her hair and pressing her close against his chest.

'It's the best thing for him, Amy,' he told her. 'This way he had the decision taken from him. He would have found a way to die, we all knew that. Now it's all over – the pain, the loneliness, everything.'

'I tried to help him,' Amy sobbed. 'I wanted to convince him . . .'

'No one could help him,' he comforted her. 'Perhaps if Lydia had lived – but no, I don't think even Lydia could have saved him from himself. Sooner or later it would have happened. Don't blame yourself, Amy; he was fond of you and I know you helped him a great deal. Just think that he's at peace now and it's what he had wanted for a long, long time.' His voice broke suddenly. 'Oh God, Amy, I'll miss him, too.'

They clung together regardless of the curious stares of passers-by, each taking comfort from the other's nearness and the knowledge of a shared affection for Ralph. They were still locked in each other's arms two minutes later when Don, only slightly the worse for drink, came out to look for Amy.

*

323

Jim Leckie was sluicing buckets of water across the floor of the cowshed when his son returned from market. He gave a shout to let Don know where he was and straightened up with one hand on his back.

'Damn back of mine!' he grumbled with a wince of pain. 'It's the bending that does it. Thought you'd be back in time to—' He broke off, seeing the downcast look on Don's face. 'What's up, lad?' he asked, surprised. Don was normally very easy-going and Jim knew at once that something was wrong.

Don leaned against the door jamb, his hands thrust into his pockets. 'Nothing really,' he said. 'At least, I don't know.' He shrugged. 'I got what we reckoned for the heifers.'

'Fine!' Jim waited. 'So?' he added. 'What's up? You might as well tell me now, because your mother will get it out of you — you know how she is.'

Don groaned. 'It's nothing really,' he repeated. 'Just Amy.'

'Amy? What's the matter with Amy?'

'I don't know what got into her,' he said, with more than a trace of belligerence in his voice. 'She turned up looking like a scarecrow — said she'd lost her hat — and then just sat there without a word to say for herself. Lord knows what Paul and Les thought about it, but I felt a right fool. Sipped her stout as though it might poison her—' He sighed heavily. 'Then this Elliot chap turned up to say Ralph Allan had died. She rushed out to meet him and didn't even finish her pie; I had to eat it myself. She didn't come back and when we got outside, there they are in the middle of the bloody street with their arms wrapped round each other, and her crying her eyes out.'

'So the poor chap died,' said Jim with a shake of his head. 'Maybe it was for the best but lordy, what a tragedy! Poor man. The day after the enquiry, too. Well, I never. Amy would be upset; they got on well, those two. Poor Amy! Mary says she kept hoping against hope!'

'Poor Amy!' said Don bitterly. 'Poor Ralph! What about poor *me*, standing there like an idiot? She's supposed to be my girl; she's not supposed to go chucking herself at other men.'

'That's hardly fair, Don,' his father said quietly, 'and you know that.'

With a snort of disgust, Don pushed himself free of the doorway and slouched across to lean on the nearest rail.

Jim said sharply, 'You didn't have words, I hope?'

'Sort of,' Don admitted. 'Oh, I know I shouldn't have said anything, but I was that fed-up!'

'What happened?' Jim asked, his heart sinking. He was as keen as Mary on the idea of a match between their son and Amy.

Don stared moodily at his father. 'I spoke my piece and she just kept on crying. Then he had a go at me and I thought, "sod it" and we just walked off and left them to it. I gave her a chance, I said, "Are you coming with me?"'

'And she said?'

'Just went on crying and he went on cuddling her as if she was *his* girl.'

'Don Leckie!' said Jim. 'You really are a first-class idiot. Of course she was upset, hearing news like that. And Elliot is Ralph's brother, remember? You really are an unfeeling wretch. Oh, I know your trouble. I can guess how it was. Too much to drink and that useless pair egging you on. You know what I think of Les and Paul – I've never been too keen on that pair. I could never understand what you see in fellows like that.'

'You wouldn't!' cried Don. 'You'd rather I didn't have any friends.'

'Oh, don't talk so daft, lad – you know perfectly well that's not it. I've just never thought they were up to much – and maybe Amy felt the same way. You know she's a shy sort of girl; she probably didn't know what to say to them, poor lass.'

'Stuck-up prig, more like it,' said Don. 'If she's going to marry me, she'll have to get used to my friends. I'm not changing my ways to suit the likes of her.'

Jim was alarmed by his son's vehemence. 'I hope to God you didn't say any of that to her,' he protested. 'I don't think she'd take too kindly to—'

'Of course I did! And I meant it.'

'Don Leckie, you're a fool!' cried Jim. 'You'd best go

round there and put things right before too much harm's done. The poor girl will be breaking her heart, she's very fond of you.'

'So you and Ma keep saying,' shouted Don, 'but I'm beginning to have my doubts. I had a lot more fun with Lorna Betts, if you must know. At least I didn't have to apologise to her for my friends.'

'Lorna Betts! Why, you were always complaining about her! Trouble with you is, you're never satisfied. You won't find the perfect woman, Don, if that's what you're after, believe me. If you want a wife you'll have to compromise, same as the rest of us. Women aren't angels and neither are we. You'll end up with nobody if you aren't careful and then you'll only have yourself to blame. If you want my advice—'

'I don't!' answered Don furiously. 'I'm not your little boy now, you know – I'm nearly twenty. Old enough to sort out my life without your help or anyone else's. So mind your own business will you, and I'll mind mine. I'm not going to chase after Amy Turner or anyone else. As far as I'm concerned, that's it. Finished!'

Father and son glared at each other for a long moment, then Jim lowered his eyes with a dismissive shrug.

'Have it your own way,' he said. 'But remember: Amy's a nice girl and you won't find a better in Gazedown. If you want to keep her, you'd better start treating her with—'

'I said I *don't* want your advice!' shouted Don and swinging on his heel, he strode out of the cowshed, leaving Jim to mutter under his breath and shake his head in despair at the intransigence of the younger generation in general, and his son in particular.

Chapter Nineteen

Amy let herself into The Lodge for the first time since Ralph's death. She had promised Elliot she would carry on with the work, and she sat down at the table and opened a letter which he had given her. Ignoring the empty chair opposite, she tried to concentrate on the contents; it was a letter written by Nigel Stanisbrooke to his first mistress, Rosa:

My dearest girl,
   Your letter touched me deeply. I am so distressed and wish I could be with you to comfort you in your sad loss. I know how devoted you were to your brother, and his passing must grieve you beyond measure. I shall think of you on Tuesday when he is laid to rest. Try to imagine that I am with you, as I shall be in spirit. Loving you as I do, it is a torment to me to be unable to give you the love and support you so desperately need, but I know you appreciate the impossible situation we find ourselves in.
   My poor Ella is becoming increasingly suspicious and any attempt on my part to be away from home while you are also absent would precipitate a crisis. It is my constant fear that our love will be discovered and that you will be summarily dismissed and how could I bear to lose you for ever? If it were not for the children . . . but that is foolish talk. My children's happiness is of paramount importance, as you well know, and I am aware of your own affection for them. We are trapped by circumstances, but at least we have our love to brighten the darkness. Ella has nothing and her illness is a great burden to her. I have to remind

myself that she is my wife and the mother of my children and as such I owe her my loyalty.

Take care of yourself, my sweet Rosa, and come back to us as soon as you are able. The children were delighted with your letter to them and ask daily about you, but I have to pretend I know nothing. I must close this letter now.

God be with you. I love you.

Your devoted Nigel

When Amy had read it she examined the letter itself. The paper on which it was written was brittle with age and browning at the edges. It had obviously been folded and unfolded many times and Amy could imagine with what mixed emotions Rosa had read it. An illicit love affair with the father of the children for whom she was employed as governess; guilt at the predicament of the suffering wife; her brother's death. Surely, Amy thought, the letter must have been of some comfort. She tried to imagine the governess, dressed in black, watching her brother's coffin being lowered into the grave, clinging to the belief that her lover was with her in spirit. They would have little hope for the future unless the wife's illness proved fatal. Amy thought, too, of poor Ella, lying helpless in her bed day after day, suspecting a liaison between her husband and the children's governess. And then Nigel Stanisbrooke himself, his loyalties divided but struggling at all costs to ensure the happiness of his children.

She re-read the letter and then laid it gently on the table, careful not to damage it. The envelope bore the same sloping, faded but still legible handwriting and she read the address: The Manse, Dorking, Surrey. The Manse? What was the brother of an impoverished governess doing at such an imposing place? Was The Manse the family home, Amy wondered? Later on, after Ella's death, Rosa and Nigel had married, but presumably it had not brought them the happiness they expected because seven years later, according to the diary of Emma Courtenay, she in turn became Nigel's mistress. Why was love so fragile and unpredictable?

Unwillingly Amy's thoughts drifted back to her own

328

predicament. She had lost Ralph and she had quarrelled with Don – or rather, he had quarrelled with her. His harsh words and lack of understanding had worried her more than she cared to admit; although she tried to make allowances for his behaviour the real trouble, she knew, lay in herself and her own inability to adapt to another way of life. She was not only unable, but unwilling. She did not *want* to like Les and Paul, nor did she want to sit for hours in a noisy public bar drinking large amounts of stout; she had not enjoyed herself and doubted if in similar circumstances she ever could. To others, the occasion had doubtless been thoroughly enjoyable – a traditional midday break in the middle of a busy market day, good food and drink shared with like-minded friends. 'It's my fault,' she said resignedly. 'I'm the one who's out of step. Oh Don, it's never going to work out for you and me. It's Elliot!'

Hearing these last words spoken aloud filled her with dismay and she buried her face in her hands.

She had known from the first moment she saw him and now she was forced to admit that he was the real reason for her disenchantment with Don. If she had never met Elliot Allan, she might well have married Don, would have been happy enough with her lot and would have made him a good wife. But she *had* met Elliot and it had finally dawned on her as they clung together just how deeply she was attracted to him. Perhaps she loved him. The realisation brought her no joy, rather the opposite. Ralph seemed to think that his brother would never marry and Amy saw no reason to disbelieve him. If her feelings for Elliot were not returned, then she faced a lonely future.

'Elliot!' she whispered. 'How could I have been so blind all this time? Ever since I first saw you . . .' Her voice trailed off.

Amy would see him again very shortly, for she was to travel up to London the next day to attend Ralph's funeral, but she imagined there would be little chance for them to talk. She presumed that her work on the book would shortly come to an end and found the prospect unutterably depressing. Without Ralph, without her work on the book

329

and without the remotest possibility of seeing Elliot again, the immediate future looked bleak indeed.

'Elliot,' she said softly, enjoying the sound of his name. 'I think I could love you, Elliot Allan,' she told him. 'No. Why try to fool myself? I already love you.'

Almost as she spoke, her expression changed again as she thought of telling Don. She assumed that she was no longer his 'intended'. Perhaps he was already rehearsing a farewell speech for her and no doubt he had already reinstated Lorna Betts as the woman in his life. Not so long ago, Lorna had apparently demonstrated to him a wish to be reconciled after their lovers' tiff.

But this daydreaming would not do, Amy scolded herself. She had come to The Lodge in an attempt to forget the present and to put in what might well prove to be the last hours of her work on Ralph's project. Tears threatened again and she swallowed hard. Tomorrow she would see him laid to rest – and she would also see Elliot. Once more her thoughts wandered and to rally them again, Amy picked up Nigel's letter to Rosa and began to read it for the second time. Around her, among the books and papers, time seemed to stand still and the anguished words of the letter reached out across the years. A sudden loud rapping at the door made her jump, but before she could move to open it Esme appeared, dressed in a dark brown taffeta skirt and matching braided jacket. Her face was very pale and she seemed no less strained than the last time they had met.

Amy stood up.

'I heard the news yesterday,' Esme told her. 'Elliot himself telephoned; it was most considerate of him.' She clasped her hands tightly as her eyes took in the workmanlike appearance of the room. 'I was terribly shocked. I had hoped to visit him in hospital. I had every intention of doing so as soon as my health permitted.'

Amy nodded politely. 'I'm glad you are recovered,' she said.

'Oh I am, yes. Quite recovered. We were very close, Ralph and I. Nobody knew.' She stared straight into Amy's eyes. 'I wanted to go to him, but the doctor forbade it. I wrote to him, naturally.'

330

'Of course.'

'Why does Elliot want you to go on working here?' Esme did not look particularly pleased at the prospect.

'It's only temporarily,' said Amy. 'Now that Ralph is dead, I expect someone else will have to finish the book.'

'I cannot abide sickness,' Esme said suddenly. She began to clasp and unclasp her hands. 'Sickness and death have always—'

She bit her lip, then went on, 'I have always found sickness and death quite unbearable. Once we had a spaniel bitch: Velvet, we called her. I must have been about six or seven. She had a litter of puppies, five of them. Born with long tails, of course. Dark brown they were and I adored them. I used to watch them for hours from the moment they were born. I saw them open their eyes for the first time. Then the gardener came in one day – "to dock their tails" my mother told me. Of course I didn't understand what that meant. He'd been drinking gin, to get his courage up I suppose.'

Esme swallowed hard and Amy was shocked to see a real horror in the beautiful blue eyes. Finally she continued jerkily, 'He had a cutthroat razor and he cut their tails. They squealed with pain and poor Velvet began to lick the blood from the stumps. I ran away.' She shuddered. 'I couldn't bear to see them afterwards. I didn't love them any more . . . they revolted me. It still affects me. Any kind of sickness affects my nerves, but Ralph and I were very close and I promised him I would visit the hospital as soon as the doctor allowed me out of bed. I feel very badly that . . .' She put up a hand to run her fingers over the smooth contours of her face. 'One has to go on, one has to keep up appearances. These things matter.'

'I'm sure they do,' agreed Amy. Now she could see that Esme was under tremendous strain. Her blue eyes were dark and her mouth trembled slightly.

Esme looked at Amy. 'Everyone needs someone,' she said suddenly.

'Yes.'

'I needed . . .' She left the sentence unfinished and Amy wondered uneasily if Esme remembered the night of the party when she had 'rescued' Ralph from the bedroom.

'My husband Gerald—' Esme began again, then shook her head determinedly. 'When I was a child, my grandmother was dying.' She stared past Amy to the window, her eyes unfocused. 'I was made to visit her, but the smell of sickness made me faint and I had to be revived with smelling-salts. I can still remember it – a sweetsour smell.' She shook her head. 'And then she died and we had to kiss her face. Her dead face.' Her voice sank to a whisper. 'It was so horrible, you cannot imagine. I was eight years old. But poor Ralph – that was different. I wanted to visit him . . .'

Amy said, 'He didn't regain consciousness. He was delirious, but never conscious.'

Esme's gaze returned to Amy. 'Not even at the very last? Didn't he speak at all at the end?'

'No. Elliot says he just slipped away peacefully.'

Esme gave a long sigh. She looked exhausted, Amy thought.

'We all need someone to love,' said Esme as though she were talking to herself. 'Someone to love. I shall attend the funeral, of course, with my husband. There will be room in our carriage, but we will be making an overnight stay at the Clarence Hotel so we really cannot offer to take you.'

'I am going up by train, thank you,' Amy told her. 'It's all arranged.'

'My husband—' Esme hesitated. 'Oh, no matter.' Turning to go, she added, 'Ah yes – the enquiry. I was so pleased when Gerald told me that your father had been exonerated of all blame. I'm sure Ralph himself would have agreed with the findings. It was an accident, pure and simple. Please tell your father that.'

'Thank you,' said Amy, surprised. 'I will.'

Esme left without another word and Amy turned back to her work. After about ten minutes she laid down her pen and inserted a sheet of paper in the typewriter, but her fingers remained poised above the keys.

'What is the point?' she asked aloud. 'Dates, names, events – all in tidy columns. It will never be read.'

Her earlier suspicions surfaced again and she groaned. 'If it was never meant to be a book . . .' she began. 'If it was

332

just a way to keep poor Ralph amused and out of trouble – did they never intend—Oh, damn!'

Pushing back the chair, she stood up and crossed to the window. Was she right? Could it be that the book had been merely a means to an end? And yet she had been officially employed by the publisher – or had she? Perhaps Elliot had really paid her out of his own pocket? The idea was so terrible that Amy could not bear it: it *had* to be a book.

'Of course it was to be published,' she said, but her voice trembled. So many hopes had resided in the book; so much of her future had been bound up within its proposed pages. But if not?

'Then it serves you right, Amy Turner,' she told herself sternly. 'You let it all go to your head. Nobody asked you to build your hopes on it. If it was a book, then it was always Ralph's – not yours.'

With a deep sigh, she looked around the room. What did it matter anyway? Soon it would all be over; the room would be restored to its previous state and Lord Stanisbrooke would be lost to her for ever.

If only she could write the book, thought Amy . . . but that was impossible. She had no understanding of military matters and no interest in them, either. All that interested her was the family – their hopes and fears, loves and hates. In her hands, it would be a different kind of book: a biography, perhaps. Slowly, she picked up the photograph of Nigel Stanisbrooke and stared into the dark eyes.

'If only you could help me,' she whispered. 'I would do it if I could. I'm so sorry.'

Still the dark eyes held hers and she felt mesmerised by them, fancying she could not look away. Was he trying to tell her something? As she looked into his eyes the photograph blurred.

'What do you want of me?' she whispered.

It needed an effort of will on her part to lay down the likeness and her hand was trembling. 'This is nonsense,' she said aloud.

But the feeling persisted – that something was required of her; that she owed the Stanisbrooke family something in return for all the pleasure they had given her.

'You're being fanciful,' she told herself. 'There's nothing I can do. I just have to walk away . . .'

Instead she sat down at the table, and propped up the photograph in front of her. Then she waited. At first nothing happened – her mind remained a frustrating blank – but then almost imperceptibly isolated phrases began to stir in the recesses of her mind. Elusive and intangible, yet they were there.

Amy hardly dared to breathe as words formed in her mind and allied themselves to others. Phrases re-formed into sentences; one idea emerged and was overtaken by another. She closed her eyes – it was all there, in her mind, waiting to be expressed. Then she opened them again abruptly and looked at the photograph.

'It can't do any harm to try,' she told him. 'There's nothing to stop me just *trying*.'

Still she hesitated, afraid of failing. How did one start to write a man's life story, she wondered? Begin with his birth, she supposed. No, that was too predictable. She frowned. Perhaps go back to his parents and explain their situation prior to his birth? Would that catch the reader's interest? Or she could begin where he was a small boy and go back from there.

The problem excited her and she tapped her fingers impatiently on the edge of the typewriter, anxious to see the first words appear on the page. She had lived with the Stanisbrooke family for so long and now she longed to bring these friendly ghosts to life; to give them substance with words.

Her fingers hovered over the keys. No one need know, she told herself. No one would laugh at her efforts. She would not tell Elliot what she was doing, therefore he would feel under no obligation to her. She would not tell him of her attempt and if he said that the book was to be finished elsewhere, she would accept it without demur.

Meanwhile, she would try her luck as a writer! A broad smile of delight lit up her face and she nodded to the photograph.

'You win!' she told him and at last her fingers descended to the keys and she began to type.

*

334

Mrs Betts' eldest daughter was not going to lose her child and for that Mrs Betts was heartily thankful. She was also heartily thankful to be back home again and freed from the company of Janet's husband, whom she had never cared for even at a distance. Close proximity over the past week had confirmed her opinion that Janet had thrown herself away on Daniel Hubbard. True, he had a regular job and provided them with a roof over their heads but he was still, in his mother-in-law's opinion, a 'shifty-eyed no-good'. He had got her elder daughter into trouble; he was weedy (Mrs Betts liked large men); he was inclined to spots and his voice was too high. Although Janet was not as attractive as Lorna she was personable and, married to the right man, might well have produced good-looking children. Now this seemed unlikely and Mrs Betts had resigned herself to an uninspiring brood of grandchildren on Janet's side.

Her only hopes lay with Lorna and her friendship with the Leckies' boy had augured well for the future. Now the silly girl had quarrelled with him and she only hoped they would soon patch up their differences. She set great store by physical appearances, for she had been pretty herself as a child and knew the power of beauty. Uncles had often slipped her an extra penny and her own father had favoured her above the other children in the family. Only the loss of her hair had spoiled her chances and she had been forced to marry the first man who asked her: Bernard Betts, God rest his soul, a wellmeaning but silly man who, after giving her two daughters, had promptly died and left her to support them. Lorna, she knew, could capitalise on her good looks if only she had the sense to do so. The thought that Don Leckie might prefer the stationmaster's daughter to her own was quite preposterous in Mrs Betts' opinion and the sooner Lorna reinstated herself in the affections of the farmer's son, the better. Mrs Betts liked the idea that one day the farm would belong to Don, and that Lorna as his wife would be established as a woman of some substance in the village. It would certainly bring home to Janet the true extent of her folly in marrying Daniel Hubbard!

All these thoughts were going through Mrs Betts' mind as she let herself in at the back door and walked through the scullery and into the kitchen, calling, 'I'm back!' as she did so. To her surprise, two faces stared back at her across the room as Lorna and Gerald Hatherley stood up to greet her.

Seeing Lorna's erstwhile employer, Mrs Betts' jangled nerves immediately cried out that here was more trouble. Instinctively, she dropped her purse and her hands went up to tighten the strings of her sunbonnet.

'Mr Hatherley!' she cried, flustered and apprehensive. 'Whatever brings you here? And Lorna, what are you doing, not offering Mr Hatherley so much as a cup of tea?'

Lorna made no effort to answer her mother's question and as Mrs Betts rambled on about just this very moment having come back from Robertsbridge and the exact state of Janet's health, she became aware of a certain tension in the atmosphere and her heart sank even lower as she sat down abruptly, prepared to hear the worst. As she looked from girl to man she kept up a rapid flow of chatter that defied interruption, thus giving herself time to collect her wits and mentally arm herself for the coming fray. She could see by the expression on Lorna's face that the news – whatever it was – would not be to her liking. So be it! Mrs Betts had fought many battles in her time, and in fact was not averse to a little conflict now and again, but today she had been looking forward to a quiet cup of tea and the chance to put her feet up and tell Lorna all about her stay with Janet.

When she finally ran out of breath, Lorna said quickly, 'I'm glad Janet's all right,' and Gerald cleared his throat importantly.

'Mrs Betts,' he said abruptly, 'I have something to discuss with you. May I sit down again?'

'Of course. Please do.' She had hardly realised he was still standing.

He exchanged a look with Lorna and they both resumed their seats.

'Something to discuss?' repeated Mrs Betts.

Perhaps they were going to give Lorna back her job, she thought. Certainly Lorna did not look too concerned.

'It's about the unfortunate matter of the . . .' He hesitated and began again. 'It arises from the night of my wife's party—'

336

Mrs Betts' hopes rose. They *were* going to take Lorna back! 'That was all very unfortunate,' she said. 'My girl is not used to strong drink. Neither of my girls—'

'Quite so,' agreed Gerald. 'As I was saying . . .' But he had lost his train of thought and looked towards Lorna for help.

She prompted him: 'About the evening of the party . . .'

'Ah yes, that evening. Well . . .'

Mrs Betts decided to be magnanimous. If they had thought better of their hasty behaviour, she would not bear a grudge. 'I believe you had no quarrel with her work before that date,' she began grandly.

'Ma!' Lorna cried. 'Don't keep chipping in. Let him get it out, for Gawd's sake!'

Mrs Betts' jaw fell open with astonishment at the over-familiarity in her daughter's words. Was the girl quite mad? If the Hatherleys were going to take her back, she could at least show proper respect.

Gerald cleared his throat again. 'The fact is, Mrs Betts, that on that occasion and while your daughter was under the influence of alcohol, someone . . .'

At this point Mrs Betts' expression froze and Gerald stopped once more.

'Go on!' hissed Lorna. 'Get it over with.'

'Someone,' said Gerald, 'took advantage of her – her inno-cence – and . . . against her will, that is. As her ex-employer – and as it took place under my roof and the man in question is obviously known to me—'

Here Mrs Betts gave a strangled cry and turned to Lorna. 'Not you, too!' she shrieked, her face colouring rapidly. 'Not you and Janet both! Oh, Lorna, surely you can't have! He doesn't mean what I think he means, does he? You're not—?'

Lorna nodded, her face pale. Mrs Betts threw up her hands despairingly and Gerald rushed on. His well-rehearsed speech was not going according to plan, but at least he had managed part of the story. He now held up a placatory hand.

'Bear with me, if you will, Mrs Betts,' he said. 'There's more to come and I hope—'

'More?' exclaimed Mrs Betts. 'My youngest daughter's been ravished while under the influence and you say there's *more*?'

Gerald swallowed and took a deep breath. 'The gentleman in question is obviously—'

'Gentleman?' she cried jumping to her feet. 'Gentleman, you call him? A man that takes advantage of a poor innocent girl? Who is he? I demand to know his name.'

'Ah, that's the problem, Mrs Betts, we don't know his name.' Gerald swallowed again. 'Your daughter only vaguely remembers him — very vaguely, I may say — but obviously he is well-born and if he knew the outcome of his little folly, he would be only too eager to make what amends he could. He would want to help financially, I am sure, to see that your daughter and the child were properly cared for.'

'The child!' groaned Mrs Betts, sinking back into her chair and fiddling with her bonnet strings. 'Where have I heard those words before? Oh Lorna! Lorna! How could you do this to me? How could you put me through all this to-do all over again? Haven't I had enough worry with that sister of yours and now—'

'I'm sorry, Ma,' interrupted Lorna, 'but it's not quite as bad as you think.'

'Of course it is,' cried her mother. 'It's probably worse than I think. All very well for Mr Hatherley to tell us what his fine friend *would* do for you, but if you don't know who he is . . . Oh, this is a fine how-d'you-do, this is!' She frowned suddenly. 'But you must remember something about him, Lorna? Was he tall, short, fat, thin?'

'I don't know,' said Lorna who, unlike Gerald, remembered her words perfectly and went smoothly into her prepared speech. 'Everything was all muzzy and it was dark in the library. My head was going round and round and I hardly knew what was happening. Maybe I fainted right away, I don't remember. When I came to he'd gone, and that's when I went downstairs and Mr Hatherley saw me and was so kind and insisted on bringing me home.'

'Was he old or young?' her mother persisted. 'You must have some idea.'

'Well, I haven't,' said Lorna firmly. 'And I wish you'd just listen to Mr Hatherley's proposition.'

'His proposition? What proposition?'

338

Gerald now stood up, his face pale, his hands clasped behind his back.

'My proposition is this,' he told the increasingly astonished Mrs Betts. 'Because the unknown gentleman is obviously of my acquaintance, I wish to assume responsibility on his behalf. I would like, with your permission, to provide your daughter with a home and a small but regular allowance. No, wait!' He held up a hand as Mrs Betts opened her mouth to speak. 'Please allow me to finish. I shall, in a very discreet way, make enquiries amongst my acquaintances and *if* the identity of the gentleman is discovered, he will then – I am quite sure – wish to take over the task of providing for your daughter and the boy . . . or girl,' he added quickly. 'If the identity of the father is not discovered, I shall continue to take care of them myself. As you know, Mrs Betts, my wife has been unable to give me an heir and it would give me great pleasure to accept a measure of responsibility for Lorna's child. I feel, in the circumstances, that it is the least I can do.'

Mrs Betts was staggered and for a while she could make no comment at all, but looked from Lorna to Gerald with a disbelief that was almost comical. Her thoughts were chaotic. Her daughter was to be provided with a home and an income and would bear the love-child of a gentleman! It was all very irregular, exciting even, but was it for the best? If Lorna was with child, she certainly would not be able to marry the Leckie boy, so that idea must be ruled out. What was left to her if she did not accept Mr Hatherley's generous offer?

'Oh dear,' she said, a hand to her heart. 'I'm knocked all of a heap, as they say.'

What she longed to do was box Lorna's ears for not telling her exactly what had happened on the night of the party. Surely the girl must have had some idea of what the man was doing to her? Could a woman be ravished and not notice it? It was fortunate for Lorna that Gerald was present to act as a restraint on her mother's temper.

'Say "Yes", Ma,' Lorna pleaded. 'I think it's ever so kind of Mr Hatherley and I've told him I'm willing.'

Mrs Betts hesitated. 'But whatever will people say?' she demanded. 'It's going to look a bit odd – and what sort of

339

a home would it be? And what sort of allowance? I mean, I've got to know a bit more about it before I can give my blessing. It's all been such a shock — and me only just back from Janet's and still in a bit of a tizzy.'

Patiently Gerald explained the details of the plan, naming a very fair figure for Lorna's weekly allowance and telling her mother about the cottage which was (by a strange coincidence!) already in the process of renovation.

Lorna watched her mother's face as Gerald spoke and could see her resistance crumbling as he went on to explain that if he should die, the cottage would become Lorna's property and a substantial settlement would be made.

'Properly invested, the money would then bring in a weekly sum very near to the allowance she will receive while I live. Your daughter, Mrs Betts, need never worry about money again. Her future and that of the child will be quite secure.'

Mrs Betts drew in a long breath, held it and then exhaled slowly.

'Well,' she said at last, 'I suppose I'd be a fool not to agree to such an offer. It's very generous of you, I'm sure, and I thank you kindly. No doubt Lorna will do the same.' She gave her daughter a meaningful look.

'Thank you ever so much,' Lorna told him. 'I'm that grateful I can't tell you!'

Gerald's colour was returning. 'I take it that's settled, then,' he said. 'My solicitors can draw up the papers early next week.'

'There's just one thing,' said Mrs Betts. 'If you do find out who the father is, will you tell us? I mean, a girl ought to know who the father of her child is.'

Gerald hesitated. 'That is most unlikely,' he said. 'I have already made enquiries and, as I said, will continue to do so. But I'm afraid you must resign yourself to the fact that we may never know the identity of the true father.'

'I see.'

'Then are we all agreed,' he asked, 'that this is the best solution to a most unfortunate occurrence? You will have another grandchild, Mrs Betts.'

'A high-born grandchild!' she corrected him with a shaky

smile. 'Life is certainly full of surprises. Yes, we're agreed. Perhaps we should all have a tot of brandy to celebrate?'

'I'll get it,' cried Lorna, rushing to the cupboard to hide the triumph in her eyes while her mother and Gerald solemnly shook hands.

'I suppose,' asked Mrs Betts suddenly, 'that your wife is in agreement, Mr Hatherley?'

'Of course,' he said. 'At least,' he amended truthfully, 'I haven't actually told her yet; I had to speak to you first. I'm sure, however,' he added less truthfully, 'that she will be agreeable.'

*

Roses. That was Harry's conclusion as he stood back to study the station garden. His muddy hands were on his hips, and his cap was pushed to the back of his head. He nodded. Red roses in each corner to give a bit of height and define the overall shape of the plot. Deep pink roses further in, to form a semi-circle open at the front edge. Pale pink within the semi-circle and white (kept low as possible) in the centre. Or reversed? How would it be, he wondered, with the red roses in the centre and white in the four corners? He pursed his lips and his frown deepened as he wiped a drip from his nose with the back of one hand and sniffed hard to discourage any more. Suppose he introduced another colour altogether – say yellow or orange? But no, that would spoil it. He would keep it simple – striking, but simple.

Harry sighed. Yes, roses would be effective, no doubt about it, but where was the money coming from? It didn't grow on trees. The station had none to spare, neither did Harry. Still, he might pluck up his courage and speak to the stationmaster about a loan. Mr Turner had been noticeably more approachable since the enquiry had acquitted him of responsibility for the accident. Perhaps a collecting tin would be in order, Harry thought, his eyes gleaming with sudden hope. They could use a cocoa tin covered with coloured paper and stick a label on it: 'For the station garden. All contributions welcome.' It wasn't exactly begging – well, maybe it was, but did that matter? No one would be compelled to contribute if they didn't want to. Such collections were purely voluntary and some members of the travelling public – the more discerning members – might welcome the opportunity to donate a threepenny-bit or even a sixpence to such a worthy cause. A beautiful station garden was a joy to behold and how pleasant, on a long and tedious train journey, to glance out of the carriage window and see a bed of roses, dark red paling to snow-white! Yes, a collecting tin was not a bad idea . . .

'How goes it, Harry?' asked Ted. 'A penny for them!'

Nothing loth, Harry outlined his current thoughts on his favourite subject and Ted listened obligingly. He was not very keen on listening to anyone but himself, but now that he had lost Arnold Harry Coombes was his only hope and Harry liked to talk, too. Ted reckoned that so long as he gave Harry a fair crack of the whip on the subject of gardens, he himself could expect equal consideration when he launched into his reminiscences. Talking or listening to Harry was infinitely preferable to being cooped up in the kitchen with 'her', otherwise known as Ellen Turner.

Ted still did his best not to converse with his daughter-in-law, although it was already becoming more of an effort to remember that he held a grudge against her. If he had not felt a duty to his dead wife's memory, Ted would have given in already, because Ellen was around more than anyone else and was also intelligent enough to appreciate an account of the Tay Bridge disaster and suchlike. And that young Toby was a bonny little lad and so like John – not only in looks, but ways. Ted grieved secretly over the loss of his errant son and the thought that he might never see him again depressed him whenever he allowed himself to dwell on the subject. Toby was a chip off the old block and Ted would have liked to befriend the boy for John's sake. He wanted to sit him on his knee and tell him stories; wanted to take the two boys fishing and show them how to fly a kite – but then Ellen would score over him and he couldn't let that happen. Leastways, not yet, he amended. Let a decent bit of time go past, he thought, and then maybe he could soften up a bit. He and Ellen had always got along so well in the early days when she and Tom were first wed. So well, in fact, that Sarah used to pull his leg and say he had taken a fancy to Tom's young bride. Still, fate had brought him John's lad and that was better than nothing. Oh yes, young Toby was a right pickle and full of fun. Sarah would have been thrilled to bits about him, even if the poor lad was born on the wrong side of the blanket.

Harry came to the end of his monologue and Ted nodded his head, for all the world as though he had been paying proper attention.

'I think you've hit the nail right on the head,' Ted told him. 'Right on the head.'

'You do?'

'Yes, I do.'

Harry looked pleased. 'I'll ask him then, first thing tomorrow,' he said eagerly.

'You do that.' Ted turned away from the garden to look up and down the station. 'Funny without Arnold, isn't it?' he said. 'Keep expecting him to pop up from somewhere, but he won't do much popping up now he's got a job. You heard about that, have you?'

Harry had not heard, so Ted was able to tell him and was gratified to see the surprise on the porter's face.

'Working for a builder!' Harry exclaimed. 'Doing what, may I ask?'

Ted chuckled. 'You may well ask,' he said, 'but I can't answer because I don't know. Nobody knows as far as I can make out. Odd jobs, I suppose. Fetching and carrying. Weeding, maybe?'

'Weeding? Builders don't weed.'

'Down at the cottage.'

It seemed Harry did not know that the cottage was being renovated, so Ted was able to tell him all about that too.

'But who's it being done up for?'

'I can't answer that either,' said Ted. 'Seems a bit odd to be spending money on the place if they've no one in mind for the tenancy, but there it is.'

'And Arnold's helping them out? Now I've heard everything. Mind you, though,' said Harry reflectively, 'it might do the lad a power of good. What Miss Dunning said at the enquiry was quite right. He's not as daft as some, and he's certainly not an idiot. Not what I'd call an idiot, anyway.

Look at the way he tries to read and he was always studying the clock over there. I miss him, really.' Smiling, he quoted, ' "When the big hand's on the twelve—" '

Both men laughed.

Seeing his chance, Ted said quickly, 'Still, the accident happened and it's cost poor Mr Allan his life. There's no gainsaying that. A locomotive is a force to be reckoned with, not like a bicycle. You could have a brush with a bicycle and live to tell the tale. You just might get run down by a horse and cart and get away with it, but you are certainly not going to survive a collision with a loco of sixty tons, not to mention the train it's pulling. I heard tell of an accident not so far from here, at Staplehurst – it was in '65—'

He paused for breath and Harry said, 'The Dickens disaster at Beult Viaduct? Aye. I was there when it happened. Terrible, that was!'

Ted's jaw dropped in dismay. Of all the accidents he could have chosen to recount, he had picked one with which Harry was familiar. His mind worked rapidly. 'You was there?' he said, his tone challenging. 'But you'd only be a young 'un in '65. How could you have been there?'

Harry grinned. 'I was in my granny's arms,' he told Ted. 'She was waiting on the station for Ma to come back from Folkestone with Pa. Home on leave he was, and she'd gone down to meet him off the Folkestone Packet and left me with her mother. Cor, I didn't half play up, apparently! Screamed blue murder from the moment she left me and my poor granny couldn't shut me up! Tried everything, she did, but it didn't work so she took me to the station to "see the lovely chuff-chuff" and hand me back to my ma. I'd never been left before, you see; I suppose I thought she was never coming back.'

Ted, resigned, nodded. ''Course, you would,' he agreed.

'Terrible thing,' Harry continued. 'Not that I knew anything about it at the time, and both my parents survived the crash, but ten poor souls went to meet their maker and forty-nine more were injured. It should never have happened, of course, but that's the way with accidents.' He shook his head dolefully. 'Replacing timbers in the bridge, that's what they were doing. They didn't know the proper times of the trains, because it varied from day to day according to the time of the tide at Folkestone. Perhaps they'd lost the time-table or some such, I don't know. Anyway, they still had the rails up when the train came along, doing fifty miles an hour!'

'Dreadful,' said Ted, determined to get a word in. 'Should never have happened.'

Harry shrugged. 'Nothing they could do to stop it then. Terrible! I heard my parents talk about it when I was older, of course, until I began to believe I'd seen it with my own eyes. Funny thing was that the loco, the tender and the brake van made it to the other side of the bridge – how, God only knows! – but the five coaches fell right through into the stream. Only ten feet deep, it was, but quite deep enough to wreck them. I could have been orphaned that day as easy as wink.'

'Which carriage were your folks in, then?' asked Ted, intrigued in spite of himself.

'The first one, luckily. Same as Mr Dickens – only they didn't know he was there, of course, until they read it in the papers. It fell on to one end, their coach, and was only partly damaged. They got out with bruises and Ma had a cut over one eye. Nothing really, but it properly shook them up and my ma wouldn't go near a train after that. "Not if you paid me," she used to say. I can hear her now. She wouldn't tempt fate a second time.'

'Can't say I blame her,' said Ted. 'They say accidents never happen unless someone makes them happen, but I don't know – seems to me it's a bit of bad luck and a bit of human error. A combination of circumstances. Let's face it, nobody's perfect.'

Harry decided to risk the question that was uppermost in his mind. 'Feeling better now, is he? Mr Turner, I mean?'

Ted shrugged. 'Hard to say really, he doesn't say a lot. He's off the hook officially but he's hard on himself, is Tom. Always has been. Then Mr Allan dying the morning after the hearing – well, that didn't help. He'll blame himself till his dying day, no matter what the enquiry found. Still, that's part of the job. If you're the stationmaster the responsibility is yours.'

'I thought it was very fair,' said Harry, 'the enquiry.'

'It was,' Ted agreed. 'Oh yes, it was very fair indeed. And he went to the funeral; Amy did too, and the Hatherleys. Dozens of people, they said, and flowers everywhere. Not his parents, though, they're not back from India yet or something. Sad homecoming that'll be for them. All that's left of their son is a mound of earth and a tombstone.'

They were silent for a while, both men busy with their own thoughts.

'So,' said Harry at last, shrugging off sombre thoughts and reverting to the matter of money and roses, 'you reckon I could ask him in the morning?'

'Don't see why not,' said Ted vaguely. 'He can't bite you.'

Chapter Twenty

Although Gerald had fully intended to tell his wife of his plans for Lorna and the child, Esme was so overwrought by the prospect of attending the funeral that he postponed the evil hour until a few days after they had returned from London. In his excitement at the glorious prospects ahead he had not really noticed Esme's increasingly odd behaviour. Had he done so, he would have attached considerable significance to it.

He broke the news to her at breakfast and much to his surprise she heard him to the end without interruption. Then, avoiding his eye, she reached for a second slice of toast with fingers that trembled slightly, although her voice was remarkably steady.

'Moral blackmail,' she said. 'I'm surprised at you, Gerald.'

'That's not quite the point—' he began.

Esme smiled up at him with cold blue eyes that held no hint of humour. 'She's a trollop, Gerald. I have always thought so. The idea is quite preposterous and you must be a bigger fool that I thought you were. I forbid it.'

She spread butter and marmalade on the toast, but made no attempt to eat it. She did not glance at him again, apparently assuming the discussion to be at an end.

'You don't seem to understand, dear heart,' said Gerald. 'I am not asking for you to give your approval. I am simply telling you what I intend to do, because I think you have a right to know.'

Esme stared at the toast. 'And you don't seem to understand, Gerald, that I will not allow it. I do not intend to

347

stand idly by while you make a fool of yourself. You must be out of your mind even to consider such a ridiculous scheme. Squander our money on a worthless chit like Lorna Betts, because one of your disgusting friends has had his way with her? Certainly not!'

'My money, Esme,' he corrected her quietly. 'It is *my* money I shall be squandering, not our money.'

Esme chose to ignore the implication of his comment and suddenly turned her cold blue eyes on him once more. 'Who is he, Gerald?' she demanded.

'I have no idea.'

'Don't trifle with me. You must know!'

'I'm afraid not. I would hardly lay aside part of my income if I knew who the father was. That *would* be very foolish.'

'Then I shall ask the girl myself.'

'She doesn't know, Esme.' He toyed with the silver napkin ring.

'She will when I've finished with her,' said his wife grimly.

At that moment Clara came in with a jug of hot water. 'Get out, Clara,' ordered Esme.

Clara looked at her in astonishment, but Esme's eyes were still fixed on her husband's face. 'I beg pardon—' she began.

'Get out of here,' said Esme, 'and don't come back until I ring.'

Clara flushed, then she resentfully banged down the hot-water jug and stalked out of the room.

'Charmingly put,' commented Gerald. 'You have a way with servants. As for Lorna, you will not ask her anything. She confided in me, which was very sensible, and I am quite satisfied that she does not remember.'

'Of course she does,' cried Esme. 'No girl could be that drunk.'

Gerald raised his eyebrows. 'What do you suggest, then? Shall we invite all our male guests to line up for an identity parade? I hardly think we would get very much response and we might lose a great many friends.'

There was a long silence; then Esme threw down her crumpled napkin, rose and walked over to the window.

'It was Harold, wasn't it?' she said suddenly. 'It was

Harold — and you know it — and you've concocted this transparent tale between you.'

'Harold who?'

'Harold Carpenter.' She swung round to face him. 'Your precious cousin. Oh yes, he's done it before, hasn't he? You thought I didn't know; you thought they'd hushed it all up, but Myra told me years ago. It's Harold, isn't it?'

'It's not Harold.'

'How do you know it's not Harold,' she asked slowly, 'if you don't know who it is?'

For a moment he almost faltered, but then collected himself. 'I don't think it's Harold,' he said. 'I believe he's learned his lesson. I don't think you will gain anything by making wild accusations and you might find—'

'Then it's Tim Barkwell! He's just the type. Young, single and rich as Croesus. She'd have encouraged Tim Barkwell!'

Gerald did not repeat his mistake. 'We shall never know,' he declared. 'You're wasting your time, Esme. Even if it was Tim, you would never prove it — you know that as well as I do.'

Esme turned back to the window, her back rigid with anger. 'How long have you known all this?' she asked, her voice controlled. 'Why did you wait until now to tell me? Why didn't you consult me?'

He had prepared his answer and it came out smoothly. 'I thought you were under enough strain already. Ralph Allan's accident had obviously caused you great distress and the doctor advised rest and quiet. It hardly seemed wise to burden you further.'

'What efforts have you made to discover the father?' she demanded.

'None at all. How should we go about it? Should we write to each one, explaining the girl's situation and asking for their comments?'

He poured another cup of tea and congratulated himself that she was taking the bombshell surprisingly well, all things considered.

Esme walked from the window to the mirror on the far wall and looked at herself with unseeing eyes, then slowly returned to the table. She did not sit down, however, but remained standing by her chair, drumming her fingers nervously along the top of the carved back.

'You say she threatened to tell the whole village if we made no provision for her?'

Gerald shook his head. 'I said nothing of the sort; I said I knew that her mother would do so once she knew of the girl's condition. Would you relish such a scandal?'

'Won't what you are proposing be a scandal?'

'But it will reflect to our credit,' he pointed out. 'One way, we allow the girl to be raped on our own—'

'Raped?'

'Don't you think that's how the mother will tell it?' he asked. 'Is she likely to suggest that Lorna agreed to her seduction?'

Esme was silent. Her face was white and drawn and her eyes had lost their steely expression. Instead she looked like a cornered fox facing the encircling hounds. Gerald hated her enough to enjoy her vulnerability and waited calmly for her next comment.

'I always knew!' she whispered. 'That girl is a calculating trollop.'

'I think you give her credit for too much intelligence,' he said. 'I doubt if any girl in her walk of life would take such a risk deliberately. We might have rejected her story completely, called her a liar and a trouble-maker and sent her away with a flea in her ear.'

'Why didn't you?' cried Esme bitterly.

'I've told you why, dear heart. Because—'

Esme lifted clenched fists above her head and screamed, 'Don't call me "dear heart" in that smug, patronising way! Oh, you don't fool me, Gerald. You're enjoying this, aren't you? You'd love to see me beaten to my knees. Oh yes, you would!'

On the last word she brought down her hands and, grasping the chair, flung it sideways. Gerald's composure abruptly deserted him as he recognised breaking point in his wife's wildly gleaming eyes. He scrambled to his feet, but too late for Esme's hands, groping wildly, seized the hot-water jug and hurled it at him across the table. The lid came off and the contents splashed over him, mercifully missing his face but scalding his right hand.

'Esme. For God's sake!' he shouted.

Her face was contorted with blind rage as she snatched up the silver teapot and threw it with all her strength towards the mirror at the far end of the room. It fell short.

'I hate you!' she screamed. 'I've always hated you. You're a pig! A loathsome smug, patronising pig!'

The silver sugar bowl followed the teapot, scattering sugar as it went. Esme then leaned forward and with her right arm swept from the table a vase of roses, the remaining cutlery and crockery, butter, jam, milk and honey, all of which cascaded on to the carpet.

'Lorna Betts!' she screamed. 'I'll make her pay for this. Oh yes, you'll see! You and she together — you've done this to spite me. You both hate me! I know you do. Well, you won't get away with it. I'll kill her first! D'you hear me, Gerald? I'll *kill* her!' With that she began dragging the long white damask cloth from the table, stumbling and almost falling as she tugged it into her arms.

Gerald watched her as a terrified rabbit watches a stoat. Her eyes flashed and her voice rose hysterically as she continued to hurl abuse at him, dredging her mind for the worst profanities she knew. When she had the entire table-cloth in her arms she paused momentarily to glare at him over the snowy mounds of linen. There were footsteps in the hall and the door opened to admit Clara, who stared in dismay at the scene before her.

'And I told *you*,' Esme screamed, 'to get out of here!'

She threw the tablecloth in Clara's direction, then picked up the oozing honey-pot from the floor and threw that too. Clara ducked and cried, 'Please, ma'am! Don't!'

'Out!' screamed Esme. 'Get out of here!' She fell suddenly to her knees beside the remains of the breakfast and began to throw knives and forks in all directions.

'I'll kill her!' she cried, 'and then I'll kill you, Gerald. I swear it!'

A knife caught the huge gilt mirror an unlucky blow and a large three-pronged crack ran upward and outward.

351

'Esme! Stop it!' cried Gerald, appalled by the destruction and his wife's frenzy. 'You'll hurt someone if—'

His words triggered a passionate response. 'Hurt someone? By Christ, I will!' she cried and snatching up a knife, she stumbled towards him.

At that moment Mrs Lester also appeared in the doorway to see what was happening and after a brief but terrifying struggle, Esme was overcome and the knife prised from her fingers. Then, without warning, she collapsed. Her body sagged, her eyes closed and with a faint moan, she fell to the floor and lay motionless.

'Oh, my God!' whispered Gerald weakly, one hand to his heart. 'My God! Esme?' He knelt beside her, afraid to touch her. 'She's not dead, is she?' he asked.

Mrs Lester, trembling in her turn, shook her head helplessly without venturing an opinion.

'Of course she's not dead,' said Clara calmly. 'Here, let me see to her.' She glanced up at Gerald. 'You'd better send for the doctor, sir. When she comes round, Mrs Lester and I can get her to her bed, but she's going to need a doctor.'

'But suppose . . .' he began fearfully, eyeing the devastation.

'The worst is over,' Clara told him confidently. 'She'll be as weak as a kitten when she comes to, take my word for it. Ah, she's opening her eyes now.'

Hastily Gerald scrambled to his feet and hurried out of the room, while Clara took hold of Esme's right hand and patted it. 'There now, ma'am,' she said soothingly. 'It's all over now.' To Mrs Lester she said, 'Would you fetch the smelling-salts? You'll find them on her dressing-table in a blue glass bottle.' To Esme she continued, 'You're quite safe now, ma'am. You had a bit of a turn, that's all. The doctor will be here directly. No, no, don't try to sit up just yet, you lie and relax. I'll stay with you and look after you, don't you fret.'

'Clara!' whispered Esme as tears rolled from her eyes. 'Oh, Clara!' She began to cry and Clara continued to murmur soothingly and pat her hand. When Esme struggled into a sitting position and caught sight of the disordered room, she gave a groan of dismay and hid her face in her hands.

352

'It's them,' she told Clara incoherently. 'They want to hurt me. They make my life a misery with their tricks. I have to be strong, Clara.'

'Of course you do, ma'am. You are strong.'

'I didn't mean it. Oh, the mess. The mess!' She began to sob.

'We'll soon clear that up, ma'am,' said Clara. 'Don't worry on that score. We'll soon have everything spick and span.'

Esme uncovered her face and looked up tearfully. 'Oh, but I do worry,' she told her. 'I do like to keep everything nice. Oh, the poor roses!'

'I'll see to it, ma'am. Clara will put it all to rights once the doctor comes. You leave everything to Clara.'

'Oh, you are a good girl,' sobbed Esme. 'I love roses, don't you? I sent roses to poor Ralph's funeral. Eight red roses. Just from me, you understand? Gerald sent separately. It was my wish that we send separate flowers. But I couldn't bear it.'

'What's that, ma'am?'

'To see him in his coffin. Some people did – to pay their last respects, they said. I couldn't. It's the smell of death. My grandmother – oh! Oh, Clara!' She began to rock very slightly from side to side.

'Now don't take on, ma'am.'

'It was that terrible girl, Lorna Betts,' whispered Esme. 'A terrible, terrible girl! It's both of them. They mean me some harm, I know they do. Oh, look at my beautiful mirror! It's ruined . . .' She broke off and glanced down suddenly towards her skirt. 'I'm wet!' she told Clara. 'My skirt—'

With a look of horror on her face, Esme scrambled awkwardly to her knees and tugged at the back of her skirt where a large damp stain was spreading. Pushing a fist into her mouth, she began to whisper, 'I've wet myself. Look, look! I've wet myself. I'm sorry. Oh, I'm so sorry!' Desperately she began to wrench and tug at the offending material.

'It doesn't matter,' Clara told her. 'Please don't worry about it, ma'am.'

'But it's dirty! Dirty!' cried Esme. 'I didn't mean to do it.'

'I know you didn't, but you're not quite well, ma'am. No one is going to scold you.'

353

Clara spoke reassuringly and instinctively put her arms round her mistress to comfort her. To her embarrassment, Esme suddenly sighed deeply and laid her head against Clara's shoulder.

'Don't tell anyone,' she begged. 'I won't do it again!'

'Of course I won't tell,' said Clara. 'It was an accident. Now you forget all about it, ma'am. I'll have that stain out in two shakes of a lamb's tail and no one will ever know.'

Esme sighed again, and her body slumped against Clara's. 'It was Gerald,' she said in a thin, tired voice. 'He made me break the mirror. He hates me, Gerald does. He made me break the cups. He made me break the saucers. He made me break—'

To Clara's great relief the housekeeper hurried back into the room at that moment with the doctor, and she was able to deliver Esme into more capable hands.

Twenty minutes later, washed and powdered, the mistress of Bates Manor lay sleeping in a bed in one of the guest rooms – a long deep sleep which the doctor had ordered, brought about by a strong sleeping draught. When he left, Gerald asked how soon his wife would be fully recovered.

'Too early to say,' said the doctor. 'Your wife is not at all well. We must wait and see; I'll call in again this evening. And hang on like grim death to that maid of hers – Clara, or whatever her name is. Your wife seems to think a lot of her and I'm afraid she's going to need her for quite some time. I am sorry to have to ask you this, Mr Hatherley, but is there any history of insanity in your wife's family?'

Gerald gasped. 'Oh God! Not that!' All the colour drained from his face, but he did not answer.

The doctor prompted him gently. 'A relation, perhaps?'

'Yes . . .' Gerald's voice came out slowly. 'It was her mother – she was in some kind of home, you know. I never actually met her. Esme's father was my closest friend. He told me, in strictest confidence of course, but I could never believe . . . Esme was so strong. There was no way of knowing, but I felt confident – the way you do when you adore someone.' He sighed heavily.

The doctor nodded. 'It's a thin line,' he said. 'Who's to say which of us is sane?'

354

'Esme's father wanted the match so desperately and I was so in love with her.' Gerald shook his head. 'I don't think she ever loved me, you see. Not really. She only loved her father – they were very close. He was older than me, but the friendship was a sincere one. I respected him, I trusted his judgement. Esme's mother was the first, you see, there was no history of it on either side of the family. Her father wanted me to marry her, because he trusted me to look after her if anything . . . if she became . . .' He fell silent, unwilling to put the calamity into words.

The doctor nodded. 'It helps to be aware of the background and get an overall picture,' he said. 'We must look on the bright side. It's early days yet and your wife is going to need long and careful nursing. That girl of yours – Clara, is it?' Gerald nodded. 'She seems very sensible, so take my advice and make sure she stays. At a time like this, a reliable girl is worth her weight in gold.'

*

Every seat in the small church was taken and 239 pairs of eyes were fastened dutifully on the Reverend Ambrose Stokes as he came to the end of his over-long sermon on the subject of the forgiveness of sins. One pair of eyes, those belonging to Eric, were not raised in the vicar's direction but cast anxiously down towards his feet where his last pear-drop had fallen.

Behind the altar a stained-glass window fragmented the November sunlight which appeared from time to time, but the sun was mostly obscured by heavy scudding clouds which threatened to release large quantities of rain as soon as the service ended and the congregation left church for their respective homes. The choir, now up to its full complement once more, sat in mahogany pews on either side; the pulpit, below the chancel steps, was of polished teak edged with brass. Most of the congregation sat in oak pews, but a few stood in the empty space at the back.

Ambrose Stokes had chosen his text with Lorna Betts in mind, for it was now the last week in November and the scandal of her seduction by an unknown member of the gentry had exploded upon the inhabitants of Gazedown like a gigantic firework. He had thought it prudent to remind his flock that Jesus himself had not scorned the woman taken in adultery. Now, as he spoke to them, his gaze moved slowly across the rows of familiar faces. Some came regularly, others not so regularly. Mary Leckie was there with her handsome son, Donald; she came every Sunday but he came, the vicar knew, only when she could bully him into it. Jim Leckie never attended divine worship.

Directly behind the Leckies but two rows further back, he saw Miss Dunning from the school and a woman friend who was staying with her. Both ladies were resplendent in feathered hats and both had their hands tucked into muffs, for the church's heating left much to be desired.

Over to the right was the stationmaster and his family which latterly had included Ellen Turner and their youngest son Toby – and occasionally even the grandfather, although he was not present on this occasion. Gerald Hatherley sat alone in the family pew – his wife was still confined to the house. Clara Midden was not in church with the rest of the Manor staff – no doubt required to stay with her mistress. Mrs Lester was in church, however, with poor little Izzie, and so were the gardener and the groom, all in their Sunday best with shiny faces well-scrubbed for the occasion. There were families from Bates Villas, some from the cottages in Hope's Lane, others from the High Street and Catts Hill, and old Bill Hodds, the greengrocer, with his enormous mother. Miss Peck sat in solitary splendour in a pew about half-way back and to the left, holding a hymn book open in front of her, which was her way of telling the vicar that she thought the sermon had lasted long enough.

This is my flock, the vicar thought to himself – the people whose spiritual welfare rests in my hands. I baptise, marry and bury them. I help them when I can. For the last two weeks Lorna Betts' predicament and Gerald Hatherley's generous solution to it had been the main topic of village conversation and although she had stayed out of sight for much of the first week, the interest with which she was now regarded had coaxed her to put in a few public appearances. Gerald's intervention on her behalf meant that whatever people might say in the privacy of their own homes, they treated her with the deference due to his protégée and she was thus spared the meaning looks and barbed comments which had been her sister's lot when her hasty wedding had been announced.

'And so I say unto you,' the Reverend Stokes continued, 'that we should love one another, help one another, tolerate one another and *forgive* one another, for how many of us are without sin? How many of us have not told a white lie at some time, or cheated just a little? How many of us have not coveted a neighbour's new horse, or even the neighbour's wife's new hat?' He waited for a titter of laughter, but none was forthcoming: another sign that he should draw the sermon to its close. 'I say unto you that God looks into our hearts and minds and sees our truest thoughts. Oh, we may smile upon the sinners but He knows if that smile is false. We can, perhaps, fool one another but our hypocrisy is known to God. "Let him that is without sin cast the first stone", he said, and we—'

Miss Peck rustled the pages of her hymn-book, dropped it to the floor and bent noisily to retrieve it. From somewhere at the back of the church there came a faint snore, followed by the gasp made by a sleeper who is suddenly awoken by a sharp elbow. That would be Willy Orford, the rat-catcher.

'So let us go forth this day determined to make a fresh start; to speak truly and to be generous of spirit, so that God may look upon us without misgivings. Let us find favour in his sight, for only by so doing . . .'

There was a scuffle behind him from the direction of the choirboys, but he ignored the distinct 'Ouch!' followed by a loud 'Ssh!' He caught Lorna Betts' eye as she reached for her hymn-book, anticipating the end of his sermon, and thought she looked very pleased with herself. Mrs Betts, re-tying the strings of her sun-bonnet, seemed also to be enjoying the spotlight which now rested on Lorna. A cottage and an income! Lorna had certainly fallen on her feet, the vicar thought somewhat resentfully, but then recalled hastily that He was no doubt looking into his heart. Shaking his mind free of such uncharitable thoughts, he brought the sermon hurriedly to an end and announced the number of the final hymn.

When the final strains of the last line of the hymn faded, a loud and thankful 'Amen!' issued from every throat. He gave the blessing and had hardly uttered the last word when the church began to empty with much whispering and shuffling of feet.

By the time the vicar had taken his place in the sporadic sunshine outside the ancient doorway, thirty or forty of his parishioners were already making their escape through the church gate into the road. Those who remained waited to be noticed.

'Mrs Benny. Good to see you. Quite fit now, are you? Good. Good . . . Ah, Mr and Mrs Coombes – so glad you could attend. Oh, you enjoyed my little homily? I'm so pleased . . . Miss Peck – er, no, I didn't think it was too long. Did you? Oh, I *am* sorry – Mr Goddard . . . Nice to see you home again, Miss Dunning. Oh, it's your sister, is it? I should have guessed; a slight likeness there! I hope you both enjoyed my sermon. Oh, you *did*. Good – Good . . .'

Lorna Betts held out her hand and he shook it courteously, saying, 'So glad you could come.'

'I never came last week,' she explained, 'because . . . well, you know. Everyone talking and all that.'

'Of course. Of course.' His smile grew wider. 'And all is well now, I understand? You really are most fortunate.'

'Oh, I know,' agreed Lorna. 'And tomorrow I'm moving into the cottage – at least, moving some of the furniture in, I should say. I'll be moving in myself at the beginning of December. I mean, I don't have to or anything—'

Mrs Betts moved closer and shook hands with the vicar. ''Course she doesn't have to,' she echoed, 'but she can't wait to get settled into her own home.' She raised her voice slightly for the benefit of eavesdroppers. 'Mr Hatherley has been that generous, me and Lorna are both quite overcome.'

'I'm sure you are.'

There was a surge of people as those still inside the church pushed forward; someone stepped on Mrs Betts' toe and caused her to stumble against the vicar, who put out a hand to steady her. As he did so, Arnold elbowed his way out of the church, grinning broadly, and seized his hand.

'I've got a job!' he told the vicar. 'A real job! I get wages,

358

I do. I get wages every Saturday. I do, Ma,' he appealed to
his mother, who now followed him out into the sunshine. 'I
do, don't I?'

'Yes, you do,' she said.

'Arnold's working on my cottage,' said Lorna. 'He's
weeded the garden and painted the fence. Done a really good
job, he has.'

Arnold positively beamed but the vicar, realising that the
rest of the congregation were getting impatient, said
hurriedly, 'Well, I shall have to pop along and see for myself,
one of these days,' to which Lorna very grandly said, 'Please
do!'

*

Greetings, my dearest mother, [wrote Nigel]

At last I have snatched a little time to write to you and
trust you will forgive the brevity of this letter. We have
now left Haiderabad and are moving towards Quetta, but
the going is very slow. Try to imagine thirty thousand
camels, nine thousand men and thousands of Indians in
attendance on the Army. Conditions are bad and cholera
and dysentery are always with us. We hear rumours of
arguments between our commanders and Macnaghten and
some of our younger officers have very little experience,
though they are not lacking in courage . . .

Amy handed the letter to Elliot and began to read aloud
from the next one which was dated May 1839:

When we finally entered Kandahar, the mood changed.
The victory has done miracles for our morale. Shah Shuja
rode in beside Macnaghten and Burnes. It was, I must
confess, a splendid sight as they rode towards the fortress.
McN. and B. in their blue-gold dress uniforms, Shah Shuja
covered in jewels riding on a white horse and soldiers all
around them with bayonets gleaming in the sun. Later,
however, I was surprised by how few people there were
in the streets for his official installation. I do not believe
he is as popular as Lord Auckland would have us believe,
but we have done our part. Now we head on towards
Ghazni and then Kabul . . .

'They mean nothing to me,' Amy confessed, 'because I don't understand what was happening at the time. He sent 27 letters home from India — at least, 27 have survived; there might have been more. Now that letter is to his mother. I've worked out that his father died in 1845 and Nigel left the Army to become Lord Stanisbrooke. From the tone of these letters, I should think he was heartily glad to get back to England and his family. Some of the families had gone out to India, but not his.'

Amy and Elliot were sitting in the little parlour-cum-study in The Lodge, discussing the book which Ralph would never be able to finish. Several weeks had passed since Ralph's funeral, during which time Amy had continued to collate the material at Elliot's insistence. Her own attempts were now out of sight and Amy intended that they should remain so. She had written and rewritten two chapters, but was uncertain of the quality of her work. Elliot had come to discuss the material with her and had explained that he was looking round for another writer to undertake the project. In the meantime, he told her, he would like her to carry on with the lists.

Now Amy struggled to keep her attention on the discussion. Seeing Elliot at Ralph's funeral had finally brought home to her just how strong her feelings were towards him. The attraction was real and very physical. Once she had thought it was merely his likeness to Lord Stanisbrooke which had appealed to her, but now she knew differently. True, she was drawn by his dark good looks, but there was also a need in her which Elliot satisfied. There was a strength in him that was lacking in her own make-up and she envied his ability to laugh at the world and the people in it. His attitude to life and his independence impressed her, and whenever they were together she was inspired by his example to be stronger and less withdrawn. She respected his intelligence, although she did not underestimate her own.

Ralph had brought out her mothering instinct and she had cared deeply for him. Elliot did not need mothering, indeed he did not appear to need anything or anyone. No doubt he had women friends — Ralph had hinted that he was never short of female company — but he had not seen fit to marry any of them. Unless he preferred married women . . . and Amy did not wish to think along those lines. She did not wish to think about him at all, because she saw no future in it. While she was alone, she could busy herself with the research and keep his bright image at bay. Now she was with him, however, her senses betrayed her and the physical longings which Don Leckie had first awoken in her returned to distract her. She was making a supreme effort to concentrate on Nigel Stanisbrooke's letters from India, thankful that Elliot seemed engrossed in the conversation and quite unaware of her feelings towards him.

'I'm finding the military aspects rather difficult to grasp,' Amy confessed. 'It was fine when all I did was type up Ralph's notes, but now I'm having to write the notes as well.'

'Let me explain,' said Elliot. 'It's not too complicated, but stop me if I'm not making myself clear.'

She nodded and he thought for a moment before beginning his explanation while Amy, her chin cupped in her hands, looked into his brown eyes and tried to follow what he was saying.

'Shah Shuja was once the King of Afghanistan,' he began, 'but he was thrown out in 1809. He fled with the Koh-i-Noor diamond, but later lost it to the ruler of the Punjab who had pretended to befriend him.'

'I thought the Koh-i-Noor was in Queen Victoria's crown,' said Amy, surprised.

'It is now, but that's another story,' Elliot laughed. 'So, poor old Shuja eventually escaped to Ludhiana, a British frontier town, and we gave him a house and a small allowance and everyone forgot about him. Now we were becoming uneasy about Russia who had moved into Persia on the other side of Afghanistan. We didn't want them any nearer, therefore we decided to put Shah Shuja back with our support.' He broke off and smiled. 'Have I lost you?' he asked, his tone teasing; Amy shook her head, not trusting herself to speak.

'A man named Burnes, however, thought Shuja would be useless after such a long exile and believed we should support Dost Muhammad, who was already ruling Afghanistan and

361

doing it reasonably well. Unfortunately, Burnes had his opponents in India and Macnaghten was one of them.'

'Ah,' said Amy, her mind beginning to work again, 'the man mentioned in the letter.'

'The same,' Elliot agreed.

'But who was Lord Auckland?'

'He was the Governor-General of British India at the time. Let me think, what happened next? Ah yes. We heard through our agents that a Russian diplomat had appeared in Kabul – in Afghanistan – and everyone began to expect the worst. At the same time Persia marched towards Herat, also in Afghanistan, and it was known that they had Russian advisers with them—' He broke off suddenly. 'A penny for them!' he said.

Amy was covered in confusion. Obviously her attempts to keep her feelings hidden were not being very successful.

'Am I going too fast?' he asked.

'No.'

'Am I boring you?'

'Oh no, of course you're not,' she protested. She was sure her face must be scarlet, but she shook her head vigorously. 'Please go on,' she insisted.

Elliot hesitated and looked as though he was about to say something, then changed his mind. Amy cursed herself for her lack of self-control and hoped he would not probe her inattention too deeply. How could she confess that being with him had thrown her into a state of such excitement that she was wasting this valuable opportunity to learn some of the background material for the book in which she had professed such an interest?

'Please go on,' she said again.

'Where was I?' he asked, with a helpless gesture of his hands. 'I'm confused now.' He stood up and moved to stare out of the window.

Amy stared at him, forbidding her heart to race. Why on earth should he be confused, she wondered. He turned back, they looked at each other and the moment lengthened unbearably while Amy struggled to remember what he had been telling her.

'The Russian advisers,' she stammered at last. 'They were marching – on Herat.'

'So they were,' he said, glancing at the ceiling for inspiration. 'Herat! Now, let me see. Yes – in a great panic we began to get an army together and it was agreed that we would march via Haiderabad and Quetta . . .' He paused and she nodded.

'Light is dawning,' she said.

' . . . and through Kandahar and Ghazni to Kabul. We would collect Shuja on the way and install him in Kabul. The whole campaign was under way when two things happened. The Russian diplomat disappeared from Kabul – presumably he went home – and the Persian army gave up the siege of Herat and they went home too.'

Amy regarded him blankly. 'Then why . . .' she began.

'Why did the British Army go on with it?' He shrugged. 'A good question. The point was that they had committed themselves to restoring Shuja to his throne and could not suddenly back out – a treaty had been signed, and so on and so forth. They went ahead exactly as planned and thousands of men died in the months that followed. They took Kabul, but at best it was an uneasy victory and in 1842 the Afghans revolted and Burnes was killed, hacked to pieces by an angry mob. Later Macnaghten died also; he was shot. The whole sorry mess dragged on for years until it ended in 1849.'

His voice trailed off into silence and Amy was conscious of an almost tangible magnetism drawing them together. He had averted his eyes as he finished the account, so she could not even guess what he was thinking. 'Stop that nonsense, Amy Turner,' she told herself frantically. 'You are nothing to Elliot Allan. No doubt a visit to Gazedown amuses him and gives him a chance to escape to the country, but he probably has a mistress waiting for him in London. He is hardly likely to fall in love with the daughter of a stationmaster. Don't even let yourself hope, or you will be letting yourself in for a bitter disappointment. He wants you to work on the book, that's all. Benwells have paid out good money and he is trying to find someone to carry on where Ralph left off. Yes, he is charming and you find him attractive, but Elliot Allan is not for you! Be sensible and save yourself a lot of heartache.'

But now he was standing beside her, leaning across the table to reach paper and pencil.

'I think it would help,' he suggested, 'if I drew you a map.' His long fingers closed round the pencil and as his hand moved, Amy could see the fine dark hairs on his wrist below the cuff edge.

'Afghan is here, with Persia to the west and Russia to the north. India is here.' His pencil moved quickly, writing in the names. 'Herat over here in the West and Kabul to the east. Here is Sind, above it the Punjab and higher still Kashmir. Karachi's right down here.'

Amy stood up and as she leaned over to follow what he was saying his shoulder brushed hers, sending a thrill through her entire body. 'Don't be a fool, Amy Turner', she warned. 'Don't let him guess'.

'Does that help?' he asked, tossing down the pencil. 'This is where they started, you see. They finally retreated to Jalalabad, here by the Khyber Pass.'

'Yes,' said Amy shakily, 'I think I've mastered it.'

They were standing very close and she turned to face him. The dark eyes stared back with a look of great intensity and again she felt intuitively that he was on the point of saying something to her. Instead he drew in his breath sharply and put his hands on her shoulders. For a long moment neither spoke and Amy dared not move as she felt the warmth of his hands through the serge of her dress. His hands moved slowly down her arms and then suddenly he kissed her – a hasty kiss, but a kiss nonetheless. Unable to believe what was happening, Amy longed to throw her arms round his neck and kiss him in return, but she held back, incredulous, waiting for him to speak.

'Amy,' Elliot said slowly, 'I want you to know that . . .' He stopped and closed his eyes briefly. When he opened them again he released her and sighed deeply. Amy's elation turned to dismay and she felt her stomach lurch with shock and disappointment.

'I've no right . . .' he began inexplicably.

'No right?' she whispered.

364

'It would be so unfair,' he said, again giving no explanation for his words. 'Forgive me, Amy. I'm sorry. Could we pretend that didn't happen?'

Amy swallowed hard.

'No, I won't pretend,' she said quickly. 'It did happen and I'm not sorry.'

'Amy . . .' he began, but again he stopped.

To hide her distress, she turned away and began to gather up letters and papers with hands that trembled.

'I owe you an explanation,' he said.

'No!' she almost shouted the word. 'You owe me nothing. Perhaps you're right. We'll pretend it didn't happen. Please don't talk about it any more.' She took a deep breath and tried to speak normally. 'My mother asked me to invite you to supper this evening. Should I say you have had to return to London?'

He hesitated, then said reluctantly, 'Perhaps that would be easier for us.'

Amy nodded. 'I'm sure they'll understand,' she said, her voice artificially cheerful. She wanted to cry out, 'Don't go! Stay and kiss me again and say you aren't angry with me,' but she put the papers away and closed the drawer.

'I have an invitation for you,' he told her. 'From my parents – they arrive in London tomorrow.'

Instantly Amy forgot her own distress as she imagined theirs. 'Oh, how sad,' she cried. 'And they have missed the funeral. What a sorrowful, empty homecoming.'

'I'm dreading it,' he confessed. 'It seems that Ralph wrote to them about you in glowing terms and they have asked if they could meet you.'

'Oh!' Taken aback, Amy stared at him. 'They want to meet me?'

'I was hoping you would spend a day or two in London with us when they have settled in. It would help them.'

Amy hesitated. More heartbreak, she thought. The sensible thing would be to decline as kindly as possible, but how could she refuse Ralph's parents? She had been close to Ralph during the last weeks of his life, so perhaps she could reassure them that he had been happy in his own way. She managed a smile. 'Of course,' she said.

365

Chapter Twenty-One

As soon as the cottage was finished, Gerald took Lorna to look at it and give her approval. As they stood at the gate, Lorna's heart swelled with gratitude.

'Oh Gerald, it's lovely!' she gasped. 'Even the garden's neat and tidy. My own little home! I can't believe it.'

'Our little home,' he corrected. 'Yours and mine.'

'And his!' Lorna patted her stomach. 'Oh, I do wish you were going to live in it with us — all the time, I mean. I know you can't, but I wish it could be like that. Me having someone to cook for and someone to come home in the evening. And then we'd sit by the fire and chat — you know.'

He looked at her anxiously. 'I will come whenever I can,' he assured her. 'You won't be lonely — you'll have the baby for company and your mother will come round — and maybe your sister will come to tea now and again.'

'I expect so.' She smiled. 'Shall we go in, then?' With a flourish, she opened the gate. 'Tarah!'

'I watched Arnold oil that gate,' he told her. 'He must have used nearly half a pint of oil!'

Lorna smiled. 'Poor Arnold.'

'Oh, he's not poor Arnold now,' said Gerald. 'Drury found him quite useful and he's going to keep him on. He's in a seventh heaven.'

'So am I,' said Lorna, giving him a quick kiss. 'So that makes two of us.' She stopped on the doorstep. 'Well, Mr Hatherley, are you going to carry me over the threshold?'

'I'm going to try,' he said gallantly. 'I'll carry you both

over the threshold! Put your arms round my neck – that's it. Now, upsadaisy.'

Lorna weighed all of nine stone, but he staggered into the hallway and set her down without injury to either of them.

'You are strong,' she told him. 'I didn't think you'd really do it. Oh, Gerald,' she looked around, 'aren't I lucky? I have to keep pinching myself.'

They had chosen most of the furniture together, but he had insisted that she did not watch it being delivered because he wanted her to see the furnished cottage when it was all finished and not before. Hand in hand they wandered from room to room, for all the world like young lovers in their first home. Lorna was being as cheerful as she could to hide the doubts that were nagging at the back of her mind – doubts that her mother had unintentionally instilled by her repeated instructions to lock all the doors and windows at night and never to open the door to strangers. The cottage was out of sight of any other dwelling except Bates Manor, and although the lights of the big house would show through the bare trees in winter, in summer they would be obscured. It was isolated, there was no denying that, and Mrs Betts' anxiety had affected her daughter more than she would admit.

'The hall looks so light!' she exclaimed. 'And the mirror! Oh, I don't remember that.'

'It's from one of the spare bedrooms at home,' Gerald told her.

'At the Manor,' said Lorna, pouting slightly. 'You just said *this* is your home.'

'So I did,' he agreed hastily. 'Of course this is my home. Take no notice; I'm just a silly old fool.'

'You're not a fool,' she told him, 'and you're not old. You're as old as you feel. That's what Ma says and if I make you feel young . . .'

'You do!' He gave her arm a playful pinch. 'Let's hurry up and look round and then we'll have time to—' He raised his eyebrows suggestively and began to blink.

' "Do the bees", you mean? Oh, you are an awful man, Gerald. Really you are!' She giggled. 'You lure me out here to this lonely place just so's you can have your evil way with me.'

'But you like it, don't you?'

''Course I like it, silly!'

They went into the kitchen and Lorna exclaimed with delight over the new range and the kitchen table and four stools.

'There's an airing rack for drying the clothes,' he said, 'and the meat safe is in the larder.'

'I'm having blue check curtains,' she told him. 'I've always liked blue. Ma's making them for me for a wedding present – well . . .' she stopped, slightly flustered. 'You know what I mean!'

Too late! His expression had changed, as she had known it would.

'Lorna, my dear, don't!' he begged. 'You mustn't reproach me. I'm doing everything I can – yes, indeed I am. I would marry you tomorrow if I could. You must believe—'

She put a finger to his lips to silence him. 'Stop it,' she said softly. 'I didn't mean that – it just slipped out, like you saying Bates Manor is your home. I know you'd marry me, but you can't and that's all there is to it. I didn't mean anything.'

'But you'll never be able to marry,' he said, stricken with guilt. 'You will never have a man of your own unless my wife dies before me, and that's not at all likely.' He thought about Esme and his gloom deepened.

'But you did say she was ill,' said Lorna a trifle wistfully.

Gerald shook his head. 'Not that sort of ill,' he said. 'Ill in her mind. Odd. Strange. Not really ill. It's hard to pin it down, but she's changed so much during these last few weeks, since poor Mr Allan's accident. She looks terrible.'

'We won't talk about it then,' Lorna told him. 'Come on – I want to see the parlour and then the nursery and then the bedroom!' She gave him a naughty wink and was relieved to see his face brighten. Linking her arm through his, she said, 'Gerald Hatherley, you're a naughty man, but I love you.'

The parlour floor was covered in brown linoleum and scattered with bright cotton rugs. Two fireside chairs were upholstered in cherry-red velvet and there was a clock on the mantelpiece. A new mahogany table stood in the window and a good second-hand sideboard was set against the wall.

'Janet's giving me a biscuit barrel,' Lorna told him. 'I've always wanted one. It's got a sort of raffia handle and a Japanese picture on it. She's bringing it the first time she comes to visit.'

The nursery contained a crib made of cane and lined with blue silk. This was on loan from Mrs Hollis, who insisted on having it back at some future date 'just in case Tim ever marries'.

In the bedroom there was a wardrobe, a double bed and a bedside table. The chest of drawers, also second-hand, had been repolished and looked as good as new.

Lorna looked at herself in the long swing mirror, turning sideways to admire her swelling body. 'I wonder if he knows what we're doing when we . . . you know,' she mused. 'Can he hear us, do you think?'

Gerald neither knew nor cared. He was pulling off his clothes with a flattering degree of urgency which set Lorna's senses tingling. He threw himself on to the bed but Lorna, still in her chemise and drawers, shrieked at him.

'Not on top of my nice new patchwork quilt! It'll get all creased up. Here, come off it, Gerald.'

She bent down to push him off the bed, but he was too quick and pulled her down on top of him.

'Oh Lorna,' he cried, 'our first time in the cottage! I thought it would never happen! I thought those wretched workmen would never finish. Come here. Oh come here, my lovely little Lorna.'

But she had leapt from the bed and was running out of the room in her underwear, a mischievous look on her face.

'You'll have to catch me first, *sir*,' she teased and they began a wild chase around the cottage. Gerald was finally allowed to corner her in the kitchen and as he dragged her off to the bedroom in triumph, he was more certain than ever before that Lorna Betts was the best thing that had ever happened to him.

Later, as they both lay on the bed, their energies spent,

they were startled to hear a knock on the front door. Lorna sat bolt upright while Gerald covered his face with his hands.

'Whoever can that be?' he gasped.

'The big bad wolf!' Lorna joked. 'I'll go.' She began to scramble back into her clothes as fast as she could. 'You stay here — and pull the curtains to.' She clapped a hand to her mouth. 'Oh, I hope it's not Ma — she'll want to see over the place.'

'Well, she can't,' he snapped, rushing to pull the curtains. 'But if she insists?'

'I'll have to climb out of the window — it's not anything to laugh about, Lorna. For God's sake, girl!'

She glanced in the mirror, straightened her hair clumsily and then went out of the room, closing the door behind her.

To her astonishment Don Leckie stood on the doorstep. 'I thought no one was here,' he said. 'Why did you take so long to answer?'

Lorna tossed her head. 'No business of yours, Don Leckie,' she said. 'What brings you here?'

'Curiosity.' He grinned. 'Thought I'd have a peek at the love-nest.'

'It's not a love-nest.' She was uncomfortably aware that Gerald was almost certainly eavesdropping. 'It's a home for me and the child when it comes.'

He grinned. 'So one of the gents put you in the family way and you don't know who it was? Still, you've fallen on your feet, you can't deny that.'

'I don't deny it,' said Lorna. 'Mr Hatherley has been a real brick and I'm very grateful to him.'

'Are you?' He leaned forward and put a finger under her chin. 'Are you grateful? How grateful? You could be very grateful and no one would know, would they?'

Lorna raised her voice. 'If you mean what I think, Don Leckie, then you've a damned cheek and you can take yourself off my property.'

'His property, you mean? Or is it "our" property?'

'I'm not talking about it,' she told him angrily, 'so you can keep your nasty thoughts to yourself. All I know is that I'd be in a fine old mess if he hadn't offered to help me and I won't hear a word said against him.'

'You used to call him a silly old woman,' Don reminded her, 'and a dry old stick – and worse. Always fiddling with you, you said.'

Her cheeks burning, Lorna made a move to slam the door but his foot was in the way.

'I'm sorry,' he said softly. 'I'm only jealous. I didn't mean to upset you, honest I didn't.'

'Well, you have upset me,' she told him. 'I don't know what you're doing here anyway. I don't think Amy Turner would be very pleased if she knew you were hanging around my cottage.'

His lips curled. 'Amy Turner!' he said. 'Stuck-up madam, that's what she is.'

Lorna hesitated, wanting to hear about the girl who had supplanted her.

'Oh dear,' she said. 'Fallen out, have you? You don't seem to have much luck with your women. Poor old Don!'

He grinned, unperturbed by her remark. 'Seems like I'm at a loose end again,' he told her, 'and I thought you might be lonely down here all by yourself.'

Remembering Gerald, Lorna said loudly, 'Well, I'm not lonely and I won't need any visitors.'

'How's that?' he asked. 'You're going to be all alone here, aren't you?'

'So what if I am?'

'I thought I'd pop in from time to time, just to keep an eye on you. Be a bit of company for you.'

'I'll have the baby,' said Lorna, 'and I won't need any company, thank you.' But she thought how handsome he was with his blond hair and large blue eyes and she remembered the feel of his mouth on hers.

'So now you know what it's all about then,' he said. 'Did you like it?'

She stiffened. 'I don't remember anything about it; now please go away.'

'Just say I can call again and I will.'

'You can't call again,' she said loudly. 'Take your foot away, Don Leckie. I want to shut the door.'

He laughed mockingly and suddenly pushed the door open

wider, pulled her forward and kissed her full on the mouth. Then he drew a long deep breath and his eyes narrowed.

'You smell all sort of warm,' he told her. 'Did you know that?'

'I don't,' she said shrilly. 'Don't talk nonsense! Get away from me, Donald Leckie, and don't—'

'That smell does things to me.'

'Go away!' she cried, kicking at his feet. 'Oh please, Don,' she begged, lowering her voice to a whisper. 'You'll *have* to go.'

He looked past her to the bottom of the stairs and gave her a questioning look, jerking his head towards the upstairs landing. In desperation Lorna nodded.

'Well,' he said loudly. 'I know when I'm not wanted. Sorry I troubled you.' He winked at her.

As soon as he moved his foot, she slammed the door before slowly going back upstairs.

Gerald was sitting on the bed, his face grim.

'If that man ever comes here again,' he told her furiously, 'you tell me, Lorna, and I'll kill him with my own bare hands!'

*

The first Friday and Saturday of November were the dates chosen for Amy's visit to London to meet Elliot's family. Clara had changed her day off so that she could run the Friday stall for her and she would also have tea with the Turner family; it would be a welcome break from Bates Manor, where Mrs Lester had agreed to sit with Esme. As she arranged the stall, Clara chatted to Tim and waved to Harry, who was on the opposite platform talking to the pigeon man. Bob Hart was repairing Ted Turner's boots while the old man sat on the seat and waited for them to be returned to him; he twiddled his toes and said, 'I wish he'd get a blooming move on! My feet are getting cold, stuck on this seat.'

Clara grinned. 'Keep you out of mischief,' she said. 'Want to buy a stamp collection? Only sixpence.' She held up a battered album for his inspection.

Ted shook his head. 'A stamp collection?' he repeated. 'No, I don't. What would I want with a stamp collection?'

'Might be worth a lot of money,' she said. 'You never know your luck. Mrs Hollis found it in a trunk full of stuff that used to belong to her husband; it belonged to his father, so that's how old it is.'

'I've no money to waste on bits and bobs,' Ted told her, meanwhile squinting across at the two men on the opposite platform. 'Isn't it time for those blooming pigeons?' he grumbled. 'Never could see the fun in racing pigeons; they're only birds, when all's said and done. Dogs now, yes. Lurchers, that's more like it; that's an exciting sport. My father used to take me to see the lurchers race. Like lightning they were, some of them – like greased lightning.'

'A lurcher?' said Clara. 'Never heard of it. Is it some sort of dog?'

''Course it's a dog!' He was delighted by her ignorance. 'It's a favourite with the gipsies. Like a shaggy greyhound, it is. Lovely dogs. Many's the shilling my old man won lurcher racing. You youngsters today don't know the half of it and that's the truth!' He sniffed. It was the afternoon of a fine November day, but the sun had lost its warmth and the evening would be cold with some mist. 'What else you got there?' Ted asked. 'Any of them mutton pies?'

'You'll have to pay for it,' said Clara.

Ted snorted. 'I won't bother, then,' he said. 'Amy used to give me one.'

'Well, I'm not Amy – and it was Mrs Turner who made them, so I can't start giving them away, now can I?'

'Amy's were better,' he said. 'More meat in them! Ellen's are all gravy.'

'Then you wouldn't enjoy it if I gave you one – oh!'

Startled, Clara put a hand to her heart as the wicker baskets on the opposite platform were opened and thirty-five pigeons burst joyfully into freedom with a clatter of wings. All eyes were on the birds as they wheeled above the station in a frenzied effort to establish their position and make a start on the long journey home.

Tim, grinning, said loudly, 'Make a nice pigeon pie, they would.'

Mr Larkin looked across and shook his fist. 'You say that in Newcastle,' he laughed, 'and you'd be lynched!'

At that moment Bob Hart descended from his signal-box with Ted's boots under his arm. 'Here you are,' he said. 'Pay me in parsnip wine if young Amy can spare a couple of bottles. Nice drop of wine, that is – got real body to it.'

'I'll ask her,' said Ted. 'If not, there's some rhubarb wine coming along. Be ready to drink in five or six weeks. Lovely colour.' He inspected his boots, muttered his thanks and began to pull them on.

Tim said, 'My ma made some strawberry wine. That was delicate; sweeter than some, but a real delicate flavour. Amy sold a few bottles for her and it went better than the jam.'

Ted finished lacing his boots, stood up and shuffled around 'to test them out' as he put it.

'Nice job,' he told the signalman. 'Many thanks. I won't forget the wine. Will tomorrow do?'

Harry and Mr Larkin began to manhandle the large pigeon baskets back across the track, so that they could travel back to London on the next train which was due in seven minutes. Tim lent a hand and Clara finished arranging the stall.

Ted stared longingly at the mutton pies but asked, 'How's the old girl up at the Manor? Gone a bit screwy, I hear.'

Clara shrugged. 'She's certainly a bit odd,' she admitted. 'Almost childish at times – then at other times, quite normal. Well, not her old self exactly, but normal enough. She gets upset easily and keeps crying, and she's everlasting putting on face creams and stuff. Scared of losing her looks, I suppose.'

Ted moved a little closer and gave her a conspiratorial look. 'What does she have to say about her old man helping the Betts girl?' he asked. 'Funny business, that, you know. I reckon there's more to it than meets the eye.'

'Could be.' Clara refused to be drawn on that subject.

'I reckon,' said Ted, 'that he knows who the father is and he's covering up for him. Bound to, isn't he, if it's a friend? Could be they all know who it is and while the father's forking out, they've agreed to keep their mouths shut.'

'Could be,' Clara said again. She had her own ideas on the subject, but it was more than her job was worth to air her views.

Luckily the imminent arrival of the train made further conversation difficult. Bob Hart closed the heavy crossing-gates and signalled its approach. The stationmaster put in an appearance and the train sounded its whistle as it chuffed into sight along the track, the smoke forming round puffs in the still air. Mr Bell slowed it to its approach speed of 15 miles per hour and prepared to apply the brakes as it drew level with the platform.

Rodney Midden had been to Hastings for the day on yet another fruitless search for his missing daughter. He had again drawn blank and had drowned his sorrows in seven pints of porter, which now churned uneasily in his stomach and made him feel aggressive towards the world in general and his erring daughter in particular. If he could find her, he'd wring her neck, he told himself bitterly. No twopenny-halfpenny trollop was going to make a fool out of him, daughter or no daughter. It had not helped matters when his wife had protested about the money he was wasting on train fares. He had soon put a stop to her bellyaching and by tomorrow she should have quite a nice black eye to prove it!

He stared out of the carriage window as the train rolled to a halt. Gazedown – the station where the girl sold mutton pies, but he couldn't fancy one right now. Gazedown. The name rang another bell, but for the moment he could not remember why. Ah! The accident. This was where he'd had a bit of an argy-bargy with the porter. Stupid idiot! That's right; someone had fallen under the train.

With an effort, he heaved himself to his feet and leaned out of the window. No sign of the accident now. Everyone smiling and . . . Suddenly he caught sight of Clara standing beside the little table and his face froze. She was talking to a man who had descended from the train. Was it really Clara? How could it be? He had spoken to the girl at that stall on a previous occasion, and it most certainly hadn't been his daughter then. But now he could almost swear to it. He opened the door and stepped heavily down to the platform. In that instant Clara half turned towards him and the horrified expression on her face was all he needed by way of confirmation. How she came to be on Gazedown

Station he could not imagine, but there she was. He had found the little trollop at last!

'Clara! You thieving little bitch!' he roared, oblivious of the startled looks on the faces of the porter and the passengers who had stepped down from the train to see what was on offer at the stall. Rodney raised his voice! 'I'll teach you to steal from your own bloody father!'

Clara's instinct was to flee, but fright had turned her legs to jelly. She dropped the stamp album and put up both hands to protect her face from what she knew was coming.

'Now, sir, we don't want any trouble,' Harry stammered, gallantly placing himself between Clara and the man who was staggering towards her with murder in his eyes. Rodney ignored him while Clara, seeing nothing else with which to defend herself, reached for the stamp album and held it up in front of her like a shield. Her father swore under his breath, put a meaty hand in the middle of Harry's chest and pushed him violently to one side, whereupon Harry – losing his balance – fell against the passenger who had been talking to Clara and both men tumbled to the ground.

'Pa! No!' screamed Clara. 'You lay a finger on me and I'll—'

'You'll what?' he snarled as he knocked the album up out of her hands and grabbed a handful of her bodice. He pulled her towards him as the book described a circle in the air above them, scattering loose stamps like confetti. With his other hand, he pushed back her straw boater and seized a handful of her hair.

'Pa!' she screamed frantically. It was not so much the beating she would get as the indignity of being punched and pummelled in front of all her new friends. Out of the corner of her eye she saw that Harry was back on his feet and her heart sank; he would be no match for her brawny father, neither would Tim, and anyway she did not want either of them to get hurt on her behalf. She was used to fighting her own battles. Her father's meaty fist was only inches from her eyes and his voice dropped to a threatening growl as he enjoyed her fear, for now he felt an all-powerful rage with her punishment still to come. He enjoyed the anticipation and revelled in the thought of the forthcoming violence.

Letting go of her hair, he drew back his fist and she closed her eyes as the first blow struck her with stunning force across the right ear. In spite of her determination to suffer in silence, a cry of pain escaped her. Half-dazed, she began to pummel at her father's chest and tried desperately to free herself from his grasp. When that failed, she began to kick him.

'I'll teach you to steal from me!' he roared. 'I'll give you one for every pound you pinched off me!' A second blow caught her mouth and she felt her lip split and tasted blood. With one part of her mind she heard the stationmaster's voice telling Tim to go for the sergeant and even in the midst of her own troubles, she thought regretfully that this would probably bring further disgrace to the station and more problems for Amy's father. There was a crash as the stall tottered and fell.

The third blow never came and Clara opened her eyes wonderingly. To her surprise, the stationmaster himself was grappling with her father and Harry was limping towards them. Clara felt a rush of gratitude towards them both, but she feared they would have no success; she had once watched her father scatter a group of four men with whom he had picked a quarrel and had seen the fierce delight on his face as he hurled himself amongst them. Today, though, he had been drinking – she had smelt it on his breath – and that might slow him down.

'Oh, be careful, Harry!' she cried, but too late, for Rodney Midden's foot came up and caught the porter's left knee, causing him to stumble and cry out in pain.

As Clara cried out her warning, her father's hands went for her neck. 'I'll choke the bloody life out of you, you rotten little cow!' he hissed and she felt his fingers close round her throat. By this time everything was blurred, but she caught a momentary glimpse of the stationmaster attempting to pin her father's arms to his sides. She swayed as a darkness swam in front of her eyes and, barely conscious, was aware only of the pressure of his fingers round her throat. Then they eased a little, but it seemed an eternity before they were torn from her neck and she fell half-swooning to the ground. Grunts and curses told her that the fight continued, but she was too weak to care any longer and willingly surrendered to the kindly hands which dragged her to a safe distance.

When she came to her senses again, she was stretched out along the platform seat and Ellen Turner was bathing her bruised face. The train had pulled out though her father, she learned, had not gone with it but now awaited the arrival of the police sergeant as he sat in the booking-office with his hands tied behind his back. He had not given in without a fight, Ellen told her, but that was no surprise to Clara. Apparently the stationmaster's left eye was badly swollen, several teeth had been loosened and he thought he might have a broken wrist.

'I'm so sorry,' whispered Clara through her torn lips. 'It's all my fault. You must all be so angry with me. He's a real brute and I hate him, but I never thought he'd keep on after me.'

'It was just bad luck,' comforted Ellen. 'If you hadn't been doing the Friday stall, he'd probably never have found you.'

'I pinched his wallet,' she said. 'I did wrong there, but he'd done me much worse. I can't tell anyone but believe you me, he done things which no self-respecting girl . . .' Tears filled her eyes, but she brushed them aside angrily.

'Don't talk about it,' said Ellen quickly. 'Some things are best forgotten. Most of us have skeletons in our cupboards, Clara — some larger than others. We're only human, after all.' She smiled faintly. 'We have to go on, whatever we've done.'

'But two wrongs don't make a right,' protested Clara. 'Whatever wrong he did me, I shouldn't have stolen from him. Now all this has happened and your husband's hurt — and poor Harry. I thought I was so clever and now I know I'm not.'

'Look at it another way,' said Ellen. 'If you did wrong, you've paid for it. He did wrong and now he's going to pay. I'm afraid he'll end up in prison — how will your mother manage without him?'

'I don't know,' said Clara. 'She'd have to manage if he was dead, wouldn't she? I'll send her a bit of my wages, but I can't spare much and she never helped me when Pa got after me — she just let him go on doing what he did, so I can't love her, Mrs Turner. I can't love either of them and that's the truth.'

'Poor Clara.'

Clara struggled into a sitting position. 'Jesus says to love one another, but they don't love me so how am I supposed to love them? I don't love anybody, Mrs Turner. Not anybody. I don't even like many people. And nobody loves me.' She shrugged. 'That's how it'll always be, I reckon, so I just have to look out for myself.'

'What about your employers?' Ellen asked curiously. 'Do you like them?'

Clara considered before answering. 'Not really *like*,' she admitted. 'I'm sorry for them, that's all. They're both unhappy people and now she's gone a bit weird. She needs me and I suppose that's something. He's like a pig in muck since he's had Lorna to fuss over – a changed man, he is. I just hope it lasts.' She sighed, swung her legs down and stood up. 'Perhaps I'm weird too and I don't know it!'

'I don't think so,' smiled Ellen. 'We're all what we are, for better or worse. I think God must be used to us by now – he made us, after all, so he can't blame us entirely.'

They both looked up as Tim came towards them, bursting with importance, his step jaunty as ever.

'It's all over now,' he told them. 'I'm afraid your father's been arrested, Clara and taken into custody. Assault, causing an affray, damage to railway property—'

'Come again?' said Clara. 'What damage?'

Tim grinned. 'He broke the window in the door of the booking-office! A right so-and-so, your father. I'm sorry I missed all the fun.'

'You were well out of the way,' said Ellen severely, 'and it was certainly not fun.'

Ted wandered up, his hands thrust into his pockets, and the stamp album tucked under his arm.

'All those mutton pies,' he said sadly. 'All over the blooming platform! Ruined, they are. I had to sweep them up and chuck them in the bin. I should have eaten one when I had the chance.'

Ellen stood up and smiled. 'All you think about is your

stomach!' she told him. 'Suppose I make a few more tomorrow for the family? How would that be?'

Ted looked at her and suddenly, inexplicably, all that remained of his animosity towards her vanished.

'I've never said "No" to a mutton pie,' he conceded, 'and I shan't start now.' He gave her a slow, lopsided grin which said more than words and held out the album. He would offer Mrs Hollis 4d for it, since it was now somewhat tattered. Then he would show it to Sam and young Toby and together they could put all the stamps back on the right pages. It would be fun — something to do now the evenings were drawing in a bit. He thought Sarah would like the idea of him and the two boys working on the album.

'I thought the boys might be interested,' he said sheepishly.

To Clara's surprise, Ellen leaned forward and kissed the old man on the cheek. 'I'm sure they'll love it,' she said.

Chapter Twenty-Two

When Amy arrived in London, Elliot was waiting to meet her. Although she had looked forward to seeing him again with conflicting emotions, he seemed for his part to be very much at ease and his manner was entirely normal. He greeted her cheerfully and told her that he was taking her first to his office, where he had a small amount of work to finish. Then he whisked her off to find a hansom cab to convey them to the publishers.

Amy's nervousness melted away as the horses made their way through the streets, weaving a rapid path through the teeming crowded traffic, all apparently in imminent danger of collision. Open-topped horse-buses raced each other, urged on by the younger and more boisterous passengers on the upper deck; hansom cabs mingled with delivery vans of all types and sizes from brewers' drays to bakers' vans. They passed army transport waggons so heavy that they were drawn by teams of six horses; road haulage waggons, catering for a variety of goods, which towered above most of the other road users, their crated loads swaying precariously and threatening to be dislodged at any moment. Exhilarated by the noise and bustle, Amy sat glued to the cab window while Elliot, amused by her excitement, watched her. Once or twice he pointed out something of interest, but otherwise he seemed content to sit back and enjoy the journey.

The weather was mild, but there was a slight breeze and Amy was warmly dressed in a tartan jacket and dark green serge skirt. Her dark green hat was trimmed with a single red flower and her dark hair swept into a neat chignon at the nape of her neck. Elliot had complimented her on her appearance and she felt unusually confident at the prospect of the approaching meeting with his colleagues. Just being away from Gazedown was a tonic in itself, although she would have felt too disloyal to put such a thought into words.

Number 37, at street level, was a solicitor's office and a small merchant bank. The first and second floors – the publishers' premises – were Elliot's second home. The stairway was painted a rather depressing shade of brown, but once inside the area rented by the publishers the decor was a little more inspiring – two shades of green picked out in cream.

'Come into my office first,' said Elliot, 'and we'll send for a pot of tea, then when you're suitably refreshed we'll go and meet the others. Go on in and I'll find Miss Braithwaite.'

Amy found herself in a small office which could best be described as a 'den' and in which organised chaos appeared to reign. The large mahogany desk which half filled the room was covered with piles of manuscripts and these overflowed on to the window-sill behind Elliot's wing-backed chair, down on to the floor and up to the shelving, where they jostled for space amongst rows of books. There was a telephone on the desk and a blotter, inkstand and pens and letters in a wire mesh tray.

Elliot came back and laughed aloud at the expression on Amy's face.

'Don't tell me!' he begged. 'I know! It's untidy, but that's how I like it. My poor Miss Braithwaite is always trying to sneak in and tidy it up, but when she does I can't find anything for days afterwards. I know exactly where everything is . . . I think!'

Amy laughed with him. 'Do all editors work like this?' she asked.

'Good heavens no! Stanley Bushy – he's our fiction editor – is the epitome of neatness and order. A place for everything and everything in its place. You could best describe Bushy's office as a model of military precision. Pencil at right-angles to the pen, which is parallel to the edge of the blotter, which is exactly in the middle of the desk!'

'I'll try not to be too impressed by him,' Amy assured him.

The door opened and a woman came in with a small round tray bearing two cups and saucers, milk, sugar, a teapot and a jug of hot water. She was about thirty, Amy guessed, and smartly dressed. She smiled at Amy as she waited for Elliot to clear a space on his cluttered desk.

'Did you have a good journey?' she asked. 'Mr Allan said you were coming up from the country.'

Amy smiled. 'Yes, from Gazedown in Kent,' she said.

Miss Braithwaite set down the tray, Elliot made the introductions and the two women shook hands.

'I thought Mr Allan was going to be late meeting you,' the secretary told Amy. 'I had to chase him out of the office.'

Elliot laughed as he began to pour the tea. 'What would I do without you, Miss Braithwaite?' he teased. His tone was friendly, almost familiar, and Amy felt a slight pang of jealousy. Was the secretary one of Elliot's lady friends, she wondered – and if so, how serious was the attachment?

Miss Braithwaite smiled at him and went out and Amy gratefully accepted a cup of tea.

'I can't offer you a biscuit,' said Elliot, 'because Miles has eaten them all, but you probably don't like Bath Olivers anyway.'

'I love them,' she told him, 'but I'm not hungry. Who is Miles?'

'Miles Ashley, one of our artists.' He put down his cup, reached out to the bookshelf immediately to his left and picked out two books. 'These are two of his,' he explained. 'Lovely, aren't they?'

Amy studied them with interest. One was a dictionary of wild flowers and the other a cookery book.

'They're very nice,' she said, 'but I can't make a very professional judgement.'

He laughed at her earnest expression. 'You don't have to,' he said. 'As a member of the book-buying public, all you have to decide is if you like it enough. If you do, you'll probably buy the book. If you don't, you won't. It's all very simple really!'

There was a knock at the door and a man came in without

waiting to be invited. He was overweight and balding, with a cherubic freckled face.

'Aha! This is the young lady, is it?' he cried, seizing Amy's hand and shaking it with enthusiasm. 'I'm Miles – oh, you're looking at one of my designs. What do you think of it?' He took the book from her and held it at arm's length, examining it critically. 'I was rather pleased with that. I thought, what is my favourite wild flower, and decided it was a poppy so a poppy design is what I did. I'm a creature of impulse!' He gave the book back to her. 'So how do you like London? Smelly, dirty London where the streets are paved with gold. Don't you believe it, my dear!'

Elliot said, 'I was just telling Amy why I couldn't offer her a biscuit,' and Miles rolled his eyes with a comic display of remorse.

'It was I,' he said. 'I cannot tell a lie. Bath Olivers are my only vice – I indulge myself, as you can see.' He patted his non-existent waistline. 'Elliot is such an obliging chap that if I run out I know I can rely on him to find me one or two when the worms are gnawing. Do worms gnaw? Maybe it's rats. Now what did I come in for, apart from a desire to meet the new author?'

Amy laughed. 'Oh dear! I'm afraid you're mixing me up with someone else,' she said.

To her surprise he seemed taken aback by this remark. Elliot, too, looked disconcerted. 'We haven't talked yet,' he told Miles.

'Ah!' Miles clapped a hand to his mouth. 'Trust me!'

There was an awkward pause while Amy looked from one to the other with growing confusion. Miles said, 'Hm!' rather theatrically and then, 'Well, I'll pop back later,' and left the room rather hurriedly.

Amy looked at Elliot. 'What on earth was all that about?' she asked.

Instead of answering, Elliot came round the table and put his hands on Amy's shoulders. 'I think you should sit down,' he suggested, pushing her gently but firmly into a chair. 'No! Don't say anything yet. I have something to say to you and I want you to listen carefully before you—'

'But Elliot! What did Miles mean by—'

He held up a finger for silence. 'Not a word,' he told her firmly. 'I promise you all will be revealed.' He smiled. 'Don't look like that, Amy. It's not bad news. Quite the reverse.'

'But, Elliot—'

'Please, Amy.'

Amy made an effort to calm herself, crossing her hands in her lap. 'I'll listen,' she promised.

Elliot went back to his chair behind the desk.

'Forgive me,' he said, 'but I have a confession to make. I was in Gazedown last week and I went to The Lodge with the intention of beginning to sort out Ralph's belongings — his clothes and things. Quite by chance I found your work and I couldn't resist reading it.' Amy gasped and opened her mouth to protest, but he went on, 'It was good, Amy. *Very* good! In fact, for someone who had never written professionally before, it was quite extraordinary. Of course there were faults and weaknesses, but it showed tremendous promise. Believe me, Amy, I say that most sincerely — tremendous promise! It wasn't the book Ralph had been working towards . . . but that brings me to my second confession.'

Amy interrupted him, her face pale. 'You never intended it to be a book,' she said. 'I know.'

It was Elliot's turn to be shocked. 'You knew?' he said.

'I guessed.'

He shook his head slowly. 'Oh Amy, this is so hard to explain. When I first "invented" the book, it was to help Ralph. There had already been an attempt to sort the material, but that had come to nothing. It seemed a good idea at the time to revive it, so to speak, for Ralph's sake. I had no idea that he would meet you, of course, nor that you would offer your services to him. By the time I realised how involved in the project you were becoming, it was too late. I didn't want you to be hurt or disappointed, but I couldn't tell you. If I had dropped the whole idea, the chances are that Ralph would have gone to Italy and I would have lost touch with him. I couldn't risk that.'

Amy smiled shakily. 'Poor Elliot, you were in a difficult position. I can see that.'

He shrugged. 'I didn't know what to do, but then Ralph's

accident happened and that changed everything. Except that you wanted to carry on with the research.'

'Were you going to tell me?' Amy asked curiously. 'That the book was only a figment of your imagination?'

'No, I thought that would be needlessly cruel. But as it happened . . .' he smiled, 'I found those remarkable first chapters.' His expression changed and he looked at Amy seriously. 'It's vivid, compassionate, evocative – believe me, Amy, I was quite overwhelmed. And I'm determined you must finish it. Oh, I'll help you, don't worry. I promise. Everyone is very eager to support you.'

Amy's heart was racing. 'Finish the book? Oh, Elliot, I would need all the help I could get,' she said. 'I want so much to say "Yes"—'

'Then say it,' he urged her.

'It's all so sudden.' She hesitated. 'I don't know—'

'Say it, Amy.'

Still she hesitated and Elliot left his chair and pulled her to her feet. 'If you don't do it, someone else will,' he warned.

'I'll do it!' cried Amy.

'I knew you would,' he smiled.

At that moment Miles returned and was the first to congratulate her. 'I'm already working on the illustrations,' he told her. 'Do you want to have a look at what we've got so far?'

'Well, I . . .'

Without waiting for her answer, he put out a podgy hand and took Amy by the arm. 'I'll bring her back in ten minutes,' he told Elliot. Then he dragged her along the corridor and up another flight of brown stairs to a studio where several people were at work. As he showed her through a file full of sketches and photographs, his obvious enthusiasm was infectious.

'Look at this!' he exclaimed jubilantly. 'Here's a newspaper cutting about his wedding to Ella – and Elliot tells me you have a wedding invitation and—'

'That's right, we have,' she told him.

'Splendid! And I thought we'd also use extracts from a number of the letters.'

'There's a mourning-card for his daughter's funeral,' said Amy, 'and a lovely portrait of him as a boy of eleven . . .'

Twenty-five minutes later when Miles escorted her back to Elliot, she had also spoken with several of the other members of the art department and was beginning to feel more relaxed. It was stimulating to have her opinions sought and to share in the project and gradually she had begun to visualise the finished book for the first time.

Miles disappeared again as soon as he had delivered her to Elliot's office, where she found him talking to a tall blonde woman. Her name was Elinor Wyatt and she was introduced as a member of the sales department. As she told Amy about her plans for the book's promotion, she too spoke to her as though she were the author. When she had gone, Amy turned accusingly to Elliot.

'You had already told them all that I'd say "Yes"!'

Elliot's laugh rang out. 'It's true,' he admitted. 'I was so sure I could convince you and so confident of your ability to do it. I didn't want you to find a way to say "No" and I'm quite unscrupulous about it. You can stay on at The Lodge – I'll arrange that – and I shall come down to Gaze-down whenever you need help and to give moral support. Amy, you are the right person for the task and what is more, when it's done and is a success, I shall give you a few weeks to recover from the shock and then I shall probably offer you another biography.'

She stammered. 'Another one! Elliot, have you gone mad? I'm not a writer, I'm a . . .'

'A what?' he asked as she paused. 'A stationmaster's daughter?'

'Yes.' Her tone was defiant.

'But that was an accident of birth,' he reminded her. 'Being a stationmaster's daughter is not a career; it's not even an achievement.' For a moment his bantering tone vanished and he regarded her with a serious expression. 'Is that all you want from life, Amy? You know you have a good brain – aren't you longing to use it? Don't you want to find out what you are capable of doing? We all need a challenge!'

She stared at him. 'You sound like my headmistress,' she told him. 'Do I want a challenge? Yes, I suppose I do. But suppose the book fails? What then? It would be too awful for you.'

A brief smile lit his face. 'The firm would stand to lose if it failed,' he said. 'Not you. We would make you an unconditional advance. But it won't fail, Amy. I've been in this business long enough to know what I'm talking about and I'm prepared to take the risks. Look, finish this book and then, if you can really say with hand on heart that you didn't enjoy it, I won't offer you anything else and I'll stop badgering you.'

She hesitated. 'But you'd be so disappointed . . .' she began.

'Amy Turner!' he cried. 'You are going to write this book! Just tell yourself you are going to write Stanisbrooke's biography. Do it for me, do it for Ralph or do it for yourself. I don't care. Just do it! I can imagine how you feel and I'm not so insensitive as you might think. I don't pretend it will be easy. I don't pretend you won't have moments of panic or despair, but I will be there to help you, whenever you want me. As I said, I'll arrange for you to stay on at The Lodge and whenever you need me, I'll drop everything and come down on the next train. I swear it. You can do it, Amy. For me. My reputation is at stake, remember!'

'Oh, Elliot!' she laughed. 'That's blackmail!'

'Of course it is.' He grinned. 'But I'm afraid I'm quite unscrupulous, as I said. Please say you'll do it, Amy.'

She made a helpless gesture with her hands. 'You win, Elliot,' she said. 'I suppose you always do.'

'Not always,' he said, 'but this time it was very important to me. Thank you, Amy.'

She stared at him. 'Thank *you*,' she said.

Now that her mind was made up to it, all her nervousness suddenly vanished and in its place came a fierce determination to succeed.

*

During the rest of the morning Amy was introduced to several other people and then Elliot took her to a nearby restaurant for lunch. While they ate, he talked about London and about the world of publishing, and Amy found it all fascinating. The conversation then turned to his parents and he told her about his childhood and went on to ask her about her own life. As usual, she found him easy to talk to and enjoyed every minute of the lunch. She noticed that he did not talk about his present life and, not wanting to appear too curious, she did not ask. However, he did ask her whether she thought she would ever like to live in London, but when she said 'Yes' he did not pursue the subject.

They left the restaurant just after 3 o'clock and walked to the Embankment to watch the boats plying to and fro along the Thames. London's waterway, it seemed, was equally as congested as her roadways and a source of fascination to anyone with the time to stand and stare. A sturdy tug pulled a string of heavily laden lighters, nudging slowly against the current, its progress almost imperceptible. Two paddle-steamers passed each other sounding their horns in greeting, riding the smooth brown water like majestic swans. Working barges moved sluggishly, their large brown sails barely filled by the sulky breeze. There were ferry-boats crossing back-wards and forwards, dodging the larger traffic with a mixture of luck and judgement, while along the edges of the river small punts and dinghies could be seen – some carrying a lone and hopeful fisherman, others a group of young people determined to enjoy a trip on the river despite the lack of sunshine.

Then a hansom took them to Elliot's home where they were admitted by the smiling housekeeper. At once a door opened and a small fragile-looking woman came into the hall, her hands outstretched to greet them.

'Ah, Elliot, at last!' she exclaimed. 'Herbert has been teasing me about my lack of patience. Hullo, my dear. You must be Amy. Ralph told us so much about you.'

As she spoke of her dead son Amy saw the hint of tears, but the handshake was firm enough. Margaret Allan was barely fifty, but years in India had dried up her skin so that she looked older than she was. Her gleaming dark hair was swept up on top of her head and her firm mouth reminded Amy of Elliot. She wore an expensive gown in black silk and her beringed hands were frequently raised to fiddle with her earrings.

'Do you like these?' she asked Amy, seeing her glance rest on the earrings. 'Ralph gave them to me for my birthday years ago – he saved up for them because he knew how I loved blue. Tiny sapphires. He was such a sensitive boy. Very quiet, but thoughtful and very affectionate.' She smiled and put an arm through Elliot's. 'Not a bit like this one. He was so boisterous and always into mischief. Weren't you, dear?'

Elliot laughed. 'I refuse to say anything that might incriminate me!' he declared.

Once more she fingered the earrings, then her smile faded and her lips trembled. 'I wear them because . . .' Her voice faltered momentarily, then she regained her composure and continued, 'So, you are Amy? Yes, I think I would have recognised you from Ralph's description. Come in and meet my husband. You must excuse his not getting up, but his back is giving him a lot of pain. The cabin was comfortable, but he's a tall man and the bunks were so small.' She paused in the doorway of the morning room and said, 'Oh Elliot, before I forget – the Lovells called in to see us – so sweet of them – and invited us to dinner this evening.'

Amy saw Elliot's expression change. 'Oh no, Mother!' he protested. 'I'm sure Amy would prefer a quiet evening—'

'Nonsense, dear,' interrupted his mother. 'Amy wants to see everything and meet everyone! That is why people come to London. Of course she'll want to go.' She smiled at Amy. 'The Lovells – Dennis and Ivy – are a charming couple and we've known them since their daughter Grace was born. They were in Karachi when we were first out there.'

She led the way into the room and her husband made as though to rise to his feet. 'No, Herbert, don't get up,' she protested. 'Amy understands all about your back.'

'Of course I do. I'm so sorry,' said Amy, shaking hands with him. He was thinner than Elliot and inclined to be round-shouldered; his eyes were smaller, his hair was medium brown instead of dark and his nose was almost hooked.

'Amy,' said Herbert. 'Yes, you look like an Amy. Pleased to meet you, my dear. Ralph thought such a lot of you. "My very dear Amy" – that's what he always called you. You were good for him; he was so upset when poor little Lydia died and we thought he would never get over it.'

'I don't think he did,' said Margaret. 'Not really.'

'Well, no, maybe not entirely. But he desperately wanted to be alone and we were so worried when Elliot wrote saying Ralph was going to shut himself away in the middle of nowhere.' He smiled apologetically at Amy. 'Please don't be offended,' he asked her, 'but I said "Gazedown? Never heard of it." '

Amy laughed. 'I felt the same way,' she admitted, 'when my father was first appointed stationmaster there.'

'And do you prefer the country to London?' Herbert asked.

'I don't know,' she confessed. 'I haven't seen much of London.'

Margaret's face lit up. 'Oh, what fun! Elliot didn't say. Why then, we must make sure you see everything before you go back! The Tower of London – you must see the Crown Jewels – and Buckingham Palace, naturally. St Paul's Cathedral – oh, and the National Gallery – and Westminster Abbey, of course. How long are you staying, dear?'

'Only until tomorrow,' laughed Amy. 'I don't think we shall fit it all in.'

'Then we'll draw up an itinerary,' Margaret cried. 'The boys used to love the Tower of London. Tomorrow, you say? Oh, no – you must stay until Sunday. I don't know how many times we had to take them; Herbert swore they were planning to steal the jewels!'

Amy caught Elliot's eye. He nodded imperceptibly and she realised that having something positive to do would help his parents through the next few days, so she expressed great enthusiasm for the extended stay and they were soon busy making plans.

She did not give another thought to Elliot's reaction to the news that they were all invited to visit the Lovells but later, when they arrived at their hosts' large Chelsea home, the reason at once became apparent. Grace Lovell, a few years older than Amy, was hopelessly in love with Elliot. Amy knew it the moment she looked into the blue eyes and wondered if her own feelings for Elliot were also so painfully transparent. So this was the woman in Elliot's life, she thought, with a terrible tightening of her throat. Well, it should come as no surprise. Ralph had told her that women found Elliot attractive and the only puzzle was that he had not married her. Grace was softly feminine, with pale fluffy hair and delicate features; her handshake was gentle and she was quietly spoken. A gown of cream lace emphasised her fragility and she reminded Amy of a Dresden shepherdess.

Dinner was a splendid affair and Amy did it justice. A perfect turtle soup was followed by *sole véronique*, which in turn was followed by succulent venison which Amy had never tasted before. An apricot mousse and cheese rounded off the meal and on the surface it was a great success. The Lovells were excellent hosts and made their visitors very welcome. It would have been a most memorable evening had it not been for the emotional undercurrents of which the older people seemed unaware. Grace went out of her way to demonstrate to Amy the strength of the bond between herself and Elliot, referring repeatedly to places they had visited together and naming many mutual friends and acquaintances. It was obvious that she had been escorted by Elliot to most of the London theatres, to Henley Regatta and to Ascot, and that they had also been invited to weekend house-parties together. Whatever the relationship between them, it covered a long period. Surely, then, an engagement could be expected, thought Amy. Elliot was nearing thirty and she guessed Grace to be in her mid-twenties, perhaps a little older. Whatever was delaying their marriage?

Occasionally Amy intercepted a look from Elliot to Grace and when she did she found it unfathomable. However, Grace made no attempt to hide her own feelings and her love for Elliot was almost tangible. Her manner towards Amy was pleasant enough, but Amy read the warning in her blue eyes. 'This man is mine. Stay away from him.'

Amy also noticed that the older Lovells talked about Elliot and Grace as though there was a definite understanding between them. Any faint hopes that she might have cherished were finally dashed, but she tried hard to conceal her sense of loss. As the coffee was brought in Grace made a comment about the silver coffee-pot, explaining that it had been in the Lovell family for well over a hundred years.

Her mother sighed. 'I'm very fond of this coffee-pot,' she said. 'I shall be sorry to part with it, but traditionally it passes on to the eldest son on his marriage. We don't have a son, so it will go with Grace when she marries.'

Amy thought she detected a wariness in Elliot's expression, but she quickly glanced away.

Dennis said, '*When* she marries,' and laughed. 'Young people today are notoriously slow about these things. In my day, if you fancied a young gal you snapped her up as fast as you could before some other blighter nabbed her.'

'Papa!' protested Grace, blushing faintly.

But her father had drunk a little too much wine and he blundered on. 'Well, we did,' he insisted. 'We didn't dilly-dally when I was young. If you found a pretty young thing, you got a ring on to her finger before she had a chance to change her mind.'

'You did,' laughed his wife, 'but not all men were so hasty.' She turned to Amy. 'I don't ever recall a real proposal,' she lamented. 'I was presented with a ring on my eighteenth birthday and Dennis told everyone we were engaged to be married. I swear to this day that he never did ask me.'

'Of course I didn't,' her husband agreed. 'You might have said "No" and I wasn't going to risk that.'

They all joined in the laughter. 'There, Elliot,' said his mother. 'Now you know how it's done. There's no excuse.'

There was an awkward silence and as it lengthened Amy kept her eyes on her coffee. It was the perfect opportunity for Elliot to announce his intentions towards Grace, with both sets of parents present. And an ideal time for a wedding too, before the Allans returned to India. 'Please,' she prayed silently, 'don't let him ask her now. I couldn't bear it.' She felt sure she would reveal her distress and then the moment would be ruined for all of them.

Elliot smiled. 'Ah,' he said easily, 'but you wouldn't just be gaining a son – you'd be losing a coffee-pot.'

And miraculously, with the laughter that followed the moment passed and Amy breathed again.

*

Tim Hollis opened the stable door and led out the shunting

horse. It was ten minutes past seven in the morning and he was not very cheerful. He did not normally meet the early train, but he had asked permission to leave early because it was his mother's birthday and Clara had also managed to get the afternoon off. The stationmaster was having a rare 'lie-in' and as luck would have it, Jim Leckie had chosen this very morning to send a horse by rail to Robertsbridge. Therefore Tim had to prepare the horse-box which would be taken on by the milk train as it passed through Gazedown. Unlike Tim, the shunting horse was in a frisky mood and came out into the late November mist with a mischievous look in his eye.

Three weeks had passed since the incident with Clara's father and the station staff had been highly complimented on their handling of the situation, the stationmaster receiving particular praise for his brave conduct. Though an unfortunate affair for Rodney Midden, who was in prison awaiting trial on a variety of charge, it had completely redeemed the station in the eyes of the Railway Board and the stationmaster was a much happier man. The local newspaper had run a front-page story with a photograph of the Gazedown railway staff posed against one of the locomotives, and the accompanying account was also highly favourable. Clara had made a good impression on the young reporter too and he had managed to word the article in such a way that her earlier actions were glossed over.

'Whoa up!' cried Tim to the horse. 'You'll have my arm off in a minute, yanking your head about like that. Stop it, will you!'

Prince ignored this last appeal and continued to toss his head. The morning mist which clothed the yard made it unfamiliar and Prince, having come out of his stable willingly enough, now decided to return to it and Tim was nearly pulled off his feet attempting to restrain him.

'Pack that up!' he grumbled, 'or you won't get your apple.' The horse's ears pricked up at this magical word and he butted Tim affectionately in the chest with his large head.

'God Almighty!' cried Tim, wishing that Harry was on hand to help him. Harry had a way with animals which Tim lacked.

'Look, here's the apple. Now behave yourself.'

With some difficulty, he managed to coax the horse into position at one end of the horse-box and eventually the harness was properly connected and the box pulled along the spur to await the arrival of the 7.34. He had just finished uncoupling the horse when Don Leckie — riding without a saddle — came into the yard on a black mare.

'Hullo, Tim.'

'Hey-up.' Tim could not bring himself to say 'Mr Leckie' since Don was only a year or two his senior.

'Damned mist! They don't like it,' observed Don.

'Now you tell me!' Tim shivered. 'It's raw — goes right through you.'

Don dismounted easily and they stood together, each holding on to their respective horses but unwilling to begin the business of getting Don's animal into the horse-box. They talked for a few moments about nothing in particular, then the subject of women came up and they discovered a mutual grievance.

'Clara?' said Tim, in reply to a question by Don. 'Don't ask me. She's a funny girl — friendly enough, but not exactly exciting. Maybe, living under the same roof, we see too much of each other. She treats me more like a blooming brother.' He shrugged. 'Not that it bothers me — I'm in no hurry to tie myself down. Ma says women are nothing but trouble and she should know. She's one herself!'

He put up a hand to pat Prince, who was fidgeting uneasily in the presence of the black mare. 'You and Amy not seeing eye to eye, I hear?'

'Oh? Who told you that?' Don's tone was aggrieved.

'A little bird. Sorry I spoke if it's a touchy subject.'

It was Don's turn to shrug. 'Well,' he said disparagingly, 'that was never really serious as far as I was concerned. My parents wanted it; you know how they will meddle! Amy's a nice enough girl, don't get me wrong, but she's a bit toffee-nosed in some ways — and so wrapped up in that daft book she's working on. Now she's supposed to be writing the damned thing herself! She's getting too big for her boots, that's her trouble. Oh, I know *you* can't say anything against her — stationmaster's daughter and all that — but she was

395

beginning to get on my nerves and when she wanted to call it a day, I was only too pleased.'

'The other brother's been coming down weekends,' said Tim, diplomatically avoiding any direct reference to Amy. 'Not a bit like poor Mr Allan—Hey! Get off me, you hulking brute.' This last was to the horse, who had finally decided he did not like the black mare and had backed away, nearly pinning Tim against the side of the horse-box. 'Clara says the Hatherleys have put the rental of The Lodge in his name now, so that Amy can go on working there.'

Don hesitated, then asked, 'Any news of the chap who put Lorna in the family way? Clara would know, wouldn't she, if they found out who it was?'

'She would,' said Tim, 'but she hasn't said a thing. Mind you, there's plenty of rumours flying around and one of them is that it was Hatherley himself.'

Don frowned. 'He'd have to be really smart to get away with it.'

'Perhaps he's smarter than he looks.' Tim gave him a quick glance. 'You still keen on her, are you?'

'God, I don't know. I've always had a soft spot for her, but she was so mean with her favours. Couldn't get near her! You know what I mean. Now this happens!'

'All you had to do was get her tipsy, you mean?'

'Something like that.' Don sighed. 'Trouble is, I suppose I do still fancy her, but it's all a bit complicated. Too many ifs and buts.'

They stared gloomily at each other until they heard Bob Hart opening the crossing gates and Tim took out his watch. 'Crikey!' he exclaimed. 'We'd better get a move on.'

He tied Prince to a convenient post and then returned to open the horse-box door and set the ramp in place. The mare was not at all sure that she wanted to go in, and the train had already been signalled when at last she responded to a whack on the rump and rushed headlong into the shadowy interior of the box.

'Good riddance!' muttered Don as the door clanged shut and they pulled the ramp away. 'Never did like that one – a bit of a temper and lazy as they come. I've been on to Pa to sell her for nearly a year now. Some chap's bought her for a small baker's cart; good luck to him, that's all I can say! We've got a nice little cob instead – real sturdy. Ah, here comes the train.'

The first train of the day, pulled by 'Tenterden', was slowing down and her whistle sounded eerily in the misty air. When the brakes had been applied, the guard's van had to be uncoupled and towed back down the line so that the horse-box could be shunted into place. The guard's van was then coupled to the horse-box and thus was still at the rear of the train as laid down in railway regulations. Tim's next job was to help unload the mailbag and the few parcels destined for Gazedown, and then to load up the milk-churns.

Mr Bell had remained in his cab while all this was going on, but he now descended briefly to hand Tim a string-bag full of coal 'borrowed' from the tender. This was to supplement the meagre allowance given by the railway authorities for the booking-office, signal-box and waiting-room fires. In exchange for the coal, Bob Hart gave him a couple of rabbits which he had snared the previous day. When these important transactions had been concluded, the green flag was raised in salute and the Rother Valley Railways No. 1 engine again took up the strain, jerked into motion once more and prepared to haul her newly extended train on towards Wittersham.

Chapter Twenty-Three

Midday on Christmas Eve found the inhabitants of Gazedown in the pre-Christmas excitement that seized the rest of the country every year. With a few exceptions, people were doing exactly what they had done the previous Christmas Eve – pinning holly and ivy around their homes, making up spare beds for visitors, or rehearsing for the evening's carol singing on the village green.

Sam Turner, no longer in the choir, was in the garden trying to teach Toby how to whip a wooden top so that it would keep spinning. With infinite patience, he wound and re-wound the string, but each time the top failed and Toby cried, 'Naughty top!' and laughed uproariously. Each time he retrieved it, Sam laughed too and prepared to explain all over again how a sudden tug would set the top in motion and how it must then be whipped ferociously to keep it moving. A strong bond of affection now existed between the two boys and their loving acceptance of each other had greatly helped the rest of the family to come to terms with Ellen's return.

Ted Turner was meanwhile taking advantage of the boys' absence to wrap up the presents he had made for them – a carved boat with sails for Sam and a smaller one for Toby. They were roughly-made but would float satisfactorily, and he was looking forward to seeing their faces when they opened the parcels the following morning.

This year it was Ellen and not Amy who was rolling pastry for the inevitable mince-pies, humming cheerfully as she worked. Occasionally as she pressed pastry rounds into the patty tins, her thoughts turned to John and she wondered what he was doing, but she was prompted only by curiosity; the agonised yearning for him was fading and the memories were mercifully blurred. His image no longer haunted her dreams and she had begun to see the episode for what it really was – a frantic desire for that elusive joy which is so often sought but rarely found . . . the crock of gold at the rainbow's end. She counted her blessings and was content.

Amy had walked round to the Leckies' farm to exchange the season's greetings and collect the goose which would be their Christmas dinner. It was now understood – and reluctantly accepted – that she would not be marrying Don, and Mary Leckie had survived her disappointment. Don and Jim were in the meadow breaking in the new cob, so the two women were able to exchange news and views while the white goose-feathers flew under Mary's nimble fingers.

Arnold, of course, was not roaming the platform of Gaze-down Station where he had previously spent Christmas Eve. He was in the village store spending some of his wages. For the first time in his life, he had money which he had actually earned and he was making sure that all the other customers were aware of the fact. Each Christmas, Mrs Betts stocked a small selection of items which would make suitable gifts – perfumes, kid-gloves, fancy hatpins and bead necklaces, handkerchiefs and pipes. Arnold spent fifty minutes in the shop before making a decision and when he finally left he was carrying a bottle of lavender water for his mother and a pipe and half an ounce of tobacco for himself!

Lorna was not in the shop because she had already moved into the cottage. Her mother had asked her to lend a hand, but Lorna had declined and they had exchanged a few frosty words on the subject. Mrs Betts would spend Christmas Day with her elder daughter in Robertsbridge, but Lorna had announced that she would stay in the cottage. This was at Gerald's insistence; he wanted to call on her loaded with presents and a bottle of champagne, and although she had suggested that Christmas Eve might be equally suitable, he would have none of it.

Clara was spending her first Christmas at Bates Manor, where she now combined the roles of maid and nurse and was paid exceedingly well for doing so. Esme's condition had improved a little, but her moods were still unpredictable and Gerald foresaw his stolen hour with Lorna as the only ray of light in an otherwise dark Christmas.

In the cottage, Lorna looked at the clock and sighed. Only a quarter past twelve and Christmas Eve stretched ahead, empty and unexciting. She almost wished she had agreed to help out in the shop, but she had wanted to assert her independence as a mother-to-be with a home of her own. Still, she thought regretfully, it might have been better than rattling round the cottage like a pea in a drum. She did enjoy her home, but the solitary life held few charms for her. Gregarious by disposition, she found it frustrating to have no one to talk to. It was unfortunate that she had moved in so late in the year, when the garden was devoid of colour and the surrounding trees were dark and leafless. The rolling Wealden countryside – beautiful though it was in its winter state – did not inspire her and she tried not to think ahead to the real winter when snow and ice would effectively maroon her from the rest of the village. For the past three weeks she had experienced a mild form of morning sickness and this had increased her self-pity. Because she was alone so much, she had had ample time to consider her future; the thrills of having the cottage and the excitement about the baby were coloured by the knowledge that she was never likely to have a man of her own. She wondered what would happen to her when Gerald died and brooded darkly on her gloomy prospects. All the eligible men in the village (and there weren't many!) would be snapped up by then, and she would still be Lorna Betts with an illegitimate child. An *older* Lorna Betts! An object of pity as her hips widened and wrinkles appeared on her face. Her son would never have a father nor any brothers and sisters, she reflected mournfully. By the time Gerald did die, she would be too old to have any other children even supposing she could find a man to father them.

She walked over to the larder and opened the meat-safe where a large chicken was waiting for the big day. There was also a pound of sausages and she meant to make some stuffing. Brussels sprouts, roast potatoes and parsnips would accompany the chicken and she would sit alone at the table

400

to serve and eat her solitary portion. Tears welled up in her eyes as she allowed her mind to dwell on this pathetic picture.

'But I still love him,' she said aloud to reassure herself. 'I do. I still love him. Dear, funny old Gerald.'

The secret fantasy she had once nurtured, in which Esme obligingly died so that she herself could become mistress of Bates Manor, did not seem even a remote possibility in her present state and Don Leckie's image rose as though to torment her with what might have been.

'But I do love Gerald,' she said again, closing the meat-safe door. 'He's kind and sweet and he does adore me.'

Lorna had never been adored before and found it a heady sensation. Her every word was law . . . well, almost; she had only to ask and her wish was granted. She knew Gerald would adore the child too, and would spoil him. They would be so happy together . . . but only for a small part of the time, thought Lorna disconsolately. Most of the time Gerald would be with Esme, and that thought rankled with Lorna. He would not sleep with Esme because they now occupied separate rooms, or so Gerald told her. Lorna wondered if she should draw Clara into conversation some day and find out whether or not Gerald was telling her the truth.

'And he does make me feel lovely,' she reminded herself. She turned her attention to the mince-pies she had made. The pastry was rather hard – she had sampled one – and had shrunk back during the cooking so that now a gap existed between the bottom and top of each tiny pie, revealing the dark and gleaming mincemeat.

Janet had given her a small plum pudding which she had made and Lorna had decided to make a white sauce to go with it. Cooking was not her strong point, but since there would be no one else to share the meal it hardly mattered if it went wrong.

Don Leckie had not been near her since the occasion on which she had sent him away, but she thought about him a lot. She even went so far as to wonder how she would feel if the child she was carrying belonged to Don instead of Gerald.

With a grimace, she closed the larder door and leaned back against it, surveying the kitchen with its scrubbed wooden table and walls hung with colanders, saucepans and trivets. There was also a string of onions and a bowl of late apples.

'Oh Don,' she whispered, 'it could have been your baby, if only I'd given in. I was such a fool.'

Or was she? She had a home of her own now and was financially independent; not many girls of her age could say that much.

Just at that moment there was a knock at the front door and she ran to open it, only to find Don Leckie standing on the front step. For a moment shock rendered Lorna speechless and she could only stare at him.

'It's me,' he said, 'turning up like the bad penny! Happy Christmas, Lorna, for old times' sake.' He thrust a small package into her hand and then, holding up a sprig of mistletoe, pulled her towards him and kissed her. It was a brief, brotherly kiss and one to which she could not possibly object.

'A present for me?' she gasped. 'Thank you, Don. Oh . . .' She clapped a hand to her mouth. 'But I haven't got anything for you,' she said.

He did not answer, but gave her a strange look which she chose to ignore. 'Aren't you going to ask me in?' he enquired.

Lorna hesitated. She was not expecting Gerald to call. He was busy with his hateful wife, she reflected.

'Come on in, then,' she said, 'since it's Christmas. Can I open this now, or must I wait until tomorrow?'

Don smiled. 'Open it now,' he said and watched as she wrestled with paper and string.

Inside Lorna found a small figurine – a shepherd boy made of china.

'Oh Don, it's beautiful!' she exclaimed. 'Oh dear – you shouldn't have! It must have cost a lot.'

'They're not cheap,' he admitted. 'So you like it?'

'Yes, I do.'

'Where will you put it then? What about the mantelpiece?'

'Oh . . .' She bit her lip. 'Perhaps I'd better not,' she said. 'He gets a bit jealous.'

'Does he?' Don was watching her closely. 'Why's that, I wonder?'

'Well, you know.'

'No, I don't.'

Lorna began to rewrap the present.

'Why should he get jealous?' persisted Don. 'He's not your husband. He's not in love with you and it's not his child.'

'No,' she said.

'Why should he get jealous then?'

'I don't know; he just does.' Too late, she remembered that Gerald had threatened Don's life.

'He's got a wife of his own,' said Don, never taking his eyes from her face. 'He should be glad if a young man takes an interest in you. He should be hoping for it.'

Lorna shrugged, afraid to speak in case she gave anything away by her tone of voice.

'So why isn't he?' said Don softly.

Lorna shook her head and her eyes beseeched him not to probe further.

'You needn't tell me,' said Don, 'because I know already.'

She stared at him, horrified, and shook her head.

'It's *his* child,' said Don, 'isn't it?'

'No.' Her voice was husky and so low it was barely audible.

'It is,' Don persisted. 'You can tell me – I'll keep it to myself.'

She shook her head.

'Then if it isn't, he would be pleased for you to have an admirer,' Don insisted. 'He won't mind at all if I call on you and bring you presents, because it's not his child and he's just doing his duty by you because of this other man.'

'Please, Don . . .' she faltered.

'Is it him, Lorna?'

'No.'

'Good. Then I can kiss you again.'

This time he held her for a long time and she did not resist as his lips moved over hers and his tongue crept between her teeth.

'Don't!' she begged weakly. 'You mustn't.'

She tried to pull away but he would not allow it. As his tongue probed deeper, his hands moved down her shoulders to her breasts and only then did she manage to draw back.

403

'Oh, please don't,' she repeated. 'I'm not very good at—'

'At saying "No"?' interposed Don. 'Oh, but you used to be! You never said anything else to me; I told you you'd enjoy it, but you wouldn't let me try. Is it different now?'

'Yes,' she whispered. 'I mean, no. I don't know what I mean. Don, you must go – he'll be so angry if he finds out.'

'But why will he be angry? I don't see that at all.'

She was silent again.

'I could come round as often as you like,' he said softly, 'and we could have wonderful times – you and me in bed together. Who's to say we can't? Who would know?'

'Don, I'd like to, but . . .' As she looked at him, he saw the longing in her eyes.

'I'm sorry about when I wouldn't,' she said, 'but now it's too late. He'd never forgive me and I can't do it to him; I can't hurt him. If he finds out you've been here . . .'

'How will he ever know?' asked Don reasonably. 'I shan't tell him and you won't say "No" to him because of me, will you? So how will he know? You like me, don't you? You like what I did?' His voice dropped. 'I can do a whole lot more than that. I promise you, you'll love it.'

He leaned nearer and put his lips to her ear. 'Don't you ever wonder what it's like with a younger man?'

She hesitated, knowing that she had wondered. 'Yes,' she confessed, 'but I don't want to talk about it. Things have changed now and I've got to say "No" to you whether I want to or not.'

But his presence, his words and the excitement were acting on her like strong wine. Her head swam and her senses reeled. She wanted him to stop talking and kiss her again, but she was afraid of what she would do and say if he did.

Don played his trump card. He moved slightly so that the gap between them widened, and then turned away.

'Well, I guess that's that, then,' he said with a sigh. 'We won't talk about it any more. What shall we talk about? Oh yes – I saw Clara at the station yesterday; I like her, she's got real spirit. She asked after you and I said I didn't really know because we're not together any more. She knew about your bit of trouble, of course.'

Lorna bit her lip. Don Leckie and Clara Midden! She

wanted to scream. Desperately, she closed her eyes to shut out the vision of Clara and Don with their arms around each other. She tried to see herself with dear, funny old Gerald. Yes, he was funny and he was old, but he was very dear to her. Gerald's roof was overhead and Gerald's child slept within her.

Abruptly she held out the present. 'Take it back,' she said. 'Honestly, I can't take it – it wouldn't be right. I've got my reasons, but I don't have to tell you. I'm really sorry, Don.'

But he would not take it back and seeing that his remarks about Clara had not had the desired effect, he quickly reverted to his earlier line of attack. 'I've always thought it would be you and me, Lorna,' he said. 'You know that, but we had that silly quarrel and then I went after Amy and you . . . well, this happened.' He sighed, his mood quite changed. 'It should have been you and me right from the start. We both made mistakes, but maybe it isn't too late?'

'It is too late,' she told him. 'You're right about everything, but it *is* too late.'

'Not if I still love you,' he persisted. 'Do you love me?'

'I can't say that. At least . . . I do, but . . . I love you both.'

'It *is* him, isn't it?'

She began to cry.

'He'll never be able to marry you, Lorna.'

'I know that.'

'I'm sorry,' he said. 'You're just a kid really. Look, I'm truly sorry – I shouldn't have said anything. I won't tell a soul. Oh, Lorna, love, please don't cry.' He put his arms round her as she sobbed. 'I swear I won't tell a soul. But – oh, God, Lorna. What are we to do? I must have time to think.'

She lifted her tear-stained face, cried, 'You can always marry Clara if she's got so much spirit!' and then went on sobbing.

'Who's Clara?' he said, stroking her hair. 'I was only teasing. I shouldn't have said that – it was stupid of me.'

'He loves me, Don, and he'll go on loving me. Nothing will change. It can never be you and me – and there's the baby, *his* baby.'

'Don't cry any more, Lorna. Please don't cry. I'll try and think of something. Just give me time; just say you love me.'

'I love you both!' she cried. 'I can't help it, I just do.'

There was a sound beyond the gate and Don looked up sharply and called out, 'Who's there?'

Lorna stopped crying and listened fearfully.

'Must have been my imagination,' said Don, pulling her close again. 'There's no one there.'

But he was wrong. Gerald Hatherley was there and he had seen them together.

*

Amy stared at the papers on the table in front of her and then glanced at the clock. She had been writing for just under three hours! Where had the time gone, she wondered in amazement. Counting the pages, she discovered that she had written seven foolscap sheets and with mounting excitement began to work out how many words she had written. Having found the average number of words on a line, she multiplied that by the number of lines on a page and then that total by seven.

'Two thousand and one hundred!' she whispered. 'Oh, Ralph!'

Earlier in the week, at Elliot's instigation, she had drawn up a very rough synopsis – chapter by chapter – and had sent it to him for his comments. Since posting it she had decided on a few amendments and had written another draft synopsis. Later, she was sure she would improve it further. Elliot had told her it would be a gradual process – 'a study in refinement' he had called it. She would write a first draft of the complete book to pull it all together and then, when satisfied with the overall form, she would write a second draft.

Sighing deeply, she closed her eyes and tried to conjure up Ralph's face but saw only the haunted eyes.

'Ralph!' she whispered. 'I can do it! I know I can do it. But I wish you were here; I wish it was still your book and I was helping you, the way it was.'

Yet even as Amy spoke, a doubt rose within her, a doubt that persisted to trouble her conscience. Of course she wished that Ralph was still alive and well. She would give anything to bring him back into her life, but would she willing relinquish the book? Now that she knew she could meet the challenge, could she bear to lose the opportunity? Guiltily she considered her feelings. Was wanting to write the book a disloyalty? Had she somehow taken advantage of Ralph's death? Surely not . . . but the uneasy feeling would not leave her and she knew that if she was to give the work her undivided attention, she must think this matter through to her own satisfaction. If she mentioned it to Elliot he would, she guessed, be genuinely astonished at such a line of thought. He had persuaded her to write it – no, he had bullied her into writing it. His words came back to her: 'Do it for me, do it for Ralph or do it for yourself.' Who was she writing it for and did it really matter? Her feelings were so confused. She wanted to please Elliot – it was all she could do to please him, she reflected ruefully. Equally, she wanted somehow to honour Ralph's memory. And then she wanted to prove to herself that she had a good brain and could use it – that she was not just 'Amy Turner, the station-master's daughter'. Not that she was ashamed of the title, but she wanted to be a person in her own right – not someone's daughter, not someone's sister, but herself.

Already she had written part of the introduction, and by the end of the afternoon she would have written more. One day she would see these words on the printed pages of a book. Smiling, she imagined Elliot's reaction when the biography was published; he would laugh triumphantly and say, 'I told you so' and she would not be able to argue with him. His parents, too, would be pleased that she had brought Ralph's work to fruition. A sudden thought occurred to her and she smiled with delight. Of course! She would dedicate the book to him. With a sigh of pleasure, she allowed herself a moment of self-congratulation as her doubts vanished. She would write the book for herself, but she would dedicate it to Ralph. Then she would deliver it into Elliot's capable hands.

Thinking about Elliot brought her once more face to face with another problem, and this was one which threatened to overwhelm her – the one thing that could ruin her future if she allowed it to do so. Because she loved Elliot Allan, he was therefore the one chink in her armour. It was ironic that she should have given her heart so completely to a man she hardly knew; a man who was no more than a business colleague; a man who did not need her and who kept her so determinedly at arm's length. Her extended stay in London had been very successful in many ways. Ralph's parents had proved warm-hearted and generous and had been so eager to talk with her about the last few months of Ralph's life. His mother had given her a photograph of him in a small silver frame as a keepsake. They had been sight-seeing and had been to a matinee of *Aida* at Covent Garden.

Elliot had been attentive, ebullient as ever and had seemed to enjoy her company. He had kissed her 'Goodbye' at the station when she left London, but it had been a quick friendly kiss. He had thanked her for the visit; it had done his parents 'a world of good', he told her, and he would come to Gaze-down in the near future to see how the book was going. Only his eyes had hinted at something deeper. He had kept his word and had visited her twice, staying overnight in The Lodge and eating in the local inn. He had been helpful professionally but restrained on a personal level.

Now, on the 28th of December, Christmas and Boxing Day were already memories. Amy had enjoyed them, but she was glad to return to The Lodge and the distraction of work. The New Year beckoned, but she viewed the prospect of 1901 with mixed feelings. Elliot did not love her — that much was apparent — and she had still to come to terms with the knowledge that she would never be more to him than a friend. What puzzled her was his relationship with Grace. Were they ever going to marry? Elliot's past was a mystery to her, at least where women were concerned. Had he had a disastrous love affair at some time, she wondered? He never spoke of anyone who might once have been close to him. Had he ever been married? Amy longed to ask him, but never would presume so far, arguing that if he wanted her to know he would tell her without prompting on her part. Was he *still* married? The unwelcome thought could not be entirely disregarded. Perhaps he had a wife who, like Ellen Turner, had abandoned him in favour of someone else. Amy could not imagine this, but she had the sense to admit that she was blind to any faults he might have. About her feelings for him, however, there was no doubt whatsoever in her mind; she loved him with every part of her being and in a way that she could never love anyone else. She remembered everything he had ever said to her, and the memory of his laughter brought an involuntary smile to her lips. She treasured the memory of her dance with him at Esme's ball, and the knowledge that once he had held her in his arms, when he had broken the news of Ralph's death.

However, it was clear that his parents expected him to marry Grace – she could draw no other conclusion – and doubtless hoped they would attend a wedding before they went back to India. Amy half-expected an invitation and the idea filled her with dread; she would open the envelope, would see their names together on the silver-edged card and then any hope she might secretly cherish would be finally dashed. It would be impossible for her to attend the wedding, so she would have to accept and then feign a last-minute illness.

With an effort, Amy pushed the unpalatable idea to the back of her mind and tried to concentrate on her writing. Scanning the sheets with unseeing eyes, she picked up the pen, dipped it into the ink and added another two lines. She thought again, took down a book from the shelf to find a reference and then wrote another line. Elliot's image would not be dismissed so easily, however, and finally she threw down the pen despondently.

'Elliot, I love you!' she whispered despairingly. 'Please don't marry Grace! I could make you happy if you would let me. I would care for you; I would love and honour you. My dearest, please don't marry Grace.'

What did it matter if she became a successful writer, she thought miserably, if there was no one with whom to share her life? No one to share the good news or make light of the disappointments? Success and money could not buy happiness and if she had to choose she would willingly forego public acclaim. A sense of desolation crept over her. Elliot would marry Grace and she was powerless to stop him.

Anger seized her suddenly and she screwed up the pages she had written and threw them into the basket.

'Write it yourself, Elliot!' she cried. 'Or talk your beloved Grace into writing it!'

Even as she uttered the words, she was ashamed. Grace loved him – it was written all over her face – and obviously had loved him for many years. What right had Amy to take him away?

Pushing back the chair, she stood up and moved over to stare out of the window. 'Hell and damnation!' she muttered and then laughed at her own foolishness. What use were words? They had no power to alter the situation and uttering them could not ease her heartache. She took a deep breath and squared her shoulders.

'Amy Turner, you are not the first woman to be crossed in love and you won't be the last,' she told herself. 'Stop wallowing in self-pity and get on with the book!'

Retrieving the crumpled sheets, she sat down at the table to smooth them out. When she had re-read them, she stared thoughtfully into space wondering how best to continue. At last she gave an almost imperceptible nod and her eyes narrowed in concentration as she searched her vocabulary for the words she wanted. Gradually, all thoughts of Elliot, Ralph and Grace were relegated to the farthest corner of her mind and Nigel Stanisbrooke filled the void, larger than life and as fascinating as ever. Amy began to write, slowly at first, but then faster. The minutes became hours as page after page surrendered to the inspired scratching of her pen and the only other sound was the ticking of the clock.

*

Not a mile away from The Lodge, Arnold's pipe was going out for the second time in five minutes. He took it from his mouth and frowned severely at the offending object in the forlorn hope that a stern look might somehow rekindle it. His mother, ironing nearby, watched surreptitiously and hoped he would soon lose interest in the wretched thing. Having a son in useful employment had disadvantages as well as advantages, and one of these was his adoption of a pipe which filled the cottage with foul-smelling smoke whenever he managed to keep it alight long enough to take a few puffs at it.

'Bloody thing!' said Arnold.

'Arnold!' she cried. His newly acquired bad language was another of the disadvantages. Lately he had used several words which he had never used before, all of which met with her strong disapproval.

'Your father,' she began, 'never—'

'Used a bad word in his life,' Arnold finished for her. He had heard it all before.

'No, he didn't, and if he could see you, he'd turn in his grave.'

Arnold had several ways of dealing with his recalcitrant pipe and now he tapped the bottom of the bowl on the wooden arm of the chair in which he sat 'reading' a copy of last week's newspaper. After tapping the pipe on both chair-arms, he squinted along the stem and then poked an exploratory finger into the bowl.

'You'll burn yourself one of these days,' she warned him, 'doing that.'

Arnold took no notice.

That was another way in which being employed had changed him, his mother thought uneasily. He took a lot less notice of her than he had done previously, which caused her more concern that she cared to admit.

With a loud sigh of exasperation, Arnold laid down the pipe and began to examine the lid of the tobacco tin in case a clue might be found there as to why the tobacco consistently malfunctioned.

'Old Holborn,' he muttered, tracing the words with his finger. His tone was puzzled. Mr Drury smoked Old Holborn and in *his* pipe the tobacco stayed alight and gave out satisfying puffs of smoke. Mr Drury was Arnold's current hero and, according to Arnold's mother, if Mr Drury chose to jump off Beachy Head Arnold would follow him over without a second thought.

'Bloody thing,' he repeated, his tone aggressive, daring his mother to remonstrate with him.

'Arnold!' she cried again. 'What did I tell you?'

411

'It keeps going out,' he complained. 'I keep lighting it and it keeps going out.'

'Give it up, then, ' she suggested. 'You know it makes you cough.'

But he appeared not to have heard and now attempted to clean out the pipe's stem with a pipe-cleaner. He pushed so hard that most of the tobacco was jerked out of the bowl and fell into his lap. Painstakingly Arnold picked it all up and coaxed it back into the bowl, his lips moving all the while in soundless entreaty. With a large thumb, he pressed it well in and squinted again through the pipe's stem.

His mother shook out a pillowcase and spread it out on the ironing blanket.

'You'll never get the hang of it, Arnold,' she assured him. 'It's a knack, pipe-smoking, and you haven't got it. My Uncle Bert, now he *could* smoke a pipe! Never had no trouble, he didn't, keeping it going. Not that it did him much good, poor old Bert. Fell asleep, he did, and set fire to the bed. But, he could always manage a pipe. He had quite a collection of pipes – he used to show them to me if I'd been good when we visited. Several clay pipes, he had, but they weren't quite so special. Oh yes, and briars, of course. And one that was all carved – a meerschaum or something, that one was.' She turned the pillowcase deftly and began to iron the other side. 'He even had one made from bone – won it in a bet, he did. Let me see now . . . oh, yes. One was a sort of china, only it had a name beginning with "p". I never could remember that name, but I remember the pipe. Very pretty and all smooth it was. Mind you, I never saw him smoke it. Too valuable, I expect.'

Arnold said, 'Waiting room starts with a double-you.'

'Oh, not that again, Arnold.'

'Gentleman starts with a gee,' her son declared.

She tutted, folded the pillowslip and took another from the pile, while Arnold took a box of matches from his pocket and prepared to relight his pipe. Match after match was struck and either went out prematurely or burnt his fingers, but his patience and determination were rewarded and at last everything worked. Finally the pipe was alight. Arnold sucked noisily and was able to send a large wreath of white smoke ceilingward. A broad grin spread over his face but when he inhaled again, the smoke caught him unawares and set him coughing. Doubled up, he heaved and spluttered, eyes streaming, while his mother tried to hide her satisfaction, her gaze firmly fixed on the ironing. When at last he stopped coughing, the pipe had gone out again.

Arnold sighed and began once more to tap it on the corner of his chair. On Monday, he decided, when he went back to work, he would watch Mr Drury very carefully and see exactly how it was done.

*

The kitchen at Bates Manor was rarely a quiet place, but on that same afternoon, at five minutes to 4 o'clock, the silence was deafening as Mrs Lester and Izzie stared open-mouthed at Clara.

'Locked himself in?' echoed the cook. 'What on earth are you talking about, Clara?'

'I'm telling you,' Clara insisted. 'The door is well and truly locked and the key must be on the inside.'

'Ooer!' cried Izzie, her fingers going to her mouth.

Mrs Lester closed the oven door and straightened up without taking her eyes from Clara's face. 'And is the master inside?' she asked. 'Are you certain sure?'

'Well, of course he is!' cried Clara. 'At least, somebody's in there. Somebody's moving around in there and it can't be anyone else.'

'Lord love us!' exclaimed Mrs Lester, sinking on to a stool. 'Now I wonder what he's up to? Did you knock at the door?'

Clara nodded. 'And I called out, but he didn't answer. I knocked again – he must have heard me – but he just ignored me.'

'Perhaps he's gone deaf,' suggested Izzie.

Clara gave her a withering glance. 'So why would he lock himself in?' she asked. 'My guess is that he's drinking to drown his sorrows.'

'What sorrows?' Mrs Lester demanded. 'Just past Christmas, the time of good cheer and glad tidings, with the New Year coming and all that.'

'Yes,' said Clara, 'but you know how he's been since

413

Christmas Eve. Barely spoke on Christmas Day and snapped my head off yesterday for no good reason.'

'Hardly spoke at all,' said the cook. 'I thought they'd had words.'

'Perhaps they had,' said Clara. 'He's been so cheerful lately, but now he's gone all moody again. I suppose the mistress being a bit queer doesn't help — bound to depress him, when you come to think of it.'

Mrs Lester looked at her doubtfully. 'He's never locked himself in before though,' she said. 'Leastways, not to my knowledge. I wonder if we should tell the mistress? I mean, he is her husband.'

Clara looked at her anxiously. 'I know, but she's having her afternoon nap and if I wake her up with news like that . . .' She left the sentence unfinished and Mrs Lester nodded as Clara also sat down at the table; she went on, 'If he *is* drinking, then there's nothing we can do about it. I mean, it's not our business really, is it? I suppose eventually he'll just sober up and come out.'

'But you'd think he would answer when you knock,' replied Mrs Lester. 'Even if he just said "Go away" or "Leave me alone" or something. I don't like the sound of it at all. Perhaps if *I* was to knock? Make out I had to ask him something — about the dinner tonight?'

Clara looked hopeful. 'That's a good idea. What could you ask him?'

They all thought hard and Izzie said, 'Ask him which wine he wants.'

'Good idea!' cried Clara, surprised.

'She's not so daft, our Izzie,' said the cook and Izzie blushed with pleasure.

After further deliberation, they all trooped upstairs and, while Izzie and Clara waited at the far end of the passage, Mrs Lester approached the study, smoothing her apron with nervous fingers. She paused at the door to straighten her cap and tuck in a stray lock of hair.

'Go on!' hissed Clara impatiently.

Mrs Lester tapped gently on the study door and said, 'Mr Hatherley, sir?'

414

There was no response. Clara called, 'He'll never hear that. Knock a bit louder!'

The second knock also failed to elicit any acknowledgement. 'Sir?' Mrs Lester called loudly. 'Are you there, sir?'

There was still no reply, so Izzie and Clara joined the cook outside the study door.

'Are you all right, sir?' cried Mrs Lester.

'Mr Hatherley? Is anything wrong?'

'Ooer,' said Izzie, looking frightened. 'Perhaps it's not him, perhaps it's a burglar.'

'Not very likely,' said Clara. 'Burglars break in at night, not in the middle of the day.'

'It is getting dark though,' whispered Mrs Lester. 'It would be awful if we were standing here like this and then the master came up the stairs behind us—' She broke off in alarm as a sudden thud came from inside the study.

Clara banged on the door with her fist. 'Sir? Answer me, *please!* Are you all right? Is it you in there?' Silence greeted this appeal.

'Perhaps he's fallen down,' said Izzie, who was still holding the potato peeler. 'Perhaps he's so drunk he's fallen over!'

They all looked at each other, dismayed and uncertain.

'Well, I don't know what to suggest,' said Mrs Lester. 'What time is the mistress likely to wake up from her nap? Could we wait until then and tell her? What else can we do?'

Clara was frowning as another idea formed in her brain. 'The window!' she said. 'We could put a ladder up to the window and see what's happening.'

Izzie's nervousness increased. 'I'm not going up it,' she told them. 'I get all funny if I go up high – and anyway, he might see me and think we're spying on him.'

'We would be,' said Mrs Lester. 'It would be a sort of spying.'

'But if he's drunk,' Clara reasoned slowly, 'he'd hardly be expecting anyone to look in at a first-floor window, would he? What if one of us stays here knocking on the door, so that he'd still be looking in that direction and then he might not notice someone peeping in at the window. We only need

415

a couple of seconds, just to make sure and then if he's drunk and not ill, we needn't worry about him.'

'Perhaps he's gone mad,' suggested Izzie darkly.

'No one's gone mad, girl!' snapped the cook. 'Don't you dare say things like that, or you'll get a clout and quick!'

Izzie's expression became sulky. 'Well, *she's* gone mad! Everyone says so.'

They stared at her. 'Who says she's gone mad?' cried Clara.

Izzie shrugged. 'Well, her mother went mad, so why shouldn't she?'

'Who says so?' Clara demanded.

'The postman. He heard it from Mrs Betts, who heard it from Tim Bagg whose brother used to be coachman to Mrs Hatherley's family. So there!'

The last two words earned her the threatened clout and she began to wail noisily. 'You get yourself downstairs!' cried Mrs Lester. 'And we'll have a lot less of your cheek in future.'

Izzie was half-way along the passage when the bedroom door opened and Esme appeared, wearing a dark blue kimono over her nightdress. Her hair was tousled and her expression vague. Clara thought uneasily about Izzie's revelation.

'All this noise!' said Esme, one hand held to her head. 'How am I supposed to rest?'

Clara thought rapidly. 'I'm so sorry, ma'am,' she said, taking Esme by the arm. 'It was just Izzie. You come back to bed now and I'll tuck you in. You know what the doctor said.'

'What's the matter with Izzie—' Esme began but Clara, with a meaningful jerk of her head to the others, steered her mistress firmly back into her bedroom. Izzie and Mrs Lester took the hint and hurried thankfully downstairs while Clara coaxed Esme back to bed, insisting that a full two hours' sleep each afternoon was what the doctor had ordered.

'And we want you better as quickly as possible,' Clara told her, smiling cheerfully, 'so I have to see that you get your rest. Or is it beauty sleep? You know what they say – good looks and good health go hand in hand!'

This appeal to Esme's vanity had the desired effect and

416

she allowed herself to be tucked up in bed again. Clara decided that she would not tell her mistress of her husband's strange behaviour unless it proved to be really necessary. If Izzie's revelation was true, then Esme must be treated with great care and not pushed further along that particular dark path. If her mistress ever became too sick for Clara to handle, she would lose her job and that prospect did not appeal at all.

When she was satisfied that Esme would soon be asleep again, Clara tiptoed out of the bedroom and went downstairs to rejoin the others in the kitchen. Having decided that Izzie should 'stand watch' so that they could not be surprised by anyone who chanced to come to the house, they sent her outside with instructions to delay anybody who came along with a story about a lost ring which might be on the drive and must not be trodden on or driven over. Meanwhile Mrs Lester and Clara went to the gardener's shed and selected the longest ladder, which they knew would reach the window because the gardener himself used it when he cleaned the windows.

The ladder was heavy, but finally they managed to prop it up against the back of the house so that the top rung was immediately below the study window.

'I'll go up,' Clara offered. 'You keep your foot on the bottom rung and steady it for me. I don't want to fall off!' Nimbly, she climbed the ladder until she was level with the window and, leaning carefully sideways, she looked into the room.

'Oh, God!' she whispered.

Gerald was sprawled in an armchair, a bottle of whisky in one hand and a glass in the other. Several other bottles stood on the floor beside him. He stared ahead of him, oblivious to his surroundings as tears rolled down his face, his nose was running, his collar was undone and so was his tie.

'You poor old basket!' whispered Clara. 'Now what's upset you, I wonder?'

She went back down the ladder and told Mrs Lester what she had seen. 'He's drunk as a lord,' she said, 'but at least we know he's not ill. I suppose there's nothing much we can do about it — not up to us to tell him what he can and can't do in his own house.'

'But when the mistress gets up — if she asks where he is?'

'I suggest we know nothing about it,' said Clara. 'We can say he's in the study and we think he's working. If he still hasn't come out, then she'll have to discover that he's locked himself in and then it's up to her.'

'I suppose so.' Mrs Lester was not entirely happy.

'Have you got a better idea?'

The cook had to admit that she had not.

'Right, then. I'll fetch Izzie and we'll all just carry on as usual.'

When Clara walked down the drive, she found Izzie in earnest consultation with Amy Turner, who was looking rather bewildered.

'What is she talking about?' Amy asked. 'She says she's lost her ring.'

'Well, I have,' cried Izzie. 'Haven't I, Clara?'

''Course you have,' said Clara, giving her a broad wink. 'Now go on back to the kitchen and Mrs Lester will tell you all about it. I'll explain to Amy.' She turned to Amy. 'There isn't really a ring,' she began.

Izzie looked indignant. 'But you said to pretend—'

'I didn't mean you had to pretend to Amy,' said Clara. 'I only meant strangers, but not to worry.'

Izzie went off in a slight huff and Clara described what was happening. Amy had called in to deliver a message from Tim Hollis, and was then on her way to the Leckies' farm.

'How are you liking it here?' Amy asked her. 'Living in, I mean? Tim is convinced you'll get fed up with it.'

'Poor Tim,' said Clara. 'Actually, I'm enjoying it. It's nice not to have to cycle backwards and forwards — especially with winter here — but apart from that, I've got a lovely big room of my own and it's better money so I can put a bit by. Tim didn't want me to come, I know, but a girl's got to keep her eye on the main chance. I said to him, you won't stay at Gazedown Station all your life. He'll move on if he wants promotion, which he does. Men are all the same; it's all right for them, but we're not supposed to rock any boats.'

Amy grinned. 'I thought once that we might be hearing wedding bells for you and Tim.'

Clara grimaced. 'Well, you thought wrong, Amy Turner! Men are the very devil, if you want my opinion, and I've better things to do with my life than wait hand and foot on some man. I'll wait on her ladyship, but I'm appreciated and I'm getting *paid* for my trouble and that's the big difference. I wouldn't give you tuppence for a husband and that's the gospel truth!' She laughed at her own vehemence and changed the subject by asking Amy about her work.

'The book?' said Amy. 'I think it's going quite well. Elliot is a great help, of course.'

She thought she had managed to control the tone of her voice when she spoke his name, but Clara was very perceptive and gave her a quizzical look.

'Perhaps the wedding bells will be yours?' she said slyly.

Amy shook her head. 'Oh, no! There's nothing at all between us. We're good friends and I must admit I do find him very attractive, but ... there's a woman in his life already.'

'What did I tell you?' cried Clara triumphantly. 'Men really are the very devil!'

When Amy left the Manor half an hour later, the riddle of the locked study was still unresolved.

*

Soon after Amy's departure, Gerald Hatherley unlocked the study door and stumbled out into the passage. He was very drunk and very unhappy and the only coherent thought he could retain for any length of time was one concerning Don Leckie. In his confusion, he clung to that thought because then he knew what he must do and that made everything much easier. It gave him a purpose.

'I've got to kill Don Leckie,' he muttered. 'I've got to kill him!'

He paused on the landing, swaying on his feet, his mind working slowly. Killing meant shooting and shooting meant guns. He frowned. Guns! After long deliberation, he began to nod his head as he remembered that his shotgun hung over the mantelpiece in the dining-room, and he made his way slowly and silently downstairs. Knowing even in his bemused state that he must not be seen taking the gun from the dining-room he listened carefully to establish the whereabouts of his wife (who was still asleep) and the staff who were in the kitchen. He staggered into the dining-room, took down the gun and loaded it. Then he stole out of the front door before anyone was aware that he had gone.

Chapter Twenty-Four

Standing at the cottage window, Lorna was watching the daylight fade as a heavy night mist settled over the landscape. Straining her eyes into the gloom, she saw only the outline of the bare trees, for the mist shrouded hedges and gates and nothing moved. She shuddered, drew the curtains together and turned back to the room where a fire blazed in the small hearth. A fire, she thought bitterly, which she had lit from kindling wood she had chopped for herself and coal she had carried in from the store outside. She had also pumped up water for the sink and done all those other jobs which should be done by the man about the house. Since Don had called in on Christmas Eve she had spoken to no one, and for her Christmas Day had passed slowly in a haze of self-pity because Gerald the provider, Gerald the father of her unborn child, had not called in as promised.

There had been no expensive presents, no champagne, no toast to the future and no love-making. Christmas had proved a fiasco and she blamed Gerald for it. She had gone to infinite pains to cook the chicken and all the vegetables and had been too angry to eat alone; she had waited hourly for Gerald to arrive and he had not come. By 4 o'clock the dinner was spoiled and she had served a plateful for herself and then let it go cold.

Two presents, from her mother and Janet, were opened at 6 o'clock – a hand-knitted scarf from her sister and matching gloves from her mother. Later the fire had gone out and, too miserable to relight it, she had gone to bed at half-past seven and cried herself to sleep.

By the morning of Boxing Day Lorna had convinced herself that Gerald had not bothered to visit her humble home because he had abandoned her in favour of Clara. She reasoned that if Don Leckie found Clara attractive, Gerald might also. After another miserable day, she had gone to bed deeply depressed, but this morning her waking emotion had been one of alarm. For the first time it occurred to her that something might have happened to him: he was either ill or dead and she would never see him again. She had waited in a fever of anxiety all day, hoping to hear his footsteps. Guilty and afraid, she now wished most fervently that she had not taken Don Leckie into her confidence. Everything was going wrong and she had no one to whom she could turn. If only she had gone to Janet's for Christmas — but she had only herself to blame.

'Where are you, Gerald?' she muttered, hugging her shawl more tightly round her shoulders. 'Why don't you come to me?' It was so quiet in the cottage that her voice became an intrusion. She wished wholeheartedly that she *had* gone to Robertsbridge and thought wistfully how much fun it would have been. Putting her right hand on her abdomen, she spoke to the baby.

'Your father, baby, is a no-good, rotten devil, you know that? Well, he is. I'm telling you. He said he'd come Christmas Day and he didn't. He didn't come yesterday either and he hasn't come today. He's deserted us, baby. He's left us stuck here in this lonely place . . .'

This reminded her that the cottage was unsecured and it was dark outside, so she made a hasty tour of the house to lock and bolt the doors and check that the windows were still fastened. Having done this, she then remembered that she had not refilled the coal-scuttle, a job she preferred to do in daylight. Only a few knobs of coal remained, so she threw these on to the fire and then reluctantly prepared to go outside. Standing on the back doorstep she hesitated, listening nervously to the drip of water from the trees and the small animal sounds from the countryside around her that were never completely silenced.

'Gerald Hatherley, I hate you!' she whispered fiercely as she stepped forward and the mist closed round her, damp and chill. She had reached the shed and was shovelling coal into the scuttle when a noise startled her. The shovel dropped from her hand and she gasped fearfully, peering into the gloom.

'Who is it?' she cried.

Gerald's voice came thickly. 'Where is he? I'm going to kill the young swine!'

'Gerald? Is it you?' Her heart hammered with relief and all her bitterness melted. 'Where are you?'

He appeared out of the gloom and as he moved into the light from the open doorway she saw that he was carrying a shotgun. He looked so haggard that she hardly recognised him.

'Gerald!' she faltered. 'What's happened? Why are you — oh, my God, Gerald . . .'

He staggered forward, keeping his balance with an effort. 'Where's Leckie?' he demanded. 'I told you I'd kill him and I will.'

With a stifled scream, Lorna backed away into the kitchen. Terrified, she slammed the door and tried to bolt it but her fingers would not function properly and he threw his weight against it. Her mind was frozen with fear and she could not think clearly. The door burst open and Gerald came into the room; in spite of her terror, she felt a rush of compassion.

'Oh, my poor Gerald!' she cried. 'What's happened to you? I don't understand.'

His eyes were swollen, his face puffy, his bald head gleamed damply and his remaining hair stuck out spikily, making him look ridiculous. His clothes were dishevelled and he breathed stertorously as he stood before her swaying, the shotgun pointing directly at her.

'Oh, Gerald!' Lorna begged. 'Put the gun down and tell me what's the matter. You look so ill. Have you been drinking? Is that it?'

Ignoring these remarks, Gerald looked round the room. 'Where is he?' he muttered. 'I know he's here. I saw you together — both of you. I warned you . . .'

'Saw us together?'

'You and young Leckie. I'm going to kill him . . .'

Her mind was clearing rapidly and she knew at once what

423

had happened. Christmas Eve when she had been so upset and Don had held her in his arms! That noise they had heard had been Gerald. 'Oh, God,' she thought frantically, 'how much did he see and hear?'

'He's hiding,' said Gerald. 'He is, isn't he?' He looked on the point of collapse.

'No, no,' cried Lorna. 'There's no one here – there's *been* no one. I've been on my own, God's honour! Oh, Gerald, do put that down; it might go off. Gerald, please! You're frightening me.'

Gerald moved unsteadily towards the foot of the stairs, tripped on the edge of the rug and fell heavily. His fingers tightened on the trigger, there was a shattering explosion and Lorna screamed as all the glass in the window flew out into the night. Gerald picked himself up and reached for the shotgun. As he turned his reddened eyes towards her, he looked like a wounded animal.

'Oh, Gerald!' she pleaded. 'Please don't be like this. I promise you there's no one here, only me. I've been waiting and waiting for you. Please stop all this, Gerald. Please love me. This is all so terrible.'

'He was holding you – in his arms,' said Gerald. 'In his arms! He's got to – I've got to . . .' His legs buckled under him and he almost fell again.

Lorna moved slowly towards him, hiding her fear with an effort. 'Sit down, Gerald, you're tired,' she coaxed. 'Sit and rest and then we'll talk about it. Put down the silly old gun and we'll have a cuddle like we always do. Just you and me and our little boy? Just the three of us!'

Gerald shook his head and the muzzle of the gun rose fractionally so that it pointed towards her heart. She saw his hands tremble and knew that she was very near to death.

Swallowing, she took a step back and raised her hands, palms towards him, until they were level with her shoulders. 'Don't shoot me,' she whispered hoarsely. 'I don't think I deserve to die. I thought you loved me!'

He shook his head again, sighed deeply and then sank down into the armchair, where he rested the gun across his knees and closed his eyes wearily.

'You and Leckie . . .' he whispered. 'How could you?'

'No!' she cried. 'He hasn't been here — except that once and then I didn't ask him to come. I . . . I told him I only loved *you*. I said I was fond of you, that you'd been so kind and everything. Oh, Gerald, don't spoil everything. Let him go — if you shoot him, they'll hang you.'

But something she had said seemed to give him new strength and he stood up again. 'I'll find him,' he said. 'I'll find him and I'll kill him and he won't come here again!'

Lorna watched with her fingers crossed, as he made his way upstairs — cursing, breathing heavily, stumbling as he went. She heard him fling open the doors and it seemed an age before he came down again.

'Gerald . . .' she began but he pushed past her restraining hand and without a word stumbled blindly out into the night.

*

At Bates Manor it was after 5 pm when Clara found the study door open and they realised that Gerald had somehow left the house unobserved. At first they were not unduly alarmed, but then Esme demanded to know where he was and Clara felt in duty bound to tell her about his earlier behaviour. When it was discovered that the shotgun was missing from above the mantelpiece, Esme decided to telephone the police. She explained to the sergeant that she thought he should know that her husband was wandering around in the dark with a gun which might or might not be loaded, adding hesitantly, that he was depressed and had been drinking. She thought he might intend to kill himself, but she kept that fear to herself.

*

Amy had called in at the farm and had spent half an hour with Mary Leckie. She left at a quarter to six and began to walk home. The darkness was intense by this time, but Mary had lent her a lantern. As she walked, she had forgotten the incident at the Manor and was thinking about Lord Stanisbrooke. If she had spared a thought for Gerald Hatherley, she would have imagined him in the study behind the locked door and was therefore quite unprepared to see him emerge suddenly from a nearby gate as she approached the level crossing. He carried a gun, which made her heart lurch uncomfortably, and he blinked owlishly at her in the lantern light.

'I want Leckie!' he said, his tone flat. 'I want . . .' He leaned forward and she could smell the whisky on his breath.

'Who's that?' he demanded. 'Who are you?'

'Amy Turner from the station,' she said quietly, her mind whirling.

He shook his head. 'Have you seen him? Have you seen Leckie?'

'No, I haven't.'

'You're lying!' he cried, with terrible despair. 'Everyone is lying to me.'

'No! I'm telling you the truth,' she assured him. Surprisingly, she felt no fear, only pity. Whatever had made him cry had driven him to this, but how Don Leckie figured in the drama she had no idea. 'I've just come from the farm,' she said, 'and he wasn't there.'

Gerald moved threateningly towards her. 'You're all lying. You – Lorna – Esme. You think you can fool me but you can't, you see. Oh no! I'm not fooled. I'm not so—' Abruptly he swung round, pointing the shotgun towards the open gate through which he had just appeared. 'Who's there?' he cried. 'It's you, Leckie – I know it is!'

'There's no one there,' said Amy.

Ignoring her, he took a few more steps until he was standing right in the gateway. 'Come out of there,' he mumbled, 'and take what's coming to you.' He swayed unsteadily and Amy thought he was going to fall. 'Mr Hatherley,' she said, 'believe me, there's no one there.'

He did not even turn his head, but stepped through the gateway into the field to be swallowed up by the darkness.

Amy hesitated. She wondered if she should try to keep an eye on him – or should she run for the sergeant? Suppose she left him and someone else came along? And was the shotgun loaded? She had no way of knowing. And where exactly was Don? Suppose he were to blunder along? If the gun was loaded, Gerald Hatherley would almost certainly kill him.

426

Reluctantly, she decided to stay and keep an eye on him. Calling his name, she followed him into the meadow where Sam had played so often.

'Dear God,' she whispered, 'don't let anything terrible happen. Please help me!'

Ahead of her she could hear Gerald making his way across the grass, mumbling incoherently and calling Don's name, but she fancied he sounded tired. She followed at what she hoped was a safe distance, hoping against hope that he would collapse with exhaustion or the effects of too much alcohol.

Suddenly she stopped and listened. Something was approaching across the field from the direction of the main road – a heifer, perhaps. Any hopes she might have cherished on that score were soon dashed, for Gerald Hatherley had obviously heard it too and he now called out Don's name.

Don's voice answered from the darkness, surprised. 'Yes. Who the devil's that?'

Amy screamed. 'Run, Don! Run back, for God's sake!' but her warning came too late and the shattering blast drowned her words as Gerald fired.

She felt her legs go weak with panic as she began to run forward, crying, 'Don! Are you all right? Oh, my God, where are you? I can't *see*.'

Ahead of her the figure of Gerald Hatherley materialised suddenly, but just at that moment she tripped and fell heavily in the wet grass. For a moment the impact of her fall drove all the breath from her lungs, but as soon as she recovered she screamed Don's name again. Scrambling to her feet, she picked up the lantern which was still alight and ran a few steps towards the place where she imagined him to be. There was no sound and she thought, 'He's dead! Don's dead and I shall have to go back and tell Mary.'

'Please God,' she prayed, 'let him live. Oh, don't let him die!' Suddenly the breath was knocked out of her a second time as she collided with Gerald Hatherley. The lantern fell and this time the flame was extinguished.

'You've killed him,' she sobbed.

Gerald's hands closed round her arm as he swayed and

nearly fell. 'I had to do it,' he told her thickly. 'I had to kill him. It was Lorna, you see. My little Lorna!'

'You had no right!' she cried. 'Whatever he had done, you didn't have to kill him!' She tried to shake herself free but he clung on grimly, insisting that he had only done what was necessary and right.

Amy struggled to prise away his fingers, but desperation had given him alarming strength. At that moment, however, they heard another voice. Amy saw the faint gleam of a lantern.

'What's going on,' cried a deep voice. 'This is the police! Are you there, Mr Hatherley? Are you all right?'

Gerald took fright and putting an arm round Amy's waist, he clapped one hand over her mouth. Holding her in an iron grip, he began to drag her across the field. The sergeant repeated his questions, but no one answered them. Amy struggled wildly, but without effect. She guessed Gerald was trying to reach the safety of the wood, but it came to her suddenly that between the gate and the wood lay the pond. Surely they were heading for the pond! Even as the thought flashed through her mind he tripped and they were both falling backwards. His hand left her mouth, but before she had a chance to scream or even to take a breath the cold water closed over her and she felt weed around her legs – and then, as she went down, it was tangling round her hands, face and neck . . . a thousand slimy cords which threatened to hold her in the cold, black depths for ever. Her lungs were bursting as she fought down her panic, desperately hoping that perhaps the water would eventually thrust her upwards again if she did not emmesh herself too tightly in the weeds by thrashing out in all directions. Surely enough, she found herself moving up; her head surfaced and she drew in long welcome gulps of air. Somewhere in the darkness towards the centre of the pond she heard a swirl of water and then Gerald's voice crying out – a frighteningly brief sound that was cut off abruptly.

'Mr Hatherley!' she cried fearfully. 'Where are you?'

There was no answer. Then, to her immense relief, the glimmer of a lantern appeared and she could make out the sergeant and see that he was standing at the edge of the pond, only a few yards away. He held out his hand to grasp hers and minutes later she was huddled on dry land, her whole body shivering, her teeth clenched to keep them from chattering. There was a warmth on her cheeks and she realised that hot tears were trickling down her face. Tears of weakness or shock or grief? She did not know. She only knew that she was still alive and was immeasurably grateful. The policeman took off his jacket and put it around her shoulders. But Don Leckie – what had happened to him?

'There was an accident . . .' she told the sergeant shakily. 'Don Leckie – I think he's been shot.'

'Christ Almighty!' he began.

'And Mr Hatherley went in the pond with me. I think he may be—'

'Jesus wept!' Sergeant Tully could scarcely comprehend further tragedy.

Just then there was a sound behind them and the figure of Don Leckie scrambled towards them out of the darkness.

'Help me!' he moaned, collapsing on the grass.

The distraught sergeant stared helplessly from Don to Amy and then past her to the pond. He could do with assistance, but none was likely to be forthcoming.

'Are you all right for a moment?' he asked Amy and she nodded. 'I'll just take a look at this poor laddie, then,' he said, kneeling beside Don's prostrate form.

With a supreme effort, Amy forced herself to follow him. 'He's not dead, is he?' she whispered as the policeman held Don's wrist.

'No, he's not dead. Leastways, he's still got a pulse, but he's bleeding like a stuck pig. What the hell was it?'

'A shotgun,' said Amy. Her voice trembled as shock set in and a great weariness seized her. She wanted to lie down and sleep where she was, but the luxury was to be denied her.

'Can you walk, do you reckon?' asked the policeman. 'Now, which way's nearest? We'd best carry him to the railway station and ask your father to telephone the doctor. If we don't get him to a doctor soon, I don't reckon he's going to make it.'

Amy never knew how she managed the few hundred yards

home, but somehow they got there. Don was only semi-conscious, but fortunately the darkness had spoiled Gerald's aim and he had not taken the full impact of the blast – had that happened, he would never have survived. As it was the left side of his face, left shoulder and arm were raw and bleeding and there was a small wound dangerously near his eye.

When the doctor arrived he sent Amy straight to bed with a sleeping draught and issued strict instructions to Ellen that she was to have two full days' complete rest in bed. Don was taken in the doctor's brougham to the cottage hospital, while the police sergeant returned to the pond to satisfy himself that Gerald Hatherley had not survived. It would be impossible to drag the pond before daylight without putting other lives at risk he decided, cursing his luck.

'Why today of all days?' he asked himself.

He had woken with a bad headache which had persisted all day. Add to that a touch of indigestion and his misery was complete. Reluctantly, he squared his shoulders and prepared to visit the Leckies at Hope's Farm with news of their son's accident. Then he would go to Bates Manor to break the news of Mr Hatherley's presumed death to Mrs Hatherley. It was a bad do, he reflected grimly – a bloody bad do! How it had all come about was a mystery, but he assumed that further enquiries would bring some enlightenment. The next few hours would not be at all pleasant and he then had a long and difficult report to write. It would be midnight, he thought resignedly, before he finally laid his aching head on the pillow.

*

When Amy opened her eyes, the sun was streaming in through the tiny attic window and she could hear a train outside. Which train was it and what was the time? It was a few seconds before the terrible events of the previous evening crowded back into her mind, and then she sat up with a start. Was Don Leckie recovering and how had Mary and Jim taken the news of his accident? Had they found Mr Hatherley's body? Sliding out of bed, she ran to the window and peered down at the scene below. Pure white steam drifted

430

upwards from the engine. It was at the up platform, so it must be either the 11.35 or the 1.07.

Had she slept all morning then? She recognised the back of Mr Bell's head as he conferred with her father – no doubt discussing the tragedy, she thought. It would be all over Gazedown by now. Several passengers were alighting and seeing Mrs Betts amongst them Amy recalled Lorna's predicament and wondered what effect Mr Hatherley's death would have on her. Further along the platform Tim Hollis was loading a selection of parcels and wooden crates into the guard's van. Harry Coombes appeared from the direction of the waiting-room and began to close the carriage doors.

Just then the bedroom door opened gently and Ellen put her head round it. Seeing Amy awake, she smiled broadly.

'Oh you are awake!' she said, coming into the room. 'Mary's downstairs to see you, but I told her you hadn't woken up yet.'

'Is Don all right, do you know?'

Ellen nodded reassuringly. 'He's going to be,' she said. 'Amy . . .' she hesitated.

'What is it?'

'Amy, I just want you to know – that is, I just want to say that . . . Oh Amy, you mean so much to me! If you'd been killed—'

Amy could see that her mother was under great stress. 'It's all right,' she said quickly. 'I know.'

'No, you don't know!' cried Ellen. 'How *can* you know that I love you when I left you the way I did? You must think – oh Amy, I don't know how to explain, but you're a woman now and not a child. Can you possibly understand how things were for me? I saw my life slipping away – I saw John as my lifeline. I was selfish, I know, but sometimes it's hard to know what to do for the best. You see a ray of light in the clouds – at least, you think it's a ray of light . . .' She was fighting back the tears. 'I just want you to know that it cost me a great deal to leave you and Sam. It was a terrible decision and I hope you never have to make such a choice. Now I can see that I did wrong; I made the wrong decision.'

'Did you?' responded Amy quietly. 'Maybe you had to

431

find out. Maybe if you hadn't gone, you would always have wondered.'

Ellen stared at her. 'I don't know,' she stammered. 'I only know that I didn't want to hurt you. I've never dared ask if you've forgiven me, and I don't suppose you ever will. It was a terrible thing – and then poor Ma-in-law dying. I've suffered so much . . . but that's only fair. I caused so much pain to you and Sam and your father—'

Amy took her hand. 'Ma, it's over now,' she said gently. 'It's all in the past. I don't know the answers, but we're all together now and I think we ought to bury the past. I'm glad you told me that you love me. And I think one day you should tell Sam, so that he knows too. And Toby is a dear little boy – you cannot wish the past undone, or you would not have Toby! Oh Ma, come here! I love you, of course I do!'

The two women hugged each other and Ellen cried with relief. When she was once more in control, she smiled shakily.

'Well, I'd best send Mary up to you and then I'll get you something to eat. You must be hungry. Do you fancy eggs and bacon?'

'Is it Sunday? I'm in such a daze.'

'No, but it'll be your lunch as well.'

So it was the 1.07, thought Amy. A lot must have happened while she was sleeping, and she was not sorry to have missed it.

Mary came bustling into the room and across to the bed, where she flung her arms round Amy and hugged her fiercely.

'You are the most wonderful girl!' she cried breathlessly. 'I love you, d'you hear me? If it hadn't been for you, Don would have been killed!' She sat down heavily on the end of the bed, making the whole bedstead creak protestingly. 'Oh, you needn't deny it,' she went on. 'He's told me all about it – how you warned him and everything. He says he was just turning away after you cried out when the gun went off. My godfathers, Amy, if old Hatherley wasn't dead already I'd strangle the old fool with my own bare hands. Drunk as a lord, they say. Oh, what a carry-on this morning, police everywhere—'

'Don really is going to be all right?' Amy persisted. 'Really all right?'

Mary's expression changed slightly. 'Yes,' she said, 'and no. Well, I don't want to think about it, but they removed some shot from near his eye—'

'Oh, no, Mary!'

'Don't say it like that, Amy,' Mary told her. 'It's only a chance and the doctor's very hopeful. "Very hopeful" were his exact words. His arm's a bit of a mess, but no bones broken. Thank heavens it was foggy, that's all I keep saying. That and you shouting out like you did. Oh, Amy, when the sergeant called last night I thought I'd die! Jim was a brick, a real brick – so calm and collected. I never expected it of him somehow. I just went like a jelly. I thought, "Now what's he been up to? Fighting or something?" Not that he's that sort of a lad,' she added hastily, 'but he's in with those two idiots – well, you know them, Amy – and nothing would surprise me. When the sergeant said he was in the hospital, you could have knocked me down with a feather.' She paused for breath and Amy took her chance.

'Have you heard anything about Mr Hatherley? Have they found him?'

'Bless you, yes,' cried Mary. 'Pulled him out an hour ago! Terrible death, that, I should think. Ugh! Gives me the creeps just thinking about it. Not that he didn't deserve it – he might have killed my Don! My God, Amy. When I think of it! Still, I'm glad I wasn't around to see it – the body, I mean. Bad enough just hearing about it. 'Course, half the blessed village was down there gawping, but pepole will; it's in their nature. Poor old Arnold was there. "I didn't do it" he kept saying. As if anyone thought he had! I saw them all as I came back from the hospital, diver and all. Mr Hatherley was laid on the bank under a tarpaulin sheet – and good riddance to him! But those divers – how they can put on those dreadful suits, I'll never know. And those huge helmets! Looked like a man from Mars or somesuch. And there was a boat sculling about with two more policemen and Sergeant Tully and the Inspector.' She stopped again, one hand to her heart. 'But look at me! On and on about this and that and never asking how *you* are! You could have been drowned by all accounts.'

'Luckily I can swim,' said Amy, 'but I must admit I did think my last hour had come. That weed! I thought I'd never be free of it. That must be what happened to Mr Hatherley. He was further in than me, and I was in deep enough! Maybe he couldn't swim or was too drunk.'

Mary tossed her head disparagingly. 'Most likely couldn't think straight, silly old sod! Mind you, he's dead and I shouldn't speak ill of him, but when I think—'

'How's his wife taken it?' Amy asked. 'Do you know?'

'Of course I know,' Mary told her with a grin. 'Everybody knows everything! You know how bad news travels. Mrs Hatherley is very calm, according to young Hollis who cycled up to the Manor and got it all from the Midden girl. Very calm. They thought she'd go into hysterics like she did when Mr Allan died, but apparently she just said "I thought he would kill himself". Apparently they knew he'd taken the shotgun, but they didn't know why. She rang the Sergeant to warn him and that's how come he turned up.'

'Lucky for us he did,' said Amy.

Ellen came in with a large wooden tray containing bacon, eggs and fried bread, a large mug of tea and a thick slice of bread and butter.

'Ah, here's my breakfast,' said Amy. 'That looks wonderful!'

Mary rose to her feet.

'Stay and watch me eat it,' suggested Amy, but Mary shook her head.

'I mustn't stop; I've got to call on Miss Betts.'

'Lorna?' Amy looked at her in surprise.

'Yes. Don made me promise I'd go over to the cottage. He thinks maybe no one will have told her about Mr Hatherley and it'll be such a shock. I mean, how's she going to manage now he's gone?' She pursed her lips. 'I think he's still fond of her – I wish he wasn't, but there it is. What can you do? She's not a bad girl, I suppose – well, I suppose she is a bad girl in a way – but it's that awful mother of hers I can't abide.'

'Don wouldn't be marrying her mother,' Amy ventured.

434

'She's a good-hearted girl, Mary, and she might make him very happy. If he's still fond of her after all that's happened, there must be some sort of bond between them.'

Mary shrugged. 'He said "Tell her not to worry". Now what's that supposed to mean? Still, he looks so awful with all those blessed bandages, I didn't have the heart to say "No". Poor girl! I wouldn't be in her shoes for all the tea in China! Oh well, best go and get it over with, I suppose.'

'Give Don my best wishes when you see him again,' said Amy.

'I will, love. Now you eat up your breakfast and then have another sleep. Doctor's orders, your Ma says. Shock can play nasty tricks and you had a real rough time last night.'

She leaned over and gave Amy another fierce hug. 'I still wish it had been you,' she whispered. 'You and Don, I mean. Is it really all over between you and him?'

Amy thought fleetingly of Elliot and nodded firmly. 'I'm afraid it is,' she said.

Chapter Twenty-Five

Mary saw the broken window with dismay but she tapped lightly on the cottage door, waited and tapped again; still having no answer, she made her way round to the back door. Perhaps the girl had gone round to the shop to see her mother, she thought hopefully, looking for an excuse to put off the meeting. Shading her eyes, she stared through the kitchen window but could see no sign of life within. The range looked dead and there was no steam coming from the kettle which stood on it. On the table stood a mug, a half empty glass milk-jug, part of a loaf of bread and a dish of butter. An apron hung over the back of one of the chairs.

Stepping back from the window, she stared up at the window above her. 'She's out,' Mary told herself. 'Well, I can tell Don I tried.'

However, her conscience rebelled at this distortion of the facts and she knew she had not wanted Lorna to hear her knock.

'Damn!' she muttered guiltily. She could not let Don down – she would have to make the effort.

She looked up towards what she assumed was a bedroom window. 'Lorna!' she shouted. 'It's me, Mary Leckie.' Almost at once the window above her swung open and Lorna stared down at her. When at last she spoke, her tone was flat and devoid of emotion.

'Mrs Leckie,' she said, 'I'm so glad – that is, I've been . . . No, wait. I'll come down.'

A moment later Mary heard bolts being withdrawn and the door was opened to admit her. She gave Lorna one glance

436

and her heart sank. More trouble, she thought – as if she didn't have enough already! The girl looked very pale and her manner was distraught; her lips trembled, her eyes were unnaturally large as she twisted her fingers together.

'He's dead, isn't he?' she said. 'I know he is and I'm so sorry. You must hate me. I was so frightened. I didn't know what to do.'

Her sentences came slowly, Mary thought, as though her mind was frozen and finding the words she wanted was proving difficult.

Lorna went on in the same level tone. 'I told him it wasn't Don's fault – I *did*! He wouldn't listen and I thought he was going to kill me too.'

Mary looked at her blankly. 'He was going to kill you?' she repeated. 'Mr Hatherley d'you mean?'

Lorna nodded. 'Yes. I thought when I saw the gun . . . he was in such a state. He wouldn't listen to me, just kept ranting and raving. When he'd gone I daren't go out after him, so I hid in the bedroom and wedged the door in case he came back.' Her voice cracked suddenly. 'Oh, poor Mrs Leckie, I'm so sorry! How can you bear it? I loved him too, I really did. We had that stupid quarrel . . .' Her lips trembled.

'Here, hang on,' said Mary. 'What are you thinking? That my Don's been killed? Because he . . .'

Lorna's eyes filled with tears. 'I really do love him, Mrs Leckie, but everything went wrong and then all this happened – poor little mite – and I'm so mixed up I don't rightly know what I'm doing these days.'

Mary frowned. 'Look,' she said, 'my Don's not dead – he's in the hospital with—'

Lorna's eyes flew open. 'Not dead!' she gasped. 'He's *not* dead? I thought—' She stopped, frowning and trying to get things clear. 'Gerald didn't shoot him, then?'

'No,' said Mary. 'At least, he tried to, but he mostly missed. Don's going to be all right in a week or so; the doctor was very reassuring.'

As the truth sank in, Lorna's face was transformed with delight. She threw her arms round Mary's neck and nearly knocked her off her feet.

437

'Steady on!' cried Mary, but she found herself warming to the girl. Lorna's joy at hearing the news of Don's survival was so obviously genuine. 'You can't keep a good man down,' she joked, returning the hug.

Lorna stepped back, her eyes glowing. 'I must see him,' she cried, but then her expression changed. 'No, perhaps I'd better not.' She sighed. 'Best leave well alone, I suppose, or there'll be more trouble. I never thought poor Gerald would be so jealous, he's such a nice little man.' Another thought struck her. 'Oh, my God!' she whispered. 'Has he been arrested? Will he go to prison? Poor Gerald! Oh, they wouldn't, would they? He didn't mean it, Mrs Leckie, I swear he didn't. He'd been drinking. He can't go to prison, not Gerald – it would kill him, I know it would.'

'Oh Lord!' said Mary, subsiding heavily on to a stool. 'Sit down, Lorna,' she said. 'I've a bit more news.'

'Couldn't you drop the charges?' Lorna asked, obediently lowering herself into a chair. 'It's asking a lot, I know, but he was not in his right mind or whatever they say. He really . . .'

'Lorna, love, Mr Hatherley's dead,' Mary told her bluntly. 'He was drowned. No one can touch him now.'

Lorna's lips worked soundlessly and Mary rushed on. 'He fell in the village pond after he'd shot at my Don. He pulled Amy in with him; luckily she managed to get out but he wasn't so lucky. It's Mr Hatherley that's dead, not Don. That's what I came to tell you. Don asked me to – and he said to tell you not to worry.'

'Gerald's dead? Oh, he can't be,' Lorna whispered. 'Are you sure?'

Mary patted her hand. 'Quite sure, love, I'm sorry. I mean, he's been very good to you, but there it is. What he did was very wrong and he's paid the price. Maybe it's for the best.'

'For the best?'

'Well, now they can't send him to prison.'

'Oh yes. Prison.'

Lorna swallowed and her blue eyes were dark with misery. Mary felt a wave of compassion for her, she was so young and she had had more than her share of troubles.

Mary moved to her and put an arm round the girl's trembling shoulders. 'There's nothing you can do for him now,' she comforted, 'except maybe pray for his soul. He's gone to a better place – at least, I expect he has. He had his faults, but he did his best for you and that'll count in his favour if anyone up there is counting. He's at peace, Lorna, love. That's more than we are.'

'I loved him too,' whispered Lorna. She looked up earnestly. 'You'll think I'm terrible, but I did. He was a funny old thing, sort of sad really, but I made him happy. I *did*, Mrs Leckie! I was the only thing in the whole world that made him happy – he told me so lots of times. Me and the baby, he said. Oh, poor Gerald!' She began to cry. 'Now he'll never see his little boy. He was so looking forward to seeing him, he had such plans.'

'*His* boy?' cried Mary. 'I thought you didn't know—'

But in her grief Lorna no longer cared what anyone thought. 'Yes, his,' she sobbed, 'and I'm not ashamed. He wanted a son and we were all going to be so happy together. You can all laugh if you want, but I don't care and the poor little mite's got no father now!' She gazed up at Mary, heartbroken. 'That is so terrible!' she cried. 'So terrible!'

Mary made comforting noises while Lorna cried out the first fierce wave of grief, but even as she held the trembling girl her thoughts were heavy. She knew how it would end – the words were written in large letters that danced before her eyes. Don would marry Lorna Betts and he would be father to Gerald Hatherley's child. 'As surely as day follows night,' she told herself. She sighed deeply. Last night she had almost lost her son, but a kind Providence had saved him. Was there a purpose to all that had happened? Was this marriage the price she and Jim must pay for having Don alive? Mary did not pretend to know any answers, but on two points she was quite clear: Don's life *had* been spared and he would almost certainly marry Lorna Betts. 'Well, so be it,' she thought. Jim would not be at all pleased, but she must work on him and win him round – she could if she tried. And they would have a grandchild before too long. Poor little mite! But Lorna's next child would be Don's. She sighed again. Amy would have been the perfect daughter-in-law, but that was not to be, so they must make the best of

439

a bad job. She found herself wondering what the first child would be like and hoped it would favour its mother!

Then there was Esme Hatherley. Mary assumed she would have to be told sometime because the baby would be her stepchild and she would have no one else in the world. Mary thought of Don, who in her eyes was still a boy himself. 'Well, Don Leckie,' she thought with a faint smile on her face. 'If this little lot doesn't make a man of you, nothing will!'

Lorna's sobs had finally ceased and Mary lent her a handkerchief.

'Now then, Lorna,' she said briskly. 'That's all the worst over. Do you think you can stand up? That's the way. Lean on me.'

'Why, where are we going?'

'Well, I don't think you should stay here all on your own,' said Mary, 'not after what you've been through. You could go back to your mother, or you could spend a few days with us at the farm.'

Lorna hesitated. 'I'll come with you,' she said gratefully.

Five minutes later the cottage was locked and shuttered and they were on their way.

*

It was nearly dark when Amy woke for the second time that day. Something had broken her sleep and she blinked hazily, trying to remember what it was. Downstairs the front door closed. The doorbell! That was the sound which had penetrated her dream, but in the dream it had become the whistle of a train. She had dreamed that she was walking barefoot along a railway track which stretched ahead and behind her into the far distance; she stepped from one rough sleeper to the next, and beneath the sleepers there was a vast emptiness. The track was like a hanging bridge with no visible means of support and she counted the sleepers as she walked: two hundred and thirty-four, two hundred and thirty-five . . . and held out her arms to steady herself, aware of that abyss yawning below her. Above her birds wheeled in vast numbers, hiding the sunlight, and the air was shrill with their cries. And then the train was coming towards her

440

along the track, very small at first – no more than a puff of smoke – but she felt the vibrations through the soles of her feet and knew it would soon be upon her. Nearer it came, and nearer, until she could see the shape and colour of it: a long black express with glaring headlights. The wheeling birds came lower as the track beneath her feet trembled with the force of the approaching train. Then its whistle sounded . . .

Amy drew a deep sigh of relief as the door opened and Sam came in with a jug of warm water.

'Ma says Mr Allan's here and wants to see you,' he announced importantly. 'She says you're not to get up – doctor's orders – and he'll be up in a few minutes when he's had a cup of tea.'

'Elliot *here*?' cried Amy. 'Oh, good heavens!' She sprang out of bed and rushed to the mirror to stare with dismay at her reflection. 'A few minutes!' she echoed. 'Tell them I've only just woken up . . .' She seized a hairbrush and began to straighten her tousled hair. 'Tell them five minutes, Sam,' she urged. 'Well, don't just stand there – go down and tell them!'

Sam went as slowly as he could, just to prove that he would not be hurried, while Amy dashed to the washstand and poured a little water from the jug into the bowl. Hastily she found a bar of scented soap, reserved for special occasions, and washed her face, neck and hands.

'Elliot here!' she repeated. 'What on earth—' Then spoke to herself sternly. 'Now calm down, Amy. You're being ridiculous – it doesn't mean anything.'

Listening at the door, she could still hear voices downstairs and the rattle of cups and saucers.

'Keep him talking,' she whispered and ran to the chest of drawers for a clean nightdress. She chose the newest one, which had a high frilled neck threaded with blue ribbon and long sleeves. Changing as quickly as she could, she then rushed back to the mirror. Pulling nightgowns off and on over her head had tousled her hair again and she began to brush it, deciding to tie it back with a blue ribbon to match the blue in the nightdress. She rummaged in the top drawer for the ribbon, failed to find it and exclaimed, 'Oh, damn!'

A sound behind her made her swing round in disbelief.

'I'm sorry,' said Elliot, looking at her humorously. 'I did knock, and I thought you said "Come in".'

Amy stood in her bare feet and stared at him. 'I said "Oh damn!",' she stammered. 'I . . . I was looking for a ribbon. I—'

'Shall I go out and come in again?' he suggested.

'No, of course not.' She made a tremendous effort not to be impressed by how tall, how fit, how handsome he looked, standing in the tiny attic room with its sloping ceiling and small dormer window. Her heart sang at the sight of him; she wanted him to think her composed and at ease, but she felt like a schoolgirl. The bed was several yards away. 'I should be in it,' she thought wryly, 'sitting up and looking like an invalid!'

Elliot was wearing a dark city suit which complemented his dark colouring. 'I should have brought some grapes,' he apologised. 'No point in being an invalid if no one makes a fuss of you.'

Amy hesitated, wondering whether to make an undignified scramble for the 'safety' of the bed or to remain where she was.

'I'm not ill,' she told him. 'It was only the doctor fussing.'

'He's quite right,' said Elliot. 'Shock can be very damaging. Your mother has told me what happened and I'm very glad you weren't hurt. It must have been a terrible experience.'

Amy nodded. 'I was terrified,' she said simply. 'I thought I would drown. Poor Mr Hatherley!'

He nodded, then neither spoke and the silence lengthened.

'Perhaps,' suggested Elliot, 'you should get back into bed? It's not very warm and your feet will get cold.'

Amy was not aware of her feet as she looked up at him and she was feeling far from cold. The thrill of seeing him again, and in such unexpected surroundings, warmed her body and made her pulse race. She was also aware of the fact that she was naked apart from her nightgown.

'Yes,' she whispered, but made no move towards the bed. She felt perilously close to losing control; her longing for him was so great that she was afraid her legs would carry her towards him instead of the bed. Praying that he could not read what was in her eyes, she said, 'I wish you'd sit down.' She attempted a light laugh. 'You're making my room look so small!'

His wonderful chuckle rang out and he glanced round him. 'I would if I could see a chair,' he said.

'Oh!' Amy looked round and then tutted. 'Sam's taken it again. I'm sorry – he will keep borrowing it. Their bedroom is rather cramped now that Toby shares and there's no room for a permanent chair, so he – he borrows . . .'

She faltered into silence as Elliot took two strides across the room towards her. He took her in his arms and kissed her. Surprise rendered her speechless for a moment, but she clung to him passionately, afraid that this could not really be happening. When he released her she asked, 'Elliot, why did you do that?' She saw that his dark eyes were no longer humorous.

'I suppose because I could not help myself,' he told her. 'I didn't intend it to happen – at least, not just yet. Amy . . .' He pulled her into his arms again, but this time his kiss was more restrained.

'I came down to Gazedown to explain about Grace,' he began. 'I have had to settle matters between us.'

Amy looked at him wonderingly. 'Do you mean that you are not going to marry her – or that you are?'

'I'm not,' he said. 'Let me explain, Amy. I've known her all my life and our parents wanted us to fall in love. Grace fell in love with me – she's a very sweet, very nice person – but I couldn't return the compliment and fall in love with her. I couldn't fall in love with anyone! I never found a woman who held my attention for long – I'm sorry if that sounds unfeeling, but it's a fact. I began to think I never would.'

'Ralph said you'd never marry,' said Amy.

'Poor Ralph – he was right. At least, he was right until I met you. Even then it didn't occur to me for some time that I was falling in love – and even then I didn't want to believe it.'

'You love me?' said Amy slowly. 'Are you saying you *love* me?'

Elliot laughed. 'Amy Turner!' he exclaimed, 'I'm telling

you that I love you, that I can't live without you and that if you don't agree to marry me, I shall just go on asking you until you do.'

'I see,' said Amy faintly, hardly daring to believe what she heard.

'I was lazy about Grace,' he went on. 'I feel very remorseful about it now that it's ended. I should have told her ages ago and then she would have looked for someone else. She's had plenty of would-be suitors, but because of me she would never give any of them a chance.'

'Is she terribly upset?'

'I'm afraid so – and so are all the parents. I'm very much out of favour at present.'

'Did you say anything about me to your parents?'

'No, I wanted to ask you first.'

For a moment neither spoke.

'Grace is a lovely woman,' said Amy. 'I don't know how you could not fall in love with her.'

'I don't know either,' he shrugged. 'It's just one of those things. Either it's there or it isn't; you can't love to order, can you?'

'No.' She could not take her eyes from his face. 'I love you, Elliot,' she told him, 'but I didn't think you felt anything for me.'

'I couldn't tell you,' he said, 'until I had spoken to Grace, I felt I owed her that much.' He sighed. 'And then today when your mother told me about last night, I knew I could have lost you. If you had been killed . . .'

'I never would have known how you felt about me!' Amy was horrified. 'Oh, that would have been too awful! It doesn't bear thinking about.'

'So you will marry me, Amy?' he asked. 'Have I actually asked you? This is all terribly unconventional. Should we go back to the beginning? I could start courting you, but it does seem an awful waste of time.'

'I will marry you, Elliot,' she laughed. 'Who cares about convention? My dearest Elliot! I'm so happy. Hold me again – don't let me go!'

They stood together, Amy with her head resting against his chest and Elliot kissing the top of her head.

Suddenly, she looked up. 'What about my family?' she asked. 'Are we going to tell them today?'

He lifted her from the ground and kissed the tip of her nose.

'We're going to tell the whole world,' he said, 'and the sooner the better!'

Chapter Twenty-Six

Amy's book was published on July 12th 1903, exactly fifteen months after their wedding and six months after they had moved out of the Allans' house and into a mews flat within reasonable walking distance of Benwells. To launch the book, Elinor Wyatt decided to give a small party; this was held at the Mayfair Rooms and began promptly at 6 o'clock.

Librarians, booksellers, critics and members of the press crowded into the small but elegant room where six waitresses served sherry and a variety of savouries. With Elliot at her side, Amy mingled with the guests. She wore a dress of ivory lace which contrasted well with her dark hair; her gold-brown eyes shone with excitement and her manner was poised and confident. Marriage to the man she loved, plus a deep sense of fulfilment, had wrought dramatic changes in her and she had waited for publication day with an eagerness that Elliot found quite charming. In fact, he found a great many of Amy's ways charming, and marvelled daily at the way the stationmaster's shy daughter had blossomed into a woman in her own right.

He moved through the crowd beside her, not because he thought she might need moral support but because he was proud of her and wanted to share in her moment of triumph.

A young reporter, notebook in hand, was talking to them.

'So if you are not a member of the Stanisbrooke family,' he asked, 'what is your connection with them? How did you become involved?'

Amy told her briefly how she had begun by working for Ralph Allan.

'Ralph Allan? The man to whom you have dedicated the book?'

'That's right.' She went on to explain that Ralph had died while the book was still in its infancy and that Elliot, Ralph's brother, had persuaded her to finish it.

'Actually, I bullied her!' laughed Elliot. '*I* knew she could do it, but Amy was not so sure.'

The reporter smiled. 'And how long did it take you?' he asked.

Amy looked enquiringly at Elliot. 'The best part of seventeen months,' he said.

'It seemed like a lifetime!' declared Amy and they all laughed.

Elliot went on, 'Meanwhile we pushed ahead with plans for publication. I had a strong feeling about the book. I couldn't wait to see it in print.'

The reporter scribbled again, then looked up at Amy. 'If I may say so, you do look very young.'

'Our youngest-ever author,' said Elliot, putting his arm round Amy and giving her an affectionate squeeze.

'And did you enjoy writing it?'

'Very much,' said Amy firmly, then amended, 'Mind you, I did have terrible moments of panic along the way. There were at least two occasions when I was ready to give up. I was lucky to have Elliot. He's had a lot of experience in the world of books and I really couldn't have written it without him.'

The reporter turned a page. 'And then you married your editor,' he smiled. 'That in itself is a very romantic story! But I must ask if you have any plans for another book?'

Before Amy could reply, Elliot answered, 'Most certainly. We have several possibilities which we shall be considering a little later.'

Amy smiled and gave him a rather enigmatic look, but said nothing, and then Miles Ashley came up to introduce a buyer from one of the large bookshops who had complimented him on the book's appearance. While they were discussing the illustrations the waiter refilled all the glasses and then Elinor Wyatt interrupted them to introduce a book reviewer from *The Times*.

Amy sipped her champagne slowly. She had eaten very little breakfast and almost no lunch and did not want to become light-headed. All the guests were important people in their own spheres and she needed a clear head to do justice to the occasion.

As a waitress passed, Amy helped herself to a square of brown bread and smoked salmon and thought how astonishing life could be. Astonishing and somewhat ironic, she reflected. This party marked the successful conclusion of all her efforts, it was her big day, yet she longed for it to be over so that she could have Elliot to herself. Surreptitiously she glanced at the clock: at least another hour to go! 'My dearest Elliot,' she thought, 'I have something to tell you and I hope you are going to be pleased.'

Behind Amy on an easel was an oval photograph of herself and next to it on a table were signed copies of her book. She allowed herself a slight nod of self-congratulation. She had done it! Advance copies of the book had been well received by the trade and – if she believed all she was told – a career as a biographer now beckoned enticingly. However, Amy knew she would not follow; she was expecting a baby and the prospect of motherhood thrilled her. She would like several children and they would fill her life for a long time to come. Later on she would write another book perhaps. She sincerely hoped so. Although she and Elliot had been married fifteen months, they had never discussed the possibility of parenthood for the simple reason that they had never had time – the book had monopolised their lives and all their energies had been directed to its completion.

Amy thought, 'I am giving you a child, Elliot, in return for all you have given me.' Their marriage had proved a happy one – they had fun together, they argued, they made love. They had established a relationship that was rewarding, full of warmth and never dull. Amy had never been happier and she counted her blessings daily. She enjoyed living in London, although often her thoughts returned to Gazedown Station and the family and friends she had left behind her. She and Elliot had gone back to Gazedown for her grandfather's funeral and been made very welcome. But she would go back on her own, she decided, to tell them about the child she was expecting.

'And now, ladies and gentlemen . . .' Elinor was beside her, holding up her hand to attract everyone's attention and Amy's heartbeat quickened as all heads turned towards them. 'I hope there are no empty glasses because it is my very pleasant duty now to propose a toast. Before I do, however, I would like to ask Amy Allan to say a few words.'

For a moment Amy's new-found courage almost deserted her as a sea of faces swam before her. Then she collected her wits and smiled.

'I promise you it will be only a few words,' she said and there was a murmur of amusement. 'I would just like to say how proud I am to be here – and how surprised!' There was some laughter. 'If anyone had suggested three years ago that I would write a book, it would have seemed the stuff dreams are made of. Now here I am and it's happened! My deepest thanks go to all at Benwells for their help and cooperation. *Lord Stanisbrooke* is obviously a team effort. On a personal level I would like to thank my husband for his encouragement.' She smiled at him and then her eyes darkened a little. 'Last, but certainly not least, I would like to acknowledge my great debt to Ralph Allan who originally allowed me to help him. I learned a great deal from Ralph, not least that imagination is no use without hard work, and I deeply regret that he is not alive to share this with us.'

Her voice trembled a little and Elinor quickly stepped up beside her and raised her glass. 'To Amy Allan, to the team and to *Lord Stanisbrooke!* We wish them all success.'

There was a murmur of endorsement, glasses clinked and Elliot stepped up on Amy's right to touch her glass with his own and to steal a congratulatory kiss.

For Amy it was a moment to remember.

*

'Gazedown Station!' yelled Tim. 'Anyone for Gazedown?'

He moved briskly along the platform with his own inimitable springy step. Harry, further along, grinned to himself because he knew Tim was showing off for the benefit of Amy, who was looking out of one of the first-class carriage

449

windows and waving to them. Before Harry could take his hands from his pockets, Tim had rushed to open the door and was helping her to alight with elaborate and highly exaggerated courtesy.

'First-class!' he mocked affectionately. 'Oh my, we have gone up in the world, haven't we?' He realised suddenly that Amy was travelling alone. 'Oh, no Mr Allan?'

'I wanted to come on my own,' Amy told him, 'so Elliot insisted I travel first-class. He sent his kind regards to everyone.' She looked very smart in a travelling suit of navy blue and grey, with a white frill showing at the neck and cuffs.

Tim looked at the large parcel on the seat and leaned into the carriage to collect it for her.

'Now let me guess,' he grinned. 'Feels like books to me!'

Amy blushed faintly. 'Well, it is,' she said, a trifle defensively. 'So many people wanted one – Mary Leckie and Papa, and then I felt I should give Mrs Hatherley a copy. Oh, hullo Harry! How good to see you again!'

After a few words of greeting, Harry slammed the door of Amy's carriage and after checking that all was in order, raised his green flag. Her next words were drowned by the rush of steam as the driver released the brake and the train began to roll forward – wheels, rods and pistons complaining as they took up the strain once more.

Harry put his head on one side enquiringly. 'I said that it seems strange not to see poor Grandfather here,' Amy repeated.

He nodded. 'It does that,' he agreed. 'We miss him and his stories; he was a good old boy. Still, he died in his sleep – didn't know a thing about it. That's how I want to go when my time comes.'

Tim grinned and cupped a hand to his mouth. 'Come in, Harry Coombes. Your time is up.'

'Do you mind!' grumbled Harry. 'Don't go giving Him ideas!'

They all stood chatting for a few moments longer and Amy duly admired the station garden, but then her father appeared to claim her. Sam and Toby were waiting and Amy felt a tightness in her throat as she looked at them. Sam was now thirteen years old and growing rapidly; his face was thinner and had lost its soft outline, his narrow shoulders showed through his shirt and his arms were too long for the sleeves.

'Sam!' she cried. 'I hardly recognised you! You look too grownup to be kissed.'

He grinned self-consciously and backed away slightly in pretended horror, saying, 'Well, Toby isn't!'

Quickly Amy handed over her parcel as Toby rushed eagerly towards her and she bent down to greet him. He was nearly six now and looked more like his father than ever.

'Do you like school?' she asked him.

Toby nodded, reconsidered and then shook his head. 'I don't like Miss Marriatt,' he told her. 'She keeps picking on me. I don't *do* anything, but she's always hitting me with her ruler.'

Amy laughed. 'And you don't do *anything*?'

Sam grinned. 'He does,' he said. 'He's even worse than I was!'

'Impossible!' Amy told him.

Ellen was at the door of the house then and there were more hugs and greetings.

'My!' said Ellen. 'You look so grand, Amy, and so well. Married life certainly suits you. She looks well, doesn't she, Tom?'

'Aye, she does,' he agreed. 'Now take off your jacket, love, and Ellen'll put the kettle on and make you a cup of tea.'

'The kettle's on, Tom. It's all ready,' Ellen protested. 'I'm dying to see the book at long, long last.'

Sam was already unwrapping the parcel and he now held up a copy with the flourish of a magician producing a rabbit from a hat.

'Amy!' cried Ellen. 'It's beautiful. Oh, Tom, isn't she a clever girl?'

'She is, indeed,' said Tom, putting an arm round Amy's waist. 'Our Amy, a famous author!' he declared.

'Papa!' Amy protested. 'I'm not famous. I'm just pleased that I managed to get it finished and haven't let Elliot or any of the others down. He was so sure I could do it.' She opened the book. 'See, I've written in it for you. I don't know if it's the sort of book you would want to read – or even have time to read – but you can glance through it when you get a moment.'

'Glance through it!' cried Ellen indignantly. 'I shall read every word, no matter how long it takes me. How can I boast about it in the village if I haven't read it?' She gave Amy a quick hug. 'Now let's see about that tea. I expect you're gasping for a drink after that journey.'

While they drank their tea, they exchanged news and gossip and Amy began gradually to relax. In a way she had dreaded this return to Gazedown, because on her last visit she had felt almost a stranger and it had saddened her to discover that she no longer 'belonged'. Today she thought that her father looked much older and even Sam was growing away from her. Ellen had put on weight, but it suited her. Toby had changed from a toddler to a schoolboy. 'And I have changed too,' she thought. 'Perhaps more than any of them. Perhaps they find me a different person – I suppose that's inevitable. We are all changing all the time and there's no way it can be otherwise.'

For some reason that she did not quite understand, she delayed telling them about the child she was expecting. Lunchtime was nearly over before she finally prepared herself to break the news, but just as she opened her mouth there was a knock at the door and Mary Leckie came in, beaming all over her face, with a basket of eggs and some honey for Amy to take back to London with her. Mary had just accepted Ellen's invitation to have some of what remained of the apple pie and custard when Amy blurted out her news.

'I've something to tell you all,' she said. 'We're expecting a baby in September!'

'A baby?' cried Sam. 'Oh, no! Babies are awful!'

Everyone started talking at once and Mary insisted that she had already guessed. 'I can always tell,' she said triumphantly. 'There's something about the eyes.'

Ellen hugged Amy. 'It's wonderful news,' she told her, 'but it makes me feel so elderly! I shall be a grandmother.'

Sam pulled a face and said, 'I shall be an uncle!' Toby giggled at this.

Her father smiled. 'I wish your grandparents had lived to see it,' he said quietly.

'How did Elliot take the news?' Ellen asked. 'I thought he had a sparkling career marked out for you.'

'He did, but he's very thrilled,' Amy assured her, smiling at the memory. 'It knocked him all of a heap, as they say. He couldn't believe it at first – kept saying, "Oh my God, Amy!" Then he couldn't stop grinning. He's very proud of himself!' she laughed. 'I don't think it had ever occurred to him that we might produce any offspring! He's treating it all as a big joke, of course. You know what Elliot's like!'

'He'll make a lovely father,' said Mary, 'and I'm glad for you both. I'll even forgive you for not being *my* daughter-in-law – I can't say fairer than that. Lorna's not a bad girl at all, bless her. Quite turned up trumps and makes a lovely little mother. The new baby's as good as gold, bless her – that's two girls, I told Lorna. You just see to it that the next one's a boy, I said. But what about Elliot's parents?'

'We've written to them,' said Amy. 'They're on their way back to India – they'll be pleased, of course.'

*

Later that afternoon Amy made her way up to Bates Manor to pay a brief visit to Esme Hatherley. She had considered sending the book by post, but had decided to go in person. Esme's behaviour in the past, particularly where Ralph was concerned, had rankled for a long time, but now Amy felt nothing but pity for her. On her last visit home, Amy had spoken to Clara and learned that Esme would never recover; the shock of Gerald's death had finally tipped the scales against her.

Amy knocked loudly at the kitchen door and was ushered inside by a delighted Izzie.

'It's Amy,' she cried, 'come all the way from London!'

'Amy Turner!' cried Mrs Lester. 'My, my, you do look smart! And we've to congratulate you, Clara tells us. The book is printed at last. I thought I'd die waiting for it to be finished. Is that it?' She nodded towards the parcel which Amy carried.

Amy nodded. 'I'm sure you'll get a chance to see it,' she

said. 'Clara can smuggle it downstairs when Mrs Hatherley isn't looking.'

Izzie darted off upstairs to fetch Clara and when she came into the kitchen, Amy could see that she too had changed. Clara wore a dark grey dress which was covered by a long lace-edged apron. Responsibility had obviously steadied her and she smiled and held out her hand to Amy instead of rushing to give her a bear-hug. Then she congratulated her on the publication of the book and Amy enquired about Esme's condition.

'She rests most afternoons,' Clara told Amy, 'but this morning Lorna brought young Penny to see her and that always gets her over-excited. I knew she wouldn't sleep, so you'll find her looking rather tired.' She shook her head as she led the way upstairs. 'The doctor says it does her good to see the child – gives her an interest – but I'm not so sure. She knows Penny is Gerald's child and she seems quite fond of her, but I wonder what really goes on in her mind.'

Clara paused on the landing and looked at Amy with a worried frown. 'She wandered off one day and I found her down at the cottage – you know Don and Lorna live there now? She was staring up at the bedroom window with tears pouring down her face.' She shrugged. 'I have to watch her like a hawk. Some days she's better than others, but she'll never be right. Sometimes she pretends not to know that Penny is Gerald's child. Other days she talks to her about her "father" and seems almost proud of the fact.'

They had reached the door of the master bedroom and Clara knocked and went in.

'I've brought Amy Turner to see you, ma'am,' she said briskly. 'Amy Turner, the stationmaster's daughter – do you remember? She lives in London now and she's written a book.'

Amy struggled to hide the shock she felt at Esme's appearance. The once beautiful woman was very thin and her eyes were dark pools of blue in her pale face. She sat in a chair with her back to the window and her expression was blank as she held out a hand to Amy.

'Hullo, Mrs Hatherley,' Amy began, recovering with an effort and shaking the proffered hand. 'I thought you might like a copy of the book Ralph Allan was working on when he stayed at The Lodge. Do you remember?'

Esme nodded slowly and when she spoke her voice, too, was devoid of expression. 'I remember,' she said. 'I remember Ralph Allan. He died.'

'I'm afraid he did, yes.'

Amy was aware that Clara was watching her mistress closely and thought that Esme was in good hands.

'Ralph Allan,' said Esme. 'I called him Ralph. We were very close you see – I think he loved me.'

While Amy hesitated, Clara said firmly, 'Of course he did, ma'am. It was all very tragic.' She gave Amy a quick look and Amy nodded. These fantasies were all Esme had left.

'Amy has brought you the book Ralph was working on,' said Clara and Amy handed it to Esme, who fumbled helplessly with the string with her claw-like hands. Clara fetched a pair of scissors and soon the book was revealed: a handsome edition bound in green leather with the words *Lord Stanisbrooke: His Life and Times* lettered in gold.

'We only had a dozen such copies made,' Amy explained. 'I was allowed four of them. The rest have the usual covers. Look here . . .' She found the dedication and Esme ran her fingers over Ralph's name, a look of wonderment on her face.

Amy and Clara waited for her comment, but she said nothing and the silence lengthened uncomfortably. Catching sight of a photograph of a little girl on the bedside table, Amy decided to change the subject.

'Is that Penny?' she asked.

From the silver frame a pert little girl smiled winningly, her round face framed with a mass of fair curls. Amy could see a likeness to Lorna.

Esme tore her eyes away from the book and glanced at the photograph.

'Penny,' she repeated. 'Yes, that's Penny Leckie. She's a charming little girl, isn't she Clara?'

'Yes, ma'am, she is. Such a happy little soul.'

'She likes to visit me,' said Esme with a little shrug. 'I don't know why, but she does. She likes the garden, you see; she picks flowers for me.' Her eyes returned to the book where her fingers still rested on the dedication. 'Poor Ralph,' she repeated. 'He found me very attractive, you know.' Slowly she raised her eyes to Amy. 'I'm not attractive now. I'm too thin, you see – much too thin.'

Clara stepped forward and gently withdrew the book from her mistress's unresisting hands. 'Of course you're attractive, ma'am,' she said. 'And we're fattening you up, aren't we? Bit by bit. A little plump bird! That's how you'll look when we've put a few more pounds on you.'

A faint smile touched the corner of Esme's lips and she turned to Amy. 'She's good to me, this girl,' she said, 'and she's never going to leave me. Never! She's promised me. You have, Clara, haven't you?'

'I certainly have, ma'am,' said Clara with a bright smile. 'You'll never get rid of me now, I'm here to stay.' She gave Amy a look which meant that Esme had had enough.

Amy held out her hand and Esme took it.

'I must say goodbye,' said Amy. 'I do hope you enjoy the book.'

'A good girl,' Esme repeated as though Amy had not spoken. 'And she'll never leave me. She won't, you see, because she's all I have.'

*

An hour later Amy stood on the platform waiting for the train which would take her on the first part of her journey back to London. All the family were with her and Tim and Harry hovered nearby. She had exchanged a few words with Bob Hart in his signal-box and now she felt a confusion of emotions. Regret that she was leaving them all, but also an eagerness to be gone. London and Elliot – they were her life now and she wanted to be back where she belonged. There was a lump in her throat as she tried to make conversation and her heart ached. This was her family, but she had stepped outside the magic circle and could never again be part of it.

The signal changed and as the train sounded in the distance, she began to hug them all with a frantic haste. Suddenly a figure came running along the platform and she looked up to see Don Leckie, slightly scarred but as handsome as ever, a sheepish smile on his face.

'Ma told me you were here and I thought I'd better say "Hullo".'

'Hullo,' said Amy, smiling.

'Ma told me the news – about the little 'un!' He grinned broadly. 'You'll have to work fast if you're going to catch up with me and Lorna. Two now, we've got.'

'I know,' smiled Amy. 'And you look very well on it.'

The train slowed and stopped and Sam and Toby rushed away down the platform shouting to Mr Bell. There was a last-minute scramble as her father helped her into the carriage and Ellen handed up the basket of eggs and honey which Mary had given her.

There were no other passengers to climb aboard and the final parting was mercifully brief. Amy felt near to tears as Harry slammed the door and the train jerked into motion once more.

'GAZEDOWN STATION'. The name-board passed as she leaned out to wave and then she saw Arnold leaning on the crossing-gate, an unlit pipe in his mouth. As she called to him, he waved both arms in a boisterous farewell. She glanced back, but the group on the platform had dwindled rapidly and then the track curved and they were lost from sight.

'I *haven't* lost them,' Amy told herself fiercely. 'They'll always be part of me!'

She stared out of the window with blurred unseeing eyes as the green woods gave way to a patchwork of fields which slumbered in the late afternoon sun. Instead of the glorious Wealden countryside, she saw Esme at the fateful party in her blue dress; Don Leckie at the market; Ralph at the dining-room table in The Lodge; Ellen and Toby standing in the kitchen like two lost souls. . . .

'Gazedown,' she whispered and for a moment – overcome with emotion – she covered her face with her hands and wept unashamedly.

When at last she recovered she wiped her eyes, blew her nose and took a few deep breaths. She thought of the child she carried and smiled. Then she thought of Elliot and her heart leaped. She was going *home*, she reminded herself. Gazedown was no longer home; it was part of her past. She was going home to a man who loved her and whom she adored. Nothing else mattered.

By the time she reached London her smile was radiant and when she stepped from the train into Elliot's waiting arms, the future closed around her, full of love and promise.